THE RECTOR'S DAUGHTER

'I find you *very* ungrateful, Sophie,' her mother said primly. 'Ungrateful *and* difficult, yes, I'll admit it. Your father and I are very surprised by the change in you since your return. You seem to take for granted all we have done and do for you.'

'I am *not* ungrateful, Mother.' Sophie gritted her teeth, and kneaded the knuckles of one hand in the palm of another.

'A penniless widow, rejected by her parents-in-law, yet whom *we* have taken to our bosoms in a true Christian spirit. You behaved as badly towards *us* as you did to them, yet *we* have not rejected you.'

'I did *not* behave badly.'

'You eloped with a man.' Her voice rose.

'I *did not* elope.'

Her mother stuck a finger in the air like an avenging angel. '*You* travelled with him *alone* on a boat all the way to Australia without being married. Imagine what people thought of *that*!'

Nicola Thorne is the author of some thirty novels, both modern and historical, many of which have been translated into most of the main foreign languages, including Japanese. She was born in South Africa but grew up in England and after spending most of her adult life in London she now lives in a small cottage in Dorset.

By the same author

The Girls
In Love
Bridie Climbing
The Daughters of the House
Where the Rivers Meet
Affairs of Love
The Enchantress Saga
Champagne
Pride of Place
Bird of Passage

The Askham Chronicles

Never Such Innocence
Yesterday's Promises
Bright Morning
A Place in the Sun

as Katherine Yorke

A Woman's Place
Swift Flows the River
The Pair Bond

as Rosemary Ellerbeck

The People of this Parish

The Rector's Daughter

Nicola Thorne

A Mandarin Paperback

THE RECTOR'S DAUGHTER

First published in Great Britain 1992
by William Heinemann Ltd
This edition published 1993
by Mandarin Paperbacks
an imprints of Reed Consumer Books Ltd
Michelin House, 81 Fulham Road, London SW3 6RB
and Auckland, Melbourne, Singapore and Toronto

Reprinted 1993 (three times), 1994

A CIP catalogue record for this title
is available from the British Library

ISBN 0 7493 1250 5

Printed and bound in Great Britain
by HarperCollins Manufacturing, Glasgow

Family Tree of the Woodville Family 1820–1898

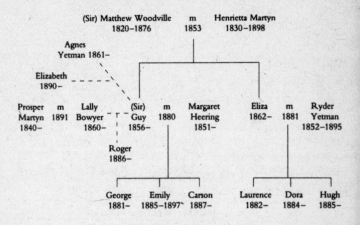

(Sir) Matthew Woodville   m   Henrietta Martyn
1820–1876   1853   1830–1898

Agnes Yetman 1861–

Elizabeth 1890–

Prosper Martyn 1840–   m 1891   Lally Bowyer 1860–   (Sir) Guy 1856–   m 1880   Margaret Heering 1851–   Eliza 1862–   m 1881   Ryder Yetman 1852–1895

Roger 1886–

George 1881–   Emily 1885–1897   Carson 1887–   Laurence 1882–   Dora 1884–   Hugh 1885–

Family Tree of the Yetman Family 1800–1898

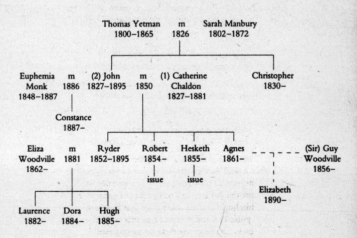

Thomas Yetman   m   Sarah Manbury
1800–1865   1826   1802–1872

Euphemia Monk 1848–1887   m 1886   (2) John 1827–1895   m 1850   (1) Catherine Chaldon 1827–1881   Christopher 1830–

Constance 1887–

Eliza Woodville 1862–   m 1881   Ryder 1852–1895   Robert 1854–   Hesketh 1855–   Agnes 1861–   (Sir) Guy Woodville 1856–

issue   issue

Elizabeth 1890–

Laurence 1882–   Dora 1884–   Hugh 1885–

CONTENTS

Prologue in Papua, New Guinea, 1907   1

Part I Return of the Widow   17

Part II Coals of Fire   125

Part III The Power of Money   311

Epilogue The Window, August 1913   467

PROLOGUE

Papua, New Guinea, December 1907.

From the shoreline there was no sign of the boat, no sign of George, and Sophie walked slowly over the soft golden sands, across the coral shingle and back to the house.

He had said he would be away ten days and now it was three weeks; a long, lonely time to be on one's own with two young children and only natives for company.

Gumbago was a small station on the north-east coast of New Guinea, fifty miles from Drogura where the main centre of the Anglican mission had been established.

Drogura had a church, a mission house and a hospital. There were white missionaries as well as black, nurses, a doctor, and frequent visits from the bishop. There Sophie and George Woodville had lived when they first arrived in New Guinea. Sophie was pregnant with Ruth, and Deborah was considered too young to be allowed to go with her parents up country, where natives addicted to cannibalistic rites still inhabited the hinterland.

Eighteen months ago George had been sent to open a solitary station at Gumbago in Collingwood Bay, and six months later Sophie, with the infant Ruth and three-year-old Deborah, had followed him. She had set up the school where she taught with native helpers, and a small clinic which a mission doctor visited once a month, or even less frequently in the rainy season, which was approaching now: December 1907.

Sawo, Ruth's nursemaid, stood at the entrance of the mission house, the baby slung in her arms native-style.

'No sign of the master yet, ma'am?' she asked in the halting mixture of native dialect and pidgin English she had learned since the Woodvilles had arrived.

Sophie shook her head and gently unclasped the hands of one of the small charges she had just been teaching, who had accompanied her to the beach. She patted the child on the head as she ran off to where her mother sat outside her hut, cooking something on the fire.

'Mr Barker said they'd be ten days. It's three weeks.' Sophie didn't try to hide her anxiety as she sank into a chair, wiping her brow. Her cotton dress stuck to her skin and the tendrils of her hair clung to her hot sticky forehead. She was a Christian soul full of the confidence of her faith, yet, at times, she was close to despair; far from home, in an alien land, without parents or friends. If she should lose George, what would happen to her then?

The Gumbago mission complex consisted of a native village of houses built on stilts to keep out the mud and water, the wild animals and, above all, the evil spirits. The New Guinea natives were primitive, Stone Age people who lived in tribes which, between them, spoke 700 languages, none of them written down. The first missionaries had come to the island in the late nineteenth century and found a deeply superstitious people to whom cannibalism was endemic. Even now, those who had been evangelised by the missionaries, or 'protected' by the British government, had tasted human flesh.

Three weeks away. It was too long.

The following day at about noon there was a commotion in the village, and Sophie, who was teaching in the school, where the recitation of the Ten Commandments in the native dialect was proceeding slowly, held up her hand. The chorus of voices obediently stopped. She went to the door of the school hut and, drawing back the curtain made of croton leaves, was unable to restrain a cry as she saw a white man, accompanied by a party of natives, cross from the beach to the shingle that covered the village street.

For a moment the face of the white man was obscured by

the drooping branches of the palm trees, but when he began to walk towards the mission compound she saw it was the Reverend Septimus Barker, priest in charge of the area, whom George had accompanied on his mission to the interior.

Without a word to her charges, Sophie flew down the steps and across the compound, arriving at the stout wooden fence at the same time as the missionary priest, who raised his helmet when he saw her.

'Good day, Mrs Woodville.'

'Is *George* with you?' she asked anxiously, without responding to his greeting.

'George will follow in a day or two.' Mr Barker's voice was that of a man not at his ease.

'How do you mean, "follow in a day or two"?' Sophie demanded, knowing somehow that her worst fears were being fulfilled. 'You haven't left George *alone* in the interior, surely?'

'Not *alone*, Mrs Woodville,' Mr Barker expostulated nervously wiping his face with a large white handkerchief. 'George has been unwell, and I have to hurry back to see the bishop. I assure you,' he added hastily, seeing the expression on Sophie's face, '*nothing* more than a touch of fever. You can be sure that I have left him safe with Kirikeu and William, and half a dozen of the strongest native boys.'

Kirikeu was George's personal servant, and William one of the lay preachers from the South Sea Islands who had run the station by himself before the Woodvilles came.

However, it was not good enough for Sophie who, through pent-up rage and frustration, stamped her foot on the ground.

'How *could* you leave George by himself, Mr Barker? How *could* you be *so* irresponsible.'

Mr Barker took a step back and, removing his helmet, wiped his heavily perspiring forehead.

'I irresponsible, Mrs Woodville? I would have you know I am *the* most responsible man alive. I nursed George for five days through a raging fever, and it was only when I was sure in my own mind that he was well, *and* at his insistence, that I took the remnant of the fellows we had brought with us

3

and came back. George is as safe as houses in an abandoned native hut, and well looked after. He is to come on a little more slowly, and I promise you that will be in not more than a day or two.'

The apprehension that had been uppermost in Sophie's breast now seemed more than justified, and the emollient words of the missionary did nothing to soothe her.

'Mr Barker, you have already been away *three weeks*, when you said ten days . . .'

'Had George not been ill . . .'

'You *now* say he was *very* ill, when a moment ago it was a touch of fever . . . You *then* leave him in a country full of savages, with a handful of natives, to find his own way back. Is *that* what you call being *responsible*, Mr Barker?'

'Mrs Woodville. I . . .'

He looked at her face and knew it was useless. She had an awesome reputation not only among the missionary wives but the missionaries themselves. She was a strong-minded, powerful woman some years older than her husband. Even the bishop was slightly afraid of her.

'The boat is waiting for me, Mrs Woodville,' Mr Barker said after putting on his helmet, and clutching his stick firmly in his hand. 'I wanted you to hear personally from me, and not from one of the natives, what had happened.'

'How *good* of you, Mr Barker.'

The scorn in her voice was its own rebuke. There was no more he could say.

'We have to trust in God, Mrs Woodville . . .'

She did not reply, but watched him, rage and contempt mingling in her heart, as he stumbled across the shingle towards the shore.

George sat on the steps of the deserted native hut and looked across the valley which, with its acres of fir trees, its lush vegetation, its masses of buttercups peering through the thick, high grass, could have been a valley in Switzerland, where he and Sophie had once spent a holiday. He sighed, and tapped the contents of his cold pipe into his hand. Useless to reflect on that time of bliss which now seemed so long ago; besides, very soon now he would see her again.

Beyond the high mountain peaks were the lower slopes of the Owen Stanley Range. The sun was beginning to set and George was aware of Kirikeu hovering behind him.

'What is it?' he asked, turning to his servant, noting the anxious expression on his face.

Kirikeu gestured towards the mountains.

'The spirits,' he said in a mixture of the native Wedanan language and the pidgin English he had painfully learned from Sophie 'The spirits, the *Dau*, come down on the mountain at night, master.'

With a fearful expression, he backed into the protective shelter of the hut.

'There is no spirit, no *Dau*, but God,' George said in a kindly tone as he got to his feet, resting a hand on the arm of his faithful servant, who bent his head as if he were a little ashamed of his fears. *Dau* was the native term for spirits, ghosts, hobgoblins, which were felt to be a potent, living force among the primitive people. Kirikeu was one of the most diligent attenders at the mission services, but he had not yet been baptised, for a long period as a catechumen was insisted upon before members of the native population were admitted to the sacrament of holy baptism.

However, George was anxious. The rest of the party had set out at noon to try and catch a wild pig for dinner and had been expected back long before sunset. He knew that the fears about spirits were not the only ones preoccupying the mind of Kirikeu. There was the savage Doriri tribe as well, whose territory this was, and who George and his companions had set out to convert; a tribe known for its ferocity and savagery, which still embraced the practices of head-hunting and cannibalism.

George and his servant made a desultory supper of yams and toro, a vegetable which looked rather like an arum lily, and whose roasted lumpy roots tasted like something between a chestnut and a floury potato. They also had left a few Huntley and Palmer biscuits which George had had pressed on him at the last minute by a thoughtful Sophie. George had been hoping for some succulent pig because he still felt very weak. To his weakness was added his nervousness about the fate of his men.

By nightfall they had still not returned and, after Kirikeu had dowsed the fire in front of the hut, George spent some time on his knees in prayer before stretching himself out on the grass pallet that served him as a bed, and attempting to sleep. But the sleep was fitful, punctuated by the cries of the nightbirds, the furtive noises of small creatures scurrying across the floor of the hut or among the sago leaves that made the roof. Thousands of cockroaches and spiders would have made their home there over the years, but George had long ago come to terms with the insect life that was part of living in New Guinea.

Except, that is, for the mosquitoes, the cause of so much ill-health and his recent bout of fever. They proliferated in the swampy marshes near the coast, harbingers of disease and, too often among the white man, death.

Across the doorway Kirikeu slept or, perhaps, tried like his master, undoubtedly listening for the footsteps which would herald the welcome return of the men who had set out earlier with their spears, hoping to ensnare a fat pig.

As soon as the faintest blush of dawn appeared in the sky, both men were up, moving purposefully about with the intention of striking camp. They still lived in hopes that their fellows, perhaps having moved too far from the camp, had decided to shelter for the night; but as the daylight grew strong their hopes began to diminish. Finally Kirikeu faced his master and threw out his arms.

'Shall I go and look for them, master?'

'What is the use?' George replied. 'If something has happened to them *you* will be in danger too.'

'At least we will have news. I shall go very carefully, master, taking care not to show myself.'

'Well . . .' George sat on his packed knapsack and thought hard and long. Finally he shook his head.

'I'm afraid that my fever will resume if we don't get home. Already my dear wife will be worried sick about me. As soon as we get back to Gumbago we shall contact the resident magistrate and ask him to find out what has happened to our friends and, if harm has befallen them, you can be sure he will punish the wrong-doers severely.'

Not long before, twenty-four Doriri had been killed and their *dubus*, or tribal huts, put to the flames in retaliation for the murder of a white rubber trader.

Putting the belongings of the rest of the expedition into a neat pile at the back of the hut, George and Kirikeu then broke camp, and just before noon headed into the forest, making for the sea.

George had made many mission journeys into the interior and was adept at finding his way with the help of the compass and the position of the sun. However, that night they had to shelter again, but this time they were attacked by hordes of mosquitoes because of the swampy nature of the land near the sea. They slept fitfully, ill protected by the mosquito nets they had erected over makeshift beds, and before dawn they were thankful to begin their trek again, reaching, by late afternoon, the narrow creek that led to the sea where they had hidden the two whaleboats, one of which had been taken by the returning party. The other, under a mound of pandaurus leaves, jutted out from the embrasure in the creek.

As soon as the men looked at the whaleboat they realised their dilemma. It needed twelve men to row it and they were but two, one enfeebled by fever.

For one of the few times in his adult life – especially since it had been touched by the grace of God – George Woodville felt like losing faith, putting his head in his hands and howling. Just in time, however, he felt himself fortified by the Holy Spirit, and also by the simple courage of his companion, who had already jumped into the boat.

'Master!' Kirikeu cried, throwing the baggage into the stern of the long, narrow boat, 'between us we can take this boat down the coast.'

George, however, sorrowfully shook his head. The whale-boat was a long, serviceable, sturdily-built craft, much used by missionaries and government officers for plying the coastal waters. As well as oars it had sails.

'I have no knowledge of sailing, Kirikeu, and nor have you, and we cannot possibly man the boat between us. She is far too heavy and I am weakened by fever. We shall be swept out to sea and drowned.'

'We can *try*, master,' Kirikeu urged, and his enthusiasm was inspiring as well as painful to see, but George, looking again round the heavy boat, knew that the task was hopeless.

'We will spend the night here, and then tomorrow we'll decide what to do, whether to press on walking down the coast or . . .' He felt in himself a sense of failure, a lack of courage, of Christian faith, as he looked at the honest, trusting eyes of his servant, who obviously believed in God-like qualities which George did not have.

'We may *have* to go back to the hut,' he said gently. 'If they come to look for us – and I know how worried Mrs Woodville will be – *that* is where they will make for. It is a hundred and fifty miles from here to Gumbago. We have insufficient food and I really do not think I have enough strength to make the journey. Anyway, my good friend, let us rest now, and see what tomorrow will bring.'

As if in answer to their prayers, the night saw the worst storm that George could recall since he had lived on the island. Had they been at sea they would have been buffeted by the waves and cast up upon the coral reefs, where their small craft would have been shattered to splinters. In the safety of the creek, and despite the tarpaulin they drew over their heads, they were soaked to the skin, and the heavy boat sank ever lower in the rising waters.

At daybreak, as the wind lowered, they raised their heads over the gunwales and saw nothing but desolation around them, the fronds of the betel-nut palm trees sodden, the vegetation waterlogged. George knew that as soon as the sun came up the swampy ground would provide a fresh breeding-ground for the dreaded malaria-bearing mosquitoes, and that their best refuge was certainly to return to the hut. God had clearly shown them the way.

8

By now even Kirikeu seemed glad to leave the half-sunk, flooded boat, its bows low in the water. One look at the surging sea convinced him that their chances of survival in it were nil.

They had a slow, wearisome trek back to the hut, and even George, steering their progress by the compass, frequently lost his bearings. They were soaked to the skin and, by the time they stopped for the night, Kirikeu's teeth were chattering and George felt as though his own fever might be returning. They had had nothing to eat all day but a few berries, and water from a clear-running stream which flowed down from the mountains. They had no time or desire to look at the beauty of the countryside around them as the wind abated and, once more, the sun shone hot and fierce on their backs. It was difficult to believe that they were in hostile territory, where their lives might be threatened by the wild, head-hunting Doriri who had probably claimed the skulls of their friends and eaten their flesh.

By noon on the following day they reached the hut, which was just as they had left it, with the bags of their companions still waiting in an abject pile in the darkened interior. A few creatures of the wild, who had hoped to be making their home in the deserted building, scuttled across the floor and out on to the safety of the sago leaves drooping from the rafters.

As he put down his bag and sank gratefully onto the floor, George was once more visited by a sense of desolation such as he had scarcely ever felt in his life before: a complete lack of faith in the Almighty, of trust in the One for whom he had deserted his native county of Dorset, his comfortable home at Pelham's Oak, for whom he had alienated his family, especially his father Sir Guy Woodville, whose heir he was.

'Oh God!' he murmured, stretching out on the grass mat and putting a hand over his eyes, 'please let this burden be taken from me.'

And then he started to sob.

After a moment he was aware of a presence near him and, opening his eyes, he saw Kirikeu squatting beside him on his haunches, his hands joined in front of him, his black eyes clouded with anxiety which seemed to mirror George's own despair.

'Master,' he said, 'I will go and find something to eat. You must take off your wet clothes and I will dry them in the sun, and then tomorrow, when we are rested, I will go and see what has happened to our friends while you stay here and wait for the rescuers who are surely on their way.'

George put out a hand and grasped that of the catechumen who, although not baptised, had a faith which seemed greater than his.

'I can't let you go into the bush, Kirikeu. If you are killed, who knows what will become of me?'

'I will be very careful, master,' the native said, taking his spear from the side of the wall. 'I will take care not to be seen, but I will try and discover what I can.'

Mr Pearce, the resident magistrate for the area, looked with concern into the eyes of Mrs Woodville. Summoned from Drogura, he did not like what he had heard.

'My husband has now been gone nearly five weeks,' she said in a low, calm voice which, nevertheless, belied her true feelings. 'How Mr Barker could have left him I do not know, but he did. Perhaps by now he is dead.'

She said the words almost without emotion, and Mr Pearce marvelled, as he often did, at the ability of the missionaries to accept the horrible fate that was frequently served up to them on these inhospitable shores.

New Guinea had a beautiful climate, but it was an uncivilised place with disease rampant; and not only disease, but the danger of attack from the inland tribes who dwelt in regions where no white man had ever penetrated, and to whom barbarism was an accepted way of life. The New Guinea savage lived by a superstitious fear of spirits and by the code of paying for a life with a life, however death occurred. It was also the custom to bless a house with human blood, and the erection of every *dubu*, every tribal dwelling, exacted its own particular form of sacrifice.

Julian Pearce was a young, ambitious graduate who wished to rise to a high place in the Colonial Service. To him New Guinea was just a stepping-stone. He had been sent there from Brisbane and, as it was his first taste of authority, he enjoyed the life, tramping through the forests with his band of well-armed native policemen and dispensing justice, which often involved the transportation of the miscreant to the capital, Port Moresby, for trial, and the exaction of the ultimate penalty: death by hanging.

Now Mr Pearce gazed solemnly at Mrs Woodville as she finished her recitation.

'Your news disturbs me, ma'am,' he said. 'I will take my men and leave at once for Doriri country.'

'You have the itinerary from Mr Barker?' Sophie asked.

Pearce nodded. 'We know that he called in at Waguni Creek, where they left the whaleboat while they went inland. Their mission to pacify the Doriri met with little success, and on the way back Mr Woodville fell ill and Mr Barker decided to leave him with half the men because he was expected back by the bishop.'

'The bishop!' Sophie exclaimed derisively.

'I'm sure that Mr Barker *thought* he did the right thing, ma'am,' Mr Pearce said gently. 'He expected Mr Woodville to start almost immediately after him, although taking a slower pace. The bishop had a confirmation service in Drogura and Mr Barker had prepared the candidates. I can assure you he is most upset by the whole incident, Mrs Woodville.'

'May he not live to regret it for the rest of his life,' Sophie said firmly. '*That* would indeed be a heavy burden.'

She walked to the beach with the RM, whom she rather liked; a brisk, practical young man of whom she had only heard good things. A few of the natives followed her, hanging on to her skirt, touching her hands as if trying to impart to her their own sympathy and sorrow for what had happened. She felt surrounded by love, by hope, and as she shook hands with Mr Pearce before he prepared to get into the dinghy that would take him to the government schooner *Merrie England* anchored in the bay, she impulsively clasped his arm.

'I am sure you will find George and bring him back to me,' she said. 'I feel that God is with you.'

'Thank you, Mrs Woodville,' the magistrate said, feeling rather clumsy and awkward as, putting his helmet back on his head, he climbed into the boat and headed for the open water, rowed on his way by four stout native policemen.

George knew that once again he had the fever. He had vomited several times, and his shivering grew more frenzied as the day advanced. He put blankets round his shoulders, but they did little to keep out the cold – though it was hot outside. It was unusual to have two bouts so close together; but maybe the mosquitoes in the swamp where they had spent the night had been particularly virulent or, maybe, he had never got over his first attack. He had also been short of quinine because he had not expected to be so long away from home, so had taken less than he should.

Kirikeu had left at first light, clutching his spear and promising to be careful in his search for a succulent wild pig, yams and toro from which to make a feast, because they were both suffering from hunger.

At first, after his servant left, George felt better, cheered by the beauty of the scene, the landscape lit as on an ideal English summer's day; and he was able to lay off his blankets and smoke a pipe after his breakfast of coconut washed down by its milk. By lunchtime he felt well enough to revel in the thought of the succulent roast with which they would assuage their pangs of hunger by nightfall.

He went out and sat on the ramshackle balcony of the hut, his pipe in one hand, his Bible in the other. He never failed to find succour from the Word, and this time he knew that his faith was doubly tried. In a way, he felt God was reproaching him for his lack of it.

George Woodville was a man who had seldom known doubt since he discovered God at school at the age of sixteen. There he felt God had spoken to him, and forever afterwards he was confident of His presence. He had also felt a strong desire to be a priest, an ambition which his parents did their best to thwart. They might even have been successful had not George first fallen under the influence of, and then in love with, the daughter of the Rector of Wenham, Sophie Lamb, six years his senior, a purposeful young woman with a strong personality who already burned with ardour to join the foreign missions.

The path of true love had not been smooth, and nor had George's attempts to be ordained after reading classics and theology at Cambridge. Candidates for the priesthood in the Church of England were not encouraged to marry, and his training would have been long and arduous.

Encouraged by Sophie, he applied to join the Anglican mission as a teacher, and to study for holy orders at the same time as he pursued his ministry to spread the Word. They sailed to Australia together and were married in Brisbane.

In Wenham the news had not been well received. Sir Guy Woodville felt his heir had betrayed him, and the Reverend Austin Lamb that his daughter was guilty of being sly and deceitful. What was more, the marriage produced a rift between the families instead of bringing them close together.

But George, far away, knew little of this, and now he leaned against the rickety balustrade of the balcony and reflected on his past; on the family he loved, yet who did not respond to his letters; on the wife and the children he adored. The world suddenly seemed black again and his frame was wracked by a fresh burst of shivering, the tobacco tasted stale in his mouth and he knew that he would once again vomit. Vomiting brought dehydration, and he was perilously short of water.

He crawled back into his hut to lie down on his pallet, and a horde of cockroaches who had decided to settle there for the afternoon, scurried out of the way.

On the balcony, the Bible lay forgotten. Oh, would that Kirikeu would return!

But it grew dark, and there was no sign of his manservant. His water-bottle was now dry and the fever was increasing. He knew he would have to crawl out of the hut to find water, or by the morning he would be dead. He had seen men dead of dehydration and it was a dreadful sight: their swollen tongues lolling out of their mouths, their lips cracked, their sightless eyes bulging obscenely.

He put aside his blankets and, with trembling hands, managed to light the kerosene lamp. At the sign of light, further creatures scuttled for the safety of the roof. A giant spider crawled rapidly up the post and disappeared into a crevice.

George's shivering grew uncontrollable, but he knew now that it was also compounded of fear.

He had managed to stagger as far as the balcony when he heard a movement and, looking up, he saw the head of a native silhouetted against the moon.

It lurched towards him, and as he had no gun – he had always refused to carry one, holding that any taking of life was wrong – he commended his soul to his Maker and, in the spirit of Christ, prepared himself to feel the shaft of the arrow pierce his skin. Suddenly the shadow disappeared and, with a mighty grunt, fell at his feet.

'Master . . .' Kirikeu exclaimed with a cry of pain. 'I am killed.'

George threw himself on the ground beside his stricken servant, and almost immediately his hand encountered the stickiness of thick, congealed blood.

'I have run, master,' Kirikeu gasped, 'run all this way to tell you to run too, master. They found me and they stabbed me; but I ran away. Oh master . . .' he reached out and feebly grasped George's arm. 'Would you baptise me into Christ before I die?'

Then George felt a surge of strength that came from he knew not where. His fever abated and his courage yet again returned.

He could hear the water trickling in the stream not far away and he lunged towards it, first slaking his thirst with giant mouthfuls cupped in his hand. Then, joining his hands together, he tottered over to the side of the dying man and, kneeling beside him, he poured the water of baptism over his head:

'I baptise thee, Kirikeu, with the name of James after the disciple of Our Blessed Lord, in the Name of the Father and of the Son and of the Holy Ghost.'

Then he clasped Kirikeu's hands between his, and under his breath began the prayers for the dying . . .

'Go forth, Christian soul, out of this world, in the name of the Father who created thee . . .'

He felt Kirikeu's hand stir in his and sensed that his servant, his beloved disciple James, wished to speak to him. He put his ear as near as he could to the dying man's mouth.

'Master,' Kirikeu whispered feebly, 'I go to join our friends who are with God too. The Doriri cut off all their heads and ate them, master. Oh, master, are they too among the saints?'

'They are,' George said in a broken voice and, as his disciple gave a great sigh and expired, George lay over him and wept.

And that was how the resident magistrate eventually found him.

Back in Gumbago, George Woodville struggled to survive. He was taken home in such a delirium that no one expected him to outlive the journey. But he did, because he wanted to see his wife. Sophie nursed him with all the skill and tenderness of which she was capable.

At times he seemed to recover, and then he relapsed and would go into delirium and talk about his dead sister Emily, his mother and father, and his regrets that he had hurt them. He would talk of Kirikeu and all those who had died on that futile and senseless expedition, which the resident magistrate with a strong police force had already gone to avenge.

Sophie sat by him whenever she could; but she thought that it was important for the children and the mission to let things be as normal as possible. A young man called Peter, also hoping to be ordained with George the following spring, was sent from Drogura and proved a great boon, a comfort to Sophie.

He and Sophie would pray by George's bed, and sometimes George joined in. Sometimes he was unconscious. But Sophie never gave up hope, or faith in the power of prayer to make him recover.

One night after Peter had gone, George took her hand as she sat beside him.

'You know, I feel better, my dear,' he said. 'And if I recover, for this miracle I will dedicate my entire life to God in the missions; but Sophie . . .'

'Yes, dear?' she said anxiously, aware of how his flesh burned, even though he said he felt better.

'If God should will that I do . . . not recover, I want you to go home. Back to Wenham. This is no place for a woman on her own with two children, and I want you to promise me you will obey my last request.'

'But my dearest,' she protested, 'it was *I* who felt the call of God first . . .'

'I want no argument, Sophie,' George said in a voice that had grown perceptibly weaker. 'I want you to promise me to go back to Wenham, and in the Church of St Mark to cause a window to be placed in my name and that of my friends who died. But next to mine must be the name of Kirikeu.' Then, as if very tired, he closed his eyes.

'Dearest, it will *not* be necessary,' Sophie said earnestly, stroking his hand, conscious of his throbbing body and his dry, scaly skin.

'Oh Sophie, how I wish I could have been ordained,' George sighed, without opening his eyes.

He never spoke again.

PART ONE

Return of the Widow

I

The return home of the rector's daughter after many years away on the foreign missions was an event of some importance in the North Dorset parish of Wenham.

There Sophie Woodville had been born, the only child of the Reverend and Mrs Lamb, to whom she had come as an unexpected gift relatively late in life. And as Sophie had first brought joy, so had she eventually brought distress, almost despair, to her parents when she ran away to marry George Woodville and caused a rift between the families which had not yet been repaired.

The living of Wenham was in the gift of Sir Guy, George's father but, though grieved by his son's behaviour, he was not a vindictive man. He knew that the rector could not justly be blamed for the behaviour of his daughter and, although Sir Guy ceased to attend his church or meetings of the parish council, he had not asked for the rector's resignation as he had once threatened to do.

The rector, though well past the age at which the Church of England expected its clergy to retire, remained in the comfortable, spacious rectory, and eventually a curate had been appointed to assist him in his duties. Hubert Turner, who was unmarried and had ample private means, lived in the house near the church, a comfortable four-bedroomed dwelling that had once belonged to Euphemia Monk.

Sophie left the mission in April and arrived home in September, having spent some time in Australia on the way, to see friends and recover from her ordeal. She was sad to part from the mission station where George and she had been so happy, found such fulfilment, and although she told herself she would return, in her heart she feared she never would.

The long sea-voyage further helped to restore her, and it was a much stronger and more confident woman who, accompanied by her two children and a nursemaid engaged in London, arrived at Blandford, where she was greeted by the Reverend Turner on behalf of her father.

Hubert felt every bit as nervous at meeting Mrs Woodville as he had when he had mounted the pulpit in Wenham to deliver his first sermon, conscious of the critical gaze of the rector, robed, sitting in the Sanctuary and listening very carefully, a hand cupped to his ear. Turner was twenty-seven years of age, a graduate of Durham where he had served as deacon in the cathedral before his ordination and his transfer to the diocese of Salisbury. He little resembled the popular notion of an Anglican divine, being rather short and stocky, with horn-rimmed glasses and the cheerful expression of a man who did not dwell overmuch on affairs of the soul, but enjoyed outdoor life and the pleasures of the table. Mr Turner was fond of walking and even played football for the town's team.

'You do not know me but I know you, ma'am,' he said, bowing deeply to Sophie and removing his hat. 'I am your father's curate, Hubert Turner, at your service, Mrs Woodville.'

Sophie looked at him in some surprise, but there was a trace of amusement on her lips as she studied him. The humour in her face was the first thing he noticed, also that she looked tired, drawn, and maybe a little apprehensive. She had the kind of reserved looks that Hubert Turner found attractive; dark brown hair, rich brown eyes where the humour lay, a determined chin; every inch the parson's daughter, with the clear light of Christian courage showing through. But there was something else: she was a woman of the world too, a woman, clearly, who had lived.

The curate in that brief instant warmed to Mrs Woodville, the admiration showing, perhaps too clearly, in his eyes. Swiftly she turned and introduced her two young children and, finally, her maid, Phoebe Nightingale.

'No relation to *the* Miss Nightingale,' she added with a smile.

''D'ye do, sir,' Phoebe said, with a neat little bob. She carried Ruth in her arms while Sophie firmly clutched the hand of the energetic Deborah whom nothing ever seemed to tire. George had had ash-blond hair and a fair skin, and his elder daughter looked like him. Like him too, she had large, twinkling blue eyes. Looking at her, it was difficult to imagine that she had so recently been struck down by tragedy. Maybe she was too young fully to take it in.

The Reverend Turner politely shook hands with the children and then demonstrated his powers of organization as he directed the porter he had brought with him from the station entrance to collect Mrs Woodville's considerable amount of baggage from the guard's van, and stow it on his barrow.

The operation even held up the progress of the train, but once everything was safely removed, the guard blew his whistle and the new arrivals stepped back to watch the train steam out on its way to Exeter.

'It is extremely kind of you to meet me, Mr Turner,' Sophie said in what the curate thought to be a particularly sweet voice. 'How are my parents?'

'In excellent health, Mrs Woodville. Your father takes Matins every Sunday. I do the Eucharist at eight and the evening service, but at that he sometimes preaches. I find the example of your father inspirational, and cannot tell you how fortunate I feel I am to have the opportunity to practise the ministry by his side, under his tutelage.'

Sophie said nothing but walked slowly along the platform, taking in the sights, sounds and, above all, the smell of Blandford Station which she had last seen nearly eight years before when, although she had not known it then, she left her home for the last time before her marriage.

Outside the station stood the familiar coach, drawn, she was sure, by the same horses, and as she went up and stroked their muzzles a lump came into her throat.

She had not realised how glad she would be to return home.

The Reverend Turner instructed the porter as, together with the coachman, he went on putting luggage into the hold until it looked as though it would burst. There was a lot of discussion, muttering and shaking of heads, coins changed hands, and it was decided to return for the rest the next day. Mr Turner gallantly handed Sophie into the coach, watched with interest by a crowd of onlookers, who with all her baggage imagined her to be, perhaps, a member of the Portman family visiting Bryanston, the local stately home.

The coach went at a brisk pace along the market place, past the Crown Hotel and over the bridge before it turned right and took the uphill road to Wenham.

'You will find much has changed in the time you have been away,' Mr Turner said. 'A few people have now purchased motor-cars. I hear your father-in-law is thinking of buying one.'

'Indeed?'

Mrs Woodville did not seem particularly interested. Hubert Turner felt uneasy. He knew that relations between the Woodvilles and the Lambs were not close. He ran a finger round his dog-collar.

'Mrs Woodville, you must understand that I am a relative newcomer to the district. What happened many years ago does not concern me.'

'Quite.' Sophie gazed at him enigmatically.

He was afraid he had offended her and, clearing his throat, said, 'May I say, Mrs Woodville, how distressed I was to hear about the death of your husband. Please accept my deep sympathy.'

'Thank you, Mr Turner,' Sophie said graciously. 'However, I am consoled by the fact that my husband was a martyr who gave his life for the souls of the heathen. One of the last things he did was to baptise his servant, to whom he was devoted. I am sure that they both sit at the right hand of God.'

Mr Turner felt dumbstruck, and remained so as the carriage bowled along and the children were instructed by their mother as to places of interest they passed, until at last she cried:

'Ah, *there* is Wenham! I hadn't realised until this moment how much I had missed it.' She put a hand to her mouth as if to restrain a sob.

The town stood on a hill overlooking the River Wen. Its most conspicuous feature was the Church of St Mark, whose square Norman tower could be seen for many miles around. Next to the church was the rectory, which could also be seen from the approach road, a large, well-proportioned house which had been built at the turn of the previous century.

A medieval bridge, with corbels in the centre of each side to accommodate pedestrians, bestrode the river, and now the carriage crossed it and then trotted up the hill, before turning into a narrow street leading off the market place and stopping in front of the church.

For a moment Sophie gazed out of the window, as if suddenly overcome with apprehension. Two familiar figures stood on the threshold of the door, gazing at her; both a little stouter, certainly older. She wondered how long they had been there.

Her mother and father.

Under the careful eye of Phoebe the children scampered on the lawn, watched from the drawing-room window by Sophie and her parents as they had tea. The Reverend Turner had tactfully withdrawn to his own house, saying that he had a sermon to prepare.

The traditional English tea, taken indoors with the September sunshine slanting through the high windows of the rectory, reminded Sophie of the days when she and George, aware of their burgeoning attraction, sat together on the bench on the lawn which sloped down towards the river. Nothing had changed, except that then it had seemed impossible that a youth of seventeen and a young woman six years his senior would eventually marry. But they had . . .

The welcome had been constrained. The Lambs were not demonstrative people, not kissers or touchers, they seldom embraced. Pecks on the cheek had been exchanged as if Sophie had been gone only a few days, and there was general chit-chat as they were taken to their rooms and allowed to rest until it was time for tea.

The children were too excited to rest. Ruth only toddled inexpertly, guarded by Phoebe, but Deborah tore around, and his grandparents watched her a little apprehensively, as though doubting her existence. Mrs Lamb, looking from one child to the other, murmured:

'Deborah is especially like George.'

'So like him,' Sophie agreed.

'Could you tell us a little . . . what happened?' Mrs Lamb dabbed at her eyes.

'George need not have died,' Sophie said firmly. 'He was left in malaria-infested country by a foolish man whose one idea was not to offend his bishop. George was accompanying the priest in charge of our mission area, Mr Barker, on a regular trip they undertook to try and bring the Word to the heathen of the interior. George, who was not strong and prone to fever, fell ill, and Mr Barker, anxious to placate the bishop, who was expecting him, left him to make his own way back.'

'Oh!' Mrs Lamb joined her hands and cast her eyes indignantly towards heaven.

'Monstrous,' the rector growled.

'He should *not* have left George,' Sophie said severely. 'Then half a dozen men, whom George had been left with, went to look for food to strengthen him and ran into an ambush set by head-hunting savages.' Sophie put a hand over her eyes. 'I can't tell you the rest.'

'Don't!' Her mother touched her arm. 'Better not. We understand.'

'Had you not behaved so unwisely, Sophie,' the rector said cautiously, 'this would not have happened.'

'We did not consider it "unwise", Father. We were moved to preach the Word. George died as he would have wished, and I . . . I do have peace of mind.'

Her eyes were bright as she stared at her parents, then her gaze fell to her wedding ring.

'It caused a lot of trouble.' The rector's tone was reproachful. 'Sir Guy was not pleased.'

'That's to put it mildly,' Mrs Lamb said with a sniff. 'It has poisoned relations between us. I must warn you, Sophie. Do not expect to be well received.'

'Oh, I shall not,' Sophie said. 'Believe me, I expect nothing of the Woodvilles.'

'Then what will you do for money?' Her mother's expression was one of bewilderment.

'Money?' Sophie too looked puzzled.

'You can hardly expect *us* to keep you, dear, on a rector's stipend. I do hope you realise that. Unless George has left you money I'm afraid you will be destitute. For we have none.'

The first day after Sophie arrived home, she took her children into the small town of Wenham just to savour its sights and smells again. It was market day and the cattle still lined the street, although there was talk of building a market. She passed the Baker's Arms, which doubled as a magistrate's court, and the haberdasher's once owned by Miss Fairchild. The butcher, the baker, the greengrocer and the saddler were still there. Little had changed. She saw few people she knew, and even fewer seemed to recognise her. Eight years was a long time.

She felt isolated and alone, except for the children, her future precarious. She knew her parents were not poor, and their remarks about destitution had wounded her.

She walked down the hill and stood for a few moments at the gates of the Yetman house where Eliza, George's aunt, had lived with her husband Ryder until his death.

A young man who had crossed the bridge and ridden up the road, stopped at the gate and took off his hat.

'Good day, madam,' he said politely. 'May I help you?'

Sophie felt a little abashed, as if she'd been snooping, and stepped back.

'I am Sophie Woodville, the rector's daughter. I think you must be . . .'

'Laurence Yetman, ma'am. Eliza's son.' The young man jumped from his horse and extended his hand. 'Do *forgive* me, Mrs Woodville, I didn't recognise you.'

'Nor I you,' she smiled. 'But I have been away eight years.'

'I would be eighteen when you left, Mrs Woodville. I am now twenty-six and a married man myself. *Do* let me introduce you to my wife. She will be so pleased . . .'

Sophie put out a restraining hand.

'I would love to meet your wife, Laurence, but not now. She

will not be prepared and nor am I; but I am glad to know there are still Yetmans in Riversmead.'

'And will be for a long time to come, I hope, Mrs Woodville, because we have two children and a third on the way.'

'That *is* most exciting news,' Sophie laughed. 'And your mother?'

'My mother is very well, thank you.'

'I hear she remarried. Is she happy?'

'Very. She married Julius Heering, Lady Woodville's brother.'

'So I heard.' Sophie's expression remained impassive. She wondered if Julius Heering would be kinder to her than his sister Margaret.

'Do give your mother my best wishes, and your stepfather.'

'You can be sure I will.'

Laurence stood with his hat in his hand, watching her for some time as she walked slowly up the hill to keep pace with the small boy hanging on to her hand, the nursemaid in the rear, pushing a pram.

Sophie Lamb back in Wenham.

What, he wondered, would the people of the parish have to say about that?

Sophie sat with her mother, her two children on either side of her, that first Sunday back in Wenham for Matins, which was taken by her father with Mr Turner assisting. It was the last Sunday in September, a pale, mellow, autumnal day in which the Dorset countryside looked at its best. As Sophie crossed from the rectory to the church, through the boughs on the heavy chestnut tree she could see the brown sheep peacefully grazing in the meadow leading up from the river.

With the full peal of bells bursting joyfully forth, and the bent heads of the worshippers who hurried towards the church, she realised it was a sight quintessentially English that she had missed during all her years in New Guinea.

The choir were in good voice, singing from the organ loft, and as Sophie sat through the age-old ritual of the Established

Church her thoughts flew to the far-off mission station and the quiet grave under the lime tree.

> Onward, Christian soldiers!
> Marching as to war,
> With the cross of Jesus
> Going on before.

George had been a soldier who had fought the good battle for which he had forfeited his life. Sophie realised her eyes were swimming with tears and, as the hymn ended and there was a rustle as the congregation sat down, her father mounted the pulpit and, clearing his voice, seemed to project it to the back of the church – just at the same moment as the double doors were flung back, and all heads turned.

Sir Guy Woodville stood at the back, his legs apart, his head held high, hat in hand, and for a moment seemed to challenge the rector whose church he had not entered for years. Then he turned and climbed into the family pew at the back of the church. For a moment he knelt in prayer, then he sat down, his eyes on the man in the pulpit.

Sophie alone did not turn. She sensed who the newcomer was to have caused such interest, and folded her arms protectively around her two children. The rector, thoroughly confused, looked as though he were about to descend the steps again, his sermon finished. Mr Turner discreetly shook his head and the rector came to his senses and, unfolding the pages of his sermon, threw back his head. His smouldering gaze, which for so many years had struck fear into the hearts of his congregation, lingered on the back pew and travelled slowly down to his daughter and infant grandchildren.

'Dearly beloved,' he began, 'I am here today to tell you of the joy of my wife and myself upon the return of our only daughter Sophie, together with her two small children born in a foreign land. It is the first time we have seen them.

'As you well know, the circumstances of our daughter's return are mingled with grief, because behind her she has left the body of her husband; and his father has today joined us in this church. We welcome him.

27

'Our hearts go out to Sir Guy and Lady Woodville in their loss but, at the same time, we have the assurance of a blessed resurrection for a man who gave his life so nobly for God.

'Because George Woodville *was* a martyr. Gladly did he lay down his life for Christ . . .'

Sophie found that the words seemed to echo above her head, coming from afar. They could not see the grave, the tiny mission station with half-clothed natives whose houses were built on stilts. For her father, for Sir Guy and the congregation, George might have died; but for her he remained alive, in her heart. Every minute of the day. She saw him in the girls. But she saw also the suffering, emaciated face, the enfeebled body of a prematurely aged man as he fought that final battle. George had not wanted to die, even for Christ.

Sophie's head sank, and her chin rested on her breast. She felt the hand of little Ruth wriggle into hers. She knew, then, a sense of doubt, of unbelief, as though a curtain were being lowered between her and the Church, between her and God. What else made one believe in Him, against all odds, but faith? And what if that faith went?

What evidence had one, after all, for the very existence of a Being who seemed to expect so much and give so little? She tried to shake the doubts away as her father descended from the pulpit, and she raised her head and smiled at him. His words had been aimed at strengthening her faith, yet she had not heard them.

She rose to sing the hymn.

> He who would valiant be
>   'Gainst all disaster,
> Let him in constancy
>   Follow the Master . . .

And she tried to put all her heart in it.

> There's no discouragement
>   Shall make him once relent
> His first avowed intent
>   To be a pilgrim.

The chords crashed to a climax, the rector pronounced his blessing and, as the organ voluntary began, she took Charles' hand while Phoebe carried Ruth, and walked slowly to the exit, thinking that now she would at last confront her father-in-law.

But it was not to be the case. The Woodville pew was empty.

During the final hymn Sir Guy had gone.

Margaret Woodville sat by the window in the drawing-room at Pelham's Oak, her feet resting on a stool. From the window she could see the town, the square tower of the church, and she knew the day would not be far off when she would rest there with her daughter Emily. She had always been an active, energetic woman until the last year, when her strength had begun to fail and an illness had manifested itself which she knew, inevitably, would prove fatal.

Guy sat slumped in a chair next to her, his eyes too, it seemed, on the church he had decided at the last minute, and against her advice, to visit, and had left so abruptly, knowing that, always a coward in his life, he had not the courage for a confrontation.

'The elder girl is just like Emily,' he murmured. 'The very image of our darling daughter. Such an *uncanny* resemblance. I would have thought Emily had come back to us.'

'Perhaps she has,' Margaret said with a sigh.

'How do you mean?' Guy looked sharply at her.

'Who knows what happens to the soul after death, Guy? Maybe God put Emily's soul into Deborah, but then I know nothing about theology.' She seemed to dismiss the notion but her expression remained thoughtful.

'And you didn't stay to see them?'

'I could not. I lost heart. The rector stared at me so hard when I came in, I hadn't the courage. All the congregation turned to stare at me too.'

'No wonder!' Margaret gave a grim smile. 'You have not been to the church since you fell out with the rector.'

'I *had* to see my grandchildren; but when I saw *her*, the

woman, I knew that I felt as strongly as ever. I hate her, Margaret, the creature who took away our son. But for her, George would be here.'

Margaret nodded, for it was she who had stoked the flames of wrath in Guy. He had been eager to forgive, but she was not. She would never forgive, never receive a person who had caused so much pain. It was a pain that she prayed one day Sophie Woodville might feel herself.

Margaret did not exactly wish her grandchildren to be taken, but she hoped Sophie would suffer. That the mysterious hand of God would strike her down.

Margaret was a Calvinist. She believed in retribution; she lived by the book and she knew she was right.

George, the perfect son, had been taken from them, first to the missions and then to the hereafter, only a few years after their darling only daughter Emily had died of scarlet fever.

'An eye for an eye, a tooth for a tooth,' she said. 'You must not weaken, George. Sophie Lamb's no good. She is not a Christian, she can scarcely be human, or else she would have known what losing George meant to us. When I am gone I do not want you to weaken. Remember George, and what we lost . . .'

Guy, who could not bear to hear her talk of her death, jumped up from his chair and began agitatedly to pace the room.

'You know I will *not* hear this talk, Margaret. The doctor says it is your time of life . . .'

'The doctor would like *you* to think it is my time of life, but *I* know better. You know, Guy, that I have a disorder of the blood, that my anaemia is pernicious; that I may get weaker and not recover. That *is* the truth.'

'Oh my darling, my Margaret.' Guy threw himself on the floor beside her and flung his arms round her waist. 'Please . . .'

'You must be realistic, Guy.'

'So *soon* after George's death is it fair you should talk of your own? Of leaving me here without you? If you go, *I* will go, Margaret. I will put an end to myself and finish a life that has brought more sorrow than joy.'

Margaret put a hand on his head and ruffled his still thick

curls. How beautiful she had thought him twenty-eight years before; what a catch! She considered herself then the luckiest woman alive. Now time and the experience of marriage had taught her differently. It was true that, in their mellow years, their affection had been mutual, and when – if – she did go, she would leave a sorrowing husband behind. There was some consolation in the thought.

'However, Guy,' she said, still resting her hand on his head, 'there is nothing to prevent us attempting to see our grand-children, so long as we do not see *her*.'

'You mean, see *them*, without her?'

'Why not?' Margaret looked at him calmly. 'She is doubtless a practical woman and she must know how we feel. It is understandable we should want to see them. George would wish it.'

'But maybe he would like us to see her too,' Guy said, looking doubtful.

'George would know *quite* well how we would feel about his wife, which is why he went off secretly in the first place.' Margaret paused and lowered her voice. 'The only despicable thing he ever did.' Then, assuming her normal tone, she went on: 'George knew how the Woodvilles felt when Eliza eloped. You did not speak to her for years.'

'Times change, Margaret.'

'*Not* in matters like this, certainly not. Morals never change, and what Sophie Lamb did, and caused George to do, was immoral. She was much older than he, and she should have known better. Never forget that, Guy.'

'No, Margaret.'

Dear Mr Lamb,

My wife and I would very much like to see our grand-children. Naturally you realise they are all that is left to us of George, and we are sure it is something he too would wish.

Unfortunately we are unable to extend this invitation to his widow, for reasons which I am perfectly sure you, and she, will understand.

If you are agreeable, we shall arrange for the carriage to be sent so that we may meet them for tea. If all goes well, it is our hope that you will allow them a longer visit in due course.

> Yours sincerely,
> Guy Woodville, Bart.

Sophie gazed at the letter, and it was all she could do to stop herself screwing it into a ball and hurling it into the fire.

'Oh!' she cried in a burst of outraged feeling, 'how *dare* he. Addressed to *you*, Father, and not to me. As if I did not exist.'

The Reverend Lamb sat behind the desk at which he so often interviewed parishioners, and gazed at his daughter. Her feeling of outrage was understandable.

'But what are we to do?' he asked her. 'This living is in his gift. I am past retirement. It is solely due to him that I am still here. In the circumstances, he has been magnanimous.'

'*Father!* You surely cannot agree to this.' Sophie looked at him in astonishment. 'Well, even if you did, *I* shall certainly not agree to it.'

The rector wriggled uncomfortably. 'You are their mother, no question. But George is their father. I think the Woodvilles *have* a moral right to see their grandchildren.'

'And what are *my* rights?'

'I think you should let them. It would show you to be a person of magnanimity and, in due course, I am sure they will come round to your point of view. Besides,' he glanced at his desk, 'the rumour *is* that Lady Woodville is far from well. She may even be mortally ill. You would not wish to deprive a woman . . .'

'Lady Woodville!' Sophie said scornfully. '*She* is as healthy as an ox. Don't be bamboozled, Father.'

'How long is it since you saw her, Sophie? I'm told she has some disease of the blood that has considerably weakened her; she moves with difficulty and quickly loses breath. *Some* say it is a very pathetic sight in a woman formerly so strong.'

'Then what am I to do?' Sophie threw the letter down on her father's desk and sat opposite him.

He looked at her carefully. It was almost impossible to accept such a great change taking place in another person within so few years. His daughter. She had always been a strong character, devout, and no beauty. But now she had the kind of authority that usually came to people a good deal older. She carried herself with poise, her expression was grave, almost majestic.

It was difficult not to imagine that here was a woman fully capable of leading an impressionable young man in a direction he might not otherwise have taken. Sophie had said that she burned with the love of God to convert the heathen. But had she not also burned to have George Woodville for a husband? And would George Woodville have made her his wife had he not been persuaded? Would he have gone to the foreign missions *but* for her? His memories of George were of a charming, intelligent, comely and, above all, *serious* young man, a little in awe of the rector's daughter but not, then, in love.

Quite easy to see that he would follow where Sophie so firmly and competently led.

'Well, Father?' She tilted her head defiantly as though she could read his mind.

'I think you *should* agree.'

'Well, I shan't. I will accompany my children, or they shall not go at all. It is not good for them to see me ignored. Besides, I wish to discuss with Sir Guy the window that George wished to be put into the church.'

'But, my dear, *I* have told you that is in order,' the rector said feebly. 'I have no objection and nor will the parish council.'

'Yes, but should not Sir Guy also have to give permission? It is his church, endowed centuries ago by his family. Besides,' Sophie paused as though she had a sudden flash of inspiration, '*who* is to pay for it, Father? I have no money and nor, you say, have you. Surely we should have the best artist, the best stained glass, and who better to provide the wherewithal for that but George's father, Sir Guy, a wealthy man?'

2

Sitting in the garden of the rectory, to which she had invited herself, Eliza Heering watched the two young Woodville children playing on the lawn, little Ruth toddling about, trying hard to keep up with her sister.

'They are beautiful children,' she said, turning to Sophie. 'So resembling Emily, and George too, when he was small. He had the same blonde hair and big blue eyes. Oh Sophie, I'm *so* sorry.' Impulsively Eliza clasped the hand of the woman who, in the opinion of the family, had brought such unhappiness to the Woodville household. But Eliza was not so sure. She, for her part, considered that George had been sound in body and mind when he made up his mind to go to the foreign missions and marry Sophie Lamb. He had certainly known what he was doing.

Eliza had been close to her nephew, and had been as shocked by his death as any member of the family. She did not share her brother and sister-in-law's hostility to Sophie but, as a woman, she puzzled her. In a way, Sophie reminded her a little of herself when young; she too had eloped with the man she loved and incurred the opprobrium of her family.

'I feel we have a little in common, Sophie,' she said, tearing her eyes away from the children and gazing steadily at their mother. 'We defied our family to marry men we loved. I am sorry, though, that once again my brother is proving difficult, even though your circumstances were different from mine. But you see, Guy so loved George . . .'

'*I* so loved George,' Sophie protested. 'Why do people think *I* married him? For money? George had not a penny! For the title

34

he would inherit? Sir Guy has, hopefully, *many* years of life left to him. I had, and have, no interest in titles and, besides, George and I intended to make the foreign missions our lives.'

'Yes, yes, I know, but my brother can't see this.'

'*He* thinks I ensnared George. I was so much older. Maybe he imagined I was frightened of being left an old maid. Is *that* it?'

'Not at all,' Eliza tried to reassure her. 'It is because George went to the missions. Guy imagines, wrongly, that, but for you, he would have been content to have been some country parson and stayed in this country.'

'But George *yearned* to be a missionary.'

'George was anxious to enter the church, but Guy is convinced the idea of the foreign missions came from you, Sophie dear.'

'Oh, so *that's* it.' Sophie crossed her arms and turned her face resolutely away. '*I* am responsible for George's death.'

'No one else would think that but a grieving father and mother. I assure you *I* don't. That is why I am here. I would like to be an intermediary between you and Guy.'

'How do you mean?' Sophie looked at her suspiciously.

'Well, I thought if *I* might take the children . . .'

'No,' Sophie said, unfolding her arms. 'If they think they can get round me . . .'

'No one thinks anything of the kind. It was purely my idea. I have grandchildren myself. Laurence's children are about the same age as yours. His wife is a sensible local girl and you would like her. I am asking you and your children to come to tea with my grandchildren and to meet Laurence's wife. Guy and Margaret will not be there. I thought that if you could meet some of the family it would be easier, eventually, for you and Guy.'

In the circumstances, Sophie thought it would be churlish to refuse.

Laurence had married at the age of twenty-one a young woman very like him in temperament, and the same age. They were a handsome, likeable young couple, and Sarah-Jane Yetman, a farmer's daughter, was as sturdy and robust as she was pretty.

Eliza was very fond of her daughter-in-law, exactly the kind of woman she would have chosen for her son. They were generous, open-hearted people, and the conflicts in the Woodville family – especially the melodrama after the return of Sophie – were quite alien to their temperaments, and they would have no part of it.

'I wonder that a man can be so hard to his daughter-in-law,' Sarah-Jane murmured a few days later, as she and Eliza sat together on the bench on the lawn at Riversmead while the young children scampered about them, well wrapped up against the autumn chill. They were all very near to one another in age, and Sarah-Jane expected a new baby any day.

'You mean Guy?' Eliza looked askance at her. 'But he behaved exactly the same way to me when I ran away with Laurence's father. But then he was dominated by our mother. Now I ask myself if it is *Margaret* who refuses to accept her daughter-in-law. Sometimes I think she's the one to blame. Guy is a doting father and grandfather. He went out of his way to go to the church to see them, but he lacked the courage to stay. He's always been a little in awe of Margaret. *She's* the strong one.'

The young Yetmans saw little of the elder Woodvilles. They thought them rather strange. Young people in love, with plenty to do, they were concentrated on the family scene, their children and each other. They lived in their own small world, utterly happy and content.

Guy Woodville, coming up the road on his horse on his way to the cemetery, could not help seeing across the hedge the little people running about on the lawn, his sister sitting with Sarah-Jane on the bench. Without hesitation, he dismounted when he came to the gate and, unlatching it, led his horse up the drive. Ted Yewell, who had been doing some gardening in the herbaceous border, looked up and saw him.

'Why, sir,' he cried jumping up. 'Mrs Yetman didn't tell me you wus coming.'

'Mrs Yetman doesn't *know*, Ted,' Guy said, looking past him to the house. 'I saw her and my sister, the children playing on the lawn . . . Say, how is Elizabeth, Ted? I hear she is turning out a beauty.'

'She is that, sir,' Ted said with pride, having long forgotten that Elizabeth was an adopted daughter.

'What will she do with herself?' Guy tried to sound offhand. 'She must be eighteen or thereabouts.'

'Exactly eighteen, sir. She has gone with her mother to Blandford today. Mrs Sophie Woodville has taken them in the rector's carriage.'

'Oh, then she is not here?' Guy sighed with relief and handed Ted the bridle of his horse. 'I wondered.'

Just then Eliza, looking round, saw him and, with a cry, jumped up. At the same time she felt a stab of guilt, because if Sophie were to appear she would think the visit was premeditated. Sarah-Jane stayed where she was, gazing rather uncomfortably at Guy, who doffed his hat to her.

'Hello, Sarah-Jane. How are you?'

'Very well, Sir Guy,' she said.

'And Laurence and the children?'

'They are well too.'

But Guy seemed to be taking little notice of her, intent, as he walked slowly across the lawn, on his grandchildren. He stopped in front of Ruth, who looked up at him with interest and stopped her game.

Guy crouched on the lawn and took her hand.

'Hello, my dear. I'm your grandpapa.'

Ruth looked questioningly past him to Eliza, who had joined them.

'Guy. I . . .'

'She *is* my granddaughter, Eliza,' Guy said stubbornly, taking Ruth in his arms and hoisting her to his shoulder. 'I have asked, begged, to be able to see my granddaughters, and Sophie will not permit it.'

'Because *you* do not wish to see *her*.'

'She has no right,' Guy said in a preoccupied way, stroking Ruth's hair from her face. 'No right at all to deprive us of the pleasure of our grandchildren.'

37

'And I do not think *you* have any right, Sir Guy, to bar her from her husband's home.'

Guy and Eliza turned and looked with some astonishment at Sarah-Jane who, remaining where she was on the bench, her hand in front of her eyes shading them against the sun, stared across the lawn.

'I am wholly on the side of Sophie.' Sarah-Jane got slowly to her feet and walked ponderously over to them, clutching her stomach. 'George was her husband. They were married nearly six years. He died a noble, martyr's death and has left her bereft.'

'But what about us?' Guy wailed as he gently lowered Ruth to the ground. 'What about his parents? Did she consider *them* when she persuaded George to go to the foreign missions? Without her he would never have considered such a step. He was far too quiet a man and, besides, his health was never robust. I could have withstood his marriage to the rector's daughter, his vocation as a country parson, all these I could have forgiven and understood. But to go to New Guinea without even letting us know! That was entirely out of character as far as George was concerned, and I can only blame the influence of his wife.'

'Then I think you're very unjust.' Sarah-Jane reached for the hand of Abel Yetman, who tucked his through his mother's. 'Sophie came home especially at George's request, to see *you*, and to arrange to have a window in his memory. She intends to go back to the missions and, if you are not careful, you will see neither her nor your grandchildren again.'

'Back to New Guinea?' Guy gasped, looking with dismay at Eliza. 'That is terrible. To take these sweet, innocent children back to a place whose climate has killed their father? That I cannot allow. I cannot tolerate it.'

'But you will *have* to tolerate it, Guy,' Eliza said with an air of sweet reasonableness. 'If you will have nothing to do with Sophie, the matter is out of your hands. If you do agree to see her you may find her more reasonable and, I assure you, susceptible to any kindness. She is lonely and vulnerable, at odds with her elderly parents. Yet the people who could be second parents to her refuse to see her. And now,' she looked quickly towards the road, 'I think you should go. If she saw you here she might think we had arranged it behind her back. Nothing would distress me more.'

'Very well,' Guy said petulantly, and stooped to pat Charles on the head and bestow a kiss on Ruth's chubby cheek. 'I'll discuss the matter with my wife. In the end the decision will be hers.'

Then, without addressing the two women further, he put his hat firmly on his head and strode to where Ted was holding the reins of his horse.

'If you ever need help with Elizabeth,' Guy said in a low voice as he put a foot in the stirrup, 'with her education, or should she want money for a dowry, you have only to let me know. You know that, don't you?'

'Very *kind* of you, Sir Guy,' Ted said, touching his forelock as he helped the baronet to mount. 'And give my best wishes to her ladyship, sir.'

'I will,' Guy said. 'But not a word about what I just said . . . to anyone.

'I understand, sir.' Ted stood thoughtfully to one side as, nudging his horse, Guy went through the gate and up the hill, out of sight.

Guy took the bridle path home across the fields, through the woods and down the narrow little lanes of his native Dorset. He had been born there and now, he knew, he would die there. Long ago he had abandoned the lifestyle, manners and dress of a dandy, a man about town, and become a simple countryman. He felt close to the soil and the people who lived there, and much of it had to do with the death of his daughter, Emily, from scarlet fever when she was twelve. Since then he had been a changed man, grieving over his past, sorrowful for his sins and, until the rector's daughter had gone off with his son and heir, a worshipper at St Mark's church and close friend of the rector.

Quite irrationally, Guy felt the rector was responsible for the behaviour of his daughter. He had turned against his former friend and scarcely ever attended Divine Service in the church which was in his gift.

Guy crossed a stream and paused, letting his horse drink from its clear water.

From where he was he had an excellent view of his patrimony: Pelham's Oak, handed down from father to son since the sixteenth century. Remodelled in the eighteenth century, it was now a Palladian mansion clad in Chilmark stone, with a pillared portico, large windows and graceful Georgian lines. It stood on a hill and was a landmark for many, and so was the huge tree on the sloping lawn, planted, it was said, as an acorn by that Pelham after whom the house was named.

Guy always had a deep sense of contentment as he gazed at his home, the feeling of love and familiarity he had for the place where he was born.

He finally took his eyes from it and, as his horse had quenched her thirst, let his gaze wander to the cottage where Ryder Yetman had lived before he eloped with Eliza. It had taken Guy a long time to forgive that, too. Was he, perhaps, in essence an unforgiving man?

He began the climb across the meadows up to the house and, skirting it, observed an unfamiliar horse tethered to a post in the drive. The stable boy, Ned, who was rubbing it down and giving it oats, respectfully touched his forelock as Guy rode up to him and began to dismount.

'Mornin', Sir Guy.'

'Morning, Ned.' Guy looked across at the horse, now with its nuzzle deep in a bag of oats.

''Tis Mr Platt's horse, sir. Farmer Platt of Nether Bend Farm.'

'Oh, I know Platt,' Guy said, tossing his reins to Ned. 'I wonder what ails him?'

Ned said nothing but began taking the saddle off Guy's horse, Daisy, preparatory to rubbing her down. At the door of the house Arthur, the butler, his face as usual impassive, greeted his master.

'I hear David Platt is here,' Guy said amiably, tossing his hat to Arthur.

'I have put him in the morning parlour, Sir Guy.'

David Platt was a tenant farmer, a good one who provided Pelham's Oak with much of its fresh meat and garden produce.

Guy strode across the hall and flung open the door before Arthur could reach it.

'Well, David,' he said, going towards his tenant, hand outstretched, 'this *is* a pleasant surprise.'

The man mumbled something and anxiously rolled the brim of his hat round in his hands.

'You don't look too happy, David.' Guy pointed to a chair. 'Please sit down.'

'Oi'd rather stand if it be all right with you, Sir Guy,' the farmer said, his eyes avoiding Guy's.

'My good fellow, I can see that there is something wrong,' Guy said anxiously. 'Is it the rent? Is it too high? Do we not pay our bills on time? Come man, out with it. What is it?'

'It is about your son, Sir Guy,' David Platt said, his voice thick with emotion. 'Oi'll be honest with you.'

'Oh!' Guy, drawing out a chair, flopped into it and, reaching in his breast-pocket for a handkerchief, began to mop his brow. 'Carson.'

'You know he's been hanging around my daughter, Susan, Sir Guy.'

'No, I didn't.' Guy sighed loudly. 'But I do know that he gets up to a lot of things in which he shouldn't concern himself. I am sorry if he is troubling your daughter.'

'It's not only *troubling*, Sir Guy,' the aggrieved father said and, as if feeling better for unburdening himself, flopped down in a chair next to Guy. 'It's not *only* as if he was bent on seduction – and who knows but what that may not have happened.' The farmer raised his eyes to the ceiling. 'But he fills her head with all kinds of ideas . . .'

'Such as?' Guy looked at him in alarm.

'Promises her *marriage* and such, Sir Guy. Fills 'er head with all sorts of notions.' The farmer wriggled in his chair and crossed one leg over the other. 'Susan is a good girl, so far as I know. She is seventeen and not averse to work. She helps her mother in

41

the house and regularly attends chapel. But ever since Carson has been hanging around,' the farmer gave an exaggerated sigh, 'her mind baint on her work, and not on her prayers neither, I shouldn't wonder.'

'Susan is, if I remember, extraordinarily pretty,' Sir Guy said thoughtfully. 'Maybe you should send her away, David?'

'Send her *away*?' The farmer looked indignantly at his landlord. 'And pray, where to, sir, and, above all, *why*? She's my only daughter, and her mother's help and companion. Why should *oi* send her, just because *your* son pesters her and fills her with notions above her station?' He leaned forward and tapped the arm of his chair with a thick finger. 'Why don't you send Master Carson away, Sir Guy? You have the means, and if you asks me, the sooner it be done the better. You will not only have him wed to someone you consider unworthy of your noble family, but you will have a number of bastard grandchildren scattered around the area, if you have not already. And that will be trouble in plenty for you, Sir Guy. Trouble in plenty.'

After the farmer had gone, Guy, suddenly feeling his years, went into the dining-room and helped himself to a glass of sherry. It was nearly time for lunch but he was not hungry. He looked out of the window at the land that he loved, clothed now in the soft mists of autumn. The leaves were slowly changing colour and falling gently down from the trees. Soon it would be winter, and the anniversary of George's death in that far-off, inhospitable climate.

George, the good, the kind, had gone, and in his mind he saw his girls scamper playfully across the lawn. Guy swallowed his sherry and was returning for another when there was a knock at the door and Arthur deferentially put his head around it.

'Will you be lunching alone, Sir Guy?'

'Is Lady Woodville not lunching?' Guy looked up from the decanter in surprise.

'Her Ladyship has decided to spend the day in her room.'

'Then I will lunch there with her.'

'Very good, Sir Guy.'

The butler withdrew and Guy, a full glass in his hand, left the dining-room and crossed the large hall, mounting the staircase to his wife's room on the first floor. He tapped quietly on the door and turned the handle before she had time to call.

To his surprise he found she was still in bed. Sometimes she stayed in her room sewing or reading, but she always rose, bathed and dressed.

Guy rapidly crossed the room and sat on the side of her bed, stretching out a hand to touch her cheek.

'My dear, are you ill?'

Margaret, who had been half-asleep, opened her eyes and looked at him in surprise.

'Today the effort was too great, Guy. I tried to get up but my maid helped me back to bed again.'

'Then I will send for Dr Hardy at once.' Guy made as if to get up, but Margaret clung onto his arm.

'Guy, dearest, what is the use? We both know what is the matter. It is merely a question of time.'

Guy impatiently shook her hand away and, getting off the bed, stood gazing down at her.

'Margaret, what nonsense you talk! You are not yet sixty, not ready to die!'

'Nevertheless, dearest, I feel that what ails me is mortal.'

'I will *not* hear such talk.' Guy stomped angrily away from her bed and stood once more gazing out of the window as if his own life were passing. What a barren landscape it would be without her! 'The doctor has pronounced no such sentence.'

'If he doesn't know, I do,' Margaret said quietly.

'Anaemia, that is all.'

'Certain types of anaemia can be a serious matter.'

'I will take you away to Germany, Switzerland, Italy . . . There, at the health spas, you will find the treatment you need. I will make arrangements for it straightaway.'

'Guy . . .' Margaret held out a hand and beckoned him to her side. 'Sit by me, Guy.'

'Not if you are going to talk . . .'

'*Sit* by me,' she commanded.

Docilely, Guy took his place by her side and gazed at the

face he had once considered so plain but now loved so much. The thought of life without his sensible, practical wife was intolerable. She not only managed him, she managed the whole estate. He took her hand and brought it to his lips.

'Without you I would be broken, Margaret. *Please* don't leave me.'

'Guy, only God knows the time and the place; but I am weak and growing weaker. Frankly, I could not make the journey to Poole or Bournemouth, never mind the Continent. Every day, my dear, I feel a little more frail. I must tell you this because I want you to be prepared, should it happen.'

Guy crashed a fist into the palm of his hand. 'But after George . . . it's too cruel!' He threw himself across his wife's body and began to weep bitterly, while Margaret lay there feeling strangely calm. Gently she stroked his forehead. What an irony it was that now, when her husband was finally hers, she should have to contemplate leaving him.

'George's death was a terrible blow to me too,' Margaret whispered. 'And I too long to see our grandchildren . . .'

'I saw them today,' Guy burst out, struggling to sit upright, dabbing his eyes with his handkerchief. 'I was on my way to the churchyard to say a little prayer at Emily's tomb and, passing Riversmead, I saw a number of children on the lawn, Eliza and Sarah-Jane sitting on a bench watching them. And there I saw the two little girls – the spitting images of our dearest boy.'

'And Sophie . . .?' Margaret stared at him in alarm.

'Sophie had gone into Blandford. Eliza was anxious that she might return and imagine Eliza had purposely contrived the meeting. Dearest, I wonder . . .'

'If you wonder if I have changed my mind about George's wife, the answer is no,' Margaret said with a sudden strength in her voice. 'However wicked it is of me to feel such hatred for the woman who took George from us, I cannot help it.'

'Not even for the sake of the grandchildren?'

'Not even for them,' Margaret said firmly. 'Even if I have to go to my grave without sight of them.'

They were interrupted by a further tap on the door and

Arthur entered bearing a tray, followed by one of the maids with another, which she arranged on Margaret's lap.

'There, my lady. The beef tea is particularly nourishing and cook says you should drink *all* of it.'

'Thank you,' Margaret said with a sweet smile and, pulling the tray towards her, reached for the cup and took a few sips.

'Delicious!' she exclaimed. 'Just what I need to restore me to health. Tell cook it is excellent.'

Guy had a more solid lunch, but his heart was not on his food and after a few mouthfuls taken at a table set near Margaret's bed, he pushed his plate away.

'There is one affliction after another in this household,' he said mournfully. 'God is punishing me for the misdeeds of my youth.'

'*Only* your youth, Guy dear?' Margaret said with a mischievous smile, but Guy ignored her.

'David Platt from Nether Bend Farm was here only a short time ago, complaining about Carson . . .'

'Oh, *who* is not forever complaining about Carson?' Margaret said offhandedly.

'But this is serious. He has told the farmer's daughter he intends to marry her.'

'But that is absurd, out of the question . . .'

'She is extraordinarily pretty, and he is over twenty-one.'

'But she is not.'

'Remember what happened to Eliza? That didn't stop her.'

'No.' Thoughtfully Margaret put down her mug of tea, recalling, as if it were yesterday instead of twenty-eight years before, the occasion when she and Guy returned home from her native Holland to be told that Eliza, just eighteen, had eloped with the son of a builder.

The daughter of a farmer was not so very different in the social scale.

'He must go away,' she said suddenly.

'That is what the farmer suggested. But where? And will he go?'

'He will *have* to. You must tell him you will disinherit him.'

'That won't worry Carson.'

It was true. The heir to the Woodville name dressed and behaved like a farm-hand, with little thought for wealth.

'We must appeal to his better nature. I know, we must send for Uncle Prosper,' Margaret said, with the light of inspiration in her eyes. 'Now, Guy, ask my maid to come, because suddenly I feel a little stronger. Maybe it *was* that good beef tea.'

Guy went slowly over to her and embraced her, holding her tightly against his heart.

If only her cure could be so simple.

Prosper Martyn was Carson's great-uncle, the brother of his grandmother who had died when he was fourteen. Carson remembered her vividly, although she was a remote, rather elderly figure, smelling of violets, whom he used to visit with his brother and sister in great state, usually with his father. His mother and grandmother did not get on.

Perhaps it was because there was a certain amount of discord in his family, undercurrents of which he could not help but be aware, that Carson, the youngest child, had become rather difficult. As he got older he grew increasingly hard to control, until in the end everyone gave up and he more or less did as he wished.

Maybe his father was not firm enough, his mother too distant; the only one he really loved and who, in turn, loved and understood him, had been his elder brother.

Now George was dead and Carson shared the family resentment of Sophie for taking George away.

Carson had had little to do with Great-Uncle Prosper. He thought him very old, but considered his wife, Aunt Lally, very beautiful, even though by now she seemed to him a little old too. In her youth she had been a dancer and, apparently, quite lovely. He liked to visit their beautiful house near Sherborne, which had originally been built by Julius Heering before he married Eliza.

An invitation to visit Uncle Prosper and Aunt Lally usually coincided with a visit by Aunt Lally's nephew, Roger, whom she and Uncle Prosper had adopted when he was twelve.

Carson and Roger were antipathetic to each other. Roger worked in the Martyn-Heering business, a wealthy conglomerate which included a bank, in the City of London. Roger was spectacularly good-looking, his colouring fair, like Aunt Lally's, and he was always well and correctly attired. His speech was clipped and polished, his manners impeccable. He had the air of a dandy, the hauteur of a grandee.

Carson, in fact, detested him.

He was therefore rather glad to arrive at the Martyns' imposing house and find that his cousin was not there. He was apparently to be alone with the Martyns for lunch. He had ridden over on horseback, but had taken unusual care to shave and wear a collar and tie.

Uncle Prosper gave him a glass of sherry on arrival to warm him, and then sent for his valet to brush his clothes while Carson combed his hair and washed his hands.

When he re-entered the lounge, Aunt Lally was there, looking, as usual, cool, elegant, even regal. Carson closed his eyes as she kissed his cheek; the fragrance always reminded him of his grandmother, though it was more sophisticated than violets; something, surely, Parisian and expensive.

They sat at the great table in the dining-room, three people served by six servants; the fare, simple and delicious, was produced by Aunt Lally's chef, whom she claimed she had poached from the Ritz in Paris. The vintage wines were from Uncle Prosper's cellar, carefully chosen and racked for years.

Carson wished that his parents would live like the Martyns; but his mother had stopped his father drinking and only water was ever served at table. The fare at home was simple, locally produced, and cooked by a motherly body called Mrs Pine whose skills were basic.

At one time his parents had kept a grand table and been waited on by servants; but now there was only Arthur, who had been at the house over twenty years, and a few housemaids who were seldom seen unless scurrying about with pails of water or scuttles full of coal, or blacking the grate or scrubbing floors.

Aunt Lally was very entertaining about her recent visit to the Continent, the scale of her purchases in Paris and Rome, bringing a fond smile to Uncle Prosper's lips because he loved her and indulged her. Carson was a little in love with Aunt Lally too, although she was more than twice his age. He listened to her quite rapt, envious of the life she led.

After lunch Aunt Lally left them in the drawing-room with brandy and coffee. She liked to rest in the afternoon, and would join them for tea. Uncle Prosper stood gazing at the door through which Aunt Lally had gone, as though still savouring her presence. Then he lit a cigar and drew on it, blowing smoke into the air.

'I love her, you know,' Uncle Prosper said, after he had got his cigar drawing to his satisfaction. He was a fine, distinguished-looking man, his hair pure white but still thick; rather bushy-browed, and as tall as Carson, who was six feet two.

'She is a fine woman,' Carson agreed politely. 'I am very fond of Aunt Lally.'

'And you, Carson,' Uncle Prosper thoughtfully considered the tip of his by-now glowing cigar. 'Is it not time you thought of settling?'

'I'm only twenty-two, Uncle.' Carson looked aghast.

'I don't necessarily mean settling to *marriage*,' Prosper said gently. 'I mean to say, settling down in general. You know what I mean.'

'I am *quite* settled, thank you, Uncle,' Carson said huffily.

'In your *own* opinion, perhaps.'

'What do you mean?' Carson paused in the act of raising the brandy glass to his lips.

'Your parents find you *very* unsettled.'

'You mean, "difficult"?'

Carson scowled. It was an ugly sight, Prosper thought. It made him look petulant, rude and uncouth. And yet he was a handsome boy and, to him and Lally, invariably charming; but towards Roger he was abrupt.

'Well, why should they find *you* difficult, Carson?'

It then dawned on Carson that he had been invited to lunch – a rare occurrence in itself – for a purpose. He was being given a grilling.

Carson, looking towards the clock on the mantelpiece, rose to his feet, hands in his pockets. 'I think I should be going, Uncle,' he said stiffly, not answering the question.

'Sit down,' Prosper commanded, inclining his head towards the chair. 'Where are your manners? Your aunt expects you to stay for tea. She would be most disappointed to come down and find you'd gone.'

'Well . . . in that case.'

It was put in a pleasant yet authoritative manner. Hard even for one as direct as Carson to refuse. Abruptly, he sat down again, and Prosper leaned towards him, replenishing his glass.

'Yes, I *have* as a matter of fact asked you for a little chat today, as you seem to suspect, Carson . . .'

'Did my father suggest it?'

There was that scowl again.

'Well.' Prosper inclined his head. 'Maybe. You are the heir, his only surviving child. He expects much from you.'

'And he thinks it is not forthcoming?' Carson growled.

'Well, perhaps not yet . . .'

'Why did he expect so much of me?'

'For the reasons I suggested. Maybe he was over-indulgent towards you when you were younger, mainly because he had every expectation that George would succeed him. The death of dear George changes everything.'

Carson pursed his lips stubbornly. 'I can't see why.'

'But you *must* see it, my dear boy,' Prosper insisted. 'You are relatively uneducated. You got yourself expelled from school. You have no particular skills and I believe – I am told – you have an unsavoury reputation in the neighbourhood.'

'What sort of reputation?'

'You know what I am talking about, Carson.' Prosper began to sound exasperated. He could recall the scene so long ago with Carson's Aunt Eliza when they had tried unsuccessfully to marry her off to a most suitable man. They were stubborn, these Woodvilles. Maybe his talk with Carson would have the same unsatisfactory outcome as the talk with Eliza who, after all, had eloped with Ryder Yetman.

'I suppose you mean women,' Carson suggested after a moment.

'I suppose I do.' Prosper suddenly chuckled, and the atmosphere between them seemed less fraught.

'My father also had a reputation when he was young,' Carson said with a smirk.

'So he did,' Prosper agreed, 'but *he* was lucky to find a good woman like your mother.'

'He married her for her money.'

'I see. So that's what you think?'

'It's what everyone says.' Carson, clearly unintimidated, stared boldly at his uncle, who began to appreciate how right his parents were to be worried about him.

'Well, whatever happened, and whatever the reason was *then*, you need have no doubt now but that your parents love each other.'

'Yes, I think they do.' Carson sat back.

'It is a good marriage, and it has grown; but, as I said, I'm not talking about marriage yet for you, Carson. I would like to offer you a position in my firm . . .'

'What?' In one movement Carson bounded out of his chair and stood facing his uncle, his expression aghast.

'At the Martyn-Heering concern, to learn the business as Roger has, to become a partner. Perhaps, in time, a man of substance . . .'

'No thank you.'

'Hear me out.'

'I don't *want* to. I have no intention of being a business man.'

'Then what is it you intend to be?' Prosper's tone suddenly grew less friendly.

'A free spirit . . .'

'Ah!' Prosper was again reminded of Eliza, who had used the very same expression. 'And how long do you think that will continue?'

'Until Father dies, maybe, and as he is still young and in good health, that will be a long time.' He tossed his head confidently. 'I mean to enjoy myself, Uncle. I will not go to the City, I will not be a business man – certainly not that! I came into a little inheritance when I was twenty-one, so I am not inclined to work.' He paused momentarily. 'In fact there *is* nothing much I wish to do . . .'

'Except upset your parents more and more. The little money you inherited – a few shares plus a hogshead of port from me, laid down at your birth – won't last for ever.'

'My parents must accept me as I am.'

'Carson!' Prosper leaned towards him and placed the stub of his smouldering cigar carefully in an ashtray. 'I wish to speak to you very seriously, and I want you to listen carefully to what I have to say.'

'Please, Uncle.' Carson reluctantly sat down again. 'I don't wish to be rude to you, but . . .'

'I'm sure you don't, and you won't. If you hear me out I think you will realise why I'm so serious, Carson.' For several moments Prosper looked steadily into his great-nephew's eyes. 'I wonder if you realise how ill your mother is?'

'Ill?' Instant alarm showed on Carson's face.

'Had you not realised it?'

'I knew she was tired.'

'She is very *ill*.'

'You mean . . .?'

'She could be dead within a year.'

'Oh *no*!' Carson gazed defiantly at his uncle. 'Are you saying this to frighten me, to get me to do as you wish?'

'I wish I were.' Prosper sighed. 'Your mother has a disorder of the blood, a kind of cancer, which is slowly killing her. No one knows how long it will take; but the fact is, Carson, that you and your behaviour are causing her great distress, and it cannot help her condition. Only recently a farmer spoke to your father about your relationship with his daughter.'

'Susie Platt!' Carson said derisively.

'Apparently you told this girl you wanted to marry her.'

'I tell them all that,' Carson said with a sly smile. 'It is sometimes the only way . . .'

'Carson!' Now the normally equable Prosper felt his patience snap. 'Please be serious. This man was your father's tenant.

Your father told your mother. Your parents are very, very distressed by such behaviour.'

'So they want me to be a business man.' Carson laughed derisively.

'It is not only that. They want *you* to assume the responsibility that George had.'

'I can never be like George.' Suddenly Carson had a stricken, vulnerable look on his face; the look of a bereaved younger sibling.

'You *can* be like George, if you wish.'

'Never, never,' Carson protested. 'George was everything that was good.'

'George *was* everything that was good,' Prosper agreed. 'He gave his life in a noble cause. You have the same parents, so why should *you* be as worthless as George was good? Tell me.'

'I cannot.' Carson, bending his head, spoke in a whisper. 'I loved George. Most truly. I was broken by his death. But Mother . . . *If* what you say is true?'

He looked hopefully up at Prosper as though wishing he would say he had been joking, but Prosper only shook his head.

'I'm afraid it is only too true. They did not want to alarm you. They thought that if they told you you would not believe them. In fact your father does not truly believe it, because he does not wish to either. But I have spoken to the doctor and it is a fact that pernicious anaemia can lead to death.'

Prosper rose from his seat and, walking over to the fire, threw a couple of logs onto it so that the flames blazed up the chimney. Then, hands in the pockets of his waistcoat, he turned and gazed solemnly at Carson. 'Your parents know that I am talking to you. It would be well to mention that I have brought up the subject of your mother's health. If God wills it, she may have, perhaps, a few more years, but if she dies . . .' Prosper shrugged. 'Imagine the effect on your father. He will be devastated. He will need you to lean on. If you continue to be so irresponsible you will not be someone on whom he *can* lean. I want you to reflect, Carson, to reform; to think about your family and your place, sooner perhaps than you think, at its head . . .'

'But Father will not die . . .'

'Who knows? Imagine his grief if anything should happen to your mother. Anyway, consider your life here.' He sat down again, looking a little contemptuously at the younger man. 'It is not much, is it? It is not *really* satisfying? Whoring and drinking? Really, at twenty-two, is that all you wish?'

'Well . . .' Carson scratched his head.

'Exactly. Now I do not wish you to become a monk but, believe me, in London you could have a very good life, work during the day, play at night. Your father did it, you know, for several years.'

'He hated it.'

'It is true he was not cut out for the life of business . . .'

'Neither am I.'

'I'm not so sure.' Prosper glanced at his watch. 'I think you're different from Guy. I think *you* could be ambitious. I think you are capable; you could even, perhaps, be very successful. Guy had a wealthy wife and felt he did not need to work. You do. Your father's fortune is not what it was. Your mother's dowry was spent long ago.

'You see,' he realised suddenly that Carson was paying careful attention to him, 'your father's indifference to business meant the estate was badly managed. Gone are the days when a man could live on capital, on the fat of the land, without either work or wise investments. Your father was good at neither. Now, what say you think about it?' Thinking the message was beginning to get home, Prosper tapped the face of his watch with his fingers. 'Your aunt will be along any minute. Please be good enough to pull the bell, as it is time for tea.'

Carson lay with his head in his mother's lap, something she could hardly recall since he was a small boy. Margaret stroked his thick ash-blond hair, thinking how fair it had been when he was small. All Guy's children were like Guy, which was fortunate. She had never been a beauty, with her over-large mouth, her long, protuberant nose; now her thin angular body was gaunt and wracked by disease. Nor had she been an overtly loving mother. But, despite that, her children were her life; in the early days of her marriage they had done much to make up for the misdemeanours of her husband.

'I am not so *gravely* ill . . .' she whispered.

'They said you were. Uncle Prosper and Aunt Lally. Oh Mother, why did you not tell me?'

'Because I do not really know myself, that is the truth,' she said with a weary smile. 'Some days I feel worse than others. I am anaemic. I must drink wine and eat plenty of red meat, and this I do.'

'Then you may still get well?' Carson raised his head, and to her astonishment she saw tears glistening on his lashes. This most wilful, recalcitrant of children cared about her after all! It was a pity he'd waited until she was nearly dead to show affection.

'Of course I may,' she said, smiling, 'and if you will reform and do as Uncle Prosper suggests . . .'

'I will do *anything* for you, Mother.'

'That will make me better, then.' Margaret raised his head with her hands and gazed into his eyes, relishing each precious, unique minute of their intimacy.

'But if I go to London you won't have me near you.'

'But, my darling, the very fact that you are engaged in some profitable activity will be like meat and drink to me. You have no idea how much your father and I have worried about you, dearest child. Your wayward behaviour has been a source of *much* misery to us . . .'

'Oh *Mother*, and has made you ill . . .'

Carson once more flung his arms around her and buried his face in her lap. 'I promise that those days are gone forever. I will do everything I can to make you well again, even if it means leaving you, Mother. I will *never* let you worry about me again.'

'Well then.' Margaret, realising that she did feel strangely better, took a clean handkerchief from her pocket and began to dab his eyes. 'We shall get you some new clothes and pack your bags. Believe me, my dearest, *nothing* will give your father and me more joy than to see you happily at work. After all, half of you is Dutch, and we Heerings have such a strong tradition of industry . . .'

But the other half? Her voice trailed off into uncertainty as she saw the look of doubt which came into Carson's eyes.

Yes, he was her son, but he was Guy's too.

3

Sophie Woodville was an unhappy, frustrated woman. She had not, it was true, exactly looked forward to her return home, but though she had tried valiantly to overcome the many obstacles confronting her, she had not been completely successful.

Her parents were elderly, her father semi-retired. He was very dependent on the Reverend Turner, who more and more came to assume the duties of parish priest.

Whatever Turner's private ambitions, he seemed a nice enough, modest man, not quite as full of the spirit of God as dear George had been, perhaps a little too worldly but, nonetheless, a diligent and worthy clergyman.

Then there was the question of her children, fatherless and now adjusting to a climate very different from the one into which they had been born. They felt the English cold, the harsh westerly winds, the snow that lay like a thick blanket over the countryside for much of the January following their return.

The main drawback, when it came down to it, was the fact that parents and daughter had not lived together for several years. And when there was added to this the fact that Sophie had left under a cloud, that the Lambs disapproved of her marriage almost as much as the Woodvilles, it was not surprising that the reunion was only moderately successful. Discord lay just below the surface, tempers were short, and Sophie decided to look for a place to rent so that she might establish a home of her own. She was a married woman, a widow, who had exercised considerable control over her younger husband. She did not now enjoy being treated like a girl, the daughter who, in her parents' eyes, had never left home.

The trouble was that she had very little money, scarcely enough to exist. George had not been well off, had spent his small inheritance on his studies, and she hadn't a penny of her own. She was dependent on the goodwill of her parents, and that rapidly evaporated when eventually, after four troubled months, she told them what she had in mind.

'I fear I may be too much a *burden* on you,' she explained, knowing how lame, how inadequate her excuse sounded.

'How can you be a burden in a house *this* size?' The rector's tone was querulous. 'We have enough room for a dozen refugees from the missions, never mind three. It is the *least* we can do to give you a home.'

'I still feel it is too much to ask of you and mother, Father, to look after two young children at your time of life.'

'But you have a nursemaid,' her mother said sweetly, 'the children are no trouble at all.'

'I really *prefer* to have my own household.' Sophie pulled her shawl across her shoulders. It was time to be honest with them. 'I thought, perhaps, a small cottage.'

'And *who* will pay?'

There was an unpleasant edge to her mother's voice, that sounded strange. It made Sophie aware of what destitution really meant. It was humiliating, deprivation of choice.

'Yes, *who* shall pay?' Her father seized at the opportunity to emphasise his daughter's dilemma. 'When we have a *vast* house here, with *dozens* of rooms, what do you think the people of this parish will say to the impoverished widow of a missionary – the daughter of the Rector of Wenham, whom everyone knows – maintaining a separate establishment?'

'You have ideas above your station, Sophie,' her mother admonished her gently. 'I thought you were a woman humbled by your harsh experiences, but now I am not so sure.'

Sophie turned away, biting her lip. Her parents knew what was wrong but they pretended to ignore it. She felt more than ever reduced to the status of an unmarried woman, dominated once again by her parents as she had been until George had freed her.

Her eyes pricked with tears and she walked quickly to the window. Despite the beauty of the scene, it was like looking out of a prison: the trees were bare, and even the birds standing disconsolately on the skeletal boughs of the trees seemed cold.

She had been wrong to return to Wenham. She should have followed her instincts and disobeyed George's wishes. She should have stayed among people with whom, at least, she was happy, fulfilling a mission that brought her close to God. Now she sometimes felt that she had somehow lost touch with Him, that, like her enjoyment of life, her faith was slowly draining away.

She leaned her hot brow against the windowpane and found herself staring straight into the eyes of Mr Turner, who appeared at the gate of the house opposite, which had once belonged to Euphemia Monk, who had married John Yetman, as his second wife.

Mr Turner raised his hand and waved, and she waved back. He was always so robust, so cheerful, that just the sight of him did one good.

'Mr Turner,' she cried, and it seemed her spirits rose.

'He will have come to talk to your father about Sunday's sermon,' Mrs Lamb said. 'How fortunate we were to have him as curate.'

Sophie and her mother turned spontaneously towards the door as Mr Turner was shown into the room. Despite the short distance he had to travel, he was heavily protected against the cold with gaiters, a long coat, a warm muffler, gloves, and his hat, which he held in his hand. He was a man who took good care of himself.

Otherwise he wore conventional clerical gear, a black suit, vest, and a white collar. He had a pleasant, affable expression and, after shaking Mrs Lamb's hand, extended his hand towards Sophie. She clasped it, and it seemed as though a silent strength flowed between them, an exchange of energy that surprised them both.

'Good day, Mrs Woodville,' he said. 'And how do you like

our English weather?' He blew between the palms of his hands before extending them to the fire roaring up the chimney.

'I was born in Wenham, Mr Turner.' Sophie, still surprised by the feeling between them, managed a smile. 'Don't forget that.'

'But eight years in the South Seas!'

'There are compensations,' she said, 'in being at home, though I shall be moving soon.'

'Oh!' He looked in surprise from her mother to her father and then back to her again.

'What nonsense,' her father snorted. 'This house is big enough for an army, and yet she talks about living separately.'

The Reverend Turner obviously thought it wiser not to comment and, after warming his hands, sat in a chair opposite the rector.

'There is a cottage in this living which is empty.'

'Oh?' Sophie looked eagerly at him.

'It belonged to the verger. It is on the other side of the school hall.'

'Oh, a *pretty* little cottage.' Sophie clasped her hands together.

'Very pretty,' Mr Turner agreed. 'And the new verger does not need it because he has a home of his own. Our last verger was unmarried.'

'Quite unsuitable for Sophie,' the rector said bluntly. 'No amenities. Freezing in winter.'

'It *does* have three bedrooms.'

'I would thank you, Mr Turner, not to concern yourself too much about our family matters.'

'Oh, I *beg* your pardon, rector.' Mr Turner, clearly ill at ease, lowered his head. Then, quickly producing some notes from his vest pocket, he said:

'Matthew five, verse three . . .'

Mrs Lamb signalled to Sophie and the two women moved silently out of the room.

As Sophie's mother gently closed the door behind her, she turned to her daughter with a reproving glance.

'You must *not* upset your father. He is not a well man.'

'Mother, *you* must not blackmail me,' Sophie hissed. 'I refuse to feel guilty.'

' I am *surprised* at you, Sophie.' Mrs Lamb propelled her daughter along the corridor towards her sitting-room at the end of the house. 'Here you have everything you could wish for. We keep you *and* pay the nurse who looks after your children. You want for *nothing* . . . nothing.' Her mother's words reverberated around the room.

'Except my *freedom*, Mother.'

'You are perfectly free.'

'I am not. I am treated like a child and not like a married woman, a widow of thirty-three years of age. When I go out you ask me where I am going and what time I shall return.'

'*That* seems to me a reasonable request. You have the household to consider, after all.'

'Well, *I* don't think it is reasonable. I want my own establishment, my own house until such time as I can return to the missions. I really don't wish to sound ungrateful, Mother.'

'I find you *very* ungrateful, Sophie,' her mother said primly. 'Ungrateful *and* difficult, yes, I'll admit it. Your father and I are very surprised by the change in you since your return. You seem to take for granted all we have done and do for you.'

'I am *not* ungrateful, Mother.' Sophie gritted her teeth, and kneaded the knuckles of one hand in the palm of another.

'A penniless widow, rejected by her parents-in-law, yet whom *we* have taken to our bosoms in a true Christian spirit. You behaved as badly towards *us* as you did to them, yet *we* have not rejected you.'

'I did *not* behave badly.'

'You eloped with a man.' Her voice rose.

'I *did not* elope.'

Her mother stuck a finger in the air like an avenging angel. '*You* travelled with him *alone* on a boat all the way to Australia without being married. Imagine what people thought of *that*!'

'Nothing untoward occurred.' Sophie also raised her voice, feeling her pulse quickening. 'George and I were Christians, who would not have dreamed of anticipating marriage, a sacrament ordained by God. I shared a cabin with two other ladies of similar virtue, bound for the missions.'

'That is *not* the point. No one in Wenham knows that.'

'Then *tell* them, Mother.' Sophie now found herself shouting. '*Tell* the whole world that I shared a cabin with *two* ladies of impeccable credentials who will vouch for the fact that I never spent a moment *alone* with George.'

'Shhh!' Her mother, her face aghast, looked towards the door. 'The servants will hear.'

'Then maybe *they* will tell the whole of Wenham.'

And with a defiant glare at her mother Sophie stormed towards the door, and banged it so hard behind her that the whole house seemed to shake.

Mr Turner unlocked the door of the verger's cottage and stood back to allow Sophie to enter. He had taken the precaution of ensuring that no one had seen them. He sensed the rector would not approve of his gesture.

It was indeed a pretty little cottage, with two downstairs rooms and three upstairs. It had no bathroom, and an outside toilet, but it was in good condition and the carpets and curtains were serviceable, if old.

'It will do,' Sophie said at once, delightedly looking round. 'It will do very well, at least until we can go back to New Guinea.'

'You really *do* intend to do that?' She thought Mr Turner looked a little disappointed.

'Oh yes.' Sophie leaned against the balustrade of the staircase which swept down into the living-room. 'It was *I* who had the call and inspired George.'

'Oh, you *did* inspire George . . . er Mr Woodville.' The curate looked at the floor. 'I wondered.'

'You mean, you wondered if the gossip you heard was right,' Sophie said sarcastically. 'That *I* seduced George Woodville and filled his head with thoughts of the missions . . .'

'No, no, *no*, Mrs Woodville . . .' The young man uncharacteristically began to stammer.

'Come, Mr Turner, you listen to gossip as much as anyone else, do you not? You have heard that I set my cap at George, who was years younger than I, and lured him from his parents . . .'

'Not *exactly*, I assure you.' But still Mr Turner sounded uncertain.

'That is what everyone says, but it is *not* true.' Sophie banged the banister. 'I resisted George even though he loved me and I loved him. But the initiative came from him, and so did the suggestion to go to New Guinea. He wanted to get away from his parents because they neither approved of his sacred vocation *nor* his desire to marry me. I would, I assure you, gladly have sacrificed my love for George if it could have prevented a rift with his family, but he would not hear of it. He was very much the man, believe me. In the end, all I could do was follow.' Sophie sounded a little, uncharacteristically, coy. 'And I am *glad* I followed, Mr Turner, believe me,' she continued. 'I would not sacrifice those seven years of perfect happiness for anything. We grew in mutual love as man and wife, and were also filled with the supreme, overwhelming love of God. My husband died a martyr's death. I regret . . . I regret nothing.'

Suddenly Sophie felt such grief, such a sense of desolation, that she burst into tears and, before she knew what had happened, Mr Turner moved quickly forward and put his arms awkwardly around her.

'There, *there*, Mrs Woodville.' He gently patted her shoulder as she leaned her head against him. 'There, *there*.'

After a while Sophie's tears ebbed and, as if aware of their compromising position, she quickly stepped backwards. She took a handkerchief from her pocket and vigorously blew her nose.

'I *do* apologise. I lost control. It was unpardonable.'

'Perfectly understandable,' he said, even though he also felt awkward. 'I think you are much maligned.'

'I *am* much maligned,' she agreed, blowing her nose again. 'I am cold-shouldered by the people of Wenham because of the evil ideas they have in their minds. I am ignored by my husband's family. My own parents *scarcely* tolerate me, and make me feel an unwelcome beggar. I am a pauper with no means of myy own and, believe me, I am tired of the situation.' She put her handkerchief away in a determined manner and flung her head back defiantly.

Hubert Turner knew that he was in the presence of a woman of strength, of inner and outer beauty, and he began to feel something approximating the emotion that had overwhelmed the young George Woodville. Maybe it had been there, lying dormant, from the day he met her at Blandford Station. A strong, good, pure woman with a love of God that had been sufficient to defy savages, wretched conditions, the torments of illness and, finally, death. An experienced woman who had mothered two children, who was no stranger to the facts of life. Such a woman was in a position of considerable power over one such as he, who had no experience of life, had been brought up in a boys' public school and a strict theological college. His feelings were confused between admiration, veneration even, and desire.

What was more, there was the same difference in age between Sophie and Hubert Turner as there had been between her and her husband. What had attracted the younger man then attracted him, Hubert, now: her strength, her character and determination.

Sophie, gazing at him, could almost read his mind. She felt embarrassed, and moved away from the staircase. Somehow she had never associated the Reverend Turner with those carnal feelings that afflicted other men, although he looked no more good and pure than dearest George had, and how George had enjoyed the pleasures of the marriage-bed.

Suddenly the idea of the Reverend Turner as a suitor seemed absurd, out of the question. It would bring upon her head more coals of fire than there were already. Think of the reaction of her fellow citizens, who would say she had been home a mere four months and already she had forgotten her dead husband and ensnared the curate!

'I think I should get back to the rectory, Mr Turner,' she said coldly. 'Forgive me for that show of emotion. I don't *think* you quite understand.'

'Oh, I understand, Mrs Woodville.' Mr Turner hastily opened the door as though feeling a little guilty himself. 'Believe me, I understand completely. I understand your position and I am sorry for you. Deeply sorry. Yet I cannot feel it right that you should deny your husband's parents sight of their grandchildren, however badly done by you feel. Quite justifiably,' he added.

'But what business is it of yours?' Sophie enquired sharply.

'No business at *all*, Mrs Woodville.' Turner's tone was humble. 'But I am just saying what everyone else says, and that is probably the reason you find the townsfolk less than friendly. There is also another matter, Mrs Woodville.' As Sophie stepped outside into the cold he stood beside her, his back to her, and locked the door. 'This cottage is in the gift of Sir Guy. Maybe you could come to some arrangement with him?'

'What do you mean, *arrangement*?' she gasped.

'He may want to see his grandchildren. You, on the other hand, would like to set yourself up as a woman of independent means . . .'

'She's asking for money,' Guy said, tossing the letter across to his wife who, despite the cold, had felt well enough to come downstairs to where Arthur had set her couch in front of the fire. 'She is nothing but a common gold-digger.'

Margaret put on her spectacles and read the letter, which had been delivered by hand.

Dear Sir Guy and Lady Woodville,

It is with some difficulty that I bring myself to write to you, but I understand that Lady Woodville is not well. Thus I can well appreciate your desire to see George's children.

I think you realise that I have suffered much personal humiliation from being excluded from the invitation to visit Pelham's Oak but, although I cannot agree with it, I can to some extent understand it. Others have helped me to understand it.

I assure you that the initiative concerning our marriage and the decision to go to the foreign missions was taken entirely by my late husband, George. I meekly concurred with his wishes. I believe that even had I not existed, George would have gone to New Guinea. It was meant by God, His will. George loved his work and the constant search for souls for Christ.

That said, my dear Sir Guy and Lady Woodville, I am convinced that it is wrong of me to deny you any longer the chance to meet your grandchildren, and I am using the good offices of Mrs Heering to arrange it.

One further point. I should like to live apart from my parents, but have not the means. I think I and my children would benefit from it. I understand that the small cottage by the side of the church hall, which is vacant, is part of the Woodville estate. With your permission, I would be glad to occupy it until such time as I have completed the business I have here and can return to New Guinea.

     Yours sincerely,
     Sophie Woodville.'

Margaret gazed for a long time at the fine writing and then, slowly folding the letter, handed it back to her husband.

'Not gold-digging. She simply wants somewhere to live.'

'That rectory has *fourteen* bedrooms.'

'She obviously is at odds with her parents,' Margaret replied. 'She is not asking us for money, merely a home of her own.' Margaret surprised herself by her own reasonableness.

'You think we should say "yes"?' Guy looked most astonished at her change of heart.

'I think you could ask Eliza to act as broker, as Sophie suggests. You might also say that if she postpones, or even abandons, her intention to return to New Guinea, we might be prepared to be even more generous.'

'How do you mean?' Guy looked attentively at her.

'Once our grandchildren return to New Guinea we may never see them again. If you give her a *very* small allowance and somewhere to live, it may be enough to keep her here or, if she is determined to return, she might agree to leave the children with *us*. We do not need to see her, but I think we can be generous with her, bend a little. Don't you, Guy? Just for the sake of dearest George?'

There was only a year in age between Roger Martyn and Carson Woodville, yet by temperament they were completely different. Roger was of medium height, with almost perfect features and fair hair that was always neatly combed. He had eyes of a most brilliant blue, a delicate, sculpted mouth and the aquiline features of an aristocrat.

Carson, on the other hand, was tall, bluff, ash-blond, and sometimes his manners seemed more like those of a farm-hand. His clothes never seemed quite to fit him, and he had the gait of a friendly, vigorous puppy. Roger, on the other hand, had all the finesse, the sleekness of a saturnine cat.

When Carson joined the Martyn-Heering firm in the spring of 1909, Roger had already been there nearly four years. He had progressed from being a mere clerk in the spice warehouse on the bank of the Thames, to the banking side of the business in Threadneedle Street.

The Martyn-Heering bank was a prosperous private concern which invested and reinvested money for men who were already rich. Much of the business was risk business, the employment of venture capital in various operations throughout the world, but particularly in the Far East. It was here that Roger had come into his own by exhibiting a flair for involved, complex transactions that delighted the senior partners and, in particular, his adoptive uncle, Prosper Martyn.

Roger had been introduced by Lally into the Martyn household when he was twelve. Up to that time his existence was supposedly unknown to Prosper who, at first, deeply resented the presence of a third person in the household he wished only to share with his adored wife or, perhaps, a child of their union. That, however, was not to be. Roger had been brought up in a slum in Kentish Town with foster-parents and a large family of foster-brothers and -sisters. Taken from this environment by Lally, he was as indignant and unhappy as Prosper Martyn. The two did not at first get on. However, he very soon took to the style of life lived by the Martyns. He was a keen pupil. He learned good manners, how to speak the King's English, and developed a taste for fine clothes.

It all seemed to be quite instinctive to him, and his schooling at Rugby completed the change. He emerged at the age of eighteen with good examination results and creditable sporting achievements. He was, in fact, the complete gentleman.

Prosper would have liked Roger to go to university, although he himself never had. But by instinct his nephew preferred the world of business that had also attracted his uncle. He was anxious to acquire wealth of his own, status in life, to obliterate the constant, hateful reminder of his humble working-class origins.

Like Lally, Roger preferred London to the country, but had mastered the gentlemanly skills of hunting and shooting; he also liked intimate dinners with interesting guests, superb foods and wines, large parties, and dressing up for stately occasions.

His encounters with Carson throughout the years had been minimal, so that when the two young men were thrown together in London, an underlying hostility, a mutual incompatibility, hitherto thinly concealed, rose to the surface. There was also the fact that Carson had to begin on the bottom rung of the business, whereas Roger had progressed well up the ladder.

But, worse, they also lived together; Roger on the second floor and Carson on the third of the Martyns' London house. They ate together and were driven to work together in the chauffeured limousine provided by Prosper, a gleaming, bronze, six-cylinder Pierce-Arrow, imported from America.

The cousins said little on the way to work. First Carson was put off in Lower Thames Street, while Roger was driven on into the heart of the City.

It was not surprising that the nascent resentment festered in

Carson's heart and the relationship between the two deteriorated.

Nor was Carson helped by his close emulation of the attitude of his father, who had been forced into similar employment many years before. Guy had longed for a life of leisure, so did Carson; but whereas his father had liked to play cards, gamble, and flirt with pretty women, Carson longed to be back riding over the land, shooting rabbits or hunting with the farmers, and tossing the farm girls in the hay.

He thus brought to his work a lack of attention to detail, a lumbering, clumsy presence, and a Dorset accent which he made no effort to correct. He quickly fell foul of most of the people in the business, who found him a strange mixture of arrogance and humility: one who found work hard and uncongenial, but cared not a whit about it.

This simmering ill-feeling between Roger and Carson naturally affected the Martyn household, particularly Lally, who was more aware of it. Prosper considered himself semi-retired, going only occasionally to the City office. He preferred travelling abroad, mainly on the Continent, where he appreciated the comfort of fine hotels and he loved his Dorset home, far more than did his wife.

One day in early summer, when Carson had been struggling in the spice office for nearly three months, Roger took a client over to the warehouse one afternoon after a handsome lunch at the offices in Threadneedle Street. As his father had, Carson too fended for himself, usually eating a few chops and drinking a pint of beer in one of the many public houses in the small alleyways leading off Lower Thames Street. Determined to prove himself, to keep his word to his mother, whose health had indeed shown remarkable improvement after he left, Carson was back at work, bending earnestly over his desk, when Roger threw open the door and, with scarcely a glance at him, ushered in a gentleman of Oriental appearance. Roger didn't introduce him to this guest but demanded, in the voice of one addressing an inferior, some ledgers appertaining to the spice trade with Java.

Carson stifled a retort and got to his feet and, finding the appropriate books, brought them over and laid them before Roger.

'I think you will find everything here, Roger,' he said.

'Address me as Mr Martyn in the office, if you don't mind,' Roger said abruptly, and then, turning over the pages, he ran his fingers expertly along a line of figures. 'You can see, Mr Sum, the volume of business we have transacted with the firm in which you are interested over the past five years. Let me see . . .' He frowned, turned the pages, and then barked at Carson.

'The latest figures for the second three months of this year appear not to have been entered, Woodville.'

Anxiously Carson rose and peered over his shoulder. Then he went to his desk and produced a sheaf of invoices from a pigeon-hole.

'They have only just arrived from the counting-house, Roger,' he said, ignoring Roger's request to use his surname. 'I was due to enter them this afternoon.'

'So you *say*,' Roger sneered.

'I tell you, it is the truth . . .'

Roger shrugged and looked at the Oriental, who was peering over his gold-rimmed spectacles with some disapproval at the clerk, who was struggling to control his anger.

'What is more . . .' Carson began, but Roger held up a hand.

'We will have a few words afterwards about this, Woodville. Mr Sum can hardly be expected to invest in a business unless he has all the particulars to hand.'

'*If* you had told me Mr Sum was expected, I would have entered them first thing this morning.'

'I *assumed* your work would be up to date.'

With that, Roger, with a courteous smile, put his hand on Mr Sum's elbow and ushered him out of the door.

'The trouble is,' Carson could hear him saying, 'that one is often *forced* to employ people of an inferior character . . .'

Carson, feeling his blood rise to boiling point, had just reached the door when Roger, turning casually to glance back at him, slammed it sharply in his face.

Carson stood there looking at the door, clenching and unclenching his hands, and then, once he had resumed his composure, returned to his desk where he slumped with his head resting in his hands.

Had he not considered it too feminine, he would have wept.

Although the limousine brought them to work, the two men made their way home separately, and that evening Carson loitered on the way to have a few drinks at various public houses en route. In one in particular, just by Blackfriars Bridge, there was a pretty barmaid called Nelly Allen. Nelly seemed to understand his woes and he had told her nearly all of them. But that evening Nelly was not there, so Carson downed his beer and caught a bus in Fleet Street which went along the Strand, up Regent Street and into Oxford Street, where he alighted for the short walk back to Montagu Square. He was not drunk, but his drinking had accentuated his sense of injustice, and when he saw Roger in the hall of the house as he entered, he seized him roughly by the collar.

'Into the dining-room, if you don't mind, Roger. I want a word with you.'

'Take your hand off *me*,' Roger said indignantly, slapping Carson's arm with his fist. 'Don't you *dare* . . .'

'And don't *you* dare . . .' Carson snarled, dragging Roger across the hall and into the room, where the table was already set for dinner. 'Don't you *ever* dare talk to me like that again, or address me in that disgraceful way, or talk about me afterwards. I want to be introduced *and* to shake hands. Is that clear?'

'You have made yourself clear,' Roger said with dignity, once he had freed himself, gently dusting the crumpled arm of his suit. 'But I think you forget just who and what you are at Martyn-Heering. A mere clerk, a nobody in the business. Also, if your work is anything to go by, you never will be anybody, just like your father . . .'

'Don't you dare – ' Carson raised a threatening hand.

'Your *father*,' Roger went on imperturbably, but taking at the same time a few steps away from Carson. 'Your father was *hopeless* at figures and spent almost six years in the counting-house. They wanted to make him a partner, but he was unfit. In the end they sacked him and, if you don't improve yourself, that is exactly what will happen to *you*.'

Roger took out a slim silver cigarette-case from the vest-pocket of his waistcoat and, casually opening it, extracted a cigarette which he put in his mouth. Before, however, he had time to light it, Carson, crossing the room, snatched the cigarette from his arrogant lips and dashed it to the floor. Then he took hold of Roger by both his lapels and effortlessly raised him a few inches from the floor until their eyes were level. He crossed to the side of the room, still carrying Roger by his lapels, and began to beat his head against the wall with such ferocity that Roger began to scream.

'You leave me alone! You'll kill me and then you'll hang . . . and I hope it takes a long time. Do you hear me, Carson . . .!'

In the face of such wrath, gripped by a strength that seemed almost superhuman and seeing that his words had no effect, Roger, growing genuinely afraid, changed his tone and began to whimper.

'Please, Carson . . . please . . . I beg you . . .'

The room began to spin round, the shapes of the furniture grew misty, and he could feel his knees buckle.

At that point the door flew open and Lally, beautifully gowned and dressed for dinner, stood on the threshold, one hand on her hip.

'What *do* you think you're doing?' she shouted in a voice fit for a fishwife and, with a few unladylike strides, she crossed the room and, taking a silver candlestick from the dining-room table, brought it down hard on Carson's shoulders. 'Take your hands off Roger, immediately . . . this instant!'

Carson, knocked almost sideways, released Roger, who fell into a crumpled heap on the floor. Immediately Lally sank to her knees and, gently raising Roger's head, laid it in her lap.

'Roger, dearest, speak to me. Are you all right? Oh, my *poor* baby, my boy, what did he do to you? Say something, Roger . . .'

'Urrh!' Roger groaned, struggling to sit up while his hand clasped the back of his head. 'My God . . . my head. Is it broken?'

Tenderly Lally ran her hands round it.

'I think it's only bruised, my dear . . . Oh Roger, what *happened* for you and Carson to have such a fight? What provoked it?'

'He insulted me, Aunt Lally,' Carson said, feeling suddenly contrite. 'He made a fool of me at work. I am sorry. I let my feelings get the better of me.'

'But that is *monstrous*, Carson.' Lally, raising her head, stared at him with an expression that almost froze his blood. Aunt Lally was a woman Carson liked and respected, and he couldn't quite believe the hatred he saw in her eyes. Gently she began to stroke Roger's head, an action which seemed to surprise Roger as much as Carson. She gazed tenderly down at him, aware of her pent-up maternal feelings, of the confusion she was undoubtedly causing in the breast of the young man she was nursing.

One day Roger would have to be told.

Roger began to struggle to his feet and Carson bent over to help him, feeling by now thoroughly ashamed of himself, also a little frightened of the way his emotions had once more got out of control. Roger refused his hand offered in help, and then turned to assist Lally to her feet.

Their close proximity made Carson realise for the first time just how alike they were. They had the same fair hair, white skin, blue eyes. Lally was so petite, and Roger too was small for a man. Carson had heard that Roger was the son of a sister of hers who had died. This undoubtedly explained the family likeness.

'I apologise,' Carson said again. 'I am sincerely sorry for my behaviour.'

'I should just think you are.' Lally, by now on her feet, was brushing down her dress. 'What a disgraceful display of ill-temper. Why, you could have *killed* Roger.'

'Oh, I don't think so,' Carson protested shamefacedly. 'I was not using much force.'

Roger gave a grunt of disbelief and began massaging his head again.

'You don't know your own strength, Carson,' Lally said, 'besides which, I *cannot* have such behaviour in this house. I shall have to consult with my husband as to what to do about you. It may be that he will feel we cannot offer you our hospitality any more.'

'Oh *please*, Aunt Lally,' Carson cried, a stricken look on his face. 'My mother will be so upset. You know it's for her that I am doing all this, and already she is improving. I love my mother and I would not wish to hurt her, or set back her recovery.'

Lally, a little breathless, sat down on one of the dining-room chairs, an exquisite piece by Chippendale who had also designed the ornate rococo mahogany dining-table with claw-and-ball feet. She held out a protective hand towards Roger and drew up a chair on which he, too, gratefully sat down. His collar was awry and his tie hung like a limp piece of string, his sartorial elegance completely gone.

'You have a *fine* way of showing your love for your mother,' Lally said severely, '*or* that you are grateful to your Uncle Prosper and to me. Not that *I* expect thanks, but we have done our best to help you, Carson, to remove the rough edges that were so distressful to your parents, and give you a little purpose in life. Above all, you do indeed owe it to your dear mother, who is not a well person.'

'I *beg* you not to tell Mother, and I promise it will never happen again.'

'But I ask again, what brought it on, what exactly caused it?' Lally, a little mollified by his repentance, gazed from one to the other.

'He attacked me as he came into the house,' Roger said, 'using a minor incident at work as a pretext. It was quite unexpected, an onslaught. I have heard sometimes that the Woodvilles *are* unstable, and now I have proof of it . . .'

'I *beg* your pardon?' Carson's voice rose and he felt his anger beginning to take hold of him again.

'It is well known that there is a mad streak in the family,'

Roger said spitefully. 'Your father was a reprobate and your aunt ran away with a peasant.'

'I don't think that is exactly madness,' Carson said thickly.

'It's certainly representing something.' Roger again dusted his shoulder fastidiously and rose from the chair. 'If you will forgive me, Aunt Lally, I have had enough of this farce and I will go to my room to change for dinner.'

'Of course, my dear.' Lally once more looked at him anxiously, then, as he quietly left the room, she turned to Carson and lowered her voice. 'Roger is ambitious,' she said more gently. 'He is proud of his achievements and maybe it has made him a little thoughtless. He surely didn't mean to offend you.'

'It is true I have no head for business and I do not like it,' Carson confessed, regretfully shaking his head. 'I know I do follow in the footsteps of my father but, unlike him, I am determined to make a success of it. The way I have hurt my parents has given me great grief. Too late have I realised it, and earnestly wish to reform. But it is *such* dull, boring work, Aunt Lally. I will never be successful like Roger, but what happened today will never happen again. I have a temper and I am determined to do all I can to control it.'

Impulsively Lally went up to him and, putting a hand on his arm, stood on tiptoe to kiss his cheek.

'You're rather sweet, Carson,' she said, 'sweet and puzzling. Today I have seen a side of you I didn't know existed, two completely different sides of the same person, each warring with the other.'

Then she held up a warning finger and shook it gently at him. 'You must be careful you don't allow the baser side to win.'

4

Sophie Woodville knelt in a pew at the rear of the church, her hands loosely clasped in front of her, her head bowed. The sounds of the organ permeated the large, light building with its long nave and narrow transepts. Although the organist was out of sight in the sanctuary, Sophie knew it was Connie Yetman practising, as she did most days of the week for an hour or two, sometimes more. Connie was the church organist and her fame had spread wide. She gave recitals at other churches in the diocese, had even played in Sherborne Abbey and Salisbury Cathedral.

The gentle strains of a Bach prelude filled Sophie's heart with such nostalgia and grief that the tears trickled down her cheeks and, unashamed, she let them. Here, in the dark end of the church, near the belfry with its celebrated peal of bells, there was no one to witness her distress.

Sophie came every day to the church to pray, and she liked, if she could, to choose the time when the organ played softly, the notes rising and falling with such sublimity as to seem to echo her own emotions, the doubts and uncertainties that tormented her soul.

The consolations of religion no longer seemed sufficient to uplift a woman who had been conscious of the presence of God all her life. She had been an ardent church-goer, a keen student of the Bible, a Sunday School teacher from the age of sixteen. Such had been the strength of her faith that it would never have occurred to her that it might diminish, might seem to drift away like the notes of the organ lost among the rafters.

There had been a coldness in her soul for months; she

repeated her prayers, assiduously trying to perpetuate the devotional mood of her youth and young womanhood, but it was not as it had been. She knew about the dark nights of the soul of the mystics; times when their faith seemed to vanish, when they were obsessed by doubts, spiritual blindness, even delusions.

Now, when she needed the hand of God so badly, it seemed to have been withdrawn. She longed for the faith to accept her fate, but the path seemed long, the horizon endless.

'Oh God, let this chalice of bitterness, of unbelief and doubts, be removed from me,' she prayed, looking earnestly at the figure of Christ crucified over the high altar.

But He hung his head, He did not look at her.

Inside, the darkness remained. The music seemed gently to fade away as though the organist were reluctant to stop. There was a lingering, rather than a sudden cessation, as though her fingers caressed the keys.

Sophie was brought back to reality. She had allowed herself to slump dejectedly in the pew, but she pulled herself up and, raising her head, smiled at Connie Yetman as she walked slowly down the aisle, a thoughtful expression on her face.

When Connie saw Sophie she halted in her steps and shyly returned the smile. She had her sheet music under her arm and, from the expression on her face, she was still thinking about it.

Sophie rose from the pew and sidled along the bench towards her.

'Good morning, Constance,' she whispered. 'I enjoyed your playing. I always do.'

'Thank you, Mrs Woodville,' Connie whispered back, blushing a little.

Connie was the daughter of John Yetman by his second marriage to Euphemia Monk, who had died in giving birth to her. At the age of eight, following the death of her father, she had been adopted by Victoria Fairchild, a wealthy spinster of the town, who had formed an attachment to the orphan child with her gift for music. Constance, whose health was delicate and who caught coughs and colds very easily, had been educated privately at home and had led a very sheltered existence.

The two women got to the door and were greeted by the warm sunshine of high summer. Connie had on a simply-made cotton dress with a pattern of cornflowers. She was no beauty, with straight brown hair and steel-rimmed glasses, but she was much liked in the town, whereas Sophie Woodville was still treated with some suspicion.

'Do come and see the design for the chapel window to be dedicated to George,' Sophie said impulsively as they stood in the forecourt.

'Oh, I *should* like that.' Connie pushed her spectacles up her nose. 'I was so attached to George, Mrs Woodville.'

'I know you were, and oh, Constance, I *do* wish you would call me Sophie. After all, we have known each other all our lives. I even remember you being born.'

Connie's blush grew even deeper. It was difficult to think of the rector's daughter, to her a very august person, as anything else but 'Mrs Woodville', just as formerly she had always thought of her as 'Miss Lamb'. Sophie was twelve years Connie's senior, and Connie had a deep respect for age. She was also a withdrawn, shy person whose sense of inferiority was acute.

As they approached the cottage into which Sophie had now moved, they could see a figure hovering outside as though uncertain whether to go or stay. When he saw them, he removed his hat and smiled with relief.

'Mrs Woodville. I was ... Good morning, Connie.' Mr Turner interrupted his explanation to turn to Sophie's companion. 'I was standing at the church door listening to you.' He sighed. 'Your playing is heavenly.'

'Thank you, Mr Turner.' Connie's blush reached down her neck.

'Heavenly,' Sophie echoed, glad to see the young parson. 'Do please come in, Mr Turner.' Hastily she put the key in the door. 'I have brought Constance to look at the design for the window to be dedicated to George; I would like to have your opinion too.'

The curate looked delighted, and ushered the two women into the cool interior of the cottage.

'Where are the children today?' he asked, looking round.

'With their grandparents. They now stay with them for several days at a stretch. Lady Woodville is far from well.' Sophie's tone was devoid of emotion.

'Most generous of you,' the curate murmured.

'It's the least I can do.' Briskly, Sophie went over to the dinning-room table where the plans lay for the window and, as she unfolded them and laid them out, she said, 'I was going to ask you, Mr Turner, whether I could prevail upon you to take these over to Sir Guy and Lady Woodville. I feel they should approve of them.'

'But would *you* not take them?'

'No. I would not.'

'I see.' Mr Turner's expression too remained impassive.

Connie, who was carefully studying the design, suddenly exclaimed:

'Oh, but it's *beautiful*.' Then she burst into tears.

'Connie!' Sophie wrapped her arms round the young woman and looked bewilderedly up at Hubert Turner. 'Whatever ails you, my dear?'

'I can . . . c-can't . . . ex-p-plain,' Connie went on sobbing.

'The design is *very* moving,' the curate said reflectively. 'I can quite see that it makes Connie weep. She knew Mr Woodville so well.'

The design depicted a reasonable likeness of George, dressed in clerical garb, with a book, presumably the Bible, clasped to his chest. One hand was extended towards the sky, to which his eyes were raised. Behind him stood a black man dressed in skimpy native costume, and then there was the representation of the sea, the betel-nut palms, together with the granadillas and limes which had surrounded the simple mission station.

The scene described to the artist by Sophie had been realised with remarkable fidelity. It was framed by a border of acanthus leaves and beneath ran the legend: 'Sacred to the memory of George Pelham Woodville, b. Wenham, Dorset, 1881, d. Gumbago, Papua, New Guinea, December 1907, where he lies buried by the side of his faithful servant and friend Kirikeu.

May they rest in peace together with . . .' and then followed the names of the six men who had been cannibalised by the Doriri. At the end of the inscription were the words, 'Martyrs for the faith'. The colouring was simple; clerical black, red, yellow, the dark greens of the palms and the deep blue of the sea.

When the Reverend Turner raised his head, his eyes too were moist.

'Very moving indeed, Mrs Woodville. *Very* beautiful.' He drew out his handkerchief and blew his nose. 'I think Sir Guy and Lady Woodville will be deeply affected. Maybe it will make them change their attitude towards you.'

'I am afraid it is too late,' Sophie said with a bitter smile. 'The chance to do that vanished long ago.'

Eliza Heering sometimes thought she carried the cares of the world on her shoulders – or rather, her small world of Wenham and its surroundings. But they were capable shoulders, everyone agreed on that. Although she was born into the minor aristocracy, she had the sturdiness and many of the other characteristics of a countrywoman, her feet firmly on the ground.

Still, she had to do the bulk of the worrying for her greatly extended family, and sometimes, robust though she was, she thought the demands made on her were too much. Yet she was expected to remain unfailingly cheerful, a feat which, on the whole, she thought she somehow surprisingly managed to achieve.

From being a headstrong girl Eliza had turned into a sensible, good-natured woman of whom much was asked. She had married at nineteen and been widowed when she was thirty-three. She had married again at the age of forty, the same year that George and Sophie were married in Australia. Her second husband Julius, who had pursued her for many years, was a wealthy Dutchman, the brother of her sister-in-law Margaret.

It was true that Margaret and Guy had suffered, but Eliza had had her own share of grief: the tragic death of her beloved husband, Ryder Yetman. He had built Julius Heering's house for him and then he fell off the roof of a cottage he was thatching in the grounds; a silly, pointless accident. Julius subsequently felt unable to live in the house and had sold it to Prosper Martyn.

Eliza did not love Julius as she had loved Ryder. There was little passion in the marriage, but there was respect and deep friendship. Each hadd been married before and, maybe, the first spouse was the most loved. But, in settling for second-best, they had achieved a measure of happiness that many couples more passionately in love were unable to find with their frequent quarrels, jealousies and petty fights.

Julius was the senior partner in the Martyn-Heering business and he travelled a lot, sometimes spending up to six months abroad, mainly in the Far East. Eliza never accompanied him. Her youngest son, Hugh, was a scholar at Oxford and came home in the vacations, and her daughter Dora lived at home. Dora was a country girl, loved horses and animals, and had shown little interest in the opposite sex. Sadly, Eliza thought, she would be a spinster. For Dora, animals took the place of people, and Eliza supposed it was maybe because of the tragedy that had come into her life when her beloved father died.

But Eliza did not lack grandchildren, whatever might happen to Dora and Hugh. Laurence and fertile Sarah-Jane had provided her with the grandchildren she adored, who were now playing with their cousins Deborah and Ruth in the shadow of the great oak from which the Woodville family home had its name.

Little Deborah Woodville had dark hair and a rather thin, grave face. She looked a delicate child and she had a tendency to fever, which had continued even after she came to England. But her sister Ruth, on the other hand, was strong and outgoing, a golden child with a loving nature and the fair Woodville hair.

It was fascinating to see George's children. Fascinating, and tragic too, because sometimes it was almost impossible to accept the fact that George's children were all that was left of him.

There *had* been much sadness in her life, Eliza thought, looking around her.

It was high summer, and the elegant white house, perched on its hill, dappled by the shadows of the surrounding trees, looked at its best. In the distance Wenham, topped by the square tower of the church, shimmered in the haze, and a short distance from where she sat now was the cottage where she and Ryder had fallen in love. It gleamed with fresh paint, having been recently occupied by Guy's new bailiff and his young wife. Eliza had no wish to see inside the cottage again or recall those memories of such happiness so long ago.

Guy was dozing in a chair while Margaret was propped up on her daybed. She wore a wide straw hat to protect her against the sun, and as usual was doing her embroidery; those fine, firm strokes of the needle which would be continued who could say, now, for how long?

The peace of the early afternoon was broken by the sound of horses' hooves in the drive and Eliza, looking up, saw a solitary horseman make his way towards the house and pass out of sight.

Eventually Arthur appeared, followed by a gentleman in clerical dress, a bundle of papers under his arm, his hat in his hand.

'The Reverend Mr Turner, Lady Woodville.'

Mr Turner bowed rather nervously as Margaret looked curiously at him. Guy wriggled and gave a loud snore, still fast asleep. Margaret leaned over and prodded him with a finger.

'Guy, where are your manners? Mr Turner is here to see us.'

Guy snorted, wriggled again and then opened his bleary eyes, frowning at the visitor. He eventually stumbled to his feet and put out a hand.

'Good afternoon, Hubert,' he said affably. 'Forgive me.'

'That's perfectly all right, Sir Guy. I am sorry to disturb you and Lady Woodville.' The curate smiled shyly at Eliza. 'Good afternoon, Mrs Heering.'

'Good afternoon, Mr Turner.'

'Mr Heering well?'

'Thank you.'

Eliza inclined her head as the civilities took place, and Guy shook himself like a dog emerging from the river.

'Now, Hubert, what brings you here? You seldom come

without a reason, and you saw Lady Woodville only a few days ago.'

It was true. Although perfectly acceptable, Hubert Turner had seldom in the past been on the list of those who were entertained socially at Pelham's Oak, maybe because he was considered tainted by his proximity to the Lambs. However, he took the Sunday services twice a month in a small church in the nearby village where Guy occasionally worshipped after his boycott of the rector. Since Margaret's illness, however, Hubert had been enormously kind. He was not stuffy, not 'churchy', and did not press religion upon her; but Margaret found his visits a comfort, and she liked him very much and had grown fond of him.

He now produced the papers tucked under his arm and held them out to Guy.

'Mrs Woodville asked me to bring these to show you, Sir Guy. It is the design for the memorial window to your son, to be placed in Wenham Parish Church.'

'What?' Startled, Guy looked at the curate. 'In the *parish church*, did you say?'

'Surely you *knew* about this, Sir Guy?' Mr Turner seemed embarrassed.

'Not a word.'

'Mrs Woodville has been talking about it, well . . . ever since she came back.'

There was a silence as everyone considered the implications.

'Did she not *write* to you about it, Guy?' Eliza broke the silence at last. 'You may have forgotten.'

'She did not.'

'I'm surprised. She told me.'

'You would think we'd be the first to be informed. George *was* our son, after all.'

Margaret held out her hand for the papers.

'May I have a glance, Mr Turner?'

'Certainly, Lady Woodville.'

The curate, perspiring freely, passed them to her as though they had been hot coals. Margaret, her face stony, her expression inscrutable, examined them carefully.

'May I . . .?' Guy got up and leaned across her shoulder, and eventually they were joined by Eliza, who placed a hand on Guy's arm.

For some moments the little tableau remained motionless, each of its members lost in thought.

Eventually Guy stumbled away from the couch and sat heavily down in his chair. He buried his face in his handkerchief and began to sob loudly. Used to such behaviour, Eliza and Margaret stared at him, patiently waiting for him to finish.

'Oh, oh, *oh*,' wailed Guy, passing his handkerchief across his face. 'Oh, oh, oh . . . my darling son. I cannot bear it. What a terrible thing . . . to be constantly reminded. The *likeness*, it is so exact. Oh my darling, my dearest George. Never did *I* think in my lifetime to see a *memorial* to him . . .'

'I think it very *wrong* of Mrs Woodville,' Margaret said sharply, 'to have inflicted this on us without notice. Extremely thoughtless.'

'I'm sure she did not mean it,' Eliza said. 'It is because of the lack of communication between you. Personally, *I* think it is high time this silly feud was finished . . .'

'It is *not* a feud, Eliza,' Margaret said icily. 'We do not receive George's widow because, if it were not for her, George would be alive.'

'I don't think you can be sure of that, Margaret.'

'Well, I am,' her sister-in-law said firmly, 'very sure. There would be no need of a window of memorial had it not been for Sophie Lamb. Why should we be pleased about it now? Can you tell me?'

It was difficult to find a reply, but Eliza went stubbornly on: 'I still think it is time that bygones were bygones . . .'

Guy wiped his eyes and sighed heavily. 'Perhaps you're right. Maybe it is *George's* way of speaking to us, asking us from the grave to receive his wife, the mother of his lovely children.' He mournfully indicated the young people on the lawn.

'Guy, don't be so sentimental,' Margaret reprimanded him. 'And please don't be *weak*. If we received Mrs Woodville now, all Wenham would laugh at us.'

'Let them laugh.' Eliza's tone was scornful. 'The opinion of the town is of little consequence.'

'Well, you might say that, Eliza, but to us it is important. People look up to us and expect us to show standards. Having taken a position, I think we would be very misguided to back down now. I, for one, will never receive Sophie Woodville.' She looked for a moment at her husband and sister-in-law, then said in a greatly lowered voice: 'She will come to this house over my dead body, and not before.'

Roger Martyn enjoyed his role of young-man-about-town, a youthful businessman on the verge of being made a junior partner.

He was keen, industrious, eager to learn. He assimilated facts very quickly. He got to work early and left late. He often ate at his club if his uncle and aunt were away, which was frequently the case these days. They spent at least half the year abroad.

When they were away, Roger enjoyed his role as head of the household, where the servants treated him with the deference usually reserved for the master. Burned on his memory was the day he had first arrived in the house, a snivelling, undersized urchin with a Cockney accent and no manners. He was given a good bath, scrubbed with carbolic soap, provided with a complete outfit of new clothes and sent to be taught how to speak without the atrocious flat vowels of an East London accent.

He had learnt quickly. From then on he had learned very quickly.

Roger had a circle of friends who liked to play cards, go to the theatre and dine either at one another's houses or at expensive restaurants. None of them were particularly interested in women but they were united by a common bond: the pursuit of pleasures of a certain kind and the spending of money.

Roger's origins were obscure, even to him, and he ensured that they were kept that way. The story was that he was orphaned at an early age and subsequently adopted and brought up by the wealthy Martyns. If any of his upper-crust, clever friends discovered the truth about the terraced house in Kentish

Town where he had been raised, Roger imagined he would cheerfully put a gun to his own head. Appearances mattered to him. They were the very stuff of life.

Roger arrived home one night just after midnight, and was paying off his cab when a similar vehicle drew up beside him and two people emerged: a man and a woman. Roger had thought his uncle and aunt were out of the country and looked round in surprise, as his cab trotted off, to see Carson reaching up to pay his own cabby. By his side stood a young woman looking up at him with a trusting, pretty face.

'Er.' Roger seemed uncertain what to say, staring hard at the woman.

'Good evening, Roger,' Carson said cheerfully, taking her firmly by the arm.

Ignoring him, Roger looked past Carson at the woman beside him. She wore a long coat, a close-fitting hat, and her hands were gloveless.

Carson stood back and, without introducing his companion, indicated the door.

'After you, Roger.'

'Are you coming in?' Roger seemed surprised.

'Of course. After *you*.'

'No, after you . . . *and* the lady.'

Carson indicated to his companion that she should precede him. She seemed nervous, and looked a little longingly in the direction of the disappearing cab.

Carson gave her a gentle prod and she ascended the steps reluctantly. By the light above the door Roger could see she was not more than twenty or so.

Carson by this time had his key in the door and, as he opened it, he flicked on the lights and the hall lit up. It was a house of some size and splendour, and the girl gasped.

'Ow!' she said, never having been inside anything like it before.

The floor was tiled in black and white stone slabs. A glittering chandelier, suspended from the high ceiling, illuminated with its myriad twinkling lights the polished sheen of the mahogany banisters. A marble staircase swept up to the first floor where the main reception rooms were, but to their right the door was open to the downstairs sitting-room where guests were sometimes received who were not expected to stay. Carson knew that a fire would have been lit there, and a tray of sandwiches left in case he or Roger were hungry.

'Go inside,' he whispered kindly to his guest, sensing her nervousness. 'Take off your hat and coat.' He then shut the door behind her and looked at Roger, who was removing his hat and coat. He wore a coal-grey business suit, whereas Carson was in tails.

'Been at the office?' Carson enquired sarcastically.

'I have, as a matter of fact.' Roger patted down his sleek hair, glancing at the watch tucked into his waistcoat pocket. 'We are expecting a large shipment of diamonds from the East and there were certain provisions I had to make about security. Things I *cannot* leave to other people.'

'Well, I'll say "goodnight" then, Roger.' Carson looked meaningfully from his cousin to the closed door and back again.

'Just one minute, my friend.' Roger put a hand firmly on Carson's shoulder.

'Yes?' Carson looked taken aback. 'What is it?'

'You can't bring that woman in here, you know.'

'Oh, can't I?'

'No, you cannot.' Roger raised himself on his toes and stared into Carson's face, his hand still on his shoulders. 'I have no idea what you mean by bringing a woman like that to this house at this time of night. Supposing the servants saw you?'

'It was bad luck *you* seeing me,' Carson retorted, 'and I'd thank you to mind your own business. A woman like what, may I ask?'

'I hardly think that a *respectable* woman would come into a man's house at this time of night. So the question answers itself. Besides, I think it *is* my business.

'And *I* think it is not. Good night.' Carson made an effort to free himself, but Roger's handclasp remained firm.

'Let me go, please, Roger.'

'I want you to tell that woman to get out. I'm afraid I cannot have her in this house, whatever she is.'

'What do you mean "whatever"?'

'She's a whore, isn't she? What would our aunt and uncle think?'

'She is not a whore,' Carson said heatedly.

'No lady of my acquaintance would accompany a gentleman to his house at this hour of night.'

'But then you don't have many "ladies" of your acquaintance, do you, Roger?'

Roger remained unruffled.

'I know what is the correct thing to do, I can assure you of that, Carson. I'm afraid I shan't leave this hall until you ask her to go.'

'And *I* tell you to mind your own business and for God's sake take your pawing hands off me. *I* am not one of your fancy men . . .'

Carson then roughly shook himself free while Roger, clearly taken aback, took a minute or two to recover himself.

'Don't you *dare* say that to me,' he said in a low voice.

'Very well, you mind your business and I shall mind mine. I shall ask no questions if *you* ask none.'

'*I* have nothing of which to be ashamed.'

'Good.' Carson straightened his necktie, looking at himself in the ornate Empire mirror in the hall. 'Neither have I. But if you mention this to Aunt Lally or Uncle Prosper, I shall tell them how I think *you* spend your free time.'

'How you "think" I spend my free time,' Roger said with a sneer. 'I *know* what you do with yours, and I can tell you that if you dare to besmirch my good name by your foul and unfounded suggestions I shall take you to court.'

'And I shall take *you* to court,' Carson raised his voice as he dug a finger into Roger's chest, 'if you besmirch *mine*.'

Suddenly the door of the sitting-room opened and the young woman who had been ushered inside stood there.

'I want to go home,' she said.

'Now you go back inside,' Carson said, trying to steer her by her shoulders. 'I shan't be a minute.'

'I don't want no trouble,' Nelly Allen said, folding her arms stubbornly.

'Don't worry, Nelly, there won't be any trouble.' Carson gave a grim smile and looked at Roger. 'My cousin is far more interested in bringing young men back to the house than young women . . .'

His sentence remained unfinished as Roger's knuckles connected with Carson's chin, catching him unawares so that he fell backwards into Nelly's arms. She, however, was too slight to support his weight and they both fell in a heap at Roger's feet.

'Ooo!' Nelly wailed, putting her hands to the side of her head. 'Oh, my 'ead. What 'ave I got meself into? Get me 'at and coat. I want to go home, Carson.'

She suddenly looked up and, seeing her gaze, the two men followed it. There, in a purple padded dressing-gown with velvet lapels, stood Roberts the butler with what looked like a small, vicious cane in his hand. He descended the stairs at a stately, measured pace, swishing his stick menacingly backwards and forwards.

'Mr Martyn, Mr Woodville,' he said sonorously, 'I am afraid I *cannot* tolerate this kind of behaviour in this household. I am answerable to Mr and Mrs Martyn, and a brawl in the 'all is not at all the kind of thing of which they would approve.'

'Quite!' Carson rose to his feet and began dusting the seat of his trousers. 'Now, Nelly, if you'd go inside while we sort this out . . .' He began to push her towards the sitting-room again.

'I *think*, sir, the young lady had better put on her coat and hat and leave, Mr Woodville, if you don't mind, sir,' Roberts said imperturbably. 'It would seem to be what she would like to do and I think it would be the best thing all round, sir. Dick will be down in a minute or so, and he can see the young lady to a cab.'

He had scarcely finished speaking before Dick, the underfootman, fully attired, quickly ran down the stairs and smiled encouragingly at the woman in the hall. 'Get your things on, dearie,' he said. 'Quick now.'

Nelly gratefully disappeared into the sitting-room and Dick followed her; and when they emerged a moment later she had on her hat and coat. Roberts moved in his customary stately manner to the door, which he opened and, with a polite bow, watched Nelly, followed by Dick, as she went carefully down the steps without looking back.

He then shut the door and put his stick on the ebony hallstand.

'Really, gentlemen, this is not the behaviour expected in this household. I am surprised at both of you, and when Mr and Mrs Martyn return . . .'

'Roberts, I should be obliged if you would say nothing of this affair,' Roger said with an authoritative expression on his face. 'It would only distress my uncle and aunt, and it is a matter which is not likely to occur again, I can assure you.' He turned to Carson, who was beginning to undo his tie. 'I think I can say that, cannot I, Carson? We would not like Uncle Prosper and Aunt Lally to become involved? It is between ourselves and it is finished, yes?'

'If you say so,' Carson mumbled and, with his tie in his hands, he pushed past the two men and rapidly ascended the stairs.

When he was out of sight, Roger took a wallet from his inner pocket and produced a large white note which he held ostentatiously before the eyes of the butler, a long-time, trusted servant of the family.

'Thank you for your co-operation, Roberts. I'm sure you could make use of this.'

Roberts hesitated only momentarily, eyeing the note, and then he took it carefully between his thumb and forefinger.

'Consider the matter closed, Mr Roger. But, in future . . .'

'There will be *no* future,' Roger said, almost between closed teeth. 'I intend to get that barbarian out of this house as soon as I possibly can.'

5

Deborah and Ruth Woodville loved going to the splendid house standing on a hill two miles from Wenham, approached by a long drive. As soon as their carriage stopped outside the great west door a footman hurried down the steps of the pillared portico to greet them, sweeping them into a world of graciousness, of indulgence and luxury that was very far from the small cottage by the church in Wenham with no bathroom and an outside lavatory. Not unnaturally, they preferred to spend more and more time there. There was plenty of space to run about, and they were almost overwhelmed by their doting grandparents who, unlike their rather strict, impoverished mother, could deny them nothing.

Because she had so little to occupy her, Sophie found, to her chagrin, that there were long periods when she had insufficient to do. She became, therefore, rather obsessional in the matter of the stained-glass window that George had so wanted in his memory and the memory of his companions. She made frequent visits to the artist, who became slower and slower because of the evident lack of the wherewithal to pay for it.

Jonathan Frost was a stained-glass artist who lived in Sherborne, almost within sight of the abbey, which was the centrepiece of the old town. He was not a greedy man but he quite rightly expected to be paid for his work because, after all, it was how he earned his living. The scale of a full-size window was large, and many hundreds, if not thousands, of pounds would be needed for the different coloured glass, the tortuous process of assembling the fragments and blending them into an artistic masterpiece that would endure for generations.

Hubert Turner had returned with the sketches from his visit to the Woodville family, with little to report but their equivocal reaction, certainly no offer to pay for it.

Some time after his visit, Sophie received a letter from Sir Guy's bailiff to say that Sir Guy and Lady Woodville were still too distressed over the matter and manner of their son's death to wish to be reminded of it by a memorial; and that was that.

For Sophie, however, it was not the end of the matter, despite the problems. A major one was that the church was in the gift of Sir Guy, and his permission would be needed, and this, together with the matter of payment, seemed to indicate that, for the time being, the matter would be in abeyance. Sophie began to feel more and more bitter and frustrated, but she had reckoned without the interest of George's aunt, Eliza.

Eliza had been close to George. She had understood him and championed him against his father. She felt she didn't know Sophie well, but mainly because the rector and she had never got on. He had disapproved of her elopement, and preached a sermon intended to humiliate her at her wedding. After that, she had scarcely stepped inside the church.

It was natural that her feelings for Sophie were coloured by the attitude of her father. Sophie was religious, and before she married George Eliza hardly knew her.

Since her return home she had done her best to make this person who was almost a stranger welcome; but Sophie was reserved, slightly prickly. One wondered if maybe some remnants of her father's attitude towards Eliza lingered in her?

Eliza had an idea about the window, but first she wanted to discuss it with her husband. On their marriage Julius Heering had bought Upper Park, seven miles from Blandford, and one of the finest examples of baroque Georgian architecture in the county. Built of Dorset brick and faced with Chilmark stone, it stood on a slight incline facing north/south, with magnificent views of the countryside on both sides. It had formal landscaped gardens, an orangery, and a small chapel shielded from the house by a copse of yew trees.

One early autumn evening, as Eliza and her husband strolled

arm in arm through the gardens of their house, she halted in front of the chapel and, stopping to unlock the door, beckoned him in.

'I want to show you something,' she said mysteriously, as Julius stepped over the threshold and looked around the tiny chapel where generations of its former owners had worshipped for centuries.

The chapel still had some pews which were in relatively good condition, but there was straw on the floor as, when the chapel had been deconsecrated, it had been used by previous owners as a refuge for farm animals.

All the glass in the chapel was plain. Whether or not stained glass had ever been removed, no one knew.

'What is it, dear?' Julius, pipe in his mouth, looked about him.

Julius was nearly sixty, and had worn well. He was a tall, grey-haired man with the strong features of a Dutch bourgeois. He had a long nose, thin lips and grey eyes; but he was always thoughtful and serious-looking rather than smiling. He had made a great success of business and was a very rich man. He had never been a scholar, but he was well-read and appreciated art and music. Eliza, his second wife, had made him very content and he wanted nothing more in life. He put an arm out and she came up close to him.

'What are you up to?' he asked with a smile. 'We haven't been in this place for years.'

'Julius,' Eliza took his hand from around her waist and moved away, 'I thought this chapel would make a nice memorial to George. You know, the stained-glass window.'

'I thought that was to go in Wenham Church?' Julius, looking surprised, removed his pipe.

'I'm afraid at the moment it is out of the question. Sophie has no money to pay for it and Guy and Margaret are unco-operative . . .'

'But surely, their elder son . . .'

'They feel differently about the matter from Sophie. They say it only accentuates their grief.'

Julius made a gesture of irritation and stuck his pipe back

into his mouth. He wore a tweed jacket and plus-fours, the garb of a countryman. With this he would wear a deerstalker or a soft trilby, carrying a stout stick when he went walking in the woods or chatting with the farmers on his estate. He ran a large dairy farm and was well versed in animal husbandry and country matters. Hugh sometimes talked of running the farm; but Julius thought he was not practical enough. He was a dreamer, a bit of an idler. He was far more likely to be a poet or a scholar than a farmer.

'I am very much aware of George's last wish,' Eliza said slowly. 'He was my nephew. We were very close. He confided in me more than in his mother and father.'

'I know he did; but, my dear, do you think it wise to interfere in these family matters?'

'George is my family too,' Eliza replied stubbornly. 'I think it may be a way out of an impasse. I also thought we might help financially by making it our gift. Sophie could then feel at rest because she has carried out the last wishes of her husband.'

Sophie read the letter with a sense of mounting rage that was hard even for one deeply imbued with the Christian virtue of humility to control. When she had finished she flung it on the table and sat down on a wooden chair beside it, staring straight in front of her.

Patronising. People always patronised her. In exchange for meekness, you had patronage. She was being offered a deconsecrated private chapel, which had been used as a shelter for animals, when George had wanted a stained-glass window in the church where he had been baptised and had worshipped all his life, as had generations of Woodvilles before him. Was it really too much to ask?

She was sure that Eliza had not meant to be offensive; but rich people sometimes couldn't help giving offence, simply by lack of thought.

Eliza Heering was well thought of in Wenham, respected and admired. But it had not always been so. Sophie had only been five when Eliza eloped, much too young to remember it. But she had always known about it even when she was a little girl, that shameful event that some people had thought Eliza survived merely because of who she was. In a way, she hadn't changed.

Gradually, as time went on, people did forget. But in country towns and villages a sense of folklore exists; stories and legends handed down in families, distorted a little in the telling but essentially the same. And the elopement of Eliza Woodville and Ryder Yetman had been like that.

Sophie sat there for a moment or two as if to recover her breath, her sense of proportion. Then, on impulse, she snatched the letter from the table and, running across the room, opened the front door; leaving it open behind her, she flew along the path by the church into Hubert Turner's house, pausing only to unlatch the gate. But as she hurried up the path towards the door of his house, it opened, and she could hear voices. Connie Yetman, smiling happily, appeared on the threshold, the usual sheets of music under one arm, a basket in her hand. Behind her stood Hubert, his face relaxed and smiling, one hand on the arm that carried the music.

Sophie felt embarrassed, and it seemed they did too, as quickly their smiles faded. Hubert immediately withdrew his hand and Connie began to blush.

Connie, as everyone knew, blushed very easily. She blushed at nothing. She was almost crimson as Sophie came more slowly up to them, the letter in her hand.

'I'm so sorry to trouble you, Hubert. If I'd known you had company . . .'

'My dear Sophie, *please* don't apologise,' Hubert said, carefully stepping to one side of the door. 'Constance was just leaving. We were discussing the possibility – only the possibility, mind – of doing *The Messiah* in the church for Christmas.'

'That sounds very ambitious,' Sophie said in the encouraging voice of a schoolmistress and, with Sophie's eyes upon her, Connie blushed even more.

'You don't think it's *too* ambitious?' Hubert wondered, his head to one side.

'You mean, you may not have the voices? I don't know. What do *you* think, Connie?'

Connie mumbled incomprehensibly and shook her head.

'Do you sing, Sophie?' Hubert asked her. 'Why, of course you do. You have a fine contralto voice. It soars above the others in church.'

'Oh, I could never sing solo in church,' she protested.

'But why not?'

'I would sing in the choir. But not solo. Never.'

'Mrs Woodville's voice *is* good enough for the solo part,' Connie said with surprising authority. 'She has a lovely voice.'

'Well, thank you very much.' Now it was Sophie's turn to blush, but only slightly, as though people seldom paid her compliments. 'I would still prefer it if you could get someone else to sing the contralto part, and I would gladly join in the choir.'

'I must be on my way,' Connie said nervously, and slipped past Sophie to the gate while Hubert showed his guest inside.

'A very nervous young lady,' he said. 'But so gifted.'

'An accomplished musician,' Sophie replied. 'I do hope I haven't disturbed you. I know Friday morning is usually devoted to your sermon.'

'Of course I don't mind.' Hubert ushered her into his study where his sheafs of notes were spread out in front of a large, well-used Bible. Outside the window the leaves were scattering lightly on the lawn like harbingers of winter.

'Do sit down, Sophie,' he pointed to a chair, 'and tell me what brings you here. You appear extremely agitated.'

'I am,' she burst out. 'Just read *that*, Hubert, and tell me what you think.'

Hubert slowly took the letter Sophie thrust at him and, just as slowly, read it. 'This *is* a surprise.'

'What do you think, though? What do you *think*?'

The resentment in Sophie's voice, her anger, seemed to unnerve him, and he read through the letter again before putting it on his desk.

'If you ask me for an immediate opinion, I cannot give you one. I was so used to the idea of the church . . .'

'It is what *George* wanted,' she said heatedly. 'Not to have it in an obscure chapel that has been deconsecrated for years and used as a cattleshed. I find the suggestion insulting.'

'I'm *sure* Eliza meant well,' Hubert murmured soothingly.

'Patronising!' Sophie joined her arms akimbo. 'Second-best because George is dead and I am penniless.'

'Oh no, I'm *sure* not . . .'

'Oh yes, Hubert. Patronising. People like her can't help it. They were born to money, to riches. They never think how other people might feel. I'm told her husband is a millionaire. Oh Hubert, I've struggled so *hard* to carry out the dying wish of my husband, so *hard* to do his bidding. Mr Frost has done his plans without charge, but he can't be expected to do more. Guy's parents . . . the very least . . .'

She took out her handkerchief and screwed up her eyes. 'It's so *hard*, Hubert. You've no idea . . . Hard, with this wall of suspicion and condescension on the part of the Woodvilles. Oh, how I wish I could go back to Gumbago and carry on the work my precious husband and I started there.'

Then, surprising even herself, she gave herself unexpectedly up to tears.

Hubert didn't know what to do. It was the second time he had seen her cry and, in a way, it was odd to see such a strong woman crumble. Yet it was reassuring, too, to know that she had a weakness. That Sophie, so strong, so rock-like, was prey to human emotions like everyone else.

'Sophie,' he ventured after a moment as he continued to gaze anxiously at her, 'I could advance you the money . . . *if* you wished. I could pay for it without any trouble at all. I would consider it an honour. Then, when you are able . . . Or.' He gulped and, feeling decidedly ill at ease even in his own home, wiped one sticky palm against the other. 'Or . . . *if* we were man and wife it would be perfectly natural. You would never need to pay me back then.'

Sophie's tears stopped almost as abruptly as they had started, and she stared incredulously at him.

'What are you saying, Hubert?'

'My dear . . . dearest Sophie . . .' He got awkwardly on to his knees beside her and attempted to clutch her hand. It was very cold and unresponsive, and he was tongue-tied and clumsy, never having been in such a situation, adopted such an attitude, in his life before.

He felt it was like a scene from Trollope and he was making himself, at the same time, ridiculous. However, here he was, an abject suitor, so he pressed on, hoping she would understand.

'I have not wanted to speak to you before, Sophie, because of your bereavement. I was deeply sensible of your loss and did not wish you to think I did *not* respect your feelings for your dead husband, was not fully conscious of the fact that it was far, far too soon for you to love another.'

'I, love . . .?' Sophie began.

'It is nearly two years since George died, Sophie,' Hubert hurried on, 'and I know how hard these years have been for you.' He made a nervous grab for her hand again, and this time her fingers curled over his. 'Is it *possible*, Sophie, that you could think of letting another have the privilege of sharing the burden with you? If you cannot return my love now, I understand, in the hope that the feeling I have for you will one day become reciprocal. In the meantime, Sophie, *if* you would allow me . . . my heart would be so full. I should be the happiest man alive.'

Sophie was aware of his hand, in her palm. It was a long time since she had touched a man or a man had touched her. His clasp was firm and she could feel, once again, his strength reaching out to her.

Oh, it would be *very* fine to have someone like Hubert by her side. He was not a ninny, namby-pamby clergyman like so many in the Church of England. He was a strong, wiry little man, a football player; a person with character. With him she could face the world, the Woodvilles, her parents, all those people who patronised her, pitied her or, perhaps, even looked down on her. The children would have a father they could respect, who would look after them and help them.

'You know,' he went on, conscious of her warm, soft skin, her full, enticing bosom an inch away from his nose, 'I have means of my own. My parents are dead and left me well off. I could provide for you, Sophie, and more. In addition of course, the window would be taken care of. Completely.'

He stared at her and, for some moments, their eyes met, as if it were impossible to tell which of them was more surprised by what had happened. 'You would *never* have to worry again,

Sophie, about anything. I would see that you had everything you needed . . .'

He removed his hands from hers and got thankfully up from his knees. Sophie too stood up and played with the belt of her pretty beige woollen dress with its wide alpaca collar, which she had made herself during the many hours she spent alone in the cottage.

She looked outside at the lowering skies, the trees heavy with rain, and she saw the coral shingle of Gumbago, the native houses on stilts, the low squat roof of the school made of sago leaves. In the distance the sun shone on the sapphire-blue sea, and inland were all those souls waiting to be converted.

'I want to make one thing clear,' she said, lowering her eyes as if the suggestion embarrassed her. 'I could never accept a bribe, Hubert. Never . . .'

'Sophie,' he said, aghast, 'I never meant . . .'

'About the window . . . it is important, but you could not bribe me with that . . .'

'Nor would I ever wish . . .' He began to blush like Connie.

'As long as you understand that,' she said, 'that's fine. I am very honoured by your proposal, and touched. I cannot, of course, reply straightaway, but I will think about it. Seriously, I promise.'

'Oh *thank* you, Sophie,' he said gratefully.

'There is another thing, Hubert, that could perhaps have some influence on me . . .' She looked speculatively at him for a moment and once again his eyes lit up with hope. 'Is there any chance that you would ever be interested in the life of a missionary . . . that you might consider going to New Guinea?'

'Oh *Sophie*,' Hubert said, putting his hands to his face, 'oh, what can I say? My dear . . .' Suddenly he lowered his hands and met the full force of her gaze. 'You have been honest with me and so I shall be with you. The answer, I am afraid, is . . . none at all. I have not the least desire to serve Our Blessed Lord in the mission field.'

For Carson Woodville, life had become a battle. It was a battle to maintain any semblance of interest in work he detested; to appear at the office on time and struggle through the day until evening. It was a battle to maintain any kind of harmonious relationship with Roger, a condition which had been exacerbated since the incident over Nelly. Ever since then it had seemed to Carson that Roger had the upper hand; he watched him carefully, as though waiting, hoping, praying maybe, to catch him out of line.

When they were in town Aunt Lally and Uncle Prosper did their best to provide suitable entertainment for the two young men with such disparate interests who lived under their roof. They held dinner parties, attended balls, soirées and parties of all kinds in order to try and find for them suitable young ladies of marriageable age. There were enough of them around. Every young girl in London seemed on the lookout for a husband, every anxious mother combed through the lists of suitable young men.

It was clear that the ladies found Carson attractive, but mothers were less interested and there was a question mark against his name. His eyes were always roaming, and the only women who seemed to interest him were older, and invariably married. Roger, although handsome and especially attractive in evening-dress, white tie and tails, seemed a cold fish, preferring to watch from the sidelines with a rather supercilious eye. Young women who were not particularly well educated – and few of them were – found him difficult to talk to, and the flirts found the distaste in his eyes rather chilling. Mothers also had a question mark against Roger. Though rich, clever and with prospects, there was the hint of mystery about him, his origins. Something not quite right.

Nelly the barmaid lived with her parents in a mean flat in a block of charity buildings in Covent Garden. She had three sisters and a brother, and her father was a porter in the market. It had never occurred to Nelly that Carson, with his rather rough manner and country accent, could possibly be a gentleman. She had accepted him for what he said he was: a farmer's son from Dorset, trying to find his luck in London and working as a clerk in the City.

After the incident in Montagu Square, she knew differently.

That was the first evening he had dressed up, and she knew he was a toff.

He told her something about his real life then, but not much, and not that his father was a baronet, and one day he would be one too.

He painted himself to Nelly as he was: a man out of sorts with himself and society. He found her a sympathetic listener; a girl with natural charm and healthy sexuality.

Nelly had a friend who was also from the country and who shared a room with another girl in Carter Lane, just behind Blackfriars. Both girls were out at work in the evenings, and Nelly had the key. On her days off she and Carson would meet in the little room in the shadow of the great dome of St Paul's, and make love.

There was a simple naiveté about Nelly that appealed to Carson. Above all, she was honest, so different from the society girls his uncle and aunt tried desperately to interest him in.

Carson had had a reputation in the Blackmore Vale for the way he chased women, and in many ways it was deserved. It was a little like a fox-hunt. He chased the women, bedded them, and that was that. Most of them he had never seen again.

But with Nelly he had established a relationship. He began to think of her as his woman, and she considered him her man. In a sense, he supposed, it was love.

Nelly was, indeed, a good listener. She was used to it, listening across the bar for hours on end to the outpourings of inebriates. But Carson was not like these; he was not the regular sort of drunk. She thought he drank – and he did, mostly too much – because he was unhappy, and gradually, over the weeks and months they spent together in the poorly furnished room with its cheap furniture and threadbare carpets, she got him to talk about it. He began to rely more on her and less on drink.

Gradually Carson became Nelly's whole life from the grime and poverty of the tenement in Covent Garden, her rather rough, uncouth father, her constantly complaining mother. Carson seemed to represent another world and, oh, how she yearned to be part of it. She added little touches to their room and tried to make it appealing with antimacassars on the chairs, a pretty fringed cloth on the table and fresh flowers that she got from Covent Garden in the vases. She was sure this was the sort of thing he was used to.

She began to fantasise about herself and Carson, and to imagine that, one day, they might have a future together in a beautiful wistaria-covered cottage in the country, with lilac trees in the garden, a cat and a dog and, perhaps, a baby of their own.

Carson, being a countryman, knew about birth control and took precautions. However, full-blooded young people are often impulsive and not as careful as they might be. Moreover, Nelly was not one of those people who suffered from morning sickness or any other symptoms, so she was perhaps two or three months pregnant before it occurred to her exactly what had happened.

She was a young woman of dignity. What had happened, happened far too early. She had not set out to trap Carson and she was horrified at the consequences of their behaviour. Of course she blamed herself. However, if maybe now they went to the country, perhaps everything would be all right.

'I've always fancied the country,' she told Carson one day.

'What makes you say that now?' Carson was lying on his back, staring at the cracks in the ceiling.

'I thought it might be a solution. You're not happy as you are. Neither'm I. I'm not suggesting . . .'

Cold terror suddenly struck at Carson's heart. But she *was* suggesting. She was *not* satisfied with things as they were. It was the same with all women. He thought Nelly was different but, in fact, she was just like the others.

They'd been together nine months. It was time, perhaps, to call it a day. He turned to look at her, and the expression on her face made him feel like a cad. She was young and trusting and vulnerable. She really did have a beautiful face; solemn and rather mysterious, like an Italian painting. Her hair was nearly black, thick and with a brilliant sheen. Her lips were full, and her eyes were very dark. She had a rounded, womanly body and full breasts. It made him hungry just to look at them. He cupped one in his hand and buried her nipple in his mouth. He was overcome by a frenzy of desire, of yearning for her, and he sank into her as her thighs parted for him.

He clasped her tightly to him and nudged her ears with his lips. 'I love you, Nelly,' he said.

That night she drank nearly half a bottle of gin, but instead of getting rid of the baby she made herself ill, and lay prostrate on her bed for several days, unable to tell Carson what had happened.

Ever since the row with Roger, Carson had steered clear of his cousin. Almost the only occasions they were together were on outings with their aunt and uncle, who continued to try, unsuccessfully, to pair each of them off with a suitable mate.

Carson no longer went to work with Roger but caught a bus. He was always there on time, if not a little early, bent over his desk at the boring task of stock-taking, or checking lading bills and balancing input of stock against output.

On a cold morning in February 1910, Carson, after reaching the office, kept on his coat because it was so cold. He lit a fire and knelt by it for some moments, rubbing his hands together and blowing on them, before sitting down at his desk and beginning his mundane task. He drew a sheaf of lading bills towards him and opened the heavy ledger.

Somewhat to his surprise, he saw it was a new ledger and not the one he'd been working on the day before. The pages were fresh and empty.

It was rather odd, and a slight feeling of apprehension overtook him, as though some ghostly presence were looking over his shoulder. Quite clearly the matter was more prosaic, and someone had been there the night before, after he'd gone, inspecting his work.

There were other signs of interference. He was not a particularly methodical person, but he kept his pens in a certain place, his different-coloured inks in another, a ruler here, a rubber or blotter there. He rose and poked the fire, which spluttered apathetically, then he walked restlessly to the window. In a few moments he had reached a decision.

He would give notice. He was being spied upon. Clearly, he was not trusted. It was a situation he could not tolerate, besides which, he knew that he loved Nelly and she suited him. He would confess the truth about his origins and he would take her to meet his parents. She would be overawed, they would be shocked; but everyone would eventually get over it. He would not be the first man to marry below his station, though certainly the first Woodville to marry *so* far below, but perhaps they would be glad he had settled down. He would ask for a farm on the Woodville estate, and he and Nelly would be like two peas in a pod. He might have been born a Woodville but, at heart, he was a country boy who liked simple country things, and his Nelly would do very well. He could visualise their life together winding peacefully along like the calm, uninterrupted water of the River Wen.

Relieved that he had come to a decision to abandon his bachelorhood and an unsatisfactory way of life, Carson resumed his seat and began drawing lines for his columns of figures. Then he wrote at the top of the ledger: *Tea, Ceylon* and, drawing a neat line under that, began to enter the amounts from the bills to his ledger until he had filled one column and begun another. After a while the room started to warm up and he removed his coat. Outside, it had begun to snow.

At eleven Carson got up to boil the kettle. Sometimes he made his own tea and sometimes one of the clerks along the corridor brought him a cup. It cheered him up to think that in a few days all this would be in the past. Gone, dull ledgers; gone, cheerless cups of weak tea. He sat down again, watching the kettle come to the boil on the fire, and mentally working on his plans.

First he would tell his Uncle Prosper he no longer wished to work for the Martyn-Heering concern. Then he would go down to see his mother and father. He would repent of his past and say he was a reformed character, and that this was mainly due to the nature of the good woman with whom he had fallen in love. He would warn them that, in the accepted sense, she was not a 'lady'. Her father was a porter at the Garden. Perhaps he wouldn't, after all, say she worked in a bar. He would remind his parents that times changed. These were modern days when even gentlemen worked for a living. He knew quite well what his parents would say to that! No matter.

His one hope was that his parents would be so happy he wanted to settle down that they wouldn't mind about his partner's social origins. After all, he was nearly twenty-three and he was sure his parents would be only too relieved that he wished to take a responsible attitude to life.

The handle of the door turned, and thinking it was Frederick, the clerk down the corridor, with his tea, he rose from his desk to remove the kettle from the fire.

He turned round with a smile, to see not Frederick but his Uncle Prosper, with a large ledger under his arm. Normally of a taciturn countenance, the expression on his face was more than usually forbidding.

'Good morning, Uncle,' Carson said politely, putting the kettle back on the hearth. 'You're just the man I wanted to see. Would you like some tea?'

'No thank you.' Prosper sat down and placed the ledger firmly on Carson's desk. 'And what did you wish to see me about?'

'I have reached a decision. I would like to give notice, Uncle.'

'Oh, have you indeed?' Uncle Prosper's expression grew, if anything, even more forbidding. And what made you reach this decision?'

'I have had enough of this life, sir. I have decided I wish to farm. I am not cut out for the City. I may even,' he paused, 'wish to marry.'

'Is that so?' His uncle's tone was laconic. 'And is there a fortunate young woman in mind?'

'There might be.'

Carson began to feel uncomfortable, not only at the sight of the ledger, but at his uncle as he drew it towards him and began slowly to turn the pages. When he came to a certain one he put his forefinger on a line and raised his head.

'And I suppose you have sufficient *funds* to begin farming and embrace matrimony?'

'I have saved a small amount, sir,' Carson said modestly. 'I am hoping my father will be relieved at my decision, and will take a tolerant view and advance me some funds. All he wished was for me to settle.'

'Before you proceed,' Prosper interrupted him, 'perhaps I should tell you the reason I am here.' With his finger still on a place in the ledger, he looked at his nephew. 'We have found some irregularities in the ledgers, Carson, and I am sorry to tell you these point to you. What you have just told me might explain the reason. I was reluctant to account for the fact that you would embezzle company funds, but now the reason is clear to me.

'You planned to leave. You needed money; funds more than you have, having spent your inheritance. You wish to marry and start a business. It is all quite clear to me now, whereas before it was not. I could not believe it . . . If only you had *asked*.'

Carson rose, and with the palm of his hand resting on his desk, stood looking down at his uncle.

'I am quite at a loss to understand what you are talking about, Uncle Prosper. I have never made false entries in the books, never embezzled funds. Frankly, I wouldn't know how.'

'Yet the discrepancies are here.'

Prosper thrust the ledger towards Carson and then drew from his pocket a sheaf of bills.

'These were found last night in a box in the cupboard behind you. They have never been entered. It is quite a simple thing to do, not complex at all. The suggestion is that you have diverted funds from the business into your own pocket by concealing merchandise, pretending it has not arrived, and perhaps making a separate transaction yourself . . .'

'That is *utter* nonsense!' Carson said indignantly. 'Malicious and false. I deny it completely.'

'But the evidence is *here*.' Prosper thrust the bills at him.

'The evidence has been planted behind my back, if you wish to know, Uncle.' Carson leaned again across the desk. 'I knew that somebody had been in here last night. The ledger was different. Things had been moved, interfered with.'

'I came here,' Prosper said, 'with a certain person, an employee of this company who entertained certain suspicions about you. I couldn't believe this because not only were you my great-nephew, but I could discern no motive. But I do now. You had a motive and, despite what you say, it appears you had the means.'

'I did *not* steal from this firm.' Carson advanced menacingly round the desk towards his uncle. 'This so-called evidence has been manufactured to discredit me.'

'Why should anyone wish to do that? Can you tell me?' Carson stood upright and scratched his head. 'No, I can't. I am mystified that *anyone* could be so malicious . . .'

He began to wonder about Frederick who, he had sometimes felt, was jealous of him; suspecting privilege from his family connections.

Prosper put the incriminating bills back into his pocket and, standing up, ran a hand wearily over his face.

'Carson,' he said, 'I am an unhappy man. You are my sister's grandson and I love you. Whatever you have done, I love you. I have supported you and spoken up for you when you seemed not to have a friend in the world. I was delighted when you decided to accept my invitation and came to London, and the improvement in your dear mother's health has been noticeable. I would keep this from her now if I could, but I can't. However, I wish to keep this matter in the family. It is not the firm's intention to press charges. Julius Heering is au fait with the situation, and he agrees.

'However, we cannot keep someone in the firm whom we do not trust. You are dismissed immediately. You will have to go home, and your parents will be informed, and that will be your punishment. Let us hope it is a lesson to you too.

'As for marriage,' Prosper swept a hand towards him, 'as for marriage, you can put that out of your mind straightaway. My suggestion will be that you are sent abroad for a while, to cool your heels. Young man . . .' He advanced towards him until Carson could feel his breath on his face. 'Many years ago your father worked in this very same room, doing a similar task. Your father did not like what he did any more than you, but he was honest . . .'

'*I* am honest too,' Carson cried, 'and I *demand* justice. I am completely innocent. I never stole. I never have and never would. It is utterly alien to me. I demand to know who my accuser is, and how these trumped-up charges against me arose. And if I am not told . . .'

'Yes?'

'I will go to the police.'

Prosper slumped into the chair again and crossed his legs, a hand dangling by his side.

'If you do that, Carson, you will be very foolish. We shall have to produce our evidence, and it is damning. Were it not, I would say so. You will then be accused of embezzlement and tried in a public court of law.

'I'm afraid the consequences for you would be ruinous. If found guilty as charged, you would without doubt be sentenced to many years in gaol, and yours and your family's good name ruined forever.'

6

All England was mourning the sudden death of the King. Edward the Peacemaker was dead: good old Teddy. Certainly not perfect, and in many ways his life had been one of controversy; but King Edward had come to symbolise an era, though that would not be known for some time afterwards: the Edwardian age.

The event of the King's death, however, did little to disturb the even tenor of life in the quiet Dorset countryside, or in the town of Wenham, where the flag flew at half-mast from the church tower. One or two people wore black, but not many. Edward, like his forebears, was largely unknown, and had certainly never been seen by the majority of his people.

Bringing in the cows for milking, Carson Woodville did not have the death of the King on his mind, or even the declining health of his own mother, which had grown noticeably worse since he had returned home under a cloud. Once again Carson had failed his family, even though they were eventually spared the truth about his dismissal. His work was considered unsatisfactory; he was not suited to it. Immediately on his return he was put to work, in disgrace, on the Sadlers' farm.

The cows climbed slowly up the track that led from the field to the milking-shed, taking their time. Some paused on the way to munch the succulent grass lining the banks and Carson, bringing up the rear with his sheepdog, thought that, in many ways, this was the kind of life he'd wanted, and he should be happy.

But no one could be happy, leaving under a cloud. Even

three months later, his heart still burned with indignation at the injustice of his treatment. He brooded and speculated about the identity of the person who had planted evidence against him. One name leapt to his mind, but there was not a shred of proof.

Then there was the question of Nelly. He had left town too suddenly to explain why. He told himself that one day he would go back and find her.

But in time Carson began to wonder whether that would be a good idea. He had nothing to offer Nelly. He would fail in her eyes, as he had in his parents'. He would see those big round eyes filled with scorn instead of love. He couldn't bear it.

Carson banished the horrible vision from his mind and pressed on up the hill. He drove the last of the cows into the shed and began to prepare them for milking. He tethered them in their stalls, observing that, as usual, Elizabeth the milkmaid had put out the stools and the pails for milking. Other cowherds would assist, and this was the time of day that Carson enjoyed.

He particularly enjoyed being near Elizabeth Yewell. He had known her all his life. Their paths had frequently crossed. She was the daughter of his Aunt Eliza's servants, Beth and Ted, and with the camaraderie of the young, which eschewed class barriers, they had played together as children.

Yet Carson had not been aware of Elizabeth as a beauty until he had come to work at Sadlers' farm, where she also worked as a milkmaid. Elizabeth to some extent helped Carson to forget about poor Nelly, to put her in perspective; in short, out of his mind.

The Sadlers had been established in the hamlet of Shepton for generations. They had originally been tenant farmers of the Barton family, who had owned the manor, the farm and a cluster of tiny houses. The Bartons had left fifteen years before, and Edwin Sadler, now seventy-eight, had bought his farm. He had not married until he was forty-five, and his bride was twenty-five years his junior. They had seven children, and the farm was now run by Tom and John Sadler. Sarah-Jane, the middle daughter, had married Laurence Yetman.

John and Tom were also married and lived on the farm with

their families. It was a large household, in which twelve to fifteen people regularly sat at the table for meals. These were presided over by Edwin, who went round the farm every week with his sons on a careful tour of inspection.

Carson had worked on the farm from time to time in the past. Tom Sadler was quite glad to have him back as he was a good worker, and he gave him a bunk and a warning to keep his mind on his work and not on the pretty young women around him.

Once the milking was under way, and a warm steam rose from the pails, these were collected and poured into large churns. The milk was then taken to the town, or turned into butter or cheese at the farm.

Carson, resting his head against the cow's flank, was aware of a neat pair of ankles on the other side. He lowered his head until he could see the owner, although he already guessed it. Elizabeth, squatting on her milking-stool, was busily working at the swollen udders of the cow. Her long work-day dress had risen over the tops of her shoes and, for a while, Carson studied them, imagining how it would be with the dres much further up or, maybe, no dress on at all. The milk spilled over his pail, and the cow's udder was flaccid in his hand. A carrier stooped down to take the pail and Carson wiped the animal's udders with a cloth. Then he stood up at the same time as Elizabeth, whose task was also finished.

The cows, released from thsir full uders, began stamping impatiently for their reward, and the cowmen began to take them from their halters and lead them out to the shed where their feed awaited them.

Carson stood watching Elizabeth as she too wiped the cow's udders, then he stared down at her hands as one of the men led the beast away. She turned, face flushed with her exertion, and saw Carson looking at her. His gaze made her flush even deeper.

She was twenty and, even though they had grown up together, she knew his reputation well enough. Her mother had urged her to be sure she kept well away from Carson Woodville when he came to work at the farm, and her father usually came to take her home, driving the trap the five miles to Shepton and the five miles back.

Carson wandered over to her and smiled.

'Any chance I can give you a lift home today, Elizabeth? I am going to visit my cousin Laurence.'

'No thank you, Carson,' Elizabeth said offhandedly. 'My father will be here shortly.'

'Very well.' Carson turned and took his jacket off the hook. 'I'll be seeing you, then.'

Carson walked out of the milking-shed and over to the bunk-house, where he flung himself down on his bed. He had a piece of straw in his mouth and he chewed it reflectively. He thought Elizabeth liked him, but pretended not to because, sure enough, she was bound to have been warned off him. He knew that Beth and Ted were protective, and whenever he visited Riversmead Elizabeth was kept well out of sight.

Yet when they were children, in the days when Eliza had lived there, they all used to play together: he and his sister Emily; Laurence, Dora and Hugh; Elizabeth Yewell and her eldest sister Jenny, her younger brother Jo.

The carefree, happy days of childhood were gone, and the age of awareness had brought awkwardness and embarrassment in their place: sex, the knowledge of good and evil.

Well, he, Carson, had taken his fill of that, and little good it had done him. In the eyes of the world he was a wastrel, a failure, and yet he knew himself to be a good man; maybe over-impulsive, passionate, but, especially since the death of his elder brother, eager to play his role as his father's heir.

No one took him seriously, and in the eyes of the world, a wastrel and a failure he remained.

He knew how faint were his chances with Elizabeth, and he thought once again of Nelly and her sweet, trusting face, her dark, limpid eyes. He felt a lump come into his throat, because he had treated her badly. He determined there and then that as soon as he had some holiday, he would go up to London and try and find her. He had been fond of her, even imagined himself in love with her, and in his panic his behaviour towards her had been shameful.

Pleased with his good resolution, Carson got off the bed, went and sluiced his hands and face, and put on clean breeches and shirt, which was required by Tom's wife, Ethel, who ran the domestic side of the farm with what some considered a rod of iron: little better than a strict boys' public school, they said. Others conceded that discipline and regularity were important on a farm of such size, with the welfare of so many people and animals to consider.

Ethel and her sister-in-law and a maid did the cooking, providing three wholesome, nourishing meals a day: breakfast, lunch and dinner. They hardly had time to recover from one meal when the preparations for the next began. Each brother had three children, so that altogether there were six under the age of five, and their needs had to be seen to as well.

The evening meal was about to start in the huge farm kitchen, and Carson took his place next to Hettie, John's wife, and a worker called Harold. Before him stood Ethel with a plate in her hand onto which she was ladling food, and as she passed his to him she gave him the sharp, fault-finding look everyone dreaded.

'Carson!'

'Yes, Mrs Sadler?' he said immediately.

'Are you going into the town tonight?'

'S'matter of fact, I am, ma'am.'

'Then would you take Elizabeth? Her father has sent word that a wheel has broken from the cart. I said he could borrow one of ours until his is mended. You can take the cart with you and come back with the horse.'

'Yes, ma'am.'

Carson felt his heart suddenly seem lighter as he tucked into his food. Then, looking round, he said:

'Where *is* Elizabeth, Mrs Sadler?'

'She's waiting in the parlour. Her mother and father expect her for dinner, so you'd better hurry.'

'Yes, Mrs Sadler.' Carson began to gulp his food, much to the amusement of his fellows, some of whom giggled silently to themselves. A few minutes later he was ready.

'Won't you have pudding, Carson?' Ethel looked at him in surprise.

'Doubtless Ted and Beth will give/me a bit of pudding, ma'am. I know they'll be anxious to see their daughter home.'

Ethel smiled grimly and handed the dish to someone else.

'And *don't* be late back yourself,' she said as he scraped his chair back from the table.

'No, ma'am.'

She watched him as he went to the kitchen door and, as he closed it, said *sotto voce* to Hettie:

'I think that lad is showing considerable improvement. Not so wild.'

'He's not what he was,' she agreed. 'Something happened to him in London.'

'Maybe it's the worry about his mother.'

'Whatever it is, he is at pains to work hard, to be seen to work hard and, above all, to behave himself. Certainly, the reputation he had would not be deserved now.'

As they started on their journey down from Bulbarrow, very few words were exchanged between Elizabeth and Carson. She seemed rather put out to find herself in his company and kept well to her side of the cart, a fact which Carson noticed.

'You need have no fear of *me*, Elizabeth,' he said, looking at her with a grin. 'I know how to behave myself. 'Sides, I'm too scared of your ma and pa.'

'I have no fear,' she replied.

'I'm a changed man,' he went on. 'I'm not what I was.'

'So they say.'

'Oh?' He reined in his horse and looked at her with interest. 'Who says?'

'My mother says, for one.' Elizabeth paused, then, relaxing, threw him a brilliant smile. 'She said, though, I should still take care.'

'Oh did she?'

'And not be alone with you.'

'And now you are.'

Carson raised his head and appreciatively sniffed the fresh evening air. The sun was sinking over the hills in the west, and a haze arose from the ground, enveloping everything in mystery. Smoke spiralled from the chimneys of the cottages and farms scattered throughout the landscape, and the fields were flecked with contented animals grazing on the lush grass. Carson sighed.

Elizabeth gazed at him sideways, perhaps a little irritated by now that he seemed to pay no obvious attention to her.

Carson's bold, attractive looks had always appealed to Elizabeth. And to someone who was as over-protected as she, his reputation for devilry was attractive too. But one had to be careful. Besides, she knew the stern eye of Ethel Sadler was always on her.

'I'll not do anything you don't *want*, you know, Elizabeth,' Carson said, suddenly betraying, after all, the fact that he had had his mind on her and not on the landscape. 'We've known each other since we were children. I notice you have been avoiding me and I assure you there's no need. But . . .' He held a hand towards her. 'I like you. I won't kiss you, and I certainly won't pester you if you don't want me to. But we've been friends since childhood and I'd like us to continue to be.'

And, to his surprise and satisfaction, Elizabeth caught his outstretched hand and held on to it.

Carson did as he promised as the summer went by. He went out of his way to seek Elizabeth's company and to be with her whenever he could. He milked the cows in the stall next to hers but he did not pester her, he did not try and kiss her. He felt that she was very special and had an important part to play in his life. Memories of poor Nelly disappeared completely.

Elizabeth only worked on the farm four days a week, sometimes three. She was much treasured by her father, and did not need to work. Both he and Beth wanted more for this special daughter than to be a mere milkmaid.

Ted and Beth had two other children, Jenny and Jo. Jenny was twenty-two, and as different from the petite Elizabeth as cloth is from silk. Jenny had worked as a clerk in the market since she left school at fourteen. Jo, who left school at the same age, was immediately apprenticed to the butcher. But Elizabeth stayed at school until she was sixteen. There was always something about her that set her apart; a sense that, whatever the fate of the other two, hers would be different.

Jo and Jenny resembled each other. They were dark, with rather blunt, country features like their father and mother; but Elizabeth was fair, fine boned, almost fragile. She looked like a lady and sometimes she behaved with the airs of one. She could be peremptory, arrogant, even rude; but she was capable of extraordinary graciousness as well. Work was her own choice because she had a passion for animals, and said she would like to work on a farm. John Sadler was Laurence Yetman's brother-in-law, and it was agreed that, as Elizabeth was so very persistent, a place should be found for her in the dairy.

For a time she helped the women in the kitchen, but her love for animals was genuine, her intentions serious, and she began to work in the cowshed, looking after the herd.

Despite her dainty appearance, Elizabeth was a tough, strong-minded young woman and she liked farm work. Her only difficulty came from her sister Jenny, who had always resented her. It was considered the jealousy of an older sibling towards a younger one; but maybe she remembered that her mother was away for a long time when she was small, and that when she returned she had a baby that people said wasn't hers. But memories are short, people forget, and it seemed to suit everyone to bury the fact that Elizabeth was adopted.

Jenny grew up resenting her little sister. She beat her whenever she got the chance, and was once thrashed by her father for her behaviour. After that, she hated Elizabeth all the more.

Jenny was always on the lookout to make trouble for Elizabeth, and one day when she saw her driving home with Carson Woodville, she hid behind a tree as they stopped just beyond the gate. Then she saw, or thought she saw, their heads come very close together until their brows almost touched. She half-imagined she saw them kiss.

That night at supper, Jenny, who had been sitting glowering at Elizabeth, said suddenly:

'How was it on the farm today, Lizzie?'

Elizabeth hated being referred to as 'Lizzie' and immediately tossed back her head.

'And why should *you* be so interested?'

'Why shouldn't I be? Or is it not the farm that is so important but the *men* who work on the farm? Or rather, *a* man.'

Ted was standing at the head of the table, carving the sirloin joint brought home that day by Jo. He placed a slice of beef on the plate held out by Beth who, in her turn, would ladle on a generous helping of potatoes and vegetables and smother them with thick gravy from the roast.

Both Ted and Beth paused imperceptibly in their tasks and exchanged glances.

'What is it you're trying to say, Jenny?' Ted screwed up his eyes at his first-born, as if he didn't understand.

'I'm not *saying* anything, Pa; but I knows what I sees.'

'And exactly what *do* you see?' Beth gave Ted a sharp nudge and he recommenced his carving, his actions noticeably slower.

'Can't say, Pa.'

'Then why bring it up?' Beth asked sharply, putting the plate in front of her daughter.

Elizabeth, perfectly composed, stared at the table. Jenny seemed to be debating to herself whether to eat her dinner or proceed with her chatter, which was causing a lot of attention, which she craved and, unlike the prettier Elizabeth, rarely got. Suddenly Elizabeth raised her eyes and gave her sister a look of such dislike that Jenny felt nettled.

'Ask Lizzie about *Carson* Woodville,' she said.

Ted dropped his fork, which clattered on to the meat platter. Beth picked it up and held it out to him.

'Careful, now,' she said, with a warning note in her voice. 'And what is there to ask, Miss Busy-Tongue?' Beth stared fixedly at her daughter.

'He be kind enough to bring Elizabeth home when I can't get there. That's all.' Ted flicked his knife against the steel and began briskly sharpening it. 'Now don't 'ee go spreading no malicious stories, Jenny. You've got a dangerous sharp edge to your tongue, like this knife will soon have.'

'Ain't *nothing* malicious 'bout it,' Jenny said, gazing defiantly at Elizabeth. ''Tis what *I* sees with my own eyes.'

'And that is?' Elizabeth spoke for the first time, keeping her voice low and controlled.

'I thought you and he had your heads together in the cart today. Very close, if I may say, or do my eyes deceive me?'

'Your eyes deceive you,' Elizabeth replied. ''Baint nothing between Carson and me except pure friendship.'

'Pure!' Jenny guffawed, and Ted held up his steel and shook it at her.

'Now don't you go sniggering there, Jenny, my girl. That's the way ugly rumours start, and a powerful lot of 'arm they do.'

'Carson has a reputation,' Jenny said. 'Surely you know that, Pa. Everybody knows it. Surprised you *ever* allowed him to bring Lizzie home.'

'I never allowed. I never asked,' Ted replied crossly. ''Twas Mrs Sadler that arranged it. Had I known she would ask Master Carson I might have thought better of it. Now, Elizabeth, my girl,' he leaned across the table towards her, 'just 'ee heed what your sister says. Carson Woodville is *not* thought well of hereabouts. You could damage your reputation if you got *too* friendly with him. Even to be seen with him is harmful. 'Sides . . .' He paused for a moment, then looked sideways at Beth. 'Your mother and I feel it's time you stopped working at the farm. 'Taint no place for a lady.'

'A "lady".' Jenny guffawed again, burying her face in her hand and squealing with laughter. 'A *lady*, be it now. Oh Pa, you *are* a caution.'

Carson stood at the door of the cowshed, looking over the heads of the milkmaids and cowherds who were squatting next to the cows, pressing the warm milk from the udder to the pail beneath. There was no sign of Elizabeth. Again. She had not been here now for a week, and discretion had made him decide not to query her whereabouts.

One of the cowherds passed him and gave him a nudge.

'No use standing around moonin', lad. She 'baint here.'

Carson sat down on his stool and, putting the pail under the udders of the cow and his head against her flank, began his task. Peeping under the belly of his cow, he saw that his neighbour was a girl called Molly, who was friendly with Elizabeth. Molly was a buxom country girl with broad hips and thick ankles, and after Carson had finished his work and the pails were being taken away and poured into the churns, he waited until Molly had finished too.

'Seen Elizabeth?' he asked casually, wiping his hands.

'She 'baint coming back,' Molly said offhandedly.

'What?'

'So they say. Best ask Mrs Sadler.'

Carson turned abruptly and hurried out of the cowshed, across the farmyard and into the large kitchen, where steam was rising from the stove as about half a dozen women bustled about getting the lunch for the family and farm-hands. It was a jovial, cheerful scene presided over by Hettie Sadler, who stood at the stove stirring a large pot, her other hand on her hip.

She looked up as she saw Carson hurry towards her.

'It's too early for your dinner, Carson.'

'It's not that, Mrs Sadler . . .' Carson stopped and twisted a large grimy rag in his hands. 'I wondered what had happened to Elizabeth.'

'She's gone,' Mrs Sadler said firmly, grasping her spoon and resuming her stirring, pausing only to savour the contents. 'That's good,' she said, smacking her lips. 'A nice hot mutton stew.'

'*Gone?*' Carson echoed. 'Where?'

'Best ask her father.' Hettie Sadler turned and gazed at him for a few moments. 'On second thoughts, better not. I hear he's not too pleased with you.'

'But I've done *nothing*!'

'That's not what I heard.'

'Nothing, nothing, nothing,' Carson said, stamping his foot on the stone floor. ''Cept drive her home sometimes as your sister-in-law asked me, if I was going that way.'

'I hear that's when it happened.' Hettie Sadler gave him a

disapproving glance. 'The incident that gave offence. I wonder my husband hasn't spoken to you, Carson.'

'I've done nothing for him to speak to me about.'

'Anyway, she's gone.'

'Gone from where?'

'Sent away, I've heard. You've only yourself to blame, Carson. I shouldn't wonder if my husband won't ask you to go too. It seems no lass is safe from you.'

Guy was slumbering in the drawing-room when his son burst in, disturbing his mid-afternoon nap. He struggled up in his chair and rubbed his eyes, spluttering as Carson banged the door and stood fuming before him.

'What's the matter now, Carson?' Guy asked testily, looking at the clock or the mantelpiece. 'What on earth is the time? My goodness, it's only *three* o'clock. Another hour before tea. What are you doing here at this time of day?'

'They've sent Elizabeth away.'

'Elizabeth? Elizabeth who?'

'Yewell. Beth and Ted's daughter.'

'Well, why should that concern you?' Guy said irritably, settling back in his chair again. 'It's no concern of yours. Or mine,' he added as an afterthought. He closed his eyes as though wishing to resume his sleep, then opened them again. 'What's it to you, anyway?'

'She worked at Sadlers' Farm. I was friendly with her.'

'You *what*?' Guy, fully awake, struggled to sit upright in his chair. 'Now, look here. You leave that girl alone . . .'

'Father . . . nothing happened,' Carson cried. 'I like Elizabeth. I've known her for years . . .'

'Then why are you so upset?' his father demanded. 'You seem terribly upset, if that was all.'

'I'm upset because she got sent away because of me.'

'*Who* sent her away?' Guy still couldn't understand. 'The farmer?'

'Her mother and father,' Carson shouted again, as if his father were deaf. '*They* sent her away because of *me* . . .'

'It's your reputation, Carson.' The voice came from behind

and, turning, he saw his mother come slowly into the room. Her face was very pale and she leaned heavily on a stick. 'You're sent away from London for unsatisfactory work, a hint of dishonesty I've since heard, and now Elizabeth is a victim of your lust . . .'

'Mother!' Carson glowered at her. 'I am innocent on *both* charges. I worked hard in London. I did not seduce Elizabeth. In the first case there was a trumped-up charge against me. In the second, all I ever did was to drive Elizabeth home at her *father's* request as his cart had broken down. I did nothing else. I swear.'

'You can't seem to help yourself, Carson,' his father said in a voice of despair. 'I don't understand why, but you can't. There is some bad blood in you which can only be inherited from the Heerings. No one in our family has behaved with such lack of regard for our name as you. You were trouble from the day you were born, Carson.' Guy's voice grew stronger as he warmed to his theme. 'You were difficult as a baby, naughty as a small boy, and as you grew up you got worse. You were expelled from school. All the farmers hereabouts criticised you, and most of them had to lock up their daughters. I don't, can't understand it. It seems you have no pride.'

Carson sat in an attitude of apparent dejection, his head sunk onto his chest.

'Part of what you say was true, Father, but no longer.' He looked tenderly over at his mother, who had sat down heavily, her eyes closed. 'When I realised how really ill Mama was, I was shocked into mending my ways. I became conscious of my responsibility as the heir, the surviving child. I swear I have done nothing of which I am ashamed.'

Carson walked slowly over to his mother. Then he knelt by her side and took her hand.

'Believe me, Mama. I did try. I did not like the work in London but I stuck to it. There was not a word of truth in the charges against me.'

'If it was not true, you should have defended yourself,' his mother murmured weakly. 'You should have stuck up for yourself like an innocent man.'

'Uncle Prosper said he would prosecute me and I thought that would only distress you. He said there was enough evidence to send me to gaol. Imagine the distress for *you* if that had happened. All I ever did to Elizabeth was drive her home in a pony and cart from time to time, beginning at her father's request.'

'Anyway,' Guy said, 'it was just as well she went.'

'Father, I wish to settle down,' Carson said gravely, sitting beside his mother. 'I am twenty-three. I realise I have caused you and Mother grief, and I wish this to cease. It appears I attract trouble. In London I formed an attachment to a young woman and I thought I would like to marry her; but now that I have met Elizabeth, who is good and virtuous as well as beautiful . . . perhaps I may be allowed to court her after all.'

'Elizabeth Yewell,' his father roared, 'is the daughter of your cousin's serving-woman. Are you mad? Have you gone out of your senses? Do you realise one day you will be *Sir* Carson Woodville? And if the way you are behaving now is continued, it will be sooner than you think. Your behaviour has already affected your mother's health, and soon it will affect mine. The very *least* you can do is to marry a woman of your own station. You may behave like a peasant, but you aren't one. You are the heir to an old baronetcy and it is high time you realised it. Elizabeth Yewell. I never heard of such a thing! Thank goodness her parents had the sense to send her away. At least *they* knew their place and will see that their daughter keeps hers.'

'I find your attitude intolerable,' Carson cried, his temper suddenly rising at the injustice of his father's words. 'This is the twentieth century, if you please. People are no longer distanced from one another in the shameful way they were. Look at Aunt Lally, a *dancer* . . .'

'Your uncle was *not* a baronet,' Guy said coldly. 'Now get out and stay out, until your mother and I have discussed the situation and have decided what to do with you.'

Carson looked down at his mother, who was staring at him, her expression so sad it made his heart ache.

'Do as your father says, Carson,' she said. 'Go for a ride, go to your room; but please *never*, ever see, or even *try* to see, Elizabeth again.' She gave a deep sigh and raised her hand towards Guy. 'My dear, would you help me upstairs to my room? I feel far from well.'

Once her maid had got her undressed and into bed and comfortable, Guy was admitted to Margaret's room, and he rapidly crossed to her bedside and sat close to her, her hand in his. For a while they remained silent, aware of a feeling of intimacy that had been absent from their marriage for many years.

Finally Guy looked at her tenderly and said:

'How do you feel now, my dear? It was too bad you came in at that moment and heard Carson's tantrums.'

'I'm glad I heard Carson,' Margaret said with vehemence. 'I am glad I heard what he said.' Her clasp on Guy's hand tightened. 'He *must* be kept away from that girl at all costs . . .' Her voice trailed off and Guy murmured:

'Yes indeed. He must.'

'And not because of the reason *you* say, Guy.' Margaret's voice was almost inaudible. 'The real reason, I know . . .'

'You know!' Guy looked at her in astonishment.

'I know Elizabeth is really your daughter by Agnes Yetman. I have known for a number of years.'

'You knew all the time and said nothing? Who told you? Eliza?'

'No, it was not Eliza. It was common gossip that Elizabeth was your daughter, and I am more aware of what people say in the town than you realise. It is known that Ted and Beth treat her differently from their other children, and why. Now let's not discuss it any more. No one now remembers; it all happened so long ago. But I know, and I forgive you. That is all. Besides,' she gripped his hand and smiled grimly, 'for many years now you have loved me as much as any mistress, and that is what matters.'

'Oh, I did. I do!' Guy exclaimed brokenly. 'I have loved you, and only you, for years, Margaret. More than you will ever know.'

'But I do know,' she said with a quiet satisfaction, pressing his hand. 'And that means more to me than *you* will ever know. It is one thing to love a man, knowing that love is not reciprocated. But to love and *be* loved is a different matter altogether. I have so much to be thankful for.'

But her face was weary as she closed her eyes, and Guy sat beside her silently weeping.

PART TWO

Coals of Fire

7

Margaret Woodville died in her sleep almost three months to the day following the death of King Edward. She was found by her maid in the morning and, from the expression of sweetness and repose on her face, it would appear that, in her last moments, she had found contentment. She was only fifty-nine.

Margaret had achieved much in her life; but her personal suffering had been enormous. She had been a foreign woman, a woman from abroad, and it took many years for the people of Wenham to accept her.

Even then, she was never one of them, nor did she strive to be. She was not as grand as her mother-in-law, Henrietta, who used to make a stately progress through Wenham in her carriage, bowing to right and left rather like a member of royalty. She had also gone regularly to church, which the Calvinist Margaret never did. Margaret was married in the church and went there for the christening of her children and formal occasions like Easter and Christmas, until Guy fell out with the rector, and then neither of them went at all.

And it was the same rector who buried her, thirty years after he had married her.

The people of Wenham were a hardy lot, and many of them recalled that day as the hearse bearing the coffin was borne slowly past, pulled by four black horses. Fifty-nine was not old, and some of them, now in their eighties, had been middle-aged when the young Sir Guy rode out with his bride, not a beauty, not young, but wealthy. It was she who was to save the family fortunes.

The Rector of Wenham liked few things better than a good

funeral. He felt such an occasion brought out the best in him, especially if the person to be interred was someone of significance in the community; and who more significant than Lady Woodville?

He had not known her very well, but that didn't prevent him giving her the best funeral of which he felt himself capable. The choir rehearsed for days, he went over the order of service again and again with the Reverend Turner, and he burned the midnight oil over his sermon.

Above all, the rector felt it was a chance to achieve reconciliation with the Woodville family. It was an occasion of social and political significance as well as a religious one.

It was a beautiful day for a funeral; a time when earthly cares are put away and the soul returns to its maker. The fields and hedgerows seemed bursting with life, the sky was of an almost Mediterranean, cerulean blue, and the sun shone down as a symbol of benediction.

The carriage wended its way from Pelham's Oak, a sad funeral procession going at a snail's pace, and Guy, his black top-hat on his knee, sat quietly weeping for the wife he had loved too late.

The rector and Mr Turner, in black copes, greeted the funeral party at the church door, and Carson helped to carry his mother's coffin down the nave to where it rested in front of the sanctuary, on a bier flanked by tall wax candles.

The choir rose and sang, most beautifully, a favourite air of Margaret's: 'How beautiful are thy dwellings'. When this was over, and after prayers, the rector mounted the pulpit and gazed round at the mourning congregation.

' "Who can find a virtuous woman? For her price is far above rubies." The Book of Proverbs, Chapter thirty-one, verse ten.'

Theatrically he flung his arm, from which hung the black stole, across the lectern, and gazed around him with an expression which, in days of old, would have struck terror into the hearts of his congregation. But now he was an old man and he frightened them no more.

'Dearly beloved, those were the words used thirty years ago when the marriage of Guy Woodville to Margaret Heering was solemnised before me. Never did I think she would predecease me . . .' – there was a loud sob from Guy and Eliza's arm stole round his shoulder – '. . . leaving a sorrowing husband.'

Mr Lamb tucked his hands into the sleeves of his surplice and gazed at the ancient rafters.

'Margaret Woodville was a Dutchwoman. She came to us from abroad, but embraced these shores. She was not a regular member of our church, being a nonconformist, and thus I did not know her very well, but virtue shone from her and she made Sir Guy, who mourns her here among us, a good and loving wife.

'She bore him three children and, alas, one is buried here in the family vault, another sacrificed his life for souls in New Guinea. George Woodville was my son-in-law, and today we praise him . . .'

Sophie sat erect in the pew behind the Woodvilles: Guy, Carson, Eliza and her children and husband. On either side of her were Deborah and Ruth, their hands tightly clutching hers. They had last seen their grandmother the previous week, and they were too young to realise they would never see her again. To be sure, it was an awesome occasion, and they sensed its importance and majesty. They also knew that she was lying in the coffin because they had been taken to see her there: a waxen face with a slight smile on her lips. It was like a doll and not the grandmama they had come to know and find a little hard to love.

Sophie listened, expressionless, to the eulogy that her father delivered on the woman she knew had been responsible for excluding her from Pelham's Oak. A good woman? A virtuous one? That, surely, was a matter of opinion. 'Her children arise up and call her blessed'? Two of them, as her father had said, were dead.

'The heart of her husband doth safely trust in her'? That was true. Who would take her place now?

' "Give her of the fruit of her hands and let her works praise her in the gates." Amen.'

The rector concluded his sermon and was pleased with its effect. Half the congregation was in tears: the sign of a good funeral oration. Satisfied, and with his Bible in his hand, he made his way creakily down the steps of the pulpit and joined Mr Turner in the sanctuary.

Sophie remembered George's simple funeral in the mission chapel in New Guinea. It had lacked the full solemnity of this, and instead of the polished tones of a well-rehearsed choir, the half-naked natives had sung their hymns in pidgin English. She looked around her at the stained glass in the windows of the nave. There was still no memorial to George. Maybe, ironically, now that his mother was dead, there would be.

Suddenly the memory of New Guinea seemed to overwhelm her and she felt that George was physically near her. It was an uncanny feeling, an intimation of the supernatural, as though George himself had come to take his mother to the throne of God. Then, in her heart, Sophie forgave Margaret for what she had done to her.

Later as they all stood around the family vault, Sophie remained at the back. She would not have gone at all if it hadn't been for the grandchildren, but would have remained in the church, thinking about George and his nearness. He was near no more, and she imagined him entering the crypt with Guy and Carson to lead his mother by the hand to God's throne. Next to her coffin would be that of Emily, her little daughter who had died when she was twelve. They were all united now. Sophie blew her nose hard.

People began to disperse. She too was about to turn away when Eliza detached herself from her husband and the little enclave made by the Woodvilles, and went up to her, bending first of all to say a few words to the children. Then she straightened and looked into Sophie's eyes.

'Guy would be very glad if you would come to the house afterwards.'

'Oh!' Sophie found it hard to conceal her surprise.

'He really would. He would like to have asked you himself . . .'

'I understand,' Sophie said. 'I think maybe I shouldn't.'

'Oh *please*.' Impulsively, Eliza took her hand. 'The family would really appreciate it. If you could bring yourself to come it would be a fine Christian gesture, one that I think you will not regret.'

'I'll come then,' Sophie said. Suddenly, once again, she was conscious of the presence of George telling her what to do. 'Would it be all right if I rode with you?'

'Of course. Gladly.' Eliza seized her arm and began to walk with her to the cemetery gates.

Sophie had been to Pelham's Oak about half a dozen times in her life, but not once since she'd been married. She could remember attending the party for the christening of Carson with her parents when she was about twelve.

Eliza and Julius took her and the children in their impressive Silver Ghost Rolls-Royce motor-car which made all heads turn wherever they went. Sophie appreciated Eliza's kindness, but as soon as they arrived at the house Eliza fell automatically into the role of hostess, and Sophie soon found herself, in the general mêlée, on her own. The children, quite familiar with the house, had immediately run off.

Sophie felt lost in the crowd but, at the same time, was grateful for the anonymity it conferred on her. She wandered round the cream-and-gold drawing-room hung with portraits of generations of Woodvilles in different poses, most of them seeming to stare rather superciliously at the throng below. She had nothing in common with these ancestors of George, nor they with her. George had been a man cast in a different mould.

By now the room was crammed with mourners, all dressed, without relief, in black. There was a solemn, sepulchral feeling to the gathering, and Sophie began to wish she had obeyed her instinct and not come. She stood for a moment by the window and saw that, as at Carson's christening, there was a marquee on the lawn for the estate workers, who were expected to drown their grief in beer, rather than the sherry or wine which was offered in the house, as well as tea and cold cordials. Beyond the marquee she could see Wenham and the tower of the church, where they had just laid Lady Woodville to rest.

Sophie turned, embittered by her thoughts. How peculiar it seemed to be in the house recently vacated by the deceased, and from which she had always rigidly excluded her daughter-in-law. Lady Woodville. It was a title that now she would never have. Not that she coveted it. Not that she coveted anything: the splendid house, the gracious grounds, the appurtenances of minor nobility.

In the distance she could see Hubert Turner and sensed that he was trying to make his way towards her. But he knew so many people that every few seconds he had to stop. Her father was talking to one group of people, her mother to another. It was only she, Sophie, who didn't fit. She was the outsider.

She went to the long buffet table and asked for a cup of tea. Gravely a servant poured her a cup from a silver teapot and handed it to her. Next to her a man handed her a plate.

'Would you care for a biscuit?' he asked and, as she shook her head, he put the plate back on the table.

'Thank you all the same,' Sophie said, 'but I'm not hungry.'

'I don't think we've met.' The man, in a black morning-suit, held out his hand. 'Bartholomew Sadler. I'm always called "Bart".'

'How do you do, Mr Sadler?' Sophie politely extended her hand. 'I'm Sophie Woodville.'

'Oh! *You're* the Sophie Woodville.'

'*The* Sophie Woodville?' She couldn't help smiling. 'And you must be a relation of Sarah-Jane.'

'I'm her brother, the only one who doesn't farm.'

'And what do you do?'

'I'm a stone-mason. I have a yard in Portland. In fact I wonder why I came today. I hardly knew Lady Woodville.'

'I was thinking the same thing,' Sophie said a little wistfully.

'I thought you looked lost.'

'Then you must know why.'

'I never listen to gossip,' Bart Sadler said softly. 'Tell me why.'

She wondered if he was teasing her. He had rather a gaunt,

stern face, like the pictures of Abraham Lincoln, a lofty brow and dark, piercing eyes.

'I was married to George Woodville. My parents-in-law were not pleased with the match and this is the first time I have been inside this house for many years.'

'I saw you with two children. *They* seemed to know their way around.'

'They have frequently visited their grandparents.'

'You must feel very bitter,' Mr Sadler murmured.

'Not at all,' Sophie said vigorously. 'Sad, but not bitter.' 'Bitterness' was a word that would get round the community, Sophie thought, far too quickly. She didn't want anybody to realise quite how bitter she was.

Just then the crowd slowly parted to reveal Guy, leaning heavily on Eliza's arm, coming slowly towards her with the shambling gait of an old man. Bart Sadler took her cup and replaced it on the table as Guy stopped in front of Sophie and took her hand.

'My dear,' he said, patting it. 'It is *so* good of you to come.'

'I was glad to come at last, Sir Guy,' she said proudly, raising her voice a little so that people could hear.

'My dear wife didn't understand, you know. She didn't *realise*. But I loved her . . . so much.'

Guy dropped Sophie's hand and, getting out his handkerchief, dabbed his eyes.

'I quite understand, Sir Guy.' Sophie realised that the eyes of most people in the room were upon her, watching, waiting, hanging on every word, sensing every reaction.

'It is very good of you, very *Christian*,' Guy emphasised. 'Today is not the time for us to speak, but I hope you will come again.'

Then, rather like a monarch making a royal progress, he moved away, and once again the crowd parted and re-formed like a mêlée of courtiers around the royal presence. Sophie stood watching him until he was completely obscured.

'You did that very well,' Bart Sadler whispered. 'You mean, you haven't *spoken* to him since you returned?'

'This was the first time,' she said with an air of triumph. 'I understood it was Lady Woodville who opposed me, and it seems I was right. George always said his father was a very gentle man.'

'You must feel most gratified.'

'Gratified?' Sophie looked at him with surprise. 'You think I should feel grateful I am invited to his wife's funeral reception? No, I should have been much more gratified if Lady Woodville had been a *real* mother-in-law; if I could have talked to her about her son. You would think a mother would like to have known how he had lived all those years away, would you not? How he died?'

'I admit I find it strange,' Bart murmured, taking another glass of sherry from a passing waiter. 'But then I know nothing of the nobility, Mrs Woodville. I am just a very simple, ordinary man of the countryside.'

Miss Victoria Fairchild also gazed upon the scene from the safety of a window embrasure, Constance by her side. Constance had played the organ for the funeral ceremony, played it most beautifully, and people had gathered round, congratulating her. Constance gazed about myopically, peering through her steel-framed spectacles, as if she found the world a bewildering place and was only happy at the console of an organ. Had she been a little girl, as she felt, and not a woman, she would have clasped Miss Fairchild's hand, but restrained herself by standing close to her; as close as she could get.

Constance had been orphaned when she was eight, and had been adopted by the kindly spinster, with whom she shared a love of music. John Yetman, Connie's father, had shown great kindness to Miss Fairchild when the romance she had briefly enjoyed with his brother Christopher ended in sadness. Christopher Yetman had proved to be a bigamist and had vanished from her life.

Miss Fairchild and Connie had a good life together. Indeed Miss Fairchild, who had lived in the shadow of her parents until she was forty-five, could only be said really to have come alive after their deaths, which were close together. Each year the two women travelled to the Continent, walking in the foothills of the Alps or painting among the lakes in northern Italy. Constance loved to visit the continental cathedrals and sit in their darkened interiors listening to music.

Miss Fairchild was now seventy-five, but she looked very much as she had fifteen years before, when she had adopted Connie. She was a rather thin woman, of medium height, with a back she kept ramrod-straight; she had a kind face with features full of character, whose only real blemish was a scar on her lip caused by a cleft palate at birth. Miss Fairchild had always blamed the blemish for the fact that she had not married and had children of her own. But after she adopted Connie this resentment vanished, because she could imagine no daughter as perfect as her ward.

Connie was now twenty-three, myopic and decidedly plain. She was a person who was unconcerned about her appearance and, certainly, she would have considered it vain and stupid to try and be other than what she was.

By any standards she did not make the best of herself, and few had any doubt that her destiny was to follow the state of single blessedness that had been her guardian's fate through life.

Miss Fairchild was sitting in the embrasure, drinking a cup of tea. She had been shocked by Lady Woodville's death, although she had never known her well. She had been dubious about accepting the invitation to the reception, but she thought that Connie did not get out enough, did not mix enough in Wenham society, and to be seen at a funeral was better than nothing.

Miss Fairchild's dearest wish was that Connie should have opportunities in life she herself had not had; the gift of love, the joy of children. In her case, her blemish had made her feel like a pariah. When her parents had had a shop, she had worked in the back. How she wanted Connie's life to be different; but in so many ways she knew Connie was like her: she lacked the ability to attract.

They had spoken to the Martyns, the Heerings – there were so many. They had chatted to Laurence Yetman and Dora and Hugh. Dora was the antithesis of Connie. She was pretty, extrovert, tomboyish, and enjoyed nothing better than riding her horses and looking after them in the stables in her mother's new home.

Miss Fairchild remarked that people seemed to be drifting away and suggested to Connie that they should be going. 'We don't want to outstay our welcome,' she said nervously. 'Maybe we can offer Mrs Woodville a lift.'

Sophie was alone again, looking awkward and out of place. Connie went over and gave her Miss Fairchild's message. Sophie said something, shook her head and smiled gratefully across the room at Miss Fairchild. Connie began to weave her way back, not looking where she was going.

Suddenly there was a mighty bump, her spectacles flew off and she felt herself clasped in the arms of a man. She peered at his face, an inch away from hers: Carson Woodville.

'Oh *dear*!' she cried fretfully.

'Connie! I *do* beg your pardon.'

'No, no, I beg yours . . .' Connie freed herself from Carson's clasp and fell to her knees, groping blindly for her spectacles upon the floor.

'Here, let me.' Carson crouched down beside her and quickly produced the spectacles, which appeared undamaged.

'There,' he said, handing them to her. 'No harm done, I think.'

'Oh *thank* you, Carson.' Connie nervously threaded the thin wire of the steel frames over her ears and adjusted the bridge across her nose. 'Oh Carson, I am *so* sorry . . .'

'But Connie, it was my fault. I wasn't looking . . .'

'No, Carson, about your mother.'

'Oh!' Carson's eyes grew bright.

'At least you knew your mother,' Connie blurted out. 'Mine died when I was born. You had all those years with her. I had none. That's something to think about, to console you perhaps.'

Carson suddenly clutched her hand. 'It does console me,' he said. 'Here, let me take you back to Miss Fairchild.'

Miss Fairchild had watched the encounter with some concern, and her relief was palpable as Carson steered Connie to the embrasure by the window.

'How kind of you, Carson.' Miss Fairchild stretched out her hand in a gesture of appreciation. 'I hope neither of you were hurt.'

'No harm done,' Carson said again. 'And Connie's spectacles are in one piece.'

'Can you see out of them, dear?' Miss Fairchild enquired solicitously, and Connie fervently nodded her head, clearly wishing the incident were over.

'It was entirely my fault,' Carson insisted. 'I . . .'

'I know.' Miss Fairchild's eyes brimmed with sympathy. 'I saw you were preoccupied. You were doubtless thinking about your dear mother. My heart goes out to you, my poor Carson. Do *please* feel that if ever you wish to speak to anyone, an older person perhaps, you can come to me.'

'Oh, how *kind* of you, Miss Fairchild.' Carson sounded sincere.

'Now.' Miss Fairchild looked briskly at Connie. 'Are we ready?'

'Yes, Aunt Vicky.'

'And is Mrs Woodville coming?'

'She is accompanying her father and mother.'

'Very well.' Miss Fairchild began to put on her gloves, continuing to smile encouragingly at Carson.

'Don't forget what I said, Carson.'

'I won't, Miss Fairchild.'

'Goodbye then.'

'Goodbye. Goodbye Connie,' he said with a smile and, as if acting on impulse, he bent and kissed her warmly on the cheek.

It was after five. The guests were beginning to drift away. Out in the marquee and on the lawn, the estate workers seemed to have forgotten that they were at a funeral, not a wedding, and sounds of merriment startled the sombre atmosphere within.

'Too much beer,' someone murmured darkly.

Sophie Woodville had already left with the rector and Mrs Lamb and her children, and after Carson had seen Connie and Miss Fairchild to their carriage, he walked back into the house and crossed the hall, going up the stairs into the drawing-room.

Lally and Prosper were chatting to Eliza and Julius Heering, Roger by their side. He stood with a hand in the pocket of his black trousers, listening with an air of deference to Julius, the senior partner of the business and someone to whom people instinctively deferred. Roger's fair, wavy hair had a neat side-parting, and his intelligent, brilliant blue eyes gazed unwaveringly at Julius. Then, aware of Carson hovering, he turned casually, acknowledging him.

'Good afternoon, Carson,' he said as Julius stopped talking.

'Good afternoon.' Carson looked around. Lally kissed him and Prosper and Julius gravely shook hands, expressing formal condolences. Lally briefly dabbed her eyes with a corner of her handkerchief, but Carson knew she didn't, couldn't, really care two figs about his mother's death.

Julius, less hypocritical, resumed his conversation with Prosper about the shipment of some items of merchandise.

Carson felt ill at ease, vividly reminded of his unjust dismissal, and began to slip away. To his surprise Roger, still with his hand in his pocket, turned to him and said casually:

'Believe me, Carson, I really *am* sorry about the death of your mother.'

'Are you really?' Carson said. 'That surprises me.'

Roger looked taken aback.

'No, seriously,' he stammered. 'I never had a mother, so to lose one must be hard.'

'And I find *your* sympathy hard to swallow.' Carson menacingly took a step nearer Roger. Lowering his voice, he said: 'The more I think about that trumped-up charge in London, the more I wonder who was responsible for it. Perhaps you know?'

Roger took his hand out of his pocket.

'I? Why should I know anything?'

'I think you know.'

'I think you're drunk.' Roger peered at him accusingly.

'I am not drunk. But as the heir, you might well have wanted me out of the way.'

'The heir?' Roger retorted. 'Heir to what?'

'Heir to the business. You would want me out of the way. Well, it killed my mother. It upset her, and now she's dead.'

Roger's beautiful eyes, now a steely blue, gazed contemptuously at Carson.

'I don't think I ever imagined for one moment that I had a rival in *you*, Carson. You were no threat to me at all. Don't flatter yourself to think that you were.'

Carson moved closer and stuck a finger into Roger's solar plexus.

'Who else but *you* had the knowledge? Who else could have fiddled the books?'

'Frankly, I think you're mad,' Roger said, turning his back dismissively on Carson.

Prosper had been watching the two young men and, as Julius had now politely turned his attention to Lally, murmured to Roger, who was flushed and agitated.

'What was that all about?'

'Nothing,' Roger said offhandedly.

'It seemed to me more than "nothing". You were quite upset.'

'The fellow's crazy. He's wrong in the head.' Roger touched his brow.

'Was it something to do with the business in London?'

'As a matter of fact, it was. *He* thinks *I* am the person responsible for his dismissal. Did you ever hear such rubbish?'

'I suppose it *is* rubbish?' Prosper looked at him shrewdly.

Roger's expression rapidly changed to one of indignation.

'What an insulting observation.'

'It's a question that has often troubled me.'

'But why should *I* do it?'

'You had no love for your cousin,' Prosper whispered, so that his voice was inaudible to the others.

'I had no fear of him either, and no respect for him. None at all. Such a gesture as you suggest would be beneath me. He was a thief, you can bank on that.'

'What are yoou two whispering about?' Lally casually turned to them.

'Business, my dear.' Prosper glanced at his watch. 'I think we should be going.'

'Is it all right to leave Guy?' Julius asked his wife as he looked across the room.

Guy was sitting talking to an old friend of the family, the Dowager Lady Mount. The windows were open but the air was oppressive. Outside, the merrymaking was getting louder.

Guy had a glass of whisky in his hand and raised it morosely to his lips.

'I think Guy's all right,' Prosper said. 'Lady Mount is in control.'

'I'd like to stay with Guy.' Eliza put a hand on Julius's arm. 'Would you mind, dear?'

'Not at all, my love,' he said, taking her hand. 'You do what you think is right.'

'Dora will stay with me, but I think Hugh wants to go back with you.'

'Will you stay until tomorrow?'

'At least, or the next day. I want to make sure that Guy and Carson can cope before I leave.'

It was good to have Aunt Eliza to rely on, but then one always had, Carson thought, watching her as she put the servants to clearing up as quickly as possible and getting the drawing-room straight again. Then he left the room to try and find his father.

Arthur had gone to the marquee to suggest to the revellers that it was time to leave and, obediently but sadly, they began to totter out, some of them still clasping glasses of ale in their hands.

As Eliza stood at the window watching the remnants lurching down the drive, she saw that Dora had already changed and was jumping in the far paddock. Her thoughts flew back nostalgically to her own girlhood, to her horse Lady, and Lady's daughter Cleopatra, both long dead.

Dora saw her mother looking at her, and waved. Eliza waved back and then turned to look at the room, now nearly straight.

This was her house, the house of her birth, her childhood,

her youth. She had always loved it, and she missed it. It was the place to which she always returned with a feeling that it was home, and now, with Margaret gone, it began to seem like days past, before Guy and she had married.

She wandered through the drawing-room, along to the corridor where she could hear the sound of men's voices coming from the study. To her concern, a row seemed in progress, and she put an ear to the door before entering.

'Of course you killed your mother,' Guy was roaring. 'Why deny it? But for you, she'd be here today. I tell you, you're no good, Carson; you're a wastrel, a womaniser, a liar, a thief . . .'

'And you, Father,' Carson's voice could be heard shouting back. 'You're a drunk . . . You're utterly unable to face the truth about anything. You wrecked the early years of your marriage with your own womanising. Everyone knows it. No one respects you.'

Guy's feeble attempts to reply were stalled by Carson, evidently in a high old rage.

'Don't think *I* don't know. You talk about *my* reputation, Father. Yours was worse. I've heard you've fathered children. I have never fathered any, to my knowledge. I've . . .'

Suddenly there was the sound of breaking glass, and Eliza threw open the door to find the two men, heads down like boxers, on the verge of a physical encounter. One of them had dashed his glass to the floor where it now lay in smithereens. Evidently both had been at the whisky bottle, which stood empty on the table between them. They were set to lunge at each other when she ran between them, forcing them apart.

'This must *stop*,' she cried, 'stop this instant! Is *this* the way to behave the day Margaret is buried? I am ashamed of you, Carson . . . to think of attacking your father.'

'I . . .' he faltered, impetuous Carson, as usual not knowing what to say.

'And I'm ashamed of *you*,' she said, turning upon Guy. 'I heard what you said to him and you know it is untrue. Margaret has been seriously ill for over a year. Her death had absolutely *nothing* to do with Carson, or you or anybody . . .'

'She got worse when he came home,' Guy said, glowering at his son. Then, with a melodramatic gesture, he raised an arm as though he were going to hurl something at him, but instead he raised a trembling finger to heaven.

'Get out of here. Get away. Sometimes I feel I can't stand the sight of you, and God knows how I am ever going to live with you.'

Then, with a sob, he collapsed into Eliza's arms.

8

The Lady Frances Roper Home for Destitute Women and Girls had been founded in the early years of the nineteenth century by a high-minded woman who, left a fortune by the early demise of her husband, had devoted the rest of her life to charity and good works.

Lady Frances, though herself childless, had a genuine compassion for more unfortunate women who had to bear unwanted children, and the object of her home was to provide refuge for those seeking somewhere to have safe and discreet delivery.

Ninety per cent of the babies were subsequently put up for adoption or sent to orphanages.

The principles governing the home were in many ways in advance of the century. When Lady Frances was alive her homes were run on strict, but compassionate, lines where cleanliness and godliness were equated. Although the fallen women were expected to show as well as to *feel* repentance for their sins, they were also advised on practical steps to avoid such a mischance occurring again.

There were also a few places in the home for elderly destitute women, those who had fallen on bad times, had committed no crimes or sins but had simply ceased to have a home, and roamed the streets with their entire possessions tied up in pathetic bundles. They were given home, shelter and food; some of the more kindly among them became substitute mothers to the luckless young women who found themselves expecting children neither they nor society wanted.

Nelly Allen was such a one. When her situation became

known she had immediately been expelled by her family. Particularly wrathful was her father, who bitterly reproached her for the shame she had brought on his humble, but honest and irreproachable, home.

Nelly, with nowhere to go, lived for some time on the streets begging, but she was rescued by a woman who worked at the Lady Frances Roper Home, found a bed and given food.

Nelly was destitute, but she was also proud. She would never have begged Carson for help, even had she known where to find him. Her only connection, had she wished to pursue it, was the house in Montagu Square where they had once unsuccessfully tried to spend the night.

In the home Nelly found many young women in the same circumstances as herself. However, since the charitable founder had died in 1875, the home had been run by a board of God-fearing men and women whose views were neither as tolerant nor as compassionate as those of Lady Frances. Remote from the practical day-to-day running of the home, a certain Christian spirit of forgiveness and charity had been replaced by a harsh regime based on condemnation. The women had sinned, and sinners they were made to feel as the regime under which they lived correspondingly became stricter and more intolerant.

After Nelly had had a few nights' sleep in a clean bed, and eaten a couple of decent meals, she began to take stock of her situation. Her baby was due in two months, and she would have to decide what to do with her own life after that. There was no question, in anyone's mind, about what to do with the baby. It would be taken away from her and sent to an orphanage, hopefully to be adopted.

This was an aspect that Nelly preferred not to dwell on too much. She loved children and had always dreamed of babies of her own. How awful to have a baby and be compelled to give it away! How unfair. Supposing she never had one again? How cruel it was to have been promised a life of bliss by a man who had then deserted her.

Nelly had been in the home for only a few days when she became friendly with another inmate by the name of Massie, who had been in the institution several times before. The institution was the nearest thing Massie had to a real home, and she rather enjoyed it, as some people are said to enjoy repeatedly going back to prison.

Massie – no one knew her real name – had led a much more deprived life than Nelly. Most of her childhood had been spent on the streets with a drunken mother and father, and assorted siblings who appeared and then disappeared.

Massie had taken to prostitution when she was scarcely at the age of puberty. By nineteen she had already mothered three children, one of whom had died; the other two had been sent to the orphanage. This was Massie's fourth pregnancy and she was the same age as Nelly. She knew no other life.

As with many whores, there was a very good heart to Massie. She thought Nelly out of the ordinary. Nelly had fine, delicate features, beautiful hair, and had it not been for her Cockney accent Massie would have said Nelly had a touch of real class.

The two girls struck up a friendship, and were together whenever they could be, although from the first light of dawn until dusk they were organised and put to work so that the institution was spotless; the floors, windows and furniture gleaming with polish. This was mainly to impress the members of the Board and other worthies, who came to visit and then went back to their comfortable homes convinced of their own remarkable Christian charity.

The board of the Lady Frances Roper Home generally paid more attention to appearances than to the well-being of the women in their care, three-quarters of whom were very young expectant mothers. Almost as soon as the women were delivered they were asked to leave, as their place was wanted. It would have been considered quite strange to oversee their post-natal care or instruct them in methods of medical hygiene. In the event, some of them subsequently found themselves in hospital with septicaemia and, not infrequently, one or two of them died.

Nelly was given the task of cleaning the lavatories, which, of course, had to be spotless. Massie was considered a good cook and her allotted place was the kitchen. The women slept in dormitories and gradually, by a process of elimination, Nelly and Massie were able to get beds next to each other.

Nelly had a feeling of kinship for Massie, the first human being that she felt she had been close to in years, apart from Carson. His abandonment of her was unexpected, painful, but she soon learned she was not unique.

Massie was small and had an elfin face, hazel eyes, and a pitted complexion due to an attack of smallpox when she was a little girl. Her hair was brown and curly, and there was an engaging wiriness about her which had come from her tough upbringing on the streets.

Strangely enough, her experience of life had not soured Massie. She lived in permanent hope, in expectation of better things.

She thought that this might at last have been realised when she met Nelly. Together they imagined life in the country, a place they had never seen and could hardly imagine. They thought that in the country there were no such things as dirt, smells and poverty. They had no knowledge at all about the deprivations of life in rural England.

Carson used to talk about his love for his home, of the beauty of the country, and Nelly passed this on, second-hand. It was all that she could do.

'Strange that he left you like he did,' Massie would venture after Nelly had repeated the story of her romance, as she did quite often. It was a real romance, not like Massie's rough experiences at all.

''E was talking about marriage, about living in the country, and I believed 'im,' Nelly would bleat. 'He wanted to be a farmer. I believed 'im, strewth, I really did.'

The two girls sat on Massie's bed in the dark dormitory, whispering into each other's ears so as not to disturb the sleepers on either side.

Whereas Massie had gladly parted with her unwanted progeny – product of a two-minute stand, usually against a wall in a dark passage – as soon as they were born, she began to realise that, because of her love for Carson, Nelly had no such intention. Carson's baby was loved before it was

146

born, as she, once, had loved him. She felt that if she hung on to the baby it would ultimately lead her to him; but at the moment there was no place in that hard world for an unmarried woman with a baby, unless it was on the streets, where the only prospects were of poverty, infection and early death.

She didn't want that, either for her baby or herself.

On the other side of London, in a very different place and in different circumstances, the Martyn family sat down with their guests to the kind of dinner an intimate of the Frances Roper Home had certainly never tasted and probably could not have imagined.

It was served on Sèvres porcelain that was almost priceless, having once been in the possession of that monarch of taste and discrimination, Louis XV. It was matched by silver and glass that Lally and Prosper had collected in the course of their many journeys abroad, and had had carefully shipped back to London. Forays that furnished both their London home and the house in Dorset were made into auction houses, to cabinet-makers, silversmiths, collectors, even the homes of impoverished noblemen who, like their counterparts in England, the Woodvilles, had spent their substance too freely. The tapered candles in their silver candlesticks, reflected in the highly polished walnut of the Chippendale table, made it seem twice as large, and the diners, peering downwards, had the uncanny sensation of seeing, like some ghostly emanation, a picture of themselves. Behind each chair stood a servant in full livery.

The food prepared by the Martyn chef was worthy of the occasion. In fact every meal he prepared was seen by him as a chance to create a work of art, and this was no exception: Soupe Tourangelle, Tourte de Saumon à la Mode Martyn, Gigot Braisé à la Septaine, a board of cheeses from the famous pastoral districts of France, and Le Klafoutis with thick Jersey cream. To drink, they had a very dry sherry with the soup, a Chassagne-Montrachet with the fish, Romanée-Conti with the lamb and cheese, and with the cherry flan an exquisite Beaumes de Venise whose sweet after-taste lingered on the palate.

The guests, too, were of an importance to justify such a

show: Admiral Sir Anthony Hill and Lady Hill, and especially their pretty daughter Emma.

Admiral Hill's father was a gentleman from Leicestershire who had never worked, but had sufficient funds to keep himself and his family in a lifestyle of great comfort. His eldest son, Anthony, however, had joined the navy as a youth of eighteen, and gone to the Royal College at Dartmouth, after which his career had been a predictable one. He had risen slowly through the navy hierarchy at a time of peace, when England acted as policeman rather than warrior. Eventually he was knighted, retired from the navy while still relatively young, and had started to dabble on the stock exchange with some of his inheritance. It was here that he came into contact with the investment arm of the Martyn-Heering bank, and Prosper Martyn and his bright young nephew in particular.

Sir Anthony had a large house, Ingleton Hall, in Leicestershire, and a small town house in Knightsbridge; and Emma was his only daughter.

Not unnaturally, she was cherished by the Hills, cherished and rather spoiled. She was just eighteen, rather small, with an appealing heart-shaped face and fluffy blonde hair. Her large violet eyes were considered her most remarkable asset.

Emma was not unintelligent, though she had not been very well educated – mostly at home by a governess, because her parents considered her too delicate to send to school. She had, however, gone to a Swiss finishing school, where she had been taught all the accomplishments considered necessary for a young lady about to embark in society: she could sketch, paint, sing, play the piano and violin, ride – she was especially keen on hunting – and she enjoyed reading. She was not an intellectual – thank heaven, no one wanted *that*! – but she was by no means stupid. But more important than that, as far as the Martyns were concerned, was her pedigree: she came from a good, old-established family, and as she was wealthy in her own right she could not be considered a gold-digger.

Perfect, in fact, for Roger.

Until that evening Roger had never met Miss Hill, but he had heard of her. She was occasionally mentioned at table, invariably as 'pretty Miss Hill', by Prosper in the hope, perhaps, of planting a seed of interest.

But Roger was not impressed, and it was not at his instigation that Miss Hill was now facing him.

In the autumn of 1910 Roger was twenty-four. He was rather effete, not particularly robust, extremely interested in fashion, and possessed of looks that fascinated women and men alike.

Lally and Prosper knew absolutely nothing of the darker side of his life, spent in the shadows of the London underworld of vice, in streets and dark alleys, in the parks or by the docks.

The young couple had been strategically placed, facing each other across the table, and Miss Hill kept glancing at Roger, not with the provocative shyness of a young unmarried woman, but openly and with considerable interest. Maybe she had heard as much about him as he had heard about her. She had a bright, lively, unselfconscious manner, and joined in the conversation. Lally thought she was absolutely delightful and, in looks only, she reminded her a little of herself when young. Lally kept on smiling at Roger encouragingly, as though to suggest what a surprise it was to them all to find pretty Miss Hill so agreeable.

Roger, knowing quite well what was in Lally's mind, smiled back.

Lady Hill was extremely taken by Roger and found it difficult to conceal her excitement. During dinner most of the attention of the diners was occupied by the excellence of the food, and lavish praise was showered on the chef and messages sent to the kitchen. There was some casual talk about the business world, murmurs of unrest abroad. Afterwards it was decided that the men would not linger after dinner at table, passing round the port, but coffee and liqueurs would be taken in the drawing-room because the older generation wished to have a rubber or two of bridge – thus leaving the young couple the better to make each other's acquaintance.

For a moment, as he found himself alone, facing Miss Hill in the drawing-room in front of a roaring fire with the curtains closed against the cold, Roger experienced a sensation of panic. But Emma had been well brought up and she knew how to handle the situation. Despite her youth, she had mixed in society; her parents liked to entertain both in Leicestershire and London and, as the only child, she was encouraged to participate.

'Do you play bridge, Roger?' she asked, seeming so confident, so at ease, that his nervousness evaporated. After all, Miss Hill was a sensible girl who probably no more wished to marry him than he wished to marry her.

'I play a little, but it's not a game I'm particularly fond of,' he replied, extracting his cigarette-case from his pocket and holding it out to her. 'Do you smoke?'

'Well,' she looked doubtfully towards the door, 'I'm not actually supposed to, but why not?'

Roger laughed and, as he leaned forward to light her cigarette, he saw that she was smiling mischievously into his eyes. Undoubtedly she liked him. He lit his own and then, tucking his case back into his pocket, placed one foot on the fender, an arm on the mantelpiece, and stood gazing down at her. Yes, she was pretty; not a beauty, but engaging and frank. She was undoubtedly modern, and would play tennis too and be a sport, the sort of woman one could feel comfortable with.

'I think our parents have thrown us together,' she said conspiratorially, after taking a few puffs of her cigarette, which showed she was not an expert. She gazed at him with a frank, slightly playful smile, and unexpectedly he found himself wishing she were a boy.

'I'm afraid they have,' he agreed. 'Only the Martyns are not my parents.'

'Oh?'

'Didn't you know?'

'No, I didn't.'

'I am Lally Martyn's nephew. My mother died when I was born and she brought me up.'

'Oh, poor *you*,' Emma leaned forward, her face creased with sympathy.

'I've had a very good life. I can't complain,' Roger said offhandedly.

'You look awfully like Mrs Martyn.'

'There is a family likeness.'

'And you, I suppose, are an only child like me.'

'I'm afraid so.' He looked at her thoughtfully for a time while she went on insouciantly pretending to enjoy her cigarette.

His respect for her grew. After all, one day, like it or not, he would have to marry; and maybe a young woman with independent means and a mind of her own would be better than some clinging, simpering female looking for love.

For the next few weeks Roger and Emma were thrown constantly and deliberately together. Emma had been presented at court in the spring, but even then many of her fellow debutantes were engaged; some were now married. It was never too early to hook your man and ensure you would not be one of those unfortunates left on the shelf until their twenties.

There were private dances and balls, one every night, and, inevitably, Roger and Emma were there with Admiral and Lady Hill in attendance, sometimes Lally and Prosper too. Naturally, there was one at the Knightsbridge home of the Hills. Emma wore a variety of exquisite couture clothes, ordered by her mother the previous winter with an eye on her only daughter obtaining a mate.

There were weekends at country houses, there was riding in The Row – both Roger and Emma were excellent riders, and both looked entirely *comme il faut* in their tailored riding outfits. People thought that, as a couple, they were ideally matched: in looks, in taste, in everything. They were fun-loving, danced well. Add to that the fact that they both had money, and what more could one want? Was there ever such a blessed couple, so destined to be together?

They were scarcely ever alone, and when they were, the conversation was of the bantering kind, nothing was ever taken seriously. But Roger saw all the women he liked as 'chums', and Emma was no different.

Emma knew very little about men, and Roger had such glamour. The instant she saw him she wanted him, knowing, like her parents before her, that he would be exactly right as her mate: he had the right background, the right schooling, the right connections – and he was no idler! A young man moving to the top of an international business, very fast.

Emma really never stopped to question anything else about Roger. She supposed all the intimate talk, 'that side of things', about which her mother darkly hinted, would come later.

The end of the autumn season drew near, and one early morning after a ball at the Langham they were driving home alone in a cab, since Prosper and Lally, their chaperones for the evening, had left before midnight.

Emma lay back with her head against the seat, eyes closed, and Roger gazed at her face, dimly illuminated by the gas-lights along Oxford Street. Her long lashes curled upwards on her cheek and tiny curls clung to her forehead, which still gleamed with perspiration from the effort of dancing in a stuffy ballroom.

Emma, who had only been pretending to sleep, suddenly opened her eyes and stared straight at Roger.

'You can if you like,' she said.

'What?' He appeared taken aback.

'You know. Kiss.'

'But, do you think . . .?' His heart began to hammer in his breast.

'Don't be silly! Why do you think *they* went early?'

She grabbed his lapel, so he bent his head and kissed her and, as an arm fastened tightly behind his back, he was struck by a feeling of nausea so strong that he thought he was going to be sick. He raised his head and then leaned it for a moment against her chest, panting.

'Roger!' she cried anxiously, lifting his head with her free hand. 'Are you all right?'

'I feel a little giddy,' he said. Then he sat upright and, getting out his handkerchief, began to mop his brow. 'It's been a very strenuous day. Sorry, darling.' Smiling wanly in the street lights, he clasped her hand.

'That's perfectly all right,' Emma said but, feeling that something was slipping away from her, she turned her head and gazed out of the window all the way home.

When they got to the door of the Hills' home in Brompton Square, the admiral hurried out, still fully dressed although it was so late.

'You're *very* late,' he cried. 'Is everything all right?'

'Everything's fine, Daddy.' Emma stepped from the cab and ran into his arms. 'Everything's *fine*.'

The admiral then wound his arms round his daughter and looked up at Roger, who was gazing out of the window of the cab, his silk scarf loose around his neck.

'Had a good time?' the admiral said.

'Simply wonderful. Everything's fine.' He tried hard to inject into his voice a sense of joy, even elation, that he didn't feel.

'Care to come in for a nightcap?' the admiral asked, still with his arms round Emma who, with troubled eyes, was gazing at Roger.

'It's terribly late, Admiral,' Roger said, stifling a yawn. 'I think I should be going home. I have to be at the office tomorrow as usual. Work all day, partying all night . . .' His voice trailed off.

'Roger didn't feel too well on the way here, Daddy,' Emma explained.

'Oh?' The admiral looked concerned.

'Simply the heat, I think, sir.' Roger passed his hand across his forehead. 'It's all go, you know, with these parties.'

'Don't *I* know it.' Admiral Hill laughed and, putting his hand through the window of the cab, shook Roger's. 'We are very much looking forward to visiting your home at the end of the month. Your aunt has very kindly invited us for a few days.'

'That's splendid news,' Roger said and, blowing a kiss to Emma, he tapped sharply on the cabbie's window.

Then, as the cab set off, he leaned back and closed his eyes. The more he saw of Emma, the more he liked her; she was jolly good fun to be with. But, as a woman, she disgusted him.

Nelly lay on her bed, clawing at her stomach, while Massie hovered anxiously beside her, every now and then bathing her forehead with a wet towel.

Nelly had been in labour for twenty-four hours and still the baby would not come. She twisted this way and that in agony on her bed in the labour ward attached to the home, where there were a couple of other groaning occupants beside herself. The beds were covered with towels instead of sheets, and the women wore shifts which could easily be adjusted whenever the midwife came to examine them.

But Nelly was a worry. As a young, strong girl she should have had no trouble. The midwife was in constant attendance on her, listening to her belly through her obstetric funnel. She thought the heartbeat sounded as though it was getting increasingly faint. To her mind, it would be no great pity if one more illegitimate soul were lost to the world.

They liked to try and avoid calling the doctor because doctors cost money. But even less did the board relish an inquest if a baby was lost, and finally the midwife decided to send for Dr Strickland, the home's honorary medical officer.

Dr Strickland arrived just after midnight, grumbling a good deal at the hour he had been called and the nature of the case – unmarried mothers being the lowest of the low on his list of priorities; but one look at the girl squirming on the bed told him she was in serious trouble.

He put down his black bag, removed his coat and put on his apron, winding the sides of his pince-nez carefully around his ears. Then, while the midwife grasped one of Nelly's legs and Massie the other, he peered inside.

'Breech,' he said, straightening up again. 'No doubt about it. The baby is the wrong way round. It is obviously in distress.'

Nelly, alert enough to hear what was being said, gave a loud scream, and the midwife slapped her face to shut her up.

'Quiet,' she commanded, 'and behave yourself. Do exactly what the doctor says.'

The doctor was sweating a little. He knew forceps were no good and, as he had seen one leg dangling out of the birth passage, already turning blue, he thought the case was hopeless. He whispered a few words to the midwife and rolled up his sleeves.

The midwife again grasped one leg, Massie clung on to the other and the doctor, as gently as he could, but firmly, wriggled his hand past the dangling foot and as far as he could up the birth-passage, where he was able to disengage the other foot and drag the infant out, not only alive but squalling lustily.

'Cut the cord, Mrs Brewer,' he ordered the midwife as he wiped the blood off his arms. 'That was a *very* near thing.'

Massie looked with some awe at the blood-stained creature lying on the towel between the legs of its mother, thrusting its tiny fists in the air as if raging against the unfairness of the world it had entered. Then she picked it up, tenderly wrapped round it the blanket the midwife had given her, and cradled it in her arms.

'Nelly,' she cooed, 'you've got a dear little boy.'

But Nelly, poor Nelly, had fainted.

The Hills arrived at the Martyn home in Dorset at the end of what had been a most exhausting season. But even here little respite was offered, or expected. Lally had engaged extra staff to cope with the influx of visitors; vans full of fresh food and provisions arrived every day.

The mixture was the same as before, only it took place in the country instead of in the stuffy atmosphere of London. There were parties, dances, private dinners, lunches; picnics, when the weather allowed, to Bournemouth and Studland Bay; and visits to the many fine houses that the county boasted, for the Hills and Martyns between them knew almost everybody.

Lally adored house-parties and threw herself into everything with vigour. Not a detail was ignored. Nothing was too good for the Hills – for the girl who, she hoped, was to be her daughter-in-law. She liked Emma, and she could see that Emma liked Roger. She was even sure that Emma *loved* Roger, but not so sure that he loved her. What went on in Roger's mind it was always difficult to know.

She tried to trap him into talking about Emma, but he was evasive. It was so hard to get him alone. He was forever on his way to this place or that, a golf club or a fishing rod in his hand, or perhaps a riding crop. He seemed to be always ascending and descending stairs, always on the run. The house was in a constant state of controlled turmoil. Not a minute of the day was free. It was almost as though no one wanted time to think.

Of course, the young people were encouraged to spend *some* time alone together, but not too much. Not long enough for anything to happen. They were sent off for walks, allowed to take a rug and a picnic-basket and be alone; but they were expected back within a certain time. One didn't want one's daughter compromised – although Lady Hill didn't have to spell that out to Lally. It was quite obvious that she was an over-protective mother and that her daughter was, as everyone expected, a virgin. It would never do for Emma to slip up before the engagement was announced.

But when would that happen? The day for the Hills' departure drew near, and the climax was to be a dinner at the house for close family and friends, followed by a dance.

If nothing happened then, nothing ever would. Emma's parents, and Prosper and Lally, were slightly worried.

Twenty-two people sat down to dinner. It was a splendid occasion. The Martyns' London chef, transported to Dorset for the important week, didn't spare himself: Carpe à la Vrai Nivernaise, Cotelettes de Veau à la Lyonnaise, Chausson aux Champignons, La Flamusse aux Pommes. To drink, champagne, Château Latour-Pomerol, Muscat de Frontignon.

Extra party staff had also been engaged to supplement the regulars employed by the Martyns, and during dinner there was a constant coming and going, doors swinging open and shut, soft commands being authoritatively called by the butler, who had never had a night such as this.

The lace cloth on the long table was of finest Brussels, the overhead chandelier blazed with a thousand tiny pieces like minute diamonds; the Sèvres porcelain had been brought down very carefully from London, packed in boxes filled with straw, the silver was polished not once but twice until it dazzled. In an anteroom the small string orchestra, engaged for the dance that was to follow, played softly: airs by Schubert, Mozart, and some of the Romantics.

Roger and Emma sat next to each other, heads occasionally together as they exchanged some comment, clearly at ease in each other's company, knowing each other well. People could hardly take their eyes off them, and the atmosphere accordingly was charged with expectation.

All the relatives were there: Eliza and Julius and Dora, but not Hugh, who was travelling on the Continent; Sir Guy, Carson, Sophie, her parents; some Martyns from Bournemouth, several big-wigs. There was a sprinkling of young people, friends mostly of Laurence, Sarah-Jane and Dora.

Dora, attractive, elegant, rather aloof, always seemed the odd one out at these occasions. She sat next to her cousin Carson and, as they invariably did, they talked about horses.

Carson, along the table from Emma, thought she was enchanting.

'Roger is a lucky fellow,' he said to Dora.

'You keep your eyes on me and your mind on horses,' she murmured with a smile. 'You know your reputation.'

'Oh, I'm sure Roger would fight for his bride,' Carson said derisively. 'Now, where were we . . .?' But he still kept glancing at Emma, surreptitiously, all during the long, long dinner.

Sophie sat on Roger's left and, after she had complimented him quietly on Emma, she turned to her neighbour, who happened to be, whether by change or design, Bart Sadler.

'So, we meet again,' she said.

'Isn't it fortunate?' He gave a sardonic laugh and raised his glass. 'To you, Mrs Woodville. You look very handsome tonight, if I may say so.'

'Thank you.' She lowered her eyes but did not blush.

After all, she was perfectly in command of herself. He was a charmer, but she didn't intend to let him get the better of her by flattery.

However, after that bold and unexpected start he seemed completely to dry up, and applied himself to the succession of delectable delicacies on the plates set before him.

Sophie decided he was taciturn, unused to small talk. He was a powerful man, undeniably attractive. She saw Hubert Turner, sitting next to Eliza, looking at her from the other side of the table, and she smiled, trying to indicate with an imperceptible shrug of her shoulders that she'd rather be next to him. Her father was talking to the wife of the Bishop of Salisbury, and her mother to the Bishop.

'This *is* the smartest occasion I have ever attended,' she observed to Mr Sadler, trying hard to find something to say.

'Really? I suppose it *is* very grand,' he agreed. 'Too grand, perhaps.'

'Why do you say that?'

'Well, as you say, it's not the sort of thing we're used to. I'm not, anyway.' He looked down at his pristine evening dress and smiled. 'I had to buy a new suit.'

Sophie put her napkin to her mouth and giggled. 'And I had to have a new dress made.'

'See?' He seemed pleased by her admission. 'All this expense, for what?'

'They are hoping for an engagement.' She put her mouth very close to his ear. 'Roger and Emma.'

'Oh!' It appeared he had not known this. 'I hope they will be very happy.'

'I'm sure they will be. She seems a *very* nice girl, and everyone is devoted to Roger.' Then she paused, and as her neighbour apparently had no comment to this, said: 'I think you told me you were a stone-mason, Mr Sadler.'

'Yes, I am, a humble stone-mason, quite out of place here, as a matter of fact. But I do some business with Prosper Martyn, so I suppose that is why they asked me; and Laurence is my brother-in-law, and I often find that where he is asked I'm asked too. That is one of the few privileges of being distantly related to a Woodville.' He gave her a sly glance and she thought he was laughing at her. She made no reply but looked along the table. Sir Guy – well in his cups, having been allowed too much champagne before dinner – was ogling the wife of the mayor. The mayoress, however, felt perfectly safe with Prosper Martyn on her other side. Anyway, when did a little harmless flirtation harm anyone? She was polite to Sir Guy, being careful not to give him any ideas.

'Forgive me if I return to what you said some moments ago, Mrs Woodville,' Sadler jerked Sophie's attention back to him, 'but you mentioned that I was a stone-mason, and I felt there was some reason for the remark.'

'I am anxious to have a memorial to my husband before I return to New Guinea.' She paused and then gave a deep sigh. 'It was *hoped* to have a stained-glass window in the church, but this has not yet been possible.'

'Why is that?' At last a look of interest replaced the boredom in Mr Sadler's rather fine, brown, hooded eyes.

'Oh, this and that,' Sophie said casually.

'But your father is the rector.'

'It's not just a question of where to put it, but . . .' She paused, as though wondering how to proceed. 'A stained-glass window is not a simple matter. It is to do with colour and design, then where to put it, and so on.' She knew she now had his complete attention and took a sip of wine from her glass. 'It is also, alas, to do with cost. I wondered,' she went on very quickly, 'if a monument made of stone . . .'

'Would do as well?' Bart put his elbows on the table and joined his hands beneath his chin. 'I should think a monument of the finest Purbeck marble possibly superior to a stained-glass window, though, of course, I'm prejudiced. As for the cost . . . I really can't say because Purbeck does not come cheap.'

'Of course not.' Sophie, flustered, looked at the custard pie which had just been placed before her.

'But please don't let that put you off.' Bart felt in the breast-pocket of his evening-jacket and drew out a card which he gave to her. 'Please do get in touch with me and I can show you my yard, some designs, what I have to offer. And . . .' he smiled at her, 'how much it would cost.'

'That *is* most kind.' Sophie gratefully slipped the card into her evening bag. 'I will be in touch with you very shortly.'

'But tell me.' Now Bart's eyes were not bored at all but enlivened by a look of genuine curiosity. 'Do you *really* intend to return to a godforsaken place like New Guinea?'

'Indeed I do.'

'For good?'

'Maybe.' She stared at him. 'I have a vocation to be a missionary and I feel I must carry on the work of my late husband.'

'Very commendable.' Mr Sadler drew out a clean white handkerchief and pressed it to his brow. 'Will your children go with you?'

'Of course.' Sophie looked surprised.

'Do you think it is right, Mrs Woodville, to bring up children in a foreign land so far from home?'

'Why not? Other missionary families have children. They usually all go to school in Port Moresby and are well looked after, I can assure you.'

'And yet your husband died of tropical fever?'

'It can happen to anyone; but in his case his illness was neglected. I assure you, our children are *very* well taken care of.'

'But supposing it should happen to *you*, did you think of that? And if you died, your children would be orphaned. Tell me, do you think that's fair?'

Sophie, who had been aware of a growing sense of irritation, found it turning into indignation. What business, after all, was it of this man, almost a perfect stranger? The intimacy of his questions annoyed her, and abruptly she turned to engage the attention of Roger, as Emma was talking to Laurence Yetman on her other side.

At that moment, however, Prosper tapped the table and, rising, proposed a toast to the monarch. 'His Majesty King George the Fifth,' he said, raising his glass.

'The King, God bless him,' voices intoned, and everyone in unison raised their glasses to their lips.

'If the ladies would like to leave the table,' Prosper said, looking around, 'the gentlemen may care to smoke.'

Lally rose with a smile, giving a signal for the women to leave their chairs and follow her from the room.

Prosper watched them go and, as Roger turned to take a cigar from the humidor being passed to him by a servant, Prosper leaned across the seat that the dowager Lady Mount had vacated between them.

'You may go too if you like,' he said encouragingly. 'You may like to accompany the ladies. *One* lady in particular, I mean.'

'But I prefer to smoke a cigar, Uncle Prosper,' Roger replied nonchalantly.

'What *is* the matter with you?' Prosper said angrily. 'You know that the purpose of this party is . . .'

'Unfortunately, you make it very obvious,' Roger replied, taking a cigar and carefully examining the tip.

'Well . . .'

'Maybe later.'

'I can't understand you.' Prosper angrily shook his head.

'And I can't understand you. What, after all, is the hurry?'

The other men who remained at the table found it difficult to pretend they were not listening, so, rising from his chair, Prosper said to the assembled company: 'Would you excuse us for a moment?' and beckoned to Roger to follow him from the room.

Roger looked as though he would ignore his uncle, but in the end, aware of the eyes upon him, reluctantly got up.

Once outside the dining-room door, Prosper closed it and walked along the corridor, which happened to be empty, casually placing his arm through Roger's.

'Now, Uncle, what *is* it?' Roger sounded bored and rather tired. 'Why the fuss? Leaving guests in the middle of port and cigars . . . *what* will people say?'

'My dear boy,' Prosper said, changing his tone completely and pressing Roger's arm, 'you like Emma, don't you?'

'Very much.'

'Well then.' Prosper stopped, disengaged his arm and looked into Roger's eyes. '*When* will you pop the question? They have been here nearly a week. You have seen her almost constantly, every day, for most of the autumn season.'

'That doesn't mean I've got to marry her, Uncle.' Roger tried to make his voice low and reasonable.

'What!' The stud fastening Prosper's collar nearly popped from its socket. 'My dear Roger, you haven't led her up the garden path, have you?'

'Certainly not.'

'Well, if this is your attitude, people will think you have. Only today the admiral and I were discussing a settlement.'

'That's very generous of you, if a little premature,' Roger murmured.

'Premature?' Prosper raised his voice again. 'How long do you need to court someone?'

'Some people take years, Uncle. I have scarcely known her six weeks.'

'Well, you can be pretty sure that if *that* is your attitude, sir, you will lose her. She has a number of young men eager for her hand, and willing to declare themselves in far less time than it has taken you!'

'I can understand that,' Roger said. 'She is a most attractive girl.'

'Then let it be *you*.' Prosper prodded his immaculate shirt-front sharply with his finger. 'Let it be *you*, Roger. You will not find a nicer girl in England, or a nicer family. You're at an age to marry, and so is she.'

'She is only eighteen, Uncle.'

'That is the right age. There you have a wife you can form, who will not cause you trouble, who will look up to you and respect you, who will let herself be guided by you completely. It is a good start in life. Moreover, you are extraordinarily fortunate in that she is an heiress. When the admiral told me the scale of her fortune, I was astonished. You will never have to worry about money in your lives, either of you. I can't tell you how lucky I think you are, Roger, and what *I*, and your aunt, expect of you is that this night you will do your duty and make us all very, very happy.' He stepped back, his head on one side, and looked critically at his heir. 'Now, what say you, Roger? The chance may not come again, certainly as far as Emma is concerned. If they leave tomorrow and you have not proposed, that will be the end of it. You will not meet on these terms again. The admiral has made as much clear. He called it "trifling" with his daughter, and I assured him that was certainly not the case, you were wildly in love. Now, what do you say?'

Wildly in love . . .

Roger leaned his head back against the wall and closed his eyes. If only it could be so. His mind raced back across the years and he saw the house in the mean street in Kentish Town, the large bed which he shared with his adoptive brothers and sisters. He heard the snores of his adoptive father coming from the room next door where, after returning as usual too drunk to mount the stairs alone, he had been helped up to bed by the boys. He smelled the stench of cabbage cooking in the kitchen, the slightly putrid aroma of decaying vegetables in the alley-way outside the back door, laced, sometimes, with the stink of stale urine from a passing drunk or the countless stray cats who proliferated in the area.

He recalled, oh how vividly, his ill-fitting clothes, his own whiney voice, the permanent drip that seemed to hang from his nose, the socks with holes, the shoes a size too big, usually, or too small.

He glanced at his legs and admired the fine cut of his evening-trousers, the sparkling white of his shirt. He glanced at the gleaming golden cufflinks that had been a twenty-first birthday present from Lally, and he inhaled the aroma of the Havana cigar between his fingers, the pungent fragrance of expensive cologne on his skin.

Yes, indeed, it seemed a small price to pay to be rid of the old memories.

'Very well, Uncle,' he said at last, opening his eyes. 'I will do what you say.'

'Oh, my dear Roger.' Prosper moved towards him and clasped him emotionally in his arms. 'I can't tell you how happy I am for you. My profoundest congratulations and best wishes to you, darling boy. I don't think this is a decision you will ever have cause to regret.'

9

The matron of the Lady Frances Roper Home was a Mrs Bland, a capable but rather unimaginative woman, well into her fifties. Whether there ever had been a Mr Bland was not known; also she appeared to have no children of her own.

Mrs Bland had been a midwife at the home for many years before she was appointed matron. The home owed much of its reputation for cleanliness to her, and certainly, in her book, cleanliness came before compassion, and probably before godliness as well.

She presided over a spotless kitchen where the frugal food was prepared. It was thought that if the inmates were nourished too well, none of them would wish to leave, so the fare, though nutritious, was basic: broth, bread and milk, vegetables and chicken or meat on Sundays.

Mrs Bland was an efficient administrator. She also didn't like to allow the mothers to keep their babies too long in case they formed an attachment to them. Sometimes, if the baby was sickly, the orphanage would not have it, so an undersized and undernourished baby stayed with its mother until, rather as an animal destined for the slaughterhouse, it was fit for the orphanage.

There were no such qualms about the baby Nelly had called Alexander. It seemed a fine name for a baby, to offer him a chance in a life where the cards were stacked against him.

Perhaps not surprisingly, seeing that his father was a robust man, Alexander weighed in with an additional advantage: he was a big, sturdy baby. He also had an extrovert personality and a bewitching smile. Given even half a chance, he appeared to exude the confidence that would take him far in life.

Mrs Bland had never shown any special fondness for babies. Perhaps it was just as well, since having to give away so many to an uncertain future might have been distressing for someone with more delicate sensibilities. To her, babies were a commodity, an unfortunate by-product of the inhabitants of her home, most of whom were there, in her opinion, entirely through their own fault.

Before they left, she would always lecture her girls on saying 'No' to the demands of a man; but it was a plea that invariably landed on deaf ears. Sometimes, without any means or prospects, the girls went from the Frances Roper straight back onto the streets, and within eight months they were back again, awaiting yet another birth.

Mrs Bland stood beside Alexander's crib with a notebook in one hand, a pencil in the other.

'He is now ten pounds,' she wrote. 'That will give him a good start in life. Did you give him a name yet, Nelly?'

'Alexander,' Nelly said defiantly. It was a far cry from the names the girls usually gave their babies, if they took the trouble to name them at all.

Mrs Bland frowned.

'That's quite a mouthful, Nelly. How about Sam, or . . .'

'Alexander,' Nelly repeated. 'That is 'is name.'

'Well, it can always be changed, and he's such a nice baby, so well-proportioned, he's sure to find a good home.'

Mrs Bland carefully made another note in her book, as though the matter was settled.

'I would like to keep the baby, mum,' Nelly said breathlessly. 'I've grown fond of 'im.'

'Don't be silly, Nell.' Mrs Bland went on writing.

'I really mean it.'

'That Massie has been getting at you, hasn't she?' Mrs Bland turned wrathfully around as though to pinpoint the corrupting influence. Whenever there was trouble, Massie was behind it. The next time she sought admission to the home – and there would be a next time, that was for sure – Mrs Bland would try and have her turned away.

'Massie has *nothing* to do with it, madam,' Nelly said stubbornly. (They always had to address Mrs Bland as though she were an employer.) 'I only made up me mind today, 'e's *such* a darling.'

'Then unmake it, Nelly,' Mrs Bland said firmly. 'Or else I am afraid that next time you seek admittance here, it will be refused.'

Nelly passed a finger across her nostrils and sniffed.

'There will be *no* next time, madam . . . I intend to keep meself clean.'

'And what will you *do* with your baby?' Mrs Bland was a portly woman, ample-bosomed and full-hipped. She wore her hair in a bun, and a pince-nez perched on the tip of her nose. She enjoyed her reputation as a person feared rather than loved; it also protected her from involvement with the inmates, many of whom were looking for a mother.

'I hope to go into service, madam,' Nelly, who had none of the cheek of Massie, said humbly. 'A good position in the country, maybe.'

'You will be extremely fortunate if that is the case,' Mrs Bland sniffed. 'I know of *no one* who would, in any circumstances, take in a serving-maid with a child.' Suddenly and unexpectedly, her features softened, and she put a hand on the young girl's head. 'Everyone *knows* it is sad to give up a baby, Nelly; but Alexander is as bright as a button, you can see that. If you allow it, he would seem to have every chance of life, given the unfortunate circumstances of his birth. He may even be only a few months in the orphanage before some lady of refinement and breeding, unable to have children of her own, sees him. Who knows . . . ?'

Mrs Bland raised a podgy hand in the air as though to suggest that Alexander's future knew no bounds.

At that moment Nelly had an idea. Something Mrs Bland had said: a lady of breeding and refinement . . . Carson had told her about such a *person*, a compassionate woman who had been unable to have children of her own. Once he had taken her to the very house in which she lived.

Well, it was worth a try. At least that way she would know that Alexander had a future and, one day perhaps, she might even see him again.

That night she told Massie of her plan, but her stalwart friend was dubious.

'It's true that I can't keep 'im,' Nelly sniffed loudly. 'He would die of cold in the streets. I love him too much, Massie, and, one day, I may get him back . . .'

'But how do you know she'll keep him?' Massie gnawed at a fingernail, torn between her doubts and a desire to help her new friend.

'If she don't, she won't fling him back on the streets. Surely she'll have him on her conscience and see that he has a home somewhere else? At least I'll *know* what's become of him.'

But Massie wasn't sure. She was touched by such sentiment, having had three babies of her own and allowed them to be taken away without the least idea of what would become of them.

Because of Nelly's obvious reluctance to part with her baby, Mrs Bland decided to hurry up the formalities for his removal to the orphanage. She had seen girls who tried to cling after their time was up, during which they usually breast-fed their babies to save the cost of milk. It was always a sad, unnerving experience, even to one as cushioned to the misfortunes of others as she was. They cried, they clung, the babies had almost to be wrenched out of their hands. Everyone suffered, and those who were next in line to give up their babies seemed to develop doubts too. It affected morale.

Mrs Bland accordingly made arrangements for an official to come from the orphanage the following day and take Alexander away.

But Nelly, too, had laid her plans, aided by Massie, who knew that if a girl said she would like to keep her baby, it mysteriously disappeared, was whisked away without the girl's knowledge. She would be given some task in the kitchen, kept well out of sight, and when she went up to feed her baby later in the day, it would have gone. That was the time of weeping, and easing of painful breasts overflowing with milk that would never be needed.

Massie desperately wanted to keep Nelly as her friend. It was lonely on the streets, lonely and dangerous, and Nelly seemed to have a little more spirit in her than most of the girls she met in the home. In some oddly indefinable way, Nelly was a cut above the rest.

Besides, Nelly talked about going away, maybe to the country, maybe to Dorset, where some day she might find Carson. Maybe, who knew, she might even see Alexander again?

That night Nelly held Alexander closely to her breast as she fed him. She had so much milk that as the baby gorged on her nipple, the milk dribbled from the sides of his little mouth. He gazed at her with such lazy contentment that the thought of parting from him brought tears to her eyes. But she had to. She had no choice. Massie had heard through the home grapevine that the man from the orphanage was due the following day. He was rather a cruel-looking man, chosen no doubt because of the unpleasant job he had to do, and no one liked him. He usually arrived in a carriage, with a woman who whisked the baby out of its crib, wrapped it in a blanket – and then they were gone.

Frequently the hapless mother ran after the carriage for some time, crying piteously, her hands flung out despairingly towards it. Sometimes the mothers leaned out of the window, helplessly watching until the carriage was out of sight or, sometimes, they just lay inert on their beds for days, clutching the sheet or blanket or pathetic piece of rag that was associated with the baby.

It was true that Alexander was such a bonnie, sturdy, thriving baby he would have every chance in life – provided he was given one. But a life with Nelly and Massie on the streets would mean he had none at all; he would frequently have to be left alone, totally deprived of the security of mother and home.

After she fed him, Nelly lay on her bed cuddling him, trying as hard as she could to impart to him the love of a mother he might never see again. If only she could tell him how she felt, why she was doing what she was doing.

Eventually, worn out, she dozed off until Massie roused her. She already had her coat on, and in her hand was the large linen bag she had stolen from the market the day before and in which they would carry the baby.

Nelly began to weep, to cling to Alexander, until with gentle fingers Massie prised him from her, wrapping him in his blanket and carefully placing him in the bag.

Nelly had already put her few pathetic possessions in a bundle and, with a farewell look round the corner of the dormitory which had been her home for several months, she tiptoed along the floor, being careful not to disturb the slumbering girls who, worn out by their labours, slept like the dead.

Massie was waiting for her at the top of the staircase leading to the kitchen and, each taking a handle of the bag, the two women tiptoed downstairs as quickly as they could. Their main fear was that Alexander would start to cry or whimper, but he seemed to know his fate depended on his silence, and not a sound emerged.

Once in the kitchen, they swiftly crossed the floor, turned the iron key in the lock and arrived in the backyard, which gave onto a maze of streets leading to the main road from Clerkenwell to the West End, the smart part of London for which they were aiming.

Then, with grim purpose, they began to stride steadily along the almost deserted streets in which only stray dogs or alley-cats prowled.

Roberts had been with Prosper Martyn before he and Lally were married. He had been engaged as under-footman and progressed to under-butler and, finally, butler.

He was devoted to his employers. He saw himself as the captain of a ship, ensuring that everything ran smoothly; and the staff were treated rather like a complement of sailors from whom instant obedience was expected.

Roger was less devoted to Roberts who, almost from his arrival in the house as nothing better than a street-urchin, had treated him with a certain arrogance and superciliousness that Roger deeply resented. The further away he got from his origins the less he wanted people to know about them, and Roberts was a constant reminder.

Roberts had never married, thinking it would interfere with his duties to his employers. He accompanied them to the country, where he ran the Dorset house as expertly as the one in Montagu Square, striking terror into the hearts of all who worked there. The easy-going staff were quite unused to the draconian measures adopted by Roberts and, if he stayed too long, one or two of them left. Occasionally Roberts formed an attachment to one of the maids in the employ of the Martyns, but it was only in order to satisfy his lust. Not one had ever yet succeeded in capturing his heart.

Roberts was always first up in the morning so that he could check on the other members of staff, and woe betide any who were a second late starting their duties. Woe betide any maid, footman, or under-footman, houseboy or tweeny who didn't start work on time. As soon as they came into the servants' hall, Roberts was there by the door with his large timepiece in his hand, checking them all in.

As usual Roberts had arisen just as the faint blush of dawn appeared on the horizon over Hyde Park. He would watch it from the attic bedroom which had been his home for so many years. He imagined he could see the tops of the highest trees in the park, waving slightly in the breeze, and he would lean on the parapet outside his window to enjoy for a moment communion with nature. This was the soft underbelly of Roberts, the only moment that indicated he had anything like a soul. He seemed to fill his lungs with air, and pretend it gave him a good start to the day.

Roberts, standing by the window in his nightshirt, flung the window open and, as was customary, craned over the parapet to view the day and inhale his measure of fresh air. The square was deserted. He knew that he was, invariably, the first riser, and not even a lazy cat lurked under the trees or a cheeky blackbird on top of them.

Suddenly his eyes were riveted by an object on the immaculately-kept steps of the Martyns' house, and Roberts, slightly horrified, leaned as far forward as he could to see what it was.

He literally could not believe his eyes. He flung his dressing-gown over his nightshirt and ran all the way down the back stairs. He emerged by the green baize door which led into the still deserted servants' hall in the basement.

Unlocking the back door, Roberts ran lightly up the steps to the pavement, where he peered at the bundle lying on the bottom step.

Cautiously, he bent down to inspect it closer. Suddenly the bundle moved and started to cry.

'"Alexander",' Lally said, reading the note pinned to the blanket which had covered the child. '"I know as how you are a good wimmin and will look after him."'

They were in a state of alarm, summoned from their beds by Roberts on a matter of urgency. They were to leave for the Continent that day on a train, mixing as usual business and pleasure, and the shock of being aroused from a deep sleep to be confronted by a baby abandoned on the doorstep, was considerable.

Certainly he was a beautiful baby, and he smiled winsomely up at Lally, stretching his tiny fists towards her as though he found her captivating. It was hard not to fall in love with him instantly.

'He is a darling,' Lally cooed and, with an involuntary smile, took his tiny clenched fist in her hand. 'But why leave him *here*?'

'And how do they know *us*?' Prosper was gaping at the ill-written note. '"I know as how you are a good wimmin . . ." How do they know *you*, Lally dearest?'

Lally was obviously mystified, but her attention was concentrated on Alexander, by whom she was clearly captivated. Roger, having inspected the baby with an air of indifference, sat with crossed legs in a chair, smoking a cigarette.

'Sheer chance, Uncle,' he said. 'Most houses in this square will be presided over by a "wimmin".'

'But why pick on us?' Lally removed her eyes from the baby to look at Roger.

Roger yawned. It was an awful time to be got out of bed.

'Well, it need not detain us long, Aunt. You must call the police and get rid of it.'

'Oh Roger . . .' Lally was by now down on her knees, cooing at the tiny thing, who was still half in and half out of the cheap bag in which he had been bundled.

'Now, Lally.' Prosper wearily ran a hand over his tired face. 'Don't think of anything *absurd* . . .'

'You're *surely* not thinking of keeping it?' Roger, with an incredulous laugh, got to his feet. 'Whatever would the Hills say?'

Oh yes, that was important. With the date of the wedding fixed, one had to be careful of the Hills.

'Oh I never thought of *keeping* . . .' Lally's voice trailed off as she gazed at Roger, and she could recall, as if it were yesterday, the day she parted with her own baby, the almost indefinable sense of desolation and loss. Also of shame and indignation that it was a thing she had to do.

And *she* had known where her baby was to go. Her heart went out to the unknown mother who had been forced to such an act of desperation as this.

In time she had got over the intense emotion of the moment in the effort of staying alive, but now she could recall the experience so vividly that it became exactly like a physical pain.

'Roberts, go and telephone the police,' Prosper ordered.

'Oh, no . . .' Lally put out her hand. 'May we just not keep him for a *little* while, dearest? He must be hungry.'

'Aunt, don't be absurd.' Roger impatiently stubbed out his cigarette. 'You could be accused of kidnapping. At *least* you must report it.' He looked at Lally and gave her a curious, again almost incredulous smile.

'Aunt Lally, I honestly do believe you would like to keep the little thing.'

The policeman was dumbfounded. A baby abandoned on the doorstep of a police station, a hospital, or some other institution, was not uncommon; but a private house in the best part of London . . .

'And you have *no* idea how the little creature came to be here, madam?' The policeman scratched his head.

'Of course we have no idea.'

Prosper, now bathed, shaved, dressed and breakfasted, felt more civilised, but his irritation remained. They were due to depart by the boat-train from Victoria in the early evening.

'Please remove this child, officer, and do . . . whatever it is you have to do. It has absolutely nothing to do with us.'

'Or *you*, sir?' The policeman turned to Roger, now dressed in his grey business-suit, with grey spats over his polished black shoes.

'Of course it has nothing to do with me.' Roger got indignantly to his feet. 'I am engaged to be married and my fiancée is a lady of impeccable virtue.'

'What a thing to suggest.' Prosper's face was like a thundercloud. 'Your superior will hear about this.'

'I am not *suggesting* anything, sir,' the officer said quickly. Then he scratched his head again. ''Tis a fair muddle. Well . . . I'll inform the authorities and have them arrange to collect him.'

'And what will happen to him?' Lally asked with a catch in her voice.

'Why, madam,' the policeman explained patiently, 'what happens to his class of person, unwanted, abandoned, found in unfortunate circumstances. He will be taken to an institution, a foundlings' home or suchlike . . . poor little beggar.' The constable gazed sadly at the waif who, as though sensing his imminent danger, made a play for him.

Lally and Prosper accompanied the policeman to the door while Roger remained in the drawing-room, looking down at the tiny scrap of humanity which seemed so curiously and unreasonably happy.

'What a start in life,' he thought, remembering his own.

He sighed, and turned as Prosper and Lally re-entered, their arms entwined. Lally sat in a chair near to the baby and Prosper stood with his arm on the mantelpiece.

'Not going to the office today, Roger?' he asked.

'Of course I am,' Roger replied, looking at the clock. 'But I wanted to do all I could here first, to support you. Poor little

173

. . . Well.' He stooped and kissed Lally. 'It *is* best that he goes. It is a sad thing, but it was not your fault it happened and it is not your responsibility.'

'It does seem somehow like fate,' Lally murmured, gripping the arms of her chair. She looked pale and close to tears.

'Fate?' Roger looked puzzled.

'Why this house? Why us? There must be some connection with us. That's what I mean by fate.'

'My dear Lally.' Prosper moved over to her again and patted her shoulder. 'I promise you anything in the world you like, but not . . . I beg you.'

'But you could never give me a baby, Prosper,' Lally whimpered, and then she suddenly burst into tears.

For the next few days the Martyn family continued in a state of crisis. Prosper, who hated any interference with his affairs, was furious at having to cancel his visit to the Continent on account of a foundling. Roger worried about what the Hill family would have to say if they knew his aunt was thinking of giving a home to a baby found on the street. The matter was very carefully kept from Emma, in the hope that Lally would be forced to come to her senses.

One didn't just adopt stray babies for no reason, he argued. The Hills would be sure to think there was some connection with the family into which they were to marry, some skeleton unearthed from the cupboard.

Unthinkable, out of the question.

Prosper offered to buy her a new kitten, as her cat, Coral, would be going to Roger after his marriage; but, somehow, she did not seem to think it a fair substitute.

The police came and went, so did the authorities from the foundling hospital. A feeble attempt was made to trace a missing baby, but such a task was invariably hopeless unless it was a kidnap, and none was reported.

Lally, meanwhile, had the baby moved upstairs and a spare room turned into a nursery. She bought a cot and baby-clothes on the pretext that while the matter was sorted out, the poor little thing might as well be comfortable.

Prosper rearranged his foreign trip again and, again, had to postpone it. It was becoming difficult to find more excuses to keep Emma away from the house.

Finally Prosper confronted Lally in the drawing-room just before dinner one night, after Alexander, having been there about two weeks, was becoming part of the family.

'My dear,' he said firmly, 'you will have to decide between that child and me.'

'What?' Gowned for dinner and looking, as usual, radiant and beautiful, she gazed at him with incredulity.

'I'm afraid the joke has gone much too far,' he said sternly. 'You seem to have taken leave of your senses, to have abandoned your normal wise and impeccable judgment. I see that, in time, the task of prising that baby out of your hands will be impossible. My dear, I am a man of seventy and you are nearly fifty. Do you *realise* what adopting a small baby will mean? What it will do to our lives? It is absurd. I forbid it. I do *not* want it . . .'

'But, Prosper darling.' She rose to her feet and amorously encircled his shoulders with her arms. 'That is how you felt about Roger. Think back, my love. How happy he has made us. Did you ever regret that decision?'

'That was . . . years ago. I was a much younger man,' he protested.

'But you don't have to *do* anything, my dearest, do you? We engaged tutors, we sent Roger to school. With this baby there will be nursemaids. You will not know he is here.'

'Of *course* I shall know he is here,' Prosper said angrily. 'His presence will disrupt our lives. Lally, this is a baby only a month or so old. Roger was twelve. Besides, *he* was your son. This case is completely different.'

Outside the door, Roger, just on the verge of entering, paused. Then he leaned his head against the door and, after a few seconds, regained his composure enough to enter.

The lights burnt very late that night at the house in Montagu Square. It had been an evening of emotional storms. There had been tears, shouts, recriminations; more tears. Lally wept bitterly, recalling her skills as an actress. She maintained a non-stop torrent. At one point Roger had seemed on the verge of leaving the house, until he was reminded of what the Hills might think, what they might surmise.

'The main thing is,' Prosper emphasised in a voice broken by strain, 'that normality should continue and be seen to continue . . .'

'And yet all this time you have treated me as a *nephew*,' Roger said in a quivering voice. 'Why could you not acknowledge *me* as Aunt's . . .' he didn't know now what to call her . . . 'as Lally's son?'

'For the same reason that we cannot adopt baby Alexander . . . Such things are not done. We had a position in society, and such a revelation would have been impossible.'

'I have been deprived of a mother's love,' Roger said bitterly.

'But, my darling, you had my love,' Lally said in a quavering voice. 'I did all I could for you, believe me. You have *always* had a mother's love, darling, always. Hasn't he, Prosper?'

'Always,' Prosper said gruffly. 'And I have loved you, and love you now as my son.'

Roger turned away and gazed out of the window at the gas-lamps flickering in the square.

The chimes of Big Ben in the distance could be heard striking midnight. He felt that he had in his hands the fate not only of himself but of one small child who, as he had been, many years ago, was a foundling.

He looked at Lally, a picture of dejection, her beauty faded, suddenly seeming old.

His mother. Maybe he'd always known it; but he experienced for her at that moment less affection than he had ever had. He felt cold and detached and angry. He felt he hated her.

'I suppose the twelve years I spent in a tenement in Kentish Town mean nothing to you . . .'

'Of course they did.' Lally stretched out her hands. 'Of course; but until I met Prosper I had no means of upkeep. And you were not sent to an orphanage, but fostered by the sister of my maid. I *always* came to see you, Roger.'

'Lady Bountiful,' he sniggered. 'With your high-handed manner and fine clothes. You should have heard what they said about you after you left.'

'Enough of that,' Prosper snapped. 'Your mother did what she could. But society is never very tolerant of . . . fallen women. Even *I* was not consulted when she brought you into the house. Ever since, I have accepted you as my adopted son.'

Roger gazed at the man on whom his life depended. After all, what would happen to him if he walked out now? Love that was not blood-love could soon wane.

'As soon as I am married I shall be leading my own life. It is all you can expect. I *am* hurt now, and angry, but I hope that, in time, that will pass. Above all, I never want this to be referred to again, or anyone to be told about it.'

'You don't *want* Emma to know?' Lally asked timidly.

'I *especially* don't want Emma or her parents to know,' Roger said angrily. 'I don't want to proclaim my illegitimacy. They may call off the marriage. They must never know.' He turned to Lally with the air of a judge delivering a sentence. 'I will never call you Mother and I will never think of you as Mother . . .'

'But, darling, Roger . . .'

'You lied to me for years and years when it would have been the simplest thing in the world to tell me the truth. You left me for years to be brought up in a slum in Kentish Town, seeing me two or three times a year at most. Why didn't you leave me for good, Aunt, and not introduce me to this world where I have never really felt I belonged? I always have one foot in the present; the other in my memories of the past. Sometimes I feel like a fish out of water, acting a part.'

Prosper went over to Roger and put a hand on his arm.

'Dear boy, once you have time to reflect . . . you will see that your mother did what she did for the best. She always had your welfare at heart. That I swear. She gave you life and, eventually, a good life. You must remember that.' As Roger continued to stare at him stubbornly, he went on: 'I did my best, too. I have helped you, made you my heir. I love you and I have a great regard for you. Forget the past, begin again.

Life is before you; you are to be married, to be a partner in a mighty business.'

Roger stood there for a moment, clearly lost in thought.

It was true, all true. He had too much to lose. Finally he held out his hand to Prosper.

'Thank you, sir,' he said. 'It is not you I blame, so much as . . .' He turned to Lally, whose face was buried in her handkerchief. 'Well, enough said.' He walked slowly to the door, opened it, and left without turning round.

The effect was deadly, even worse than all the shouting that had preceded it.

Lally and Prosper sat for some time after Roger had departed. The lights were low and the room had grown cold. Prosper was worried about Lally's immobility and he moved over to sit beside her, and raised her pale, limp hand to his lips. He bent and kissed her cheeks, but they were cold too. He was alarmed about her. He tenderly put his hands around her face. The expression in her eyes was tragic.

'My darling Lally,' he said. 'Tonight has been an ordeal for us all. For you, Roger and for me. We have all lost. We should have told Roger years ago. That is the part he resents. But he will get over it, I'm sure, because he is sensible, and he will have Emma's love. That will reassure him, as yours has always been of such comfort to me. Meanwhile, I have been thinking. I can see Alexander means a lot to you. I shall not be pleased, it may cause a distance between us; but you *may* adopt him if you wish. He will console you for Roger's alienation, his eventual loss when he is married.

'After all, two wrongs don't make a right, and I hope that, maybe, after all this misery and confusion, out of it can come a little good. Maybe God has spoken to us through the means of a helpless child.'

IO

Sophie had known the Reverend Angus Maclean since she and George had first approached the Society with the purpose of going to the foreign missions. He was now about fifty, but appeared hardly to have aged in the last ten years. He was a kindly-looking Scot with thinning hair and a lean, earnest face. He was a true ascetic who had spent many years preaching the Word in the most inaccessible and rugged parts of the world.

The Reverend Maclean had agreed to see her although Sophie had given no hint in her letter of what she wanted.

It is not improbable that he guessed.

Sophie travelled to London and arrived at the office in Queen Victoria Street a few minutes before eleven. The gaunt red-brick Victorian buildings, stretched on either side of the thorough-fare, gave no hint of the river that ran as an arterial lifeline at the bottom of the slight incline although, every now and then, a barge would hoot or a ship anchored in the docks further down-stream would sound its siren.

It was a mellow, late autumnal day and Sophie, who had spent the night at a temperance hotel near Waterloo Station, felt a heightened sense of excitement; a sense that this would mark a turning-point in her life.

She had to wait only a few minutes in the rather desolate lobby of the Missionary Society's headquarters before she was shown into a lift that slowly creaked its way to the fourth floor, past hideous brown-and-cream-coloured walls that reflected mid-nineteenth-century taste, as well as a lack of cash to freshen them up. The stone steps were chipped, and the corridor was of polished granite marked with scratches and deep holes which were almost lethal traps for the unwary.

Hearing the lift stop, the Reverend Maclean came to the door of his room and warmly held out both hands to Sophie in greeting.

'Welcome, dear sister. It is *so* good to see you again.'

He drew her into his office, which gave a surprising panoramic view of St Paul's Cathedral and the steeples of the churches of St Andrew-by-the-Wardrobe and St Stephen Walbrook.

Sophie did not at first register the woman who rose from a seat in the corner of the room and came over to greet her.

'I don't think you know Miss Grace Purdy.' The Reverend Maclean stretched out a hand and drew her forward. 'She is the assistant missionary secretary and has recently returned from India.'

'How do you do?' Sophie was a little surprised to find a third party present, but took the chair her old friend and colleague held out for her and sat down, smiling at Miss Purdy.

'I am *so* glad to meet you, Mrs Woodville,' Miss Purdy said in a voice throbbing with emotion. 'I was so moved and touched by the testament you gave of your work in New Guinea, where you carried the Word of Our Lord so boldly.' She bowed her head, and clasped her hands in her lap. 'I was devastated to hear of the death of your dear husband, now – ' she pressed her hands earnestly together ' – a shining soul for Christ.'

Sophie, who had been brought up in the traditions of the English Church as by law established, was averse to the fulsome expressions of Evangelical Christianity, but Miss Purdy was obviously a person whose support she needed, and she smiled her thanks. Angus Maclean had returned to his desk where he sat rereading Sophie's letter. Then he removed his spectacles, joined his hands and smiled at her, a smile in which she saw understanding and sympathy. Surely there was also room there for hope?

'Now, my dear Mrs Woodville, how have you been? How are your children? Above all,' he put his head on one side like a bird, 'have there been any changes in the attitude of George's family?'

What a lot of questions. Sophie wondered to herself how many of the mission's staff were privy to the intimate details of her domestic life.

'It *has* been a difficult two years,' she acknowledged. 'Two years almost to the month since I returned to Wenham.' Mr Maclean and Miss Purdy nodded in unison. 'My parents-in-law were not disposed to encourage me, but my mother-in-law has since died. My father-in-law has welcomed me, and especially my children.' As her emotions came to the fore she moved awkwardly. 'I will confess, Angus, that they have *not* been easy years. My children have settled, but not I. I have missed my beloved husband and, of course, I have missed my vocation: New Guinea. I miss that dear country more than I can say, and my reason for coming here today is to ask if I may be allowed to return.'

For a moment silence reigned in the room, a heavy, pregnant silence like the lull before a storm. Then the minister pulled a file of documents towards him and went through them slowly, turning over each page, as if his mind were on something else.

After a while he shut the file firmly, folded his hands on his desk and looked obliquely at his colleague.

'Miss Purdy, would *you* like to say something?' he said.

Miss Purdy seemed not only prepared but willing, and looked straight at Sophie.

'Mrs Woodville, we at the mission, knowing of your devotion to Our Lord, had anticipated your request. When you wrote to Mr Maclean he thought that this was indeed what you might have in mind. We realised your burning ardour to serve in the mission field, and were reinvigorated by it, our faith renewed; but I am afraid that, in the circumstances, we could not grant your request.'

'But that is disgraceful,' Sophie cried indignantly, rising from her chair. 'What can *you* know . . .'

'I am entrusted by the board as the assistant secretary, Mrs Woodville.' There was a slight edge to Miss Purdy's voice. 'I have studied your circumstances with particular care and womanly sympathy; but the Society feels it cannot permit a single woman – one moreover with the onerous responsibilities of two young children – to undertake such arduous work alone.'

'You *must* understand, Sophie –' the Reverend Maclean, having left his subordinate to do the dirty work, finally found his voice ' – that your situation *is* a difficult one. We send a number of single women who are unencumbered, without dependants.' He turned to his companion. 'Miss Purdy was abroad for many years. We send many married couples, as you know. We are not against women, indeed we are not. But to send a mother with children . . .' he shook his head '. . . out of the question, I am afraid. We would be heavily criticised, if not actually censured.'

'And if I were to leave my children here?' Sophie asked. 'Their grandfather would be delighted to have them, besides which, both my parents are still alive.'

There was another ponderous silence, during which Miss Purdy and the Reverend Maclean again exchanged glances.

'You would not seriously consider doing that, *really*, would you, Mrs Woodville?' Miss Purdy's tone of voice was almost one of disapproval. '*Surely* you would not consider leaving such small children parentless? Suppose, for example, you followed the fate of your husband and did not return?'

Sophie stared defiantly in front of her; her head was beginning to throb.

Angus Maclean rose from his desk and walked round to Sophie, remaining standing slightly behind her.

'I do so *beg* you to accept, dear sister, the wisdom of the decision of the board. A Christ-like acceptance can only win adornment to your heavenly crown.'

'Then the board's decision is irrevocable?' Sophie felt her tremendous fighting spirit had gone, stamped out like a flame beneath a harsh heavy boot.

'When we had your letter asking for a meeting, we naturally anticipated your request. It could of course have been for money, but knowing your husband's wealthy connections we dismissed that. A board meeting was being held a few days later, and we considered what action we should take if you did ask to return. That is why I asked Miss Purdy to attend today so that, as the board's secretary, she could confirm its unanimous decision. I am so *very* sorry, Sophie; but perhaps, in a few years, when the children no longer need you . . .' He shrugged.

It seemed a vain hope, she thought, getting stoically to her feet. Besides which, by then they would probably tell her she was too old.

Sophie returned to Wenham on a slow train which gave her plenty of time to think. In many ways the decision had not surprised her, and had left her with a number of hard alternatives. She took stock of her life in recent years.

In the first place, she considered she had achieved very little during her time at Wenham. She had not settled; she had not encouraged a man who wished to marry her, despite his worth, integrity and the undoubted honesty of his intentions. She had no money, no home of her own and, worst of all, she had not even set up a memorial to George. In this small, dying request she had failed him.

Maybe in her mind she had thought it would be the last thing she would do before she left to return to his burial place. In fact, how could she have gone back without doing it? Sometimes the task, quite a simple one really, seemed insuperable. It was as though, in some mysterious way, the hand of God had intervened to delay it.

Sophie arrived in Blandford and, although she had ordered a cab to meet her, she saw, with mixed emotions, that Mr Turner had arrived with his pony and trap, and sat looking expectantly towards the entrance to the station. He was, she thought, decidedly an agreeable man, and he had a pleasant smile of anticipation on his lips.

He got down when he saw her, and raised his hat.

'Any luck?' he enquired anxiously and, as she shook her head, he took her hand and helped her up into the seat beside him.

'I thought they'd say "no",' he said when he had positioned himself beside her.

'Well, you were right.' Sophie avoided his eyes but gazed

about her instead at the people in the streets, as Mr Turner set off at a brisk trot through the town. 'It appears the fault is that I am not single, and I am not married. The responsibilities of my children preclude me from any activity in the mission field, that is, until the children are grown up, by which time they will probably tell me I am too old.'

Mr Turner, sensing her profound disappointment, said nothing, following the progress of his pony, who seemed to know his own way through the town which was much larger than Wenham. They passed the Crown Hotel and crossed the bridge over the Stour, turning to the right just after the imposing gates to the Portman estate at Bryanston. The pace slowed as the pony began to pull the trap and its occupants up the hill. A slight breeze had sprung up, and Sophie put her hand on her hat, grateful for the silence, for Hubert's understanding presence, so that she could collect her thoughts.

It was just over two years since she had been met at the same station by the same man on her return from New Guinea. Now, as then, the countryside looked beautiful and inviting, the greens merging into the browns and golds of autumn, the leaves forming a thick carpet on the ground, the neat fields being prepared for sowing.

Yet the golden beach at Gumbago was just as vivid to her, and the sight of the pink coral shingle mixing with the fronds of the overhanging palms, the green of the granadillas and crotons and, as a superb backdrop, the splendour of the mountains towering towards the far-off Owen Stanley range. How small and inconsequential did the undulating hills of Dorset seem in comparison to these! She looked sideways at Hubert and observed that he too appeared lost in thought. He glanced at her and smiled. She felt comforted by his presence; he was an undemanding sort of person to be with, yet loyal, reliable and true.

She wished she could love him. How convenient it would be.

When they reached the cottage, Hubert jumped down first with her overnight case and extended his hand to help her alight. She put the key in the door and turned to thank him, but saw, from his expression, that he was going to accompany her inside.

'Will you have a cup of tea?' she asked, unpinning her hat and putting it on the table. It seemed only polite in view of the fact that he had met her.

'I took the liberty of putting a jug of milk in your pantry,' Hubert said, putting her case by the table. He seemed quite at home.

'That's *very* good of you, Hubert. You're so thoughtful.' She secured the pin in her hat so that it would not get lost, and stood looking at it, then at him. The atmosphere seemed charged with emotion in a way she had not anticipated.

'You know . . .' Hubert paused and cleared his throat. She noticed for the first time how prominent his Adam's apple was. 'You know, I made an offer to you once. Maybe it was made too early, and you thought I didn't mean it . . .'

'Oh, but I *did*.' She sat down on the chair next to the table. 'I judged it too soon after George's death.'

'And now?' He looked down at her, aware of an almost irresistible impulse to take her in his arms. It was something he had never done to a woman; didn't really know how to do. One of the many attractions of Sophie was that she would know, and would help him. 'But Sophie, it is nearly three years since George . . .'

'I don't want to marry you because I have no choice,' Sophie burst out. 'I don't want *you* to feel you must marry *me* out of pity, or that I should marry you solely because of need.' She gazed at the pin stuck in the hat, which seemed to mesmerise her. 'I am poor, it is true, very poor, but that is only because I choose to be independent of my parents. I have my pride, you know. Besides,' she looked to one side so as to avoid his gaze, 'I don't *love* you, Hubert. Not in the way I loved George.'

'I don't mind that.' He made as if to grasp her arm but she moved quickly away from him.

'There must be many women in these parts, Hubert, who would be glad to be your wife, who would make you a much better one than I.'

'Oh no, Sophie there is *no one* like you, no one at all.' Hubert stood with his arms stiffly by his side as though afraid, now, to move.

'But I am much *older* than you, Hubert.'

'That is no barrier. I love you and I want to take care of you, and your children. I believe a few years separated you and your husband. I have means above my stipend and I know I can make you very comfortable. The object of my life, next to the love and service of God, is your happiness. I wish you would give me the chance to prove it to you.'

It would be so easy to say 'yes'. And why should she refuse? She liked him; in fact, she liked him very much. But it was not love. It was affection, respect, even admiration. Yet a woman who had known passion, the true union in flesh and spirit with a man, yearned for that experience again. However much she wished it, she knew in her heart that the Reverend Hubert Turner, good, pious, worthy man though he was, would never awaken her in that way; and yet she did not wish completely to burn her boats so, impulsively, her hand reached out for his.

'Will you give me more time, Hubert? I need it, you know, to consider my position.'

Once more, unfairly perhaps, she had given him hope.

Sophie made tea, changed her travelling-dress, and then it was time to go to Pelham's Oak to pick up the children. Hubert appeared encouraged by her reply and she thought that, indeed, he was a man of exemplary patience, of true Christian hope and optimism.

But they said very little on the short journey; and as the pony and trap bowled up the drive to Pelham's Oak, the front door opened and Deborah and Ruth, as if they had been looking out for her, ran headlong down the steps towards their mother. They clambered onto the cart and flung themselves into her arms, and she burst out laughing with sheer exhilaration and happiness. The love of her children, and hers for them, was very precious. Better by far, she thought, hugging them close to her, than the love of man.

Sophie felt now that the future, if not settled, was not as bleak as it had been; that even if she did not love Hubert as she would have wished – as she had loved George – he was a friend; a good and true friend who would never let her down.

Hubert too seemed quite happy at the outcome of their talk, despite its inconclusive nature, and handing the reins of the pony to the groom, he followed her into the house with a positively jaunty air.

Arthur hovered in the hall. He had been devoted to Margaret and had not recovered from her death. She had given him his first job as under-footman, and he had served her for her lifetime at Pelham's Oak, a span of thirty years.

'I hope the children have behaved themselves,' Sophie said, looking towards the door.

'Oh yes indeed, madam,' Arthur smiled. 'Sir Guy is so devoted to them. He is a changed man when they are with us. He is waiting for you in the drawing-room, Mrs Woodville, and hopes you will stay for tea.'

'I should be delighted to stay for tea.' Sophie looked around at her companion. 'Hubert? Have you the time?'

'Well, if that is all right with Sir Guy?'

'I'm sure it will be all right with Sir Guy,' Sophie said briskly. 'I was merely wondering whether you were in a hurry to get back to your parish duties.'

'I have the time.' Hubert held out a hand to Deborah, who clutched it. Sophie knew how much her children liked Hubert, but it was still not sufficient reason to marry him.

The door of the drawing-room opened and Carson came out, dressed for riding. He smiled politely at Sophie and Hubert.

'Hello, Sophie. Father says you have been to London. Was it a successful visit?'

'I came away disappointed,' Sophie said with a sigh. 'I was hoping to return to New Guinea, but it is not to be.'

'If that's what you wanted, then I'm sorry.' Carson rather astonished her by his apparent concern. 'But I know Father will be pleased. Ruth and Deborah give him such happiness. I, by the way, have been teaching them to ride. I hope you don't mind. I think they will be very good.'

'Oh, do take care, they are so small.' Sophie looked apprehensive.

'Don't worry,' Carson replied soothingly. 'Deborah has a natural seat on a horse, and Ruth is already quite accomplished, just like her Great-Aunt Eliza. Did you ever ride, Sophie?'

'No, I never learned.' Sophie's tone was offhand. 'But do take care with my two.'

She smiled at him and proceeded past him into the drawing-room, where Guy was sitting in his chair close by the fire.

He was not an old man, not by any means, but he looked like one and, Sophie thought as she sat down by his side, behaved like one.

'How are you, Sir Guy? How were the children?'

'My dear, they are never any trouble,' Guy said. 'I love having them. Carson has been taking the girls riding.'

'So he told me.'

'Carson is *so* good with the children.' Guy sighed loudly. 'I wish he'd have some of his own. He is too irresponsible to settle and have a family, sweet boy though he is, and a comfort to me since poor Margaret died.

'If Carson had an interest in this estate, how much more relaxed I should feel. Compare him to his cousin Roger. Now *there's* a fine young man for you. I believe he is to be made a junior partner on his marriage, and he is not yet twenty-five.'

'Is the marriage date arranged, then?' Sophie asked with only formal interest.

'I believe it's to take place in London in the spring. Her family wanted it at their seat in Leicestershire, but St Peter's, Eaton Square has been decided upon, as that is also near where the couple are to live. Prosper and his parents have bought Roger and Emma a most *handsome* house in Eaton Place as a wedding present. Ah, there is no shortage of money there.' In his frustration, Guy banged his knee. 'Now why could not Carson have been like that? Why did he have to be like *me*?'

The door opened and Arthur, followed by a maid, entered bearing the tea-things.

Although Margaret, the mistress of the house, was dead, the staff endeavoured to keep up her high standards. But though she had never been there when Margaret was alive, Sophie could not help noticing a slight sloppiness in the service, the fact that the sandwiches were not as wafer-thin as they would have been, she was sure, in Margaret's time, or the cakes quite so light.

Sophie also thought that the uniforms worn by the staff were not so crisp or correct as they would have been in Margaret's day. As for Guy, there was a stain on the front of his jacket that, even when she was very ill, Sophie was sure his wife would not have tolerated.

To Sophie, the great house and the people in it looked as though they had lost a woman's touch.

'Tell me about London, my dear.' Guy, with a trembling hand, put his cup up to his lips. 'Did you go to shop? Who did you see?'

Sophie put her arm around the legs of Deborah, who huddled up to her. 'I have no means to shop, Sir Guy. I went with the object of seeing if I could return to my beloved missions in New Guinea.'

'Oh, my dear.' Guy unsteadily put his cup down. 'Oh, don't tell me that now, just when I am getting to know you. *And* the children . . . my little grandchildren. They are almost all I've got left and are so precious to me. Don't tell me you are even considering taking them away.'

'Well, not now, Sir Guy.' Sophie, who had never enjoyed any intimacy with him before, who had not so much as pecked his cheek, put a hand comfortingly on his arm. 'I am going to stay here in Wenham for the time being, though I may have to seek a position to bring in money. My missionary society which sent George and me out to New Guinea would not have a single woman, a lone mother. Women completely on their own *are* acceptable as missionaries, and we have many great and good ones in the field; but mothers with young children . . .' Sadly, she smiled and shook her head. 'I'm afraid not.'

'I must say, I'm glad to hear it.' Guy pressed her hand, and she felt a curious kinship with him.

'My dear,' he went on, 'I have not been a very good man in my life. I did a lot of bad things when I was young, and I have been weak. I have tried to make up for it in recent years, but not always successfully. Your father was very good to me and I quarrelled needlessly with him; I was unforgiving towards you when you took George away; and now that I am a widower, and will soon be an old man, I should like to try and make up for the harm I have done. My dear Sophie . . .' he held up his free hand and waved it around the room '. . . I don't know how long we shall be here, or what will happen, but it will give your father-in-law the greatest pleasure in the world if, while you can, you and the dear children would consent to live at Pelham's Oak with me. To take your rightful place as George's widow by my side. Would you do that, dear?'

At the other end of the room, almost unnoticed by the company, Hubert Turner put his head in his hands. Once more, when it was just within sight, he felt he had been denied his prize.

But Sophie felt momentarily overwhelmed. At last she was accepted, and acceptable; a Woodville not merely in name. Here she was, being invited to live in the family home; George's home, where he had been born. Had he lived she would have been its chatelaine, and now she was to be its housekeeper, her purpose to take care of a bereaved, perhaps rather sickly man.

No matter.

'Of course I will,' she said. 'Gladly.'

It was what George would have wished.

II

Guy Woodville, despite his age, his local eminence as the holder of a title over two hundred years old, always stood in some awe of his Uncle Prosper Martyn, his mother's brother.

He was a man who had not only once given Guy the sack from the Martyn-Heering business, but had gone on to marry his discarded mistress, Lally.

All that had happened a very long time ago, and if Lally and Guy continued to feel uncomfortable in each other's presence, at least they did not meet very often, and then always in a room full of people.

In time Guy had completely forgotten that, for him, she had once been the most precious object in the world, that he had held her in his arms.

The Martyns and the Woodvilles, despite the fact that their houses were only a few miles apart, saw one another infrequently. There was no particular need, especially since Margaret had died, and they had little in common.

Guy had been stirred slightly by the fact that Lally had adopted a foundling, and brought him to Dorset because of her husband's apparent disapproval. It made him think a little guiltily of the child that he and Lally had had, and whom she had shortly afterwards given away. Guy's memory was conveniently selective about certain parts of his life, and he had whole areas of total amnesia.

Prosper called at Pelham's Oak shortly after the Christmas and New Year festivals were over. He had put off an unpleasant task, not wishing to ruin that period of blessing for Guy and Carson, who were spending their first Christmas without Margaret, and their first with Sophie and her children.

Carson had been riding before his great-uncle arrived, and when he saw his chauffeur-driven motor-car process up the drive he dug his heels in his horse's flank and cleared a fence with ease. He galloped across the field and then turned sharply back, to find that Prosper had alighted from his car and was standing, hands joined in front of him, watching Carson with every sign of approval. It was nice, even unusual, to see such an expression on his great-uncle's face, and Carson halted before the fence, uncertain whether to jump it again and again turn round; but one dared not be rude to Great-Uncle Prosper. It would be tempting fate, and his father would be angry.

'Hello!' Prosper hailed him, his hands cupped to his mouth.

'Hello!' Carson called back and, tapping his horse, easily cleared the fence, despite the short distance. He then rode up to within a few paces of Prosper, who smiled a greeting.

'You've a very fine seat on a horse, Carson.'

'Thank you, Uncle.'

The young man jumped down as a groom ran up and took the reins from him.

'Tell me.' Prosper put an avuncular arm around his shoulder as they strolled round the side of the house towards the front. 'Did you ever think of a career in the army?'

'The *army*!' Carson gasped, stopping for a moment to stare at the man beside him.

'I've been thinking, and I have reached the conclusion that it would suit you, Carson,' Prosper continued imperturbably. 'The army is a fine career for a man. You've the spirit of adventure and you like the outdoor life. You could be sent abroad to all kinds of interesting places: India, Africa, any of the colonies. The British Empire circles the world. You're a first-class horseman. I dare say we could buy you into a cavalry regiment, and your future would be made. What do you say?'

'I *say*,' Carson said, falling again into step beside his uncle, 'that I have *never* thought of it and, frankly, I don't think I ever would.'

'Oh come, Carson.' Prosper's hand again clasped his shoulder as they entered the house. 'Don't make a decision too rashly. Think about it.'

'I would hate the discipline, Uncle.' Once more Carson paused as they were about to enter the drawing-room. 'I hate being told what to do.'

'Don't I know *that*.' Prosper laughed a little grimly. 'But I think it would do you good. You would have every chance of succeeding in it, of making a name for yourself before the time came to inherit. What do you say, Guy?'

Guy, hearing voices, had come to the door and took Prosper's outstretched hand.

'Say to what?' Guy enquired amiably, looking disapprovingly at his son's jodhpurs and riding-boots. 'I do think you might have changed, Carson,' he said tetchily. 'You know Sophie gets *most* concerned about muddy riding-boots in the hall.'

'I wiped them.' Carson looked unconcernedly at his feet.

'Sophie, ah yes.' Prosper looked approvingly around him. 'I can see her influence already. Nothing like a woman's touch.'

'She *is* an excellent housekeeper,' Guy murmured. 'She has transformed the place, and brought the servants to heel in no time.'

'She's a martinet,' Carson said, but his expression was benign. 'However, it is an improvement; a bit like having Mama back: meals on time, beds made, that sort of thing.'

'A man can't run a house, you know, Prosper.' Guy went over to the sideboard and removed the stopper from the whisky decanter. 'Carson and I were floundering until Sophie came to live with us.'

He poured generous measures of whisky into three glasses and handed one each to Prosper and Carson, keeping one for himself. 'However good a butler, the servants take advantage over you, which they never dared with Margaret. No, Sophie is a blessing.' He sat down, crossing his legs, and looked at Prosper. 'She is also a very nice, sensible young woman. Now that I know her better, I cannot say that I blame my son for marrying her. My opinions have decidedly changed in that direction. And justice has been done,' he added as an afterthought. 'We should not have behaved towards Sophie as we did; but my dear wife was adamant . . .' He fumbled in his pocket and, shaking his head, drew out a large handkerchief. Both his companions knew what to expect. As soon as Guy mentioned Margaret's name, his eyes filled with tears. He gave his nose a hearty blow before stuffing the handkerchief back into his pocket again.

That little ceremony over, Prosper put his whisky-glass to his lips, aware of a feeling of unease. As a rule he had a reputation for not mincing his words, and he relished it. Straightforward, out-spoken – people knew where they were with Prosper Martyn. But . . . on this occasion he found his task peculiarly difficult. These were his nephew and great-nephew, not strangers met in the course of business.

He thought he would start obliquely. 'We were saying as we came in – ' he casually crossed one leg over the other ' – that a military career might not be a bad thing for Carson.'

'A military career?' Guy's eyes boggled. 'And how long do you think Carson would stand that, or they would stand Carson?'

'Exactly what I said, Father.' Carson looked gratified.

'Beggars can't be choosers,' Prosper said severely.

'How do you mean exactly?' Guy, sensing Prosper's unease, felt increasingly ill at ease himself.

'Carson has no job and you, Guy, I'm sorry to say, have almost no money. I don't think you can possibly realise how very grave your situation is. Margaret's fortune, or what was left of it, has reverted to the Heering estate.'

Guy sat staring at Prosper, his mouth hanging open.

'*All* of it?'

'All of it, I'm afraid.' Prosper uncrossed his legs, then re-crossed them. 'You may recall that when you were newly married her father formed an opinion about you: you were too profligate with your wife's money, having none of your own. He rearranged her affairs into a family trust. Each of your children would receive a small portion when they were twenty-one, and you and Margaret would be able to live com-fortably on the rest.

'It has taken us some time to work it all out.' He raised

his glass to his lips and finished his whisky. 'But that is how matters stand, I'm sorry to say.'

'I had no idea that Margaret's money would not come to me on her death,' Guy said. 'And, I'm sure, nor had she. I consider it *most* unjust, as that undoubtedly would have been her wish.'

'I'm sure it would have been,' Prosper agreed. 'But it is not what happened. What her father did many years ago is irrevocable. The Heerings, I may say, have a very different attitude from mine. I would have released some money – an annuity, say – but they will not. The leopard cannot change its spots, and you would soon whittle it away, Guy. Neither do they have any confidence in Carson after what happened in the City.'

'I was *not* a thief,' Carson said, roused by anger to his feet. 'Was not and am not. Someone did what they did to get rid of me . . .'

'Well, we won't go over all that ground,' Prosper parried. 'I haven't come to talk about the past, but the future. All I can say is that it is a pity that what happened happened, that's all. If, on the other hand, you were seen to be taking an active, constructive part in the management of the estate, Carson . . . But you are not. It is all suffering from neglect.'

'I do what I can,' Carson said grumpily. 'I wasn't trained to manage estates.'

'Well, you could find out,' Guy said, leaning forward and poking him with his finger. 'All you do all day is ride horses and drink in the local public houses.'

'You're always picking on me,' Carson shouted. 'Whatever I do is wrong. It's unfair. I cannot be something I am not. I am not a businessman, I am not an administrator . . .'

'*And* you do not want to be a soldier? Not even try?' Prosper's tone was one of sarcasm.

'I can hardly bring vast sums of money into the family on a *soldier's* pay,' Carson objected. 'I believe it costs more to be in the army than to be out of it. Polo ponies can cost an awful lot of money. Mess bills are enormous. I should need a large allowance.'

'I was thinking of a *career*,' Prosper snapped. 'Of serving king and country. Whatever happens to the house and estate, you will be provided for if you buy a long-term commission. And you would be expected to work, not play polo all day.'

'What do you mean, "whatever happens to the house"?' Guy's mouth remained open in shock.

'Dear Guy.' Prosper thrust out his legs before him and folded his arms across his chest. 'Your only asset is this house, and believe me, it *is* an asset. You have farms, cottages, and two thousand acres. There are many men in the City whom the prosperity of our times has made supremely rich. It is new money, and most of the men who have made it are socially inferior to the Woodvilles. But they aspire. They would love to own a country house and all that it entails. *And* they have the means. You would get a very good price for Pelham's Oak, a price which would enable you to live in comfort for the rest of your life.'

'And where would that be, may I ask? Since I would have no home.'

'Well . . .' Prosper produced some documents from his inside pocket and proceeded to unfold them.

'Oh, so it's all been worked out, has it?' Carson sneered. 'We might have known the groundwork would be done, Uncle.' Then he turned to Guy. 'Careful, Father, that they don't bamboozle you with figures.'

'There is *no* intention to deceive,' Prosper said coldly. 'Our only idea is to help. Having said that, however, we see no reason to bail out with our money a man rich in assets.' He looked around him. 'You have pictures and other pieces in this house that alone could raise several hundred, maybe thousands of pounds. I assure you that the Heerings and the Martyns, having a close interest in the welfare of this family, have gone into the details with great care. As your brother-in-law, Julius, in particular, has put in a vast amount of work. Naturally, we have the well-being of the Woodville family *very* close to our hearts. Now see . . .' He spread the papers on his lap and pointed with a finger. 'You have a very fine farm at the boundary of your estate, Guy.' Prosper then vaguely turned towards the window in a south-easterly direction. 'It is at present put over to beef-farming and makes a profit. It has a very nice Georgian farm house with four bedrooms, drawing-room, dining-room, study. It is let to Farmer Phelps, but he is very old and his sons are not interested in farming. We have reason to believe that he will be happy to retire to a cottage on the estate, so that we can take over the house to make a comfortable home for you, Guy. After all, you are unlikely to marry again, are you, and if Carson does the sensible thing I have suggested . . .'

'Why am *I* unlikely to marry again?' Guy demanded. 'You were not so young when you married Lally. Do you suppose me to be past it, Prosper?'

'Not at all.' Prosper remained unrattled. 'And if there *is* a lady fortunate enough to become the new Lady Woodville, I shall be among the first to congratulate you Guy, you can be sure of that. It may be that she would also find the commodious nature of Low Farm sufficient for her purposes. I dare say Sophie, who has come from a tiny cottage, would feel quite at home again too.'

During his uncle's speech Carson had moved over to his father's side and sat down next to him, as if to lend him support.

'And if Father or I do not do the things you suggest, what then? It is, after all, asking us to make a substantial change in our lifestyles.' He chuckled. 'You have certainly been most thorough, Uncle. Oh, I can see all those overworked clerks in Threadneedle Street beavering away on facts and figures – not a stone left unturned.' Prosper looked at him coldly and then, as if ignoring his remarks, went on:

'If you do not agree, you are, I am afraid, on your own. The family, having done its best to help you and, as you say, worked very hard, will naturally feel it can do no more. We may even have a purchaser interested in Pelham's Oak among our clients: a wealthy financier, a friend of the late king, who advised him on several financial matters.'

'Oh, adding interest to altruism, Uncle?' Carson chided. 'What's in it for you?'

Prosper looked at his watch and stood up. 'I do not propose to take any notice of your offensive remarks, Carson. I assure you, we as a firm are *quite* above mercenary transactions of that nature. Despite your sarcasm, you can have no doubt of that.'

Victoria Fairchild, though in many ways as upright and vigorous as ever she had been, and in good health and spirits, was nevertheless seventy-six years of age. She worried a good deal about her adopted daughter, Connie, and what would become of her after she died.

In the opinion of most people in the town, that time was undoubtedly a long way off. But one never knew. Sometimes people were struck down without any warning, and the older one became, the more one felt the cards stacking up against one. Any little pain or creaking joint made one conscious of the passage of time and its ultimate end.

Not that Miss Fairchild had not made every provision for Connie who, in any case, had inherited a house and a fortune of her own from her father, John Yetman. Her inheritance had been carefully invested by the same solicitor who took care of Miss Fairchild's own not-insubstantial inheritance. Thus between them the two ladies were worth a considerable amount of money.

It was not, however, so much about Connie's material well-being that Miss Fairchild was concerned, but about her emotional happiness. She would have liked Connie to marry; to have that kind of close, personal union with a person of the opposite sex that she herself had never had.

Once she had come near to it. Her heart had almost been broken by Connie's uncle, Christopher Yetman, a fine, strapping, swashbuckling, wicked character who had kissed her on the lips. Once. It was the one and only time in her life it had happened.

Christopher had subsequently spent seven years in gaol for bigamy, and then he had disappeared to the other side of the world, never to be seen or heard of again.

But Miss Fairchild never forgot Christopher, or that brief

moment of passion in the back of the haberdashery shop she used to own in the main street of Wenham. Despite the silence, the passage of years, she did not doubt that, if he appeared on her doorstep or at her garden gate, she would feel now as she had then, thirty years ago, before Connie was born, and she would welcome him as though he had never left.

To her, Connie was the daughter she and Christopher might have had. Connie was a Yetman and she looked like one; the same blood that had flowed through Christopher's veins flowed through hers. It made her thus doubly close.

People often wondered how much Miss Fairchild's devotion to Connie was due to the fact that she was Christopher's niece, because, of course, her relationship with Christopher had been part of Wenham folklore; like the elopement of Eliza Woodville, and the marriage of the rector's daughter to Sir Guy's heir.

Connie was by now twenty-four. She had straight brown hair without the slightest kind of a wave or a curl in it. She was myopic, and wore unbecoming steel-framed glasses. She even had a very *slight* suspicion of a squint. Above all, she was shy to the point of incapacity. It almost amounted to a real physical handicap. The one place where she didn't blush continually was in her home, and even then, if someone unknown came to the door she went as red as a beetroot and rushed for cover. For her to go to parties or mix with crowds was an agony.

Connie's shyness was a blight; it diminished her enjoyment of life. The only time she ventured outside was to creep down to the church to practise on the organ – and then scuttle home again as fast as she could. She was never seen in the shops, at fairs or any other social events unless she was in the protective custody of her aunt. In fact, if it had not been for her playing in church and the occasional recital, she would scarcely have been known at all, except as a recluse, a hermit, a creature of mystery.

Miss Fairchild fretted about Connie; but what could she do? The child – she always thought of her as a child – *said* she was happy. She made no complaints. She wanted nothing more in life than her music. If Miss Fairchild had been bold enough to mention the subject of men, Connie would have sunk beneath the floor. It would simply not have done.

On a cold January day in 1911 Miss Fairchild was sitting in front of the fire when her maid entered to say that Mr Potts was on the telephone. Not many people had telephones in Wenham but Miss Fairchild was one of them. She liked to keep up with business, with the stock-market and world affairs. She read the *Daily Mail* every day and knew what was happening. It was quite natural that a woman with such modern attitudes should own a telephone.

She heard the voice of Mr Potts, her solicitor, crackling over the wire. He wished to come and see her.

Was it trouble? She sounded worried. He assured her it was not trouble, but the very opposite. In fact he sounded most excited. Miss Fairchild suggested Mr Potts should come that afternoon, and returned to her sitting-room with a frown on her face. Mr Potts rarely displayed emotion of any kind, and she couldn't help a feeling of mild agitation over the purpose of his visit.

Connie had heard the wobbly bell of the telephone, and came downstairs and into the sitting-room with her sheet music under her arm. *The Messiah* at Christmas had gone very well. The soloists were almost professional, the choir had been strong. It had made Mr Turner, who acted as choirmaster, rather more ambitious, and they were considering *The Creation* or, maybe for Lent, Mozart's *Requiem*.

'Who was that on the telephone, Aunt?' Connie asked, flopping down by Miss Fairchild's side. Truthfully, telephone calls were a rare event.

'It was Mr Potts, dear. He wants to come and see me.'

'Not any trouble, I hope, Aunt?' Like Miss Fairchild, Connie was a pessimist.

'He didn't *sound* as though it was trouble.' Miss Fairchild sounded dubious. 'But I'm worried, all the same. Europe is in a very unsettled state, Connie. Trouble in the Balkans. Trouble in Russia. The noise made by the suffragettes here does *nobody* a favour.' Miss Fairchild sniffed disapprovingly.

'Do you *not* think women should have the vote, Aunt?' Connie had never before properly considered the matter.

'Of course I think they should have the vote! A woman is just as good as a man; as a businesswoman, I know that well. We are able to look after ourselves and manage our debts as well as any man; but this is *not* the way to go about it, provoking public disorder. It will only put back their cause, not advance it. Now, Constance dear.' Miss Fairchild made a visible effort to put aside her worries and smiled. 'What plans do you have for the day?'

'I am meeting Mr Turner this afternoon, Aunt, to discuss performing Haydn's *Creation* at Easter, following our success with *The Messiah*.

'*Meeting*? Where are you meeting him?' Miss Fairchild asked anxiously.

'Why, at his house, Aunt.' Connie seemed surprised. 'Then we are going to the church to run through the score.'

Miss Fairchild was a clever embroiderer, president of the Ladies' Guild, and she and the ladies were working on the church vestments, replacing them one by one. It was to be their gift to the church, and she herself was embroidering an exquisite cope to be used when the new rector was presented to the church, whenever that should be. Miss Fairchild sighed.

Now she laid aside her embroidery and took off her spectacles. 'You must be *very* careful, you know, my dear. Mr Turner is a single man, and it would not do to be seen too frequently in his company. People might consider you flighty.'

'Aunt!' Connie said in a shocked voice. 'Whatever are you suggesting? Who could consider *me* flighty?'

'Just that you must take care, my dear,' Miss Fairchild said, getting up and patting her ward's hand. 'Mr Turner is in many ways a most suitable mate for you, but you must be careful not to . . . Well, people's tongues will wag.'

'Not about *me*, Aunt,' Connie said with a resigned smile. It was true this was rather a delusion on Miss Fairchild's part. 'Mr Turner is head over heels in love with Mrs Woodville. Everybody knows that.'

'Mrs Woodville!' Miss Fairchild sat down again abruptly. 'But she is years older than him.'

'Nevertheless, he loves her. He conducted her almost exclusively when she sang in *The Messiah*, and she wasn't even a

201

soloist. His eyes scarcely ever left her face. Everyone noticed it, and now that she lives at Pelham's Oak he finds every excuse he can think of to go and see her. I can assure you, Aunt, no one would ever read anything into my seeing Mr Turner alone. He scarcely even notices that I am a woman.'

'Oh!' Miss Fairchild sounded as though a puff of wind had thrown her off course. 'Oh, I see.'

Why was it, she thought, that some women attracted men, and went on attracting them, and others didn't?

It was a little like the Bible: 'For he that hath, to him shall be given: and he that hath not, from him shall be taken even that which he hath.' It seemed most unfair.

After lunch Connie went off to her appointment with Mr Turner, sidling along the streets as though she were terrified of whom she might see, and Miss Fairchild awaited the arrival of her solicitor, Mr Potts of Potts, Bootle and Potts of Blandford, whose firm had been her family's solicitors since the time of her parents' marriage.

Mr Horace Potts was the third generation to be in the family law practice, and he was considered a go-ahead young man, ambitious to prosper and do well, to expand his own and the firm's fortunes.

'Good afternoon, Mr Potts.' Miss Fairchild held out her hand as he crossed the room, and was surprised by the vigour with which he seized it and pumped it up and down.

'Good afternoon, Miss Fairchild. A very *good* afternoon I think you will find it. Do I find you well?'

'Very well, thank you, Mr Potts, and you?' Miss Fairchild sounded a little surprised by his animation.

'Excellent, thank *you*, Miss Fairchild.' He gave her a broad smile as he drew a large folder from his portmanteau. 'And Miss Yetman?'

'Constance is very well, thank you. Practising her music.'

'What a *fine* musician.' Mr Potts raised his eyes reverentially to the ceiling. 'In the opinion of my wife she is of professional standard.'

'That is most kind of your wife,' Miss Fairchild said, 'but

nevertheless, not quite true. If she had been, I would have had her trained; but she is a good amateur, and that is quite sufficient in Connie's case.'

Not for the first time, Mr Potts felt deflated in his enthusiasms by Miss Fairchild and, taking the seat she indicated, he sat looking at her with an air of expectancy.

'Now, Mr Potts,' she said, 'what brings you here?'

'Well . . .' Mr Potts dived into his folder and produced a certificate which he passed to Miss Fairchild, who gazed at it uncomprehendingly.

'Gold shares.' She looked enquiringly at him. 'So?'

'They were purchased by your parents in a remarkable act of foresight in the year eighteen sixty. I don't know whether my father or grandfather advised them or what, but for many years that particular mine in South Africa remained undeveloped and the shares thus practically worthless. I now have to tell you the astonishing good news that a rich vein of gold has been discovered in the mine, one of the best and largest in South Africa. The shares have gone up tenfold since this was announced, and as you have ten thousand they are worth over a hundred thousand pounds.'

'A hundred thousand pounds!' Miss Fairchild breathed. 'What a lot of money.'

'These,' Mr Potts went on enthusiastically, 'together with your various properties, this house and the shop in Wenham, and your many other investments, make you a very wealthy woman, madam. In fact, I should think you are the richest woman in Wenham.' He paused and then said dramatically, 'Miss Fairchild, you must be worth close to a million pounds.'

'A *million* pounds!' At last Miss Fairchild took a very deep breath. 'Did you say a *million*?'

'Well, close.' Mr Potts looked quickly at his calculations. 'Say, eight to nine hundred thousand. Nevertheless, a considerable sum of money. Now.' He sat back and, returning the share certificate to its folder, tapped his knee. 'The thing is, what shall we do with it all?'

'*Do?*' Miss Fairchild echoed shrilly. 'Why, leave it where it is. It seems to be doing very well.'

'Shares rise and fall, Miss Fairchild.'

'I know that.'

'Well, I have been talking to your broker and he advises Russia, Miss Fairchild. He feels that Russia offers an attractive prospect for investment. He says, sell South Africa and buy Russia. There are gold fields in Russia too.'

'Is he mad?' Miss Fairchild said with a trace of impatience. 'What sort of broker is he exactly? Does he not read the papers? Does he not know, for instance, that together with China and the Balkans, Russia is in a ferment? The whole country boils like a cauldron.'

'Why, nothing would unseat the Tsar. He is a cousin of our king, a grandchild of Queen Victoria.' The notion seemed to appal Mr Potts.

'Cousin or not, grandchild or not, Russia, young man – ' Miss Fairchild shook her finger at him as one on the brink of a lecture ' – is poised on the verge of revolt and, let me tell *you*, the rest of Europe might well follow . . .'

'Oh, I hardly think . . .'

'You leave my shares where they are. South Africa, lately unionised and well out of Europe, is a very safe place to be. If the price has only just begun to rise, you may be sure it will go higher.'

'But, Miss Fairchild, the shares have soared . . .'

'Then let them go on soaring, and while you're talking to your broker and putting him right about prospects for investment in Russia, based on my advice, ask him to purchase another five thousand of those excellent South African shares for my ward as well. There is no reason why we both should not benefit. Is there, Mr Potts?'

'None at all, Miss Fairchild.'

'Excellent. Do it, man, and get them before the price is even higher.'

Mr Turner was not at his house. He had forgotten Connie. His maid was full of apologies and tried to explain that the curate had so many things on his mind: the rector had not been well, and this doubled his workload, no, trebled it, because the rector did very little parish work anyway. Poor Mr Turner, out all day visiting his parishioners, attending this meeting and that. She did not mention that this day his duties had again taken him to Pelham's Oak.

Connie left a message and went on her way to the church, where she began to sight-read Haydn's *Creation*, hoping that no one was listening in the church.

It was a difficult piece. Difficult to play and, surely, much too difficult to sing? *The Messiah* was so much easier; besides, everyone knew the tunes. It was always being sung in some local concert hall or church. Everyone knew its rousing choruses, its sublime solo pieces.

'I know that my Redeemer liveth, for in my flesh shall I see God.'

She strummed a few notes extempore on the organ and then she began spontaneously to sing, lifting up her head and opening her mouth wide as her voice echoed through the chancel, across the altar to the very rafters and beyond. She sang like an angel.

'And though worms devour my body . . .'

Connie had not sung with such freedom, such abandon, for years. Her soul felt indeed free and exalted, her body was uplifted, liberated from awkwardness and embarrassment, short-sightedness and the slight squint; above all, from the curse of perpetual shyness.

'Yet in my flesh shall I see God.'

Of course Mr Turner preferred the experienced Mrs Woodville to someone so naive and gauche. Which man of good sense would not?

Connie, once she had finished the aria, sat silently for a moment, head bent, realising she was close to tears. The rain had started to thud on the roof, and the inside of the church grew dark. It was also very cold. Yet for that moment she *had* seen God, *had* had a vision of heaven, *had* realised that there was more to life than being a spinster of the parish, a woman meekly accepting her destiny, never to know the happiness of marital love, the fulfilment of motherhood.

She took the heavy copy of *The Creation* from the organ and, getting off her stool, walked slowly through the sanctuary and along the centre aisle of the church. Suddenly she stopped and her heart literally seemed to freeze with horror, for there, crouched at the back against the wall, lurked a man.

Aunt Vicky's warnings now came back to her: '*Never* go to the church alone when it is dark. Never . . .'

But Aunt meant at night. She would certainly never go at night. This had just been an overcast day.

Connie gazed, petrified, at the form which, like her a few minutes before, appeared to be in a trance. As he straightened up and ran his hands through his hair, she realised who it was. She breathed a sigh of relief and, as she breathed, so she blushed. The blood rose in her cheeks and flooded her face.

Thank heaven it was too dark for Carson Woodville to see her. He now came towards her and she saw that his hands were silently clapping together.

'Well done. That was *divine*, Connie. I can't tell you when I have been so moved.'

'Oh *thank* you, Carson,' Connie said diffidently. 'I don't know what made me do it. It was a sudden impulse. I thought I was alone.'

'You were,' he said. 'I was visiting the tomb of my mother and little sister Emily when I heard this heavenly sound.' Carson raised his eyes to the church roof, a hand behind his ear. 'I thought it must come from heaven. Then it began to rain and I was brought down to earth, but the wonderful sound persisted. So I took shelter inside. Do you often sing like that?'

'Never.' She shook her head violently. 'I don't know what made me do it. I sing sometimes with Aunt Vicky, or when the choir is practising and I'm playing for it; but what I did today I have never done before. I can't think what got into me.'

'Well, whatever it was, I'm glad.' Carson smiled down at her and she wished she could melt; he made her feel so inadequate, so gauche.

She was not too naive to know that Carson had a bad reputation in the neighbourhood. Any girl who saw him was warned by her parents to avoid him at all costs, and to hurry home.

He was considered a bad lot, the black sheep of the family. But she had always liked Carson. She thought he was very handsome, almost beautiful, wild-looking as she imagined Heathcliff must have been; and yet she discerned an air of melancholy in him, of which others appeared not to be aware. She remembered him at his mother's funeral, and as she was motherless herself she knew just how sad and bereft he really was.

It seemed curious that she, Connie Yetman, could understand Carson Woodville so well, yet she could; she did. She felt a sense of hero-worship for him, as the comparison with Heathcliff already showed.

Carson opened the door and they looked out onto the sodden scene. The wind had risen and the rain lashed the stone of the church like a curtain.

'Well,' Carson said, 'we shall have to stay here until it stops, Connie.'

'My aunt will be worried,' Connie fretted. 'She'll wonder if I'm all right.'

'Would you like me to run ahead and tell her where you are, and that you're all right? I could even bring you back an umbrella and escort you home.'

'Oh Carson, how kind. How very, *very* kind.'

He was really like a knight in shining armour.

Carson really *was* kind. Miss Fairchild shared Connie's opinion. In the pouring rain he had run all the way for an umbrella and then had escorted her home. He had also taken a mackintosh and a pair of galoshes. People said a lot of bad things about him, but he was a gentleman. For himself he had no thought at all, and arrived soaking wet; the two ladies had fussed over him, divesting him of his jacket and insisting that he cover his shoulders with a blanket as he sat in front of the fire, drinking hot tea.

Miss Fairchild had shared the common opinion of Carson

Woodville as some kind of villain. But every time she'd encountered him – and it was true these occasions were few – he had been quite charming. He had been attentive and polite, and now he had gone out of his way again to assist Connie.

Connie couldn't do enough for her deliverer. She made sure he was as near to the fire as he could get without burning himself, and she plied him with tea and hot muffins. Miss Fairchild noticed how animated and confident Constance appeared to be in his presence. So far there had not been a single blush.

'How opportune you happened to be in church,' Miss Fairchild murmured, pouring fresh tea into his cup. 'Are you a worshipper, Carson?'

Now it was Carson who blushed.

'Not what you would call a *regular* worshipper, Miss Fairchild, although, of course, I accompany my father to church, which he attends more regularly now that George's widow is living with us.'

'And how *is* dear Sophie?' Miss Fairchild asked with concern. 'I seem to see her so infrequently.'

'Sophie is very well,' Carson said. 'I think she likes living with us, and we certainly like having her. It is good to have a woman there again. The house is almost as it was when dear Mama was alive. In fact I was visiting our family vault today when the heavens opened, and for that reason I had to seek shelter in the church. That was my real reason for being there. And how lucky I was,' he turned to the girl beside him and smiled, 'for the church was suddenly filled with the most wonderful song, as though the heavens had opened. I couldn't believe it . . .'

'And it was *Constance* singing?' Miss Fairchild opened her eyes wide with pleasure.

'Like a lark. Its beauty reminded me of my Mama, and of dear Emily and George in heaven. I could have wept.' And he brushed a hand across his eyes as though there were, indeed, tears.

'Oh, you poor boy,' Miss Fairchild cried solicitously. 'You have been bereaved, Carson, haven't you? Your mother and brother dying so soon after each other, and dear little Emily . . . well, we all recall that tragedy.

'Now,' she said, suddenly practical, 'we are getting a little morbid. There's no need for it, as they are with God. We mustn't allow our love and concern for the dead to spoil this occasion of having you for tea. You must come and see us more often, Carson,' she went on. 'That's, if you like.'

She sounded as if she thought it doubtful a young man like Carson would enjoy the company of two single ladies.

'I should like that, Miss Fairchild.' Carson appeared enthusiastic as he accepted another muffin smothered in butter and honey from the tender hands of Connie. 'However, we might be moving . . .'

'*Moving* . . .' Miss Fairchild said shrilly. 'Moving, did you say?'

'I did.' Carson sank his teeth into the muffin.

'You don't mean, moving from Pelham's Oak?'

'Yes.' Carson wiped his lips on his white linen napkin.

'But the Woodvilles have lived there for centuries.'

'True.' Carson dabbed a spot of honey from his chin and wiped each finger carefully. 'The first Woodville lived there in the time of Queen Elizabeth, as Father never tires of telling us.'

'Is Sir Guy tired of living there, then? Surely it's your birthright, Carson? You are the heir?'

'I don't have much say in the matter, Miss Fairchild, to be frank. My mother's death has left us unexpectedly impoverished. It is not as she would have wished, we're sure; but the Heerings have always been rather mean-minded. They are business people, you know, who think of little else but money. While Mama was alive there was plenty, but on her death it reverted to her family.'

'Nothing for you?'

'Nothing at all, except some bequests of a personal nature. Naturally, she thought we were taken care of financially.'

'What a dreadful story.' Miss Fairchild, amazed, sat back and gazed at Connie.

'It is. My father is a broken man. He has no stomach to fight or argue with the Heerings. They are too clever. He has been offered a farmhouse on the estate, quite large, but rather than demean himself he is considering living abroad. Italy perhaps. The income from what he will get for the estate will be ample for his needs.'

'And what of you, Carson?' Miss Fairchild, still startled, gazed at him thoughtfully.

'I shall probably go abroad too, Miss Fairchild, and try my luck overseas. Or I may go to London and look for work.' Sadly he shook his head. 'There will be nothing left for me to do here.'

12

For Eliza, the news about the possible disposal of Pelham's Oak to a gentleman from the City, a *nouveau riche* with no association with the neighbourhood, was almost as much a blow as it was for her brother and nephew. She had been born at Pelham's Oak, and the shock was more bitter for being learned in a roundabout way when she visited Lally after Prosper's departure for London in the New Year.

Lally had brought her adopted baby, Alexander, to Dorset, thus sentencing herself to a life in the countryside she professed to dislike so much. Despite his acquiescence, the adoption had provoked a rupture in her relationship with Prosper, who felt she preferred the baby to him. He had come down for Christmas, but Roger spent the festive season with the Hills, and for Prosper and Lally, despite dinners and parties, and presents galore, it had not been the same.

Eliza had been puzzled by Lally's behaviour, but she respected it. She did not know that Roger was Lally's son – the secret had been kept from almost everyone – and she thought it was because she had no children of her own. She admired her for what she had done, and went to see her and keep her company often. Eliza's generous heart always went out to people who performed acts of personal courage, and she knew that the adoption of Alexander had caused a crisis in Lally's relationship with her beloved husband.

'Of course we were too close,' Lally confided to Eliza, who had driven over to see her. 'Prosper allowed nothing to come between us. He was jealous of Roger, and I should have realised how he would feel about Alexander. However, Christmas wasn't too bad.'

'Isn't it a little strange to adopt two children and expect your husband not to mind?' Eliza leaned forward and made baby noises at the gurgling infant. 'I can't blame you for what you did. I would have done the same myself. He is a lovely little fellow, and gets lovelier all the time.'

'Doesn't he?' Lally gazed dotingly at him. 'I love him so much and, in time, I'm sure, dearest Prosper will too. He's only a little jealous, and smothered him with presents at Christmas. It is a pity that we did not have a child of our own. That way he would have learned not to be so selfish. He is a man who from birth has always had his own way, been cosseted, deferred to, and never kept short of money. Even I at one time was a toy – ' her eyes glinted dangerously – 'until he realised there was more to me than what he admired on the surface.'

With the maximum of fuss Lally tucked the warm blanket round Alexander in his crib and then, taking Eliza's arm, walked with her to the window of the nursery. The beautiful country-side of Dorset stretched out before them with its valleys, fields and ridges tipped with stately trees. It was ideal riding country, and Dora had come over with Eliza in order to try a new pony Prosper had bought. Lally was a townswoman, nervous about country pursuits and unable to ride. Below them, now, Dora was slowly putting the pony through its paces, unaware of the two women gazing intently down at her.

'I wonder what will become of Dora?' Lally put her head on one side and gazed at Eliza. 'Are you not worried about her?'

'Because she hasn't a husband?' Eliza laughed good-humouredly. She was a woman who had kept her looks, Lally thought. Her dark hair was without a thread of silver, her skin healthy with the olive hue that gave her the look of a Spanish gypsy rather than the traditional English rose.

'I would like *my* daughter to be married if she were . . .' Lally put a finger thoughtfully to her chin '. . . let me see, how old is she now, Eliza? Twenty-six?'

'Nearly twenty-seven,' Eliza replied offhandedly. 'I assure you, Lally, I don't mind at *all*.'

'You mean, you wouldn't mind if she never married?'

'No. Why should I, so long as she's happy?'

'And Julius doesn't mind?'

'Julius is not her father,' Eliza replied. 'What Ryder would think about it I am not sure, but I think that he would probably feel the same as I do. As long as Dora is happy, that's what I care about, and she is. She loves her horses and dogs, her country pursuits.'

'Dora will be most unhappy when Pelham's Oak goes,' Lally sighed. 'She adores the stables there, as you did. But, of course, your own stables are superb, and she is welcome to come over to us as often as she wishes. Shall we go down and have a word with her?'

'I beg your pardon?' Eliza clasped Lally's arm. '*What* did you say about Pelham's Oak? I think I must have misheard.'

'Oh dear.' Lally looked crestfallen. 'I do *hope* I haven't got the wrong end of the stick; but Prosper told me that there was nothing left from Margaret's estate and he had suggested to Guy that the house should be sold.'

'He suggested to Guy? When?'

'It was just after Christmas.' Lally began to look uncomfortable. 'Oh dear, I feel I may have spoken out of turn. I assumed you knew. I was told Julius had insisted on it. That a possible purchaser was a *nouveau-riche* banker. Maybe they didn't wish to worry you . . . Eliza!' Lally called after her as, without a word, her guest hurried to the door. 'Where are you running off to?'

'To have a word with my husband,' Eliza called back angrily. 'He must be party to all this. Prosper would never have acted alone. Julius is at home at the moment, but later he leaves for the Continent . . .'

'Oh dear, I wish I hadn't . . .'

But, with a wave, Eliza was gone, and shortly after, as she walked disconsolately down the staircase, Lally heard her car purring along the drive towards the gate.

Julius Heering was a man well pleased with what life had given him. After the death of his first wife there had been a time, inevitably, of loneliness and sadness, but he had compensated for this by hard work, which in time had returned dividends.

The Martyn-Heering empire, of which he was president, was one of the largest trading concerns in Europe. It had its own fleet of ships, its own bank, and a virtual monopoly of the spice trade with the Far East. It also imported gold and silver, precious stones, and more mundane materials such as cotton, hemp, tea and animal furs.

And then, to his good fortune and joy, Eliza had come into his life – only, at the time, she was happily married. After her husband was killed in an accident he had to wait a few years more and then, finally, obtained his heart's desire and made her his wife.

After that, his cup was full. He had three step-children whom he liked, three step-grandchildren, and a beautiful house, Upper Park, with extensive gardens and greenhouses. As he grew older and could relax the burdens of high office, Julius became more and more fond of horticulture and began to specialise in the cultivation of rare botanical specimens, most of which came from the East and had to be cared for under glass.

Thus most days of the week when he was at home Julius could be found in one of his heated greenhouses, lovingly tending his delicate, unique plants, many of which were brought over by his ships after being traced by overseas specialists constantly on the lookout for him.

London had not the fascination for Eliza that it had for Lally, so there was no Heering town house. When he was there alone, Julius stayed at his club, and when they were together they stayed at a hotel, usually the Carlton in the Haymarket or Claridges in Brook Street.

Julius was busy in his greenhouse when he saw the car, with Dora at the wheel, come up the drive. He gave a grunt of pleasure and, putting the species he was attempting to propagate to one side and collecting his pipe, went to the door of the greenhouse and waved; but they didn't see him. They were in earnest conversation and Eliza, in particular, seemed agitated about something.

Julius stood at the door, lighting his pipe. He never hurried.

He thought it was unlike Eliza to seem so excited. After an impetuous youth she was the calmest, most philosophical of women; he prided himself, in fact, that she had grown to be almost as phlegmatic as a Dutchwoman. He strolled along the path towards the lawn in front of the house, by which time Eliza had seen him and hurried over to him.

'Julius!' she called when she was still a way off. 'I want a word with you, urgently, if you please.'

'Certainly, my dear,' he said and, as she approached him, he attempted to encircle her waist with his free arm, but she brushed it away.

'Not here, please, Julius! Let's go inside. It's freezing.'

She then hurried ahead of him while Dora, poised still at the wheel of the car, watched them.

'Dora drives well?' Julius asked, attempting to catch Eliza up.

'Very well.'

'I must buy her a car of her own.'

Eliza said nothing, but rushed up the steps of the house and into the hall, where a footman was waiting to take her coat and hat.

'And please bring some coffee into the drawing-room,' she instructed him.

She then turned her attention to Julius, who was gazing at her in some bewilderment. Dressed in his gardening clothes, with his old pipe in his mouth, his grizzled Dutch features making him seem cold and remote, he could have passed for the gardener. His pipe was now cold and, sticking it in his pocket, he ambled after his wife, who was standing by the fire, her hands outstretched towards the flames.

'Goodness, it *is* cold, even for the time of year,' she said, glancing up as he came towards her.

'How was Lally? You look terribly upset. Something wrong?'

'There *is* something wrong,' she replied acidly, 'but not with Lally or the baby. It's what *I* heard there today, Julius, that made me hurry back to see you.'

'And what is that, my dear?' He didn't try to touch her again, but eased himself into a chair and began to take off his boots, which were dry but dusty.

'I have heard that Prosper has suggested to Guy, at your insistence, that he puts Pelham's Oak on the market. If so, you must deliberately have concealed this from me. Please tell me I am wrong, Julius?'

For a moment or two Julius said nothing, but went on easing his boots from his feet. When that was done he wriggled his toes in his hand-knitted grey socks and then he reached slowly for his pipe again, like a baby reaching for its comforter. This delaying procedure always irritated Eliza but with difficulty she restrained her impatience.

'In a *way* you are wrongly informed, Eliza.' He looked up at her at last. 'I do know, but I have not *insisted* Guy sell the house. I didn't mention it to you because nothing is settled.'

'Well, thank heaven for that.' Eliza relaxed and gave a sigh of relief as the footman came in with a silver coffee-pot on a tray. A maid followed behind with cups, biscuits on a plate, cream and a bowl of sugar.

'Just put it down, I'll see to it, thank you.' Eliza dismissed the servants with a smile which vanished as soon as they had left the room, and then she went to the table to pour.

'Coffee, Julius?'

'I think I'll have a schnapps,' he said. 'I feel I may need it.' And, rising, he went over to the table where a range of bottles bore witness to his catholicity of taste; but chief among his favourites was Dutch sloe gin which was brewed by an offshoot of the Heerings in Holland.

'Now, *if* you'd kindly explain, Julius,' Eliza said, sitting down. She wore a cardigan-suit and sensible shoes, as she had thought that she and Dora might take a walk. Despite what she told Lally, she was a little worried about Dora's future. For a woman, even a wealthy one, spinsterhood was a bleak prospect, and Dora was not wealthy. Everything she had she got from Julius. Eliza watched her husband over the rim of the cup, observing that he'd helped himself to quite a generous measure of the Dutch fire-water.

The unease she'd felt all the way home recurred.

'My dear.' Julius sat down again and stretched his feet in

front of him, wriggling his toes. 'I think you know that when my sister married your brother, he had no money.'

'Of course I know it,' she snapped.

'He had none at all, and there was the possibility *then* that the house might have to be sold.'

'It *was* considered, I believe.'

'Margaret brought a fortune to the Woodville family, and over the years Guy got through every penny.'

'Oh, that's not *fair*,' Eliza protested, placing her coffee cup on a table and getting up. 'The money went on the estate. On their children . . .'

'*And* on Guy's other interests. I won't specify them.'

'Such as?' Eliza raised her eyebrows but Julius shook his head.

'I'd prefer not to say. But for years Guy got through an enormous amount of money. However . . .'

Julius, looking as though he was recovering his confidence, began to light his long Dutch pipe and sucked away at it for a time.

'Before George was born, and after he realised what sort of man Guy was – that is, an irresponsible spendthrift – my father in his wisdom restructured Margaret's financial status. He was helped by the eventual passage in England of the Married Woman's Property Act, which enabled her to keep her own fortune. Only, in the settlement, my father arranged matters so that, in the event that Margaret should die before Guy, which seemed possible as she was older, her estate would revert to the Heerings who, of course, would see to the welfare of the children should they not have grown up. After the age of twenty-one they were deemed old enough to be on their own, although each would inherit a little money when they came of age.

'And that, my dear, is what has happened. Guy is free of debt, thanks to Margaret, but I understand he has no capital, no investments and no savings. His debts will mount again. Carson, as you know, we tried to help, but instead of gratitude he attempted to steal from our company; bite the generous hands that had fed him.'

'I never believed that,' Eliza said indignantly. 'My nephew's no thief.'

'The evidence was pretty damning, I'm afraid. He was very lucky we didn't prosecute him. It was only because he was family that we didn't.'

'There *is* a hard side to you, Julius,' Eliza said slowly, gazing at him. 'I'm only beginning to see it now.'

'Please don't think that, my dear.' Julius lowered his voice. 'I am not a hard man, you of all people should know that; but I am a man of business. I am responsible for a great deal of other people's money and I also have a duty to the Heerings who, unlike the Woodvilles, have always husbanded their money and conducted their financial affairs with wisdom and acumen. In fact they do not need all the money that reverts to them from the death of our dear sister; but I have no intention of letting Guy have it. It will go to many deserving charities.'

With that, he joined his hands across his stomach and, pipe still in his mouth, puffed defiantly away, staring at Eliza as if to challenge her to argue with him. After a moment's contemplation she rose from her chair and wandered across the gracious, elegant room, pausing every now and then to finger the various ornaments and *objets d'art* scattered on the tables. None of them had been hers. None of *this* was hers. Occasionally she felt like a visitor.

'Guy does not deserve this, Julius,' she said at last, turning to him.

'And why not, pray?'

'Because he has never understood money. He left that to you and Prosper, and he trusted you.'

'My dear, we made it very clear over the years that Margaret's money was not *Guy's*. In the beginning it was, but not for long. The Act changed all that. I agree that as he got older he settled down and spent less; but he had still wasted a fortune, and would have gone on wasting it, as far as I can see, throwing most of it away, probably on that good-for-nothing Carson. Prosper was good enough to suggest that Carson should think of joining the army. He is an adventurous lad, a wonderful horseman. He has some assets, and was clearly not cut out to be a banker.

We would have bought him a commission and helped him to settle. And what did he say?'

'He said "no", I suppose,' Eliza observed with a slight smile. 'I can't really see Carson settling to the life of a soldier.'

'Well, that is his affair.' Julius shrugged. 'Frankly, I can't see him settling to anything, whereas Roger . . .' Julius paused and began to pack more tobacco into the bowl of his pipe. '*Roger* is to be made a junior partner on his marriage. Roger is the complete opposite of Carson. He is hard-working, polite, truthful, loyal. He has a touch of genius when it comes to business, and he doesn't like to spend his time thwarting and opposing people. He is to marry a *very* nice girl of whom we all approve, and who is also, incidentally, an heiress. You could hardly have two more different men.'

'Roger and Carson are different, but I think you're straying away from the point, Julius. That is, I am most disturbed about what is to happen to my brother, every bit as much as I am about losing our family home. In your own logical, unemotional Dutch way it all sounds very reasonable, no doubt. But for me, to see my brother – who, in the end, loved your sister and appreciated everything she had done for him – in *this* situation . . . It's terrible. His nerves are weak. He is not a well man, and I think the shock of disposing of the family home might kill him.'

'Well, I don't.' Julius stood up and went and helped himself to more schnapps. 'I think Guy is very hardy, and Carson likewise. You are over-indulgent about your brother, and most of what is wrong with him is the consequence of drinking too much, a failing he has never succeeded in curing himself of. Many families who do not husband their wealth, or extend it in some way, have to give up something. The Woodvilles have no "divine right" to keep Pelham's Oak if they cannot afford it.'

'But a Woodville, one of my ancestors, *built* it.'

'I see the family pride is still very strong in you, my dear,' Julius sighed. 'Well, I'm very sorry. I truly am.'

'Of course it's strong in me.' Eliza walked restlessly over to him and stood in front of him, hands on her hips. 'I *am* a

Woodville, Pelham's Oak is my birthplace. I believe you are to offer it to some member of the newly rich, some crony of yours, doubtless, who will use it to flaunt his wealth.'

'I do not know who will be the ultimate purchaser of Pelham's Oak,' Julius said loftily. 'Nor have I any interest in the matter; but if he is "new" money, what is wrong with that? The Martyns *and* the Heerings were once new money, and so, even if it was very long ago, were the Woodvilles, ennobled for mercenary service to the king.

'What is wrong with money honestly made with honest toil? If a man wants to use it to improve his status, by all means let him. Many in this country have done so. I have time for them; but none at all for the decayed members of the aristocracy who rest on laurels they never earned themselves, and spend fortunes they no longer have.'

Then, beginning to look as annoyed as his wife, Julius stalked from the room.

The Woodville girls were the pride and joy of their doting grandfather. They were taught at home by their mother, but the time was soon approaching when they would have to go to school. There were a number of good schools in the area, but the distance even then was several miles each way every day, and a decision would have to be made about sending them eventually to boarding-school.

Guy couldn't bear to think about this, and Sophie was reluctant too. The children had had a number of changes in their young lives and who could tell what effect these would have on them? It was true that, for them and for her, the months they had spent at Pelham's Oak had so far been the happiest since the death of George. At last they felt settled and secure, and there were the attractions of a large house with plenty of space to move about in after the cramped, spartan quarters of the mission house, or the tiny cottage in Wenham next to the church with no bathroom and an outside lavatory.

But more than this was the happiness of living in the house where George, husband and father, had been born, and which, had he lived, he would have inherited. That now would fall to Carson, but Sophie accepted the plan, the will of God, and had no unchristian sense of jealousy or envy. She felt that, until such time as Guy died, she would be happy in Pelham's Oak.

She had a bedroom and sitting-room on the first floor. Next to her were the children's rooms – they had the luxury of one each – and the room for their nursemaid. Then there was the schoolroom, freshly painted primrose. At the end of the corridor was Guy's room and study, and on the next floor Carson's. The servants occupied quarters in the attic, except for the groomsmen and gardeners who slept in outbuildings above the stables.

Sophie relished her role as housekeeper, and she was good at it. She was thorough and meticulous, used to giving orders and being obeyed, but in a way that was not obnoxious to the servants. She was pleasant, without allowing them to think of her as an equal. For all that, she was not very popular; she was too exact and exacting. In many ways she was herself a worthy successor to Margaret who, had she overcome her prejudice while she was alive, would have deeply approved of her daughter-in-law.

And what of Mr Turner? The more Sophie settled in at Pelham's Oak, the less did he consider his chances. His trump card had been that she had need of him, but now that was true no longer. He continued to call and hope, but his hopes appeared to have waned.

Hubert Turner was a man almost weighed down by goodness. He was so nice and so good, so correct about everything that he could have been an obnoxious bore, the tedious sort of person that people avoid.

But no one did; everyone liked him and sought his company. He was not boring; he was jolly and intelligent, an active type who even played football.

However, it was not surprising that his nature, together with an overwhelming appreciation of the presence of God, had decided him from youth to be a priest. It was a decision he had never regretted.

Hubert was the child of rich and indulgent parents, the only son in a family of five daughters, and on the death of his father he inherited everything, as was normal. This did nothing to hinder his vocation, except to render him the antithesis of the impoverished clergyman of fiction. If he had a weakness – for it could not be called a vice – it was that he liked the good things of life.

He liked fine food, vintage wines, Gothic churches, and the comfort of grand hotels on his many holidays abroad. Above all, he appreciated beautiful women, though he had never had a love-affair or ever been in love.

Because he was a parson, and Connie Yetman was deeply religious, it was thought that they would suit. Yet this was far from being the case. On the contrary, Hubert Turner did not admire shy spinsters like Connie, but striking women with minds all their own, and as soon as he met Sophie he was attracted by her. As well as her physical good-looks, he was attracted by her age and experience; but above all, perhaps, by the fact that she'd been married.

Sophie sat at her desk in her sitting-room, from which she conducted the affairs of the large house. She was thinking of undertaking a complete process of redecoration, and had been in consultation over this matter with the bailiff, a man with whom she sometimes crossed swords as their paths overlapped. Invariably in their battles, she won.

She looked at her watch and saw that it was nearly time for tea, which she usually took with her father-in-law, either alone or with Carson. The children had nursery tea and then spent an hour in their grandfather's company before going to bed.

Sophie finished making the neat list of questions she wished to discuss with Ivor Wendor, the bailiff, and then looked around her pretty room with a deep sense of satisfaction. This had once been Eliza's room, and was at the end of the house with a view across the fields to Wenham. The lights were beginning to come on in the little town, and the landscape had that crepuscular aspect of mist and shadows that was somehow inviting and mysterious, but made one grateful at the same time to be indoors.

She had had the room, and the bedroom next door, decorated to her own taste when she moved in, with pretty wallpaper and cretonnes. It had an open fire and two easy chairs on either side, a table, and the desk at which she worked. On the wall was a bookcase full of her own books, mostly works of devotion. Many of them had once belonged to George, and in them he had inscribed his name. There was, in addition, a *prie-dieu* where she knelt every night and morning to say her prayers, usually with the children, but sometimes to meditate on her own.

That strong and abiding sense of God that had sent her to the far-off mission fields had been sorely tested, but had never completely left her.

She rose from her desk, her notes in her hand, and switched off the main light, leaving the lamp burning on her desk. Before she left she drew the heavy velvet curtains and placed a guard round the fire; then she went out of the door and along the corridor to peep into the playroom, where nursery tea was in progress. The nursemaid got up and bobbed, and Ruth and Deborah also rose, greeting their mother respectfully.

'Please sit down, dears, and get on with your tea,' Sophie called out. 'I am going to see Grandpapa, after which you may come down and play with him for a while. I believe he has a nice story to read to you tonight.'

'Oh Mama, may we have Jonah and the *whale* again,' Deborah called out excitedly, clasping her hands, while Ruth shook her head just as emphatically but had difficulty in getting out the name of the story she wanted.

Sophie smiled at the nursemaid and gently closed the door, walking to the head of the stairs, where she paused a minute, looking around as if to savour the feeling of the house, the particular thrill it gave her.

Pelham's Oak, home of the Woodvilles for nearly three centuries. Yes, she did belong here very bit as much as the children. It was their home, and now it was hers too.

When she reached the drawing-room, Guy was already helping himself to tea.

'I'm sorry I'm a little late, Father,' she said, closing the door and, going up to him, kissed him lightly on the top of the head.

Guy was an affectionate man, as she had discovered soon after she had taken up residence. He liked to touch, to kiss and be kissed. He loved fondling his grandchildren, sitting them on his knees and patting their chubby legs.

Sophie, brought up by undemonstrative parents, was normally reserved in her show of affection; but in her desire to please Guy and be accepted by him she had overcome this, and now found it quite instinctive to respond warmly to her father-in-law, and she had quickly agreed to his suggestion that she refer to him as 'Father'.

Guy had once been a handsome man, but he was so no longer. He was overweight, and the self-indulgence he had enjoyed all his life showed only too plainly. But he was a lovable man; in Sophie's opinion, a good man; and in the time she had lived here, not only had she become fond of him but she thought her feelings were reciprocated.

She too helped herself to tea, selected a cake and went over to the fire, drawing up her chair opposite Guy.

'Is Carson not joining us today, Father?' she asked, raising her cup to her lips.

'Carson has gone to Blandford,' Guy replied. 'He has to see about something. I'm not sure what . . .'

'Father.' Sophie leaned over and passed him her list. 'I thought we should start to think about redecorating the house. Some of the paint is actually peeling in the ballroom. I . . .'

Guy showed no interest in her list, took it from her but didn't even glance at it.

'Later, dear,' he muttered, and put it on the table by his side.

'But it *is* important, Father. You don't want . . .'

'My dear Sophie, I have a lot of things to think of at the moment. Redecoration is the least of them.'

There was something about the tone of his voice – a truculence, an irritation – that disturbed her deeply and, putting her cup and saucer down, she attempted to retrieve the list so that it didn't get buried under a mass of papers, pipes and tobacco pouches, and all the paraphernalia with which Guy liked to surround himself.

'Are you not *well*, Father?' she asked anxiously. 'You don't seem yourself. Should I call Dr Hardy?'

Guy passed a hand wearily over his brow, and she could see the pain in his face.

'Sophie, Dr Hardy can do nothing for what ails me.'

'Then can *I* help?'

He looked across at her and reached for her hand. 'My sweet girl, my dear daughter-in-law, how truly fond I am of you. How good you are to me, and what a misfortune it was that my dear Margaret was unable to appreciate your goodness.'

At the mention of Margaret's name his eyes once again filled with tears and, extracting a handkerchief from a pocket, he began to dab at them. Today, however, his sorrow seemed deeper than usual; there were real, prolonged tears, and Sophie sought desperately to think of a reason for his melancholy. Relatively speaking, he was a young man; but he had not taken care of himself and had allowed himself to age. Sometimes he looked as old as the Rector of Wenham, who was twenty years his senior.

'I do feel there is something wrong, Father.'

'Yes, there is.' He ponderously nodded his head. 'But nothing, alas, that you can do anything about.'

'But could you not tell me?' By now she was thoroughly anxious. 'Is something else amiss with Carson?'

'Oh no,' Guy managed a smile, 'that dear boy is a much reformed character, intent on helping his papa as much as he can. However – ' Guy dabbed at his eyes again ' – I fear it is too late. Much too late.'

Suddenly there was a disturbance in the hall, the sound of doors opening and closing, and voices.

'I think Carson has returned.' Sophie raised her head, but when the door opened it was Eliza who stood on the threshold, in the act of drawing off her gloves.

'Eliza!' Guy said, struggling to sit upright in the chair into which he had slumped. 'My dear, what . . .?'

'I came as soon as I could, Guy.' Eliza rapidly crossed the room. She still had on her coat and hat, and a footman hovered uncertainly at the door. She paused to greet Sophie, then she called out to the footman to shut the door.

'But your coat, madam?'

'I'll keep it on for the moment, until I get warm,' she said. 'I shan't be staying long.' Then she turned to Guy while removing her hat, and threw it on the sofa.

'Why did you not tell *me*, Guy?'

'Tell you? Tell you what?' Guy looked puzzled.

'About the house. I only heard today, a few hours ago, in fact. I came straightaway.'

'The house? *This* house?' Sophie sat upright in her chair. 'Something has happened about the house?'

'Oh, so you don't know either?' Eliza sank to her knees beside Guy. 'Why do you keep these things to yourself, Guy? Sophie is here to help you. *I* am here to help you. We are the people you love and who love you. Why not confide in us?'

'Confide. Confide what?' Sophie, seriously alarmed, stood up. 'Will you have tea, Eliza?'

'I'd love a cup,' Eliza replied. 'It is absolutely freezing in that motor, even with a rug over one's knees.'

'Did you drive yourself?' Guy looked doubtfully out of the window. 'It's pitch dark.'

'No, my chauffeur brought me. He knows the way blindfold. He is now in the kitchen, getting some warm tea inside him. Thank you,' she said, taking the cup and saucer from Sophie. 'I'm absolutely *incensed* by what I heard, Guy. I had to come and see you at once.'

She looked across at Sophie, who appeared to be at a loss and stood gazing at her.

'I'm sorry, Sophie. You must be bewildered. Naturally, I thought you knew.'

'I know nothing except that Father is obviously very unhappy, and has been for some days. I wondered if he were unwell . . .'

'Guy has been advised to sell Pelham's Oak,' Eliza said. 'Margaret's will left him nothing . . .'

'I cannot believe it.' Sophie sat down quickly again.

'Pelham's Oak, our home for three centuries,' Guy intoned. 'Carson's inheritance. It is all he has, poor boy.'

'There is nothing for the upkeep.' Eliza perched on the arm of Guy's chair and put her arm around his neck.

'But *I* thought this family was very wealthy,' Sophie stammered. 'I was about to bring up again the question of a suitable memorial to George.' She stressed the word 'suitable' in case Eliza remembered that the deconsecrated chapel had not been considered suitable.

'The family *is* very wealthy,' Guy stuttered. 'The Heerings and the Martyns are millionaires many times over; but I, a close relation, am a pauper, and they make sure they let me know it. I was raised a gentleman and I have remained one. I could never stoop to commerce, whereas they thrive on it.' He raised his eyes with an expression of distaste.

'It's absolutely *monstrous*.' Eliza bent to kiss his cheek. 'I had sharp words with Julius today.'

'And what did he say?' Guy looked hopefully at her.

'I saw a Julius I never saw before.' There was a note of sadness in Eliza's voice. 'I saw a man who has made a fortune in the City several times over; but I also saw a man lacking in compassion, who was a stranger to me: a stranger *and* a disappointment.'

'He gave you no hope?' Guy shook his head.

'I haven't finished with him, nor have I begun on Prosper Martyn,' Eliza said spiritedly, and then she paused. 'But I don't hold out very much hope. The trust was drawn up by Julius and Margaret's father Willem who, as you know, thought you spent too much money when you were young, Guy. He said you dissipated Margaret's fortune. He didn't want that to happen again. I am sure he didn't *mean* to leave you without the means to live or maintain the house after his death. After all, your children were *his* grandchildren too. And I am quite, quite sure that Margaret wouldn't have wanted it.'

'Margaret would have been horrified,' Guy said. 'She loved Pelham's Oak and wanted it for this family, her family.'

Sophie had listened carefully, her expression one of intense shock.

'And can *nothing* be done?'

'Well, obviously we have not exhausted all possibilities.' But Eliza's expression was not hopeful. 'I do believe my husband to be adamant. He and Prosper have obviously thought the whole matter over very carefully. It is not an impulsive, ill-considered act; nothing they do ever is. Had Carson proved more satisfactory in the business . . . Unfortunately,' she bit her lower lip, 'not only was he *not* a success, but they believe that he was a thief.'

'I do *not* believe that,' Guy said firmly. 'Carson, a foolish boy in many ways, is *not* a thief. No Woodville is a thief. The idea is scandalous. Someone wanted to get rid of Carson and manufactured evidence against him. Some clerk, somebody who wanted to better himself no doubt, or who was jealous of Carson's family connections. That's what he thinks, and I agree. A proper enquiry should have been instituted, but the Heerings and Prosper Martyn were too eager to think ill of my boy.' Sadly he shook his head. 'It hastened Margaret's end. I am quite sure of that.'

'They think there is no future in Pelham's Oak with Carson either,' Eliza said. 'They know Guy has never been interested in estate management, and Carson will be no better.'

'But Ivor is an excellent bailiff,' Sophie exclaimed. 'I do battle with him, but it is only in your interests. If anything can work, he will make it work.'

'But it is not the same as capital – ' Guy looked sadly at her ' – and we have none; no savings, nothing. The kitty is empty.'

'All they have is the house – ' Eliza nodded in Sophie's direction ' – and many acres of land, the farms and cottages on the estate. When realised, the sum will be sufficient to keep Guy in comfort well into his old age and maybe leave something for Carson too . . .'

Sophie suddenly proceeded to the fireplace and remained there for some time, gazing thoughtfully down at the flames.

'And what of me?' She did not look round. 'Me and my children? We did not ask to come here, we were asked. Shall we so soon be made homeless again?'

Eliza went up to her and slid an arm round her waist.

'Dear Sophie, you are *so* good and kind. You have been unlucky, and also badly used. I am sure there will be money put aside for you, enough for a little house. But you see, I myself have no money. Julius is most generous with me and I want for nothing, but he gives me an allowance which is sufficient for clothes and my small personal needs. Anything larger I have to ask him for. It would be gladly given, but it would never be enough to keep Guy.'

'Of course, I am not his family,' Sophie said with a note of bitterness. 'I am only a Woodville by marriage. I am the daughter of a clergyman who has only ever had enough for his own needs.'

'We will always look after you,' Eliza assured her. 'A house will be found for you on the estate.'

'Is that fair to the wife and children of the man who would have succeeded his father had he lived?' Sophie protested. 'Is it proper?'

'My dear, we all have to make sacrifices.' Guy's voice had begun to tremble. 'Besides, it has not yet happened. Carson has gone to Blandford to see a man who might be able to assist us.'

'Assist? How?' Eliza opened her eyes wide.

'He is a money-lender of some description . . .'

'No!' Eliza thumped the table next to her. 'You must *not* borrow money. With no income, you will never be able to repay it. You must keep out of the hands of money-lenders . . .'

'*And* sell the house?'

'I will talk to my husband again. I will talk to Prosper. I will do what I can. However . . .' she reached out a hand towards Guy, who clasped hers '. . . however, I must tell you that I don't hold out much hope. Business is business, and when it comes to figures the Martyns and Heerings have few human sympathies. I know that now.'

13

Roger sat in the gracious drawing-room where he had first been introduced to Prosper and, indeed, his whole new life at the age of twelve, thirteen years before. After a brief fit of pique, when Lally revealed she was his mother, he had taken a flat in Pimlico, but he soon moved back. By now he was used to servants and the pleasure of being looked after. In a bachelor flat he missed too many of the good things in life to which he had become accustomed.

He had now lived in the house in Montagu Square for longer than he'd lived in the small, overcrowded house in Kentish Town, but he still dreamed about the place, and his memories of it were as vivid as when he had been that small urchin boy who wiped his nose on the back of his finger.

Thirteen years – and now that same undernourished scrap of a boy was on the verge of being made a junior partner in a firm of international stature and reputation, about to be married to a girl whose father was a knight and an admiral.

Roger wore a grey suit made by Prosper's Saville Row tailors, a blue shirt from a shop in Jermyn Street, and a pearl-grey tie with a pearl tie-pin his mother had given him for his twenty-first birthday. He looked, and he felt, the quintessential young man about town; only he was more. He was a businessman who was not only the heir to a fortune – two, if one counted that of his wife – but he was in line to succeed Prosper and Julius as head of the huge Martyn-Heering combine. He had specialised in finance, the purchase of bonds and the transfer of stocks and shares; he was an acknowledged expert in the Far Eastern money market. Quite an achievement for a man whose formal education had not begun until he was twelve. Life, indeed, looked very rosy. Or rather, it *should* have looked rosy.

On his lap was the cat Coral, who had first welcomed him when he had come to Montagu Square. In the imperious way that cats have, her greeting had at first been rather frosty, as though she sensed that his dubious origins meant he had possibly more in common with an alley cat than with a well-bred tabby such as herself.

But after that, love had grown, and from being Lally's cat Coral became exclusively Roger's, utterly and completely devoted to him. His solely, to spoil and love.

Coral was now an old cat who had all the grace and dignity of a dowager. She came down the stairs with caution, as though a touch of arthritis had begun to stiffen her bones. Sometimes she had to be helped onto Roger's knee, her spring not quite what it was. But her silky, lustrous coat, lovingly tended by Roger, was just the same, and that look of disdain in her eyes only turned to hero-worship when she gazed at Roger.

Roger's long hand lay on Coral's back and he was murmuring to her in the language only they understood, when the door opened and Prosper came in, a bundle of letters in his hand.

'Ah, Roger.' His eyes lit up with pleasure. 'I wanted to talk to you, my dear boy.'

'Yes, Uncle.' Roger, with his hand still on Coral, gazed imperturbably at him.

'The rehearsal for the wedding.' Prosper sat opposite his nephew and consulted a paper in his hand. 'It is scheduled for next Tuesday, but that is the day we have called the board-meeting to have you elected a partner. Now, which is the more important? Which shall we change?'

'Change the rehearsal,' Roger said without hesitation, picking up Coral and giving her a hug, whereupon he placed her tenderly in the centre of the sofa. He then went over to the fireplace and gazed at himself in the large ornate mirror over the mantelpiece, stroking the silky moustache he had recently grown.

In the background, Prosper chuckled.

'First things first, eh? Business before pleasure.'

'Oh definitely, Uncle. Call the rehearsal for the morning and the board-meeting for the afternoon.'

'There will be a lunch.' Prosper frowned at the cat, who had started scratching the sofa. 'I think the board-meeting in the morning, then lunch. The rehearsal, perhaps, the following day. Would you see if it will suit Emma?'

'Oh, it will suit her,' Roger said casually, gazing at Coral.

'I wish you'd stop allowing that cat to scratch the furniture, Roger,' his uncle said a little testily. 'That sofa is Pompadour.'

'That's why she likes it,' Roger said, going across to unfasten the cat's claws, then returning to the mirror to continue his self-appraisal. 'She has such good taste.'

'Now then, Roger.' Prosper gave a slightly nervous laugh. 'I wish your mother would take the damn thing to Dorset, together with that wretched baby . . .'

'Come, come, Uncle.' Roger looked at him with raised eyebrows. 'In the first place, Coral is *mine*, and she will come with me to Eaton Square. And "wretched" baby . . . really, Uncle. How *can* you say that of your adopted son?'

'Your mother is quite absurd.' Prosper's tone was churlish. 'How do we know where it comes from? What its antecedents are? It might have inherited defects. How can we tell?'

'Well, it *seems* perfectly healthy.' Roger languidly ran a finger along his fine blond moustache. Yes, he thought, it gave him character, made him look older, sagacious and responsible. It would be sure to impress the board.

'How does Emma like your moustache?' Prosper looked with interest at Roger's face in the mirror.

'Who knows?'

'Haven't you asked her?'

'Why should I?' Roger seemed surprised by the question. 'Whether I have a moustache or not has nothing to do with Emma. Frankly, *I* rather like it.'

Prosper crossed one leg over the other. He too was in grey, but wore a winged collar and cravat, and a double-breasted waistcoat with his morning-coat. He was a Victorian, and still wore formal dress to the office.

'Roger, far be it from me to ask,' he began diffidently, 'but when I was first in love with your mother I was most concerned to know what she thought about me. Indeed I still am. Are you sure of your affections for Emma?'

Roger finished his self-inspection in a leisurely manner and then, turning to face Prosper, put his hands in his pockets.

'And if I am not? After all, it was you who practically forced the engagement on me.'

'I was merely asking. It is not a good thing to marry someone one does not love. There is no need for it. In your case, none at all. I imagined you needed a little push; there was no force, I assure you. But if you are not in love, do not love her *at all*, it can lead to all sorts of trouble later on.'

'But if I withdrew now, Uncle, would you like the publicity that a possible breach of promise case brought in the courts might cause? The cancellation of the wedding? What an uproar!'

'My dear boy,' Prosper continued in deep earnestness, 'I would prefer it to a lifetime of misery for you and for the girl, who I really like.'

'Oh, I shan't be miserable,' Roger said offhandedly. 'And I shall try not to make Emma miserable. I assure you, I shall do my best to make her happy. I think she will be – she already is. As for love . . .' he shrugged his shoulders '. . . frankly, I'm surprised you place such high store on it where marriage is concerned . . .'

'But I adored your mother . . .' Prosper protested.

'Oh, I'm not for a moment suggesting you did not. Far from it, and I believe you took your time about popping the question.' (Roger in fact knew that Prosper had lived for years with his mistress before proposing to her.) 'Yours, in fact, is one of the truly happy marriages I know, or was until the advent of Alexander which banished Mother to the country.'

Prosper put his finger to his mouth and began to gnaw a nail.

'I confess I was angry, maybe a little unjust. Your mother is the kindest of people . . . But to take an urchin off the street . . . At first I couldn't understand her.'

Roger returned to the chair facing his uncle, and Coral took a leap from the sofa onto his lap again, where she settled down happily. Once more one of Roger's long, elegant hands began rhythmically to caress her back.

'Was *I* not an urchin off the street, Uncle Prosper?'

'Certainly not,' Prosper snapped. 'You were your mother's child and she knew who you were, and had kept an eye on you.'

'After abandoning me . . .'

'She did not abandon you, Roger. I'm surprised to hear you say that. You don't know how hard those early years were for her. *She* was the one who was abandoned and at her wits' end, and she placed you with the Mountjoy family, who were known to her through her maid.'

'Her maid!' Roger said scathingly. 'And when at last she married you, why did you not take me out of that wretched place?' In the last few seconds Roger's tone had hardened.

'We did not marry for some time, Roger.' Prosper sounded nervous, as well he might, wondering how to explain a basic situation with delicacy. 'To begin with, as you know, I protected your mother . . .'

'Knowing nothing about me?'

'No.'

'So that must have been a shock?'

'It was. It was a shock.' Prosper got out his handkerchief and passed it over his upper lip with a hand that trembled slightly.

'You knew nothing about me, and yet you adopted me?'

'I knew quite a lot about you. For example, that you were Lally's son . . .' He paused. 'Roger, *why* are you putting me through all this?'

'Did you know, in that case, who my father was?'

The question was so unexpected that it took Prosper completely unawares; his mouth sagged.

'I . . . er . . .'

'You do know who my father is, don't you, Uncle Prosper?' Roger's eyes narrowed. 'He was *not* some man my mother met on the street, as has been suggested . . .'

'Oh come, that was *never* suggested.'

'Oh come,' Roger mimicked his uncle's tone, 'I know that

234

at one time my mother was no better than she should have been, no ordinary dancer . . . A prostitute, shall we say?'

'Really!' Prosper stood up and threw the letters he had retained in his hand onto a table. 'I find this conversation deeply distasteful, Roger.'

'Nevertheless – ' Roger also stood up and put his hands in his pockets, apparently still at ease ' – it is the truth, and high time we spoke of it. The trouble is that in this household there have only ever been half-truths, or downright lies. It is not "nice" to ask and, for so many years, I was so afraid of being sent back to Kentish Town that I never dared question my origins. But whatever happened made my mother feel so guilty that when she found an urchin on her doorstep, instead of packing it off to a foundlings' home as anyone else would have done, she took it in and gave it a home. Maybe the plight of baby Alexander reminded her of *me*.'

'I think it did,' Prosper murmured. 'There is no doubt that your mother was reminded of the similar situation, though in fact there was no comparison. Your father was a gentleman, there's no doubt about that, and had your mother been able to keep you she would most certainly have done so.'

'Ah!' Roger held up a hand. 'An admission. My father was "a gentleman". You know who, don't you?'

Prosper was silent.

'You do know who, Uncle Prosper,' Roger said accusingly. 'Who now *is* this fine gentleman who failed to support my mother, and thus condemned me to twelve years of poverty and deprivation when I was certainly not brought up as the son of a gentleman? Oh no. How I would like to exchange those twelve years of hardship for the life that *he* undoubtedly had. My God, if I knew who my father was now I should like to make him suffer!'

'You will not be surprised, then, that we do not tell you.'

Prosper had never seen this aspect of Roger, and he was shocked by it. All he had ever seen was a boy, then a man, who had done all he could to fit in, to conform, trying hard to please, and succeeding. Who had worked hard not only at school but in the business, where he had mastered the intricacies of money and commerce not only skilfully, but with ease. People had a high regard for his expertise.

Roger had set out to charm, and he had succeeded; to be obedient, dutiful, everything that one could expect of a son. Indeed, he had been better than most sons. It occurred to Prosper, who had never been a father, that for all those years Roger had behaved very much as though he were his son, and as the mask fell off and the bitterness was exposed, Prosper realised how insecure he really was, how much he had suffered.

Roger, clearly disturbed now by his outburst, began furiously to stroke Coral who, unperturbed by the commotion, settled herself more comfortably on his lap.

'I apologise, Uncle,' he said softly. 'I let my emotions get the better of me. I did not mean to. You have been very good to me, very kind, the best father one could have hoped for. You have given me *every* chance and I believe you have loved me.'

'I *do* love you, Roger,' Prosper said earnestly, 'as much as if you were my own son. Believe me, I have done all I could to blot out the memories of those wretched early days from your impressionable mind, but I have obviously not succeeded, because today you showed me a very bitter man.'

'But you have succeeded, Uncle, you truly have.' Roger nodded his head several times up and down. 'You have been more than one could have wished. It is simply that in my heart, at times, I did feel bitter. I would like very much, one day, to know who my father is . . . I promise you,' he held up a hand, 'there would be no reproaches, no violence. I would just like to know, and now that I am to be married I think I have a right to know.'

Prosper came and sat beside Roger and took his hand in his. 'I am sorry, Roger, but I can't tell you who your father is, except that he was a gentleman of whom you would not be ashamed. His desertion of your mother was caused by circumstances beyond his control, and I have reason to think he regretted it. His family came to hear of it and a stop was put to the affair. But it all happened a long time ago. Such a long time ago now.'

'Is he still alive?'

'I'm afraid, again, I can't say. You see, I don't feel a free agent in this matter. It is your mother's prerogative to tell you the truth.'

Roger's hand remained in Prosper's, but he felt drained of all emotion, of all hatred, all desire for revenge. The only creature he truly loved in the world was his cat. Only she spoke to him, and only she had awakened in him feelings of altruistic love. The rest of his heart remained empty and barren. He had no emotions, no feelings. Even his soul was cold, like the tundra untouched by human footsteps.

Sometimes he felt he was the unhappiest man alive, because when he really tried to look into the innermost recesses of his being, he found only emptiness.

Between Marylebone High Street and Baker Street ran a number of side-streets containing various different kinds of dwelling. Some were small, terraced private houses in the late-Georgian style; others had been built by charitable trusts to house the poor of the area.

The main focus of a district that contained a mixed population of the well-to-do, the fairly well-to-do and the downright destitute was the Parish Church of St Marylebone, whose imposing classical portico faced Marylebone Road and Regent's Park.

It was to a street just behind the church that Roger came after his talk with his uncle. Perhaps the purpose of his visit there had something to do with the mood he'd been in when, as he now realised, he had let his uncle see a far less attractive side of him, the dark side that he usually kept well hidden.

But Roger had learned to be a consummate actor on the world's stage, managing for the most part to contain his true emotions and feelings, sometimes even from himself.

He walked the short distance from Montagu Square, crossing the busy thoroughfare of Baker Street on his way. He stood for a moment gazing up at the windows of the houses next door – always on the lookout for curious neighbours – and then he knocked at the door and, after a while, it opened and he was ushered in.

It was what was known as a 'town house'. Not a very grand town house, like the one belonging to the Martyns in Montagu Square, or the even grander one owned by the Woodvilles in Chesterfield Street, Mayfair. This was a small town house built in the early years of the nineteenth century when a George was still on the throne.

Roger greeted the sole inhabitant of the house and, after a few words, followed him up the stairs to the sitting-room on the first floor, where a fire burned in the grate.

'Will you take a drink, Roger?' Frederick enquired, going to a side-table on which there was a display of bottles.

'Whisky, please, Fred,' Roger said. 'A stiff one.'

'Oh, trouble?' Frederick took the stopper out of the bottle and poured. Then he crossed the room and gave the glass to Roger with a faint smile.

'No, not really. There's a board-meeting next week on the same day as the rehearsal for the wedding. Uncle said which did I think should have priority and I replied, the board-meeting! He appeared rather bemused.'

'Oh!' Frederick, also with a glass in his hand, sat opposite Roger and grimaced sympathetically.

'He later asked me if I loved Emma.'

'And what did you say?'

'Something non-committal.' Roger leaned forward and beckoned to Frederick with his finger. 'Don't you worry about it. Come here and sit beside me.'

Dutifully, Frederick obeyed and Roger, placing his glass carefully on the table beside him, turned and began to caress him, kissing him finally, passionately, on the lips.

'Oh Roger!' Fred murmured in an agonised voice after their embrace. There were tears in his eyes.

'What's the matter?' Roger took up his glass and had another large sip of his drink.

'Well . . . you know.'

'I *have* to get married, Fred. It's expected of me. A lot is at stake. A lot of money, as well as my seat on the Board.'

'I know that. It's just . . .' Fred put his hand in Roger's, and Roger leaned over and kissed him again.

'Come to bed,' he said gently, taking the glass out of his lover's hand. 'Let's try and forget our sorrows.'

The bed that they had shared for a number of years, ever since they had met when Roger worked in the warehouse in Lower Thames Street while he was learning the business, was on the top floor of the house. It was quite a big, light room with a view over the rooftops of Marylebone. In the nearby churchyard the tops of the trees could just be seen, waving gently in the breeze. Night was falling, and Fred drew the curtains firmly across before switching on the lamp.

By the time he turned round, Roger had begun to take his clothes off, laying each garment neatly on a chair. Then he sat on the bed, removing his socks and suspenders, and when he was completely nude he lay on the bed, his head resting on his arms propped up by the pillow.

For a long time Fred looked at him. He was beautiful, and he had loved him for a very long time. He gave Roger love, and Roger looked after him. He wasn't sure he loved him in return because Roger seldom showed emotion. But Roger was very good to him, and until his engagement Fred had been content.

But ever since then he had been edgy, living on his nerves. And now the event he'd been dreading was approaching, and what was going to happen then?

'Come here, Fred,' Roger said, holding out his hand, and Fred approached the bed and sat beside Roger and began to caress him.

Afterwards the lovers lay close together, Roger with his arms round Fred's waist. He then let a hand travel lightly over Fred's body, and when it reached his face he uttered a sharp exclamation.

'Fred!' he cried. 'What is it? You're crying.'

'It's nothing, Roger,' Fred said in a stifled voice, rubbing his face in the pillow.

'But it *is* something! What is it?'

Roger gently disengaged himself and sat up. 'Is it about the wedding, Fred?'

Fred, his face still pressed to the pillow, nodded.

Roger sat there thoughtfully for a moment or two, then he took Fred's face gently between his hands and licked his mouth. Fred trembled all over, his eyes closed, his expression fraught.

Roger got purposefully off the bed, covered Fred with the sheet and went to the neat pile of clothes lying on the chair by the window. He took his cigarette-case out of his inside pocket and lit a cigarette with fingers that shook slightly. He sat on the chair and, cigarette between his lips, began to put on his socks.

When he was dressed and the cigarette was half-smoked, Fred still hadn't moved, and Roger went back to the bed and, sitting beside him, put a hand on his shoulder.

'Fred?'

'Yes?' in a muffled voice.

'I have to go.'

Fred buried his face in the pillow again.

'Fred,' Roger said, this time with a note of urgency, 'I have to go out to dinner and I want to talk to you. I have something quite important to say.'

'What is it?' Fred muttered, his head still in the pillow.

'Sit up, there's a good chap. I want you to listen attentively.'

Reluctantly Fred heaved himself up and pulled the bedclothes over his shoulders as though he were very cold, though with the gas-fire on it was quite warm in the room.

'What is it?' He asked again, looking curiously childlike and vulnerable, his face still streaked with tears, his dark hair tousled.

'I want you to have this house, Fred. I'm making it over to you so that it belongs to you.'

'Oh Roger . . .'

'Don't say anything.' Roger took a firm grip on Fred's arm. 'It's a gift. An outright gift for all that we've been to each other for the past few years. I want you to know that I'm grateful, Fred, and that I love you . . .'

'But . . .' Fred began sobbing again, and Roger strengthened his grip.

'Don't say anything, please, Fred, until I've finished. It isn't easy for me, and I know it's not easy for you.'

Roger got up and lit a fresh cigarette, then he began to pace up and down the room in front of the bed, his eyes fixed on the floor.

'This has to end, Fred. I'm getting married, and I want to make a fresh start. I want to try and make it work. I have to.'

He sat on the bed and gazed with tormented eyes at his lover. 'I can't make it work if we go on like this. Emma would know.'

'*How* would she know?'

'She'd know. Any woman would know.'

'She'll know, anyway, that you're not straight.' Fred's voice was bitter.

'Why should she know that?' Roger's voice was indignant. 'Doing it from the front is just the same as doing it from behind.'

'How do you know if you haven't done it?'

'The principle's the same.' Roger tried to hide his unease. 'It must be. I shall close my eyes and think it's you.'

'*Don't!*' Fred flung out his hand and vigorously tried to push Roger away. 'You're deliberately tormenting me, Roger. I don't know how you can.'

'I wanted to be fair and honest with you, Fred. I also want to be fair to Emma. She might not know I prefer men to women, but she surely knows I don't love her. I feel sorry for her.'

'Then *why* do it?' Fred sounded perplexed. 'A lot of men don't marry. Your uncle didn't marry until he was over forty . . .'

'I have to. For the family. There's a certain amount of pressure. I feel if I don't, they'll *know*. They were already uneasy. They pushed me into it, as if to test me.'

'I can't understand it.' Fred buried his face in his hands.

'It's one of the dictates of society. It's expected, and I've always wanted to swim with the stream, not against it.' Roger reached out and fondled Fred's head, but Fred pushed him away.

'Does she love you?' Fred gave him a cynical smile. He was very dark, with an eager though rather crafty face, and it was his Lothario-like good-looks that had first appealed to Roger.

'Emma is a very well-brought-up girl,' Roger said cautiously. 'Too well brought up to reveal her feelings.'

'Have you kissed?'

'Of course we haven't kissed!' Roger grimaced with disgust. 'Not in the way you mean. Emma would be shocked. But I think she is "in love" with me in the conventional sense. She has told her mother she thinks I am very handsome.'

'You are,' Fred said peevishly. 'And you know it.'

'You don't look bad yourself, Fred,' Roger said fondly, putting out a hand to stroke his arm. 'You know how I feel about you; but I can't lead two lives. I want to give the marriage every chance and, who knows, I might like it.'

'You? Like it?' Fred put back his head and began to laugh. 'You're as bent as a pin, Roger. You'll never be straight. It's impossible. The whole thing will absolutely disgust you.'

Roger got stiffly off the bed, his face flushed, though in the half light Fred couldn't see it.

'Don't make it difficult for me. I'm being honest. I'm giving you the house. It's worth three or four thousand pounds. I'm making the freehold over to you and you'll have security all your life. I'll see to that. If ever you're in want I'll see you're all right, you have only to let me know; but, other than for business, I don't want you to come near me again. If word of this relationship ever got round, I'd be ruined. Now Fred – ' he leaned against the tallboy, arms akimbo ' – don't make it awkward for me, and don't *ever* try anything. I would deny absolutely everything and, what's more, I'd make sure you never worked again. If you want me to be mean I can be mean, but I don't want to be, believe me. I feel I am doing the right thing by you and my future wife. I'm being honest with you both. And if you trust me and leave me alone, I'll make it worth your while. Is that clear, Fred?'

'Clear,' Fred said quietly, nodding his head. 'But you can't expect me not to mind.'

'Of course you mind, and I mind too because we've had a good time together, and I shall miss you.'

Roger took the hand of his lover of many years and pressed it.

'Fred, some of the employees are coming to the wedding and I'd like you to come, if you wish. It's a gesture. There . . .'

'I'd like that,' Fred said. 'I'd like to see you make a new start.'

'That is handsome of you, Fred.' Roger bent over and lightly kissed his cheeks. Then he jumped off the bed and stood looking down at him.

'Until then, *au revoir*.'

'For the time being,' Fred said in a quiet voice. 'But the leopard doesn't change its spots, you know. Remember that.'

Roger ran down the stairs into the hall and took a final look round. It was a grubby little place and he wouldn't miss it. Nor would he miss Fred with his clerk's mentality, his lack of culture. They had strayed too far apart since those days when, still with his feelings of inferiority and insecurity, he had started to be inducted into the mysteries of stock control at the warehouse, by Fred, who was a few years his senior . . . He opened the front door, gently closed it, and ran lightly down the three steps into the street.

Goodbye to the past.

He walked rapidly along Nottingham Place into Paddington Street, cutting through the old churchyard on his way towards Baker Street. The night was dark. It was now very cold. A woman approached him out of the shadows, and rather harshly he pushed her away.

He hated himself; he felt confused. Far from being the happy bridegroom, he sometimes felt that he was entering a long, long tunnel without light at the end.

'And by the power invested in me by God, I pronounce you man and wife.'

A collective sigh rose from the congregation, the organ

crashed out and Roger turned to Emma and, raising her veil, kissed her on the cheek.

Then, joining hands, they turned to face the packed congregation as man and wife, and began the slow march up the aisle to the doors, which had been flung wide open.

The pews on either side were packed with the smiling faces of people invited from all sections of society, the business world, the professions and the arts. Right at the back, out of sight, were two pews filled with estate workers from the Martyn house in Dorset, and a sprinkling of employees from the Martyn-Heering London offices, including Fred, spruce in a new suit.

It was April, and the sun shone. The bells pealed forth and the crowd of onlookers gathered at the gate began to throw confetti. The official photographer was there with his camera and tripod, and there were a couple from the newspapers. It wasn't the wedding of the year, but it was an important social occasion. The guests began to stream out of the church, to gather behind the happy couple while the bride and groom paused for photographs, first alone and then with Lally and Prosper on one side, Admiral and Lady Hill on the other. Everyone looked almost unbelievably happy.

A huge Silver Phantom Rolls-Royce took the newly-weds off to a reception at the Savoy, and the rest of the guests followed by various means: car, cab and carriage.

Such a large party took some time to reassemble in the ballroom overlooking the river. The bride and groom, the bride's parents, Lally and Prosper stood for an hour in the receiving line, greeting the guests.

By any standards Emma looked the part of the bride. A good bone-structure, a pretty mouth; and although her expression was naturally haughty, it was softened by the sparkle in her violet-blue eyes. Her fair hair was caught up by her veil and the tiara that was her parents' gift to the bride. Her wedding-dress, made entirely of lace, was cut to accentuate her slim body, her pointed breasts. Next to her wedding-ring was the cluster of amethysts Roger had given her for her engagement; flawless jewels imported by the Martyn-Heering concern and set in pure platinum. She carried a small bouquet of roses, freesias and camellias grown in the greenhouse of her family home.

She was nineteen, six years younger than Roger, but she looked older. She looked poised, mature, even serene, and all the men thought how lucky Roger was, and the ladies envied her.

Beautifully-gowned women passed along the line, escorted by men in grey morning-suits, pearl-grey cravats and spats. There was a sprinkling of Far Eastern businessmen and diplomats dressed in exotic Oriental garb, their ladies gorgeously attired in rare silks fashioned into beautiful dresses and saris, according to the custom of their countries.

Connie followed Miss Fairchild around like a lamb its mother sheep. She knew she was totally out of place amid all the glamour, and was sorry she'd come. Her first instinct had been to refuse, but Aunt Vicky had been horrified. In the first place she had not wished to travel to London alone and, secondly, not everyone in Wenham had received an invitation to The Wedding. To have refused would have been foolish, out of the question. Besides, 'It would *never* do to offend the Woodvilles' was the argument that clinched the matter.

Connie, feeling small, inadequate, badly dressed and ugly, shuffled up the receiving line praying for self-effacement, and when she saw the bride smiling brilliantly at her she was so startled that she almost dropped a curtsey. The bridal pair were startlingly beautiful, other-worldly, in special dress which was a sort of uniform that set them apart. Both shook hands with her, Roger also kissed her cheek although she hardly knew him. They then gave the identical treatment to the person following her and, murmuring inaudibly, she passed on down the line – Lally shaking hands, Prosper giving her a kiss on the cheek, Admiral and Lady Hill a stiff handshake, merely a glance.

Miss Fairchild, on the other hand, revelled in the occasion. She often dreamt of worldly events like this, but seldom attended them. She had chatted to the bride and groom until almost forcibly moved on. But after all, she had sent them an expensive present of hand-blown glass and thought she deserved a few words in appreciation.

Miss Fairchild also felt she *looked* nice. This was important – to feel at one's best, at one's ease – and she had gone to some trouble about dresses for herself and Connie. They had not been made by the local dressmaker, but bought at a shop in Bournemouth which catered for the quality. Connie was so thin, her mauve silk did just *hang* on her a little; maybe a tuck or two before the next big occasion.

Now, as she cast her eyes round, she wondered where her poor, shy little ward had hidden herself. There were so many people. A waiter pressed a glass of champagne into her hand. Someone waved. It was Sophie. Thank heaven for a familiar face. Sophie was with Laurence and Sarah-Jane Yetman, and with them was a tall, quite handsome but surly-looking man who was one of the Sadlers, Miss Fairchild knew; she wasn't sure which one.

'Bartholomew Sadler, my brother-in-law.' Laurence introduced them and they shook hands.

'I never forget a face,' Miss Fairchild said, 'but are you one of the brothers who farm, or . . .'

'I'm the stone-mason, Miss Fairchild.'

'Of course,' her brow cleared, 'the odd one out, and I *do not* mean that unkindly.'

Bart laughed perfunctorily.

'Have you seen Connie?' Miss Fairchild turned anxiously to Sophie. 'She's slipped away. She's a little shy, you know. I'm so afraid that she may try and go back to the hotel.'

'Oh, I'm sure she wouldn't. On her *own*?'

'She's not really happy among so many people.'

'Carson . . .' Sophie beckoned to her brother-in-law, who stood apparently entertaining a group of unattached young women, all most fashionably dressed and hanging on his words. Carson excused himself to them and joined Sophie, who whispered in his ear.

'Miss Fairchild is worried about Connie. Could you try and find her?'

'Of course.' Carson stopped a passing waiter and exchanged

his empty glass for a full one. 'When did you last see Connie, Miss Fairchild?'

'Only a few moments ago, as we shook hands with the bride and groom. I stopped to chat with some people I knew and when I looked up Connie had slipped away. A crowd like this terrifies her, you know.'

'Leave it to me,' Carson said, and adroitly melted into the crowd.

'He *is* so kind,' Miss Fairchild breathed, watching him make his way through the throng. 'Such a genuinely kind young man. One day he and Connie got caught in a rainstorm in the church, and he came all the way back for an umbrella to escort Constance home. He was drenched to the skin.'

'I'm glad you find him kind,' Sophie said approvingly. 'I do too. There is a very nice side to Carson that not a lot of people see. We are privileged. Tell me, Miss Fairchild, are you enjoying yourself?'

'Oh, very much.' Miss Fairchild's face was flushed. 'I would not have missed this for the world.' She gestured about with her hands. 'The hotel is like a palace, and the people . . . It is a real occasion. So different from anything we have at Wenham.'

Carson meanwhile was walking about the crowded room, peering over the heads of people for a sight of mauve silk. It was a little unbecoming for Connie, who might have looked better in blue or pale green.

One or two people he knew tried to detain him, but he slipped past them with a nod. He felt almost as uncomfortable here as Connie, out of place at the wedding of Roger and his pretty bride, out of sorts in morning-dress. He was stopped by a hand on his arm and looked up with surprise at a familiar face. At first he couldn't place it.

'I didn't think you'd remember me, Carson.'

'Of course I remember you . . . Frederick . . .' Carson shook the hand of the clerk who had worked in the room next to his in the Martyn-Heering warehouse. He clearly recognised the face but, in fact, he had almost forgotten his name. 'How are you keeping?'

'Very well. And you? Not married yourself yet?'

'Not yet.'

'Me neither.' Frederick put his glass to his lips. 'I never thought Roger would, but he did.'

'Yes, it's done now.' Carson was surprised that someone low down the social scale like Frederick knew Roger well enough to use his Christian name. 'He's rather grand now, a partner.'

'A partner, yes.' Frederick nodded. 'I knew him when he didn't know a thing about the business, but – ' Frederick sighed ' – he's left me well behind. I wish him luck. I wish Roger lots and lots of luck.'

Carson decided Frederick was rather drunk. 'Good to see you again,' he said. 'Excuse me. I'm looking for someone.'

'Good to see you too,' Frederick said, stepping to one side, a confused, unhappy man.

Carson continued his search in the ballroom for Connie, but his thoughts were on Frederick. It had surprised him to see the junior clerk from the warehouse who sometimes used to bring him a cup of tea. Otherwise they had little to do with each other. Yet, oddly, Carson had always felt that Frederick resented him, seemed to regard him in a way that was detached, and rather suspicious. This encounter now seemed to explain it. Frederick had taught him, and he had taught Roger who was now a partner.

Maybe Frederick, a man of humble origins, had resented the young men from good families who would climb the company so easily, while he himself, a warehouse clerk, would remain just that all his life, with yearly increments, a small pension and a gold watch at the end.

Carson wondered if Frederick had resented him enough to have him sacked? Was Frederick the man who had doctored the books? But would he know how and, now, did it matter?

Here and there was the odd familiar face; but there were few. They were mostly Prosper and Lally's friends from the smart London set, a host of younger people who were familiars of Roger, and friends of the Hills who were rather county and stuffy. There was a sprinkling of military and naval uniforms, plenty of scarlet, and gold braid.

There must have been five hundred people in the room, and

Carson had almost despaired of finding his quarry when he saw a flash of mauve amid all the pastel colours, and just managed to reach the door as Connie was in the act of sidling out.

'Connie!' he called above the hubbub and, like a startled fawn, she turned towards him.

'Carson,' she murmured, hand to mouth. 'I was just . . .'

'Your aunt's worried about you, Connie,' he said kindly and, taking her firmly by the arm, he propelled her back into the room. 'She wondered where you'd got to.'

'It's so *hot*.' She put a hand to her forehead. 'I decided to take a walk. I . . . I don't really like it here,' she burst out, eyeing him wildly. 'I *don't* like these people and I wish I'd never come.'

'I'm not enjoying myself much either,' Carson said, drawing her into an alcove where two seats had just been vacated by an animated couple who now appeared to be joining those who were getting ready for dancing. 'I feel totally out of place here.'

'Oh, do you really?' Connie was clearly surprised by his admission. 'I thought it would be the kind of thing you liked.'

'But why should you think that?'

'You know . . .' Connie faltered. Then a blush spread slowly from her neck and began to suffuse her face.

'Come on, let's dance,' Carson cried, seizing her hand as the floor cleared and the small orchestra in the corner began to make the dissonant sounds of tuning up.

'Oh, I can't *dance*.' Connie sounded appalled at the idea. 'Besides,' she glanced furtively around, 'Aunt Vicky might see.'

'But why should Miss Fairchild mind you dancing? I'm sure she'd like to think of you enjoying yourself.'

'Perhaps I should ask her first?' Connie appeared to hesitate.

'Don't be silly, Connie,' Carson said sharply. 'You're not a little girl now, are you?'

'No.' She hung her head.

'You're a woman of . . . how old?'

'Twenty-four,' she mumbled.

'The same age as me. We were born in the same year, Connie. That's a good sign, isnn't it?'

'Why?' she looked puzzled.

'It means we get on. I think we have a lot in common, Connie.'

'Really?' She took a deep breath and, as he held out his arms for the waltz that had begun, she slipped rather clumsily into them.

First the newly married couple took the floor, waltzing expertly around the circumference of the ballroom while the guests looked on admiringly. They completed a circle, gazing all the time into each other's eyes, and then Prosper and Lally and the Hills joined in sedately – three couples gyrating round the floor to give the signal that everyone else could begin.

Couples flocked onto the floor and, very gingerly, Connie and Carson joined them.

'I've only *ever* danced at the church socials,' she whispered.

'I have only ever danced at the young farmers' ball,' he whispered back and, as if to prove it, trod on her toes.

Miss Fairchild, happily engaged in animated conversation with the small contingent from Wenham, saw the flash of mauve pass before her eyes like a mirage.

'Goodness me!' she cried, startled out of her wits. 'Is that . . .?'

'Carson and Connie dancing together. Well, well.' Sophie, who wore a smart dress of grey chiffon with an ankle-length skirt, seemed equally impressed.

'Well, at *least* he found her,' Miss Fairchild said, and at that moment the couple caught her eye and Carson waved back.

'How happy Connie looks.' Sarah-Jane was waiting for her husband to invite her to dance; but he had disappeared to the bar with Bart, where he had met some cronies.

'Connie has a *very* soft spot for Carson,' Miss Fairchild confided. 'He is terribly kind to her.'

'It seems to me as though Carson has a soft spot for Connie too.' Sarah-Jane looked anxiously towards the bar, hoping that Laurence wasn't having too much of a good time in the company of Bart. However, at that moment they could both be seen wending their way through the crowd, with a waiter behind them with a tray on which were precariously balanced a bottle of champagne and glasses.

Sophie turned as Bart and Laurence reached them, and immediately caught Bart's eye.

'Are all your family here?' she asked with a smile, as they drew instinctively to one side.

'Besides Sarah-Jane and Laurence, only me.'

'Your brothers and sisters-in-law weren't invited?' Sophie seemed surprised as Bart shook his head, adding: 'I do a little business with Mr Martyn.'

'Oh do you indeed?'

'Yes, I do. Champagne, Mrs Woodville?'

'Thank you, but I don't drink,' she smiled.

'Religious reasons?' He took a glass of champagne from the waiter and held it to his lips.

'No. I do believe in temperance as it happens, but I have never tasted alcohol. It doesn't appeal to me.'

'That does surprise me. I understand your father likes a drop.'

'Only with meals.' Sophie was immediately on the defensive. 'A little wine at dinner.'

'Pardon, I should have said your father-in-law.' Bart, who seemed a little under the influence himself, hiccoughed. 'I meant Sir Guy.'

Sophie didn't reply. She found herself at a loss in her judgment of Bart Sadler. One half of her admired him and the other half didn't like him at all. She was repulsed and attracted; a curious, haunting, inconvenient and altogether puzzling sensation.

From the corner of her eye she could see Guy clearly enjoying himself with Prosper and some friends. Guy had a very short memory. He was still under notice to quit Pelham's Oak, and Prosper was pressing him, while Guy found one excuse, then another, and stalled with a list of fictitious would-be purchasers.

'Maybe he thinks "laugh and be merry, for tomorrow we die",' Bart said, as if he'd read her thoughts.

'I don't know what you mean.'

'That surprises me.' Bart took another sip of his drink. 'I heard Pelham's Oak was for sale.'

'Nothing is decided,' she replied stiffly.

'I heard it was definite. But tell me what will happen to *you*, Mrs Woodville, if the family home is sold?'

'I have been promised that I will be looked after.'

'What are promises?' Bart scoffed. 'They haven't done much about the memorial to your husband, have they? Why, it must be nearly over years since the poor fellow died.'

'It is over three years,' she said, as if a few months mattered.

'And no memorial? I call that a scandal.'

'Really, Mr Sadler, I find this conversation out of place at a wedding.'

'Mrs Woodville.' Bart leaned confidingly towards her, 'I know you want a window, but a window has difficulties. I have an *excellent* piece of marble that I thought would just do for a memorial for your husband. It is a beautiful piece from the Isle of Purbeck. You remember you once thought you might be interested in stone?'

'I am afraid I couldn't possibly afford it . . .'

'Don't worry about that. I think we could come to some arrangement. Would you at least like to see it?' He seemed so excited, so eager to please, she felt astonished.

'It's *very* kind . . .' she began, and noticed that Sarah-Jane was looking at her strangely.

'It's about the stone for George,' Sophie explained. 'Your brother has very kindly reminded me of my obligation. I have had so much on my mind that I feel I have been unfaithful to poor George, neglectful of his memory.' She then turned to Bart and gave him a smile of singular sweetness.

'You really are extremely kind, Mr Sadler. I would love to see the stone. I'm most grateful to you for thinking of it.'

'Then you have only to name the day, Mrs Woodville. Let me know as soon as you have decided.'

He gave her an old-fashioned courtly bow, low from the waist, and straightening up, walked away. Soon he was lost in the crowd.

'What a kind person your brother is,' Sophie said to Sarah-Jane.

'He is kind,' Sarah-Jane agreed dubiously. 'But he is his own man.'

'Oh? Really?' Sophie felt alarmed.

'None of us in the family understands him particularly well. Bart is a law unto himself, Sophie.' Sarah-Jane put a hand on her arm and looked into her eyes. 'You might remember that before you have any dealings with him.'

'What a strange thing to say,' Sophie said. 'You make me quite nervous.'

'Don't be nervous, just be careful.' Sarah-Jane pressed her arm reassuringly. 'But then I am sure you are a woman well able to look after yourself.'

It was getting dark, and Carson held the door of the cab open for Miss Fairchild and Connie as they got into it at the embankment entrance to the Savoy.

'Won't you come back to Brown's and have some refreshment, Carson?' Miss Fairchild asked, leaning out.

'Thank you, I think I have had enough for today.'

'That's true. We have all had enough.' Miss Fairchild turned and smiled at Connie. 'And Connie has had a lovely time. She will be tired. Thanks to you, she has enjoyed herself so much. Haven't you, Connie?'

'Yes,' Connie said from the depths of the cab.

'You must come and have tea with us again when we all get back to Wenham.'

'I should like that, Miss Fairchild.'

'Make it soon.' Miss Fairchild gave the cabbie the name of the hotel and then leaned back, her hand fluttering out of the window.

'Oh Connie, what a wonderfully *happy* day we have had. How friendly everyone has been, and what a really very *nice* man Carson Woodville is.' And, although she did not say so, how very fond he seemed of her beloved ward. She had watched them dancing. Who could doubt it?

And, at that very moment, an idea was born.

14

There were days for Sophie when everything seemed possible, and others when it all looked hopeless. Her moods waxed and waned like the tide, at one moment optimistic, the next sad, even fearful.

She felt that since she had returned from New Guinea she had never really found peace; nor had she succeeded in finding herself. She no longer knew who she was, or her purpose on this earth.

The God in whom she formerly placed such trust seemed to have rejected her, and she was no longer buoyed up by her Christian faith. She even found it hard to pray.

In her misery she believed that George, whose faith had been so strong, would have been disappointed in her, and even that in death she had failed him. Three years after returning from New Guinea she had put up no memorial to him; its continuing absence seemed to accuse her. Maybe that was why she had no peace.

These dismal thoughts were uppermost in her mind as she picked her way among the huge masses of Purbeck stone littering the floor of the quarry around which Bart Sadler was escorting her. Sometimes she reached out for his strong hand to steady her because the ground was so uneven. It was a few weeks after Roger's wedding, and he was keeping the promise he had made then. He had called for her in his carriage and driven her over, saying very little on the way. He was a steely man; a man of few words. Ahead of them stretched the wide expanse of the Channel, flecked with angry waves that seemed to grow larger under a lowering, threatening sky. A few drops of rain had already spattered the ground, and she pulled her scarf more securely about her.

'Cold, Mrs Woodville?' She felt his hand on her back, and even such an impersonal gesture disturbed her.

Bart Sadler made her uneasy. He was a brooding, thoughtful man, and she had seldom seen him smile. He was tall and lean, with the hands of a man who laboured. Yet it was obvious that, if not a scholar or thinker, he was intelligent. She remembered what Sarah-Jane had said about him; that even his family didn't know him. She wondered if he had ever married, and if not, why not.

'There,' Bart said, pausing at last in front of a monolithic piece of stone which lay on its side as though it had been there since some prehistoric upheaval of the earth.

'That?' she enquired, pointing.

'Oh, it doesn't look much now.' Bart sat on the stone and ran his hands sensitively over it. His gesture had all the intimacy of a lover. 'But wait until I've hewed it and honed it. Have you any ideas for the design?'

'The *design*?' Sophie perched uneasily on the stone, taking care not to sit too close to him. Her sense of unease continued, and in many ways she wished she hadn't accepted his invitation. But she had been thinking of George; she was sure she was thinking of George.

'Did you have a cross in mind, Mrs Woodville, or something more subtle?'

'Subtle, how?' She knew she was talking in monosyllables and felt foolish.

'Maybe I could do a few designs.' His voice began to show a trace of impatience. 'I should like to know the wording, too.'

'I feel I've wasted your time, Mr Sadler,' she said, getting up from the stone.

'Not at all, Mrs Woodville.' He stood up also beside her, and looked down. 'What makes you think that?'

'I can tell it from your voice.'

'You mean, you don't *really* want a stone?' He put his hands on his hips, and now his face showed a sense of impatience too.

'I don't know what I want,' she said with a feeling of despair. 'Yes, yes, of course I want a stone. It is better than no memorial at all.'

'You *really* want a window, don't you?' he asked, his voice sounding more gentle.

'My husband wanted a window.' She felt close to tears. 'It was his dying wish.'

'Then you shall have a window, Mrs Woodville,' he said, leaning forward. 'You shall have a window *and* a fine stone memorial. I shall see to both myself.'

'But, Mr Sadler . . . I cannot accept all that. Not possibly.'

'Why not?' He busied himself about the stone with a measure, and then smiled up at her. 'I am a man of substance, you know. I have no family and no one to spend it on. I would regard it as a civic duty, as well as a Christian one, to spend the money on a tribute to George Woodville who, as far as I can tell, was worth two of his father.'

'What makes you say that?' Sophie, crestfallen, stared at the ground.

'What sort of man lets his affairs get into such disarray that he has to sell his house?'

'Sir Guy has never been good at business. Never pretended to be.'

'Good at nothing, from what I hear. Led his wife a dance when he was young. Spent all her money and then was unfaithful to her . . .'

'Oh, I'm sure *not* . . .' Sophie started up.

'I'm sure *yes*, Mrs Woodville,' Bart said firmly. 'Though I will not sully your ladylike ears with the stories I've heard. His son Carson is no better. Now . . .' he put a foot on the stone and leaned one arm on it '. . . why does one turn out so good and the other so bad? Can you tell me?'

'Oh, George was heroic.' Sophie clasped her hands together, her eyes filling with tears. 'He was so good, I can't tell you; so responsible. He was like an angel, and so God took him. He never spared himself.' She gazed up at Sadler. 'You know what they say, Mr Sadler? Only the good die young.'

'Beats me.' Bart scratched his head. 'But then I'm not religious, Mrs Woodville. I don't want you to think I am. I never go to church. I don't really think I believe in God.'

For a long time there was silence between them, broken only by the gentle, far-off sound of the sea.

'Sometimes I wonder if I do,' she burst out.

'*You*, Mrs Woodville? A missionary?' Bart made no attempt to hide his incredulity.

'That is how it seems to be sometimes.' She had a sense of relief that now she was telling him all this. 'I wanted *so* much to return to New Guinea, but the mission society which sent me would not have me. That was a sore test of my faith in God. I wished *then* I'd never come back. And why did I come back?' She looked up at him but he knew she didn't want an answer. 'Why, to carry out George's wishes. I imagined I would be received, welcomed by his family, but I was not. I imagined they would want news of him, how he died, his last words; but they did not. I imagined they would *welcome* a memorial to their eldest son, but they rejected the idea as too painful. I had to wait until George's mother died before I could set foot in the house . . . and now I am to be turfed out of it again.

'I tell you, I have had nothing but heartache since my return, Mr Sadler, and I wonder after all if there *is* a God to comfort us?'

And anxiously she peered at the sky as if seeking an answer. 'As for your offer, Mr Sadler,' she went on hastily, 'I could not possibly accept it. Not possibly. Eliza and Julius Heering offered a stained-glass window in the old chapel in their grounds, but I turned it down. It used to be a cowshed!' Her voice rose with indignation. 'But now that Lady Woodville is no more and Sir Guy may go and live abroad, perhaps Mrs Heering and her husband, who I know is very wealthy, will subscribe to a window in the church. I could not possibly accept a window from you. But your very kind offer of a stone – ' she gave him a sudden, brilliant smile that transformed her features from being merely handsome into a kind of beauty ' – may well be acceptable. Indeed, it would be churlish to turn it down.'

'*That's* settled, then.' Bart leaned down and gave her his

hand. 'I have a business project with Laurence Yetman and I'll discuss it with him this very evening. There now, let me drive you back. Maybe we could pause at an inn for a bite of lunch on the way?'

'Business with Laurence Yetman?' she enquired. 'May one ask its nature?'

'A client of mine wants to build a factory this side of Dorchester.'

'What kind of factory? I hope I'm not being too curious.'

'Not at all. It's to do with farm machinery. He has great plans.'

'How very exciting.' With her hand in his, Sophie daintily picked her way across the yard again, watched with interest now by one or two of Bart's workmen who were eating their lunch.

'It will make Laurence a fortune. I shouldn't wonder if he didn't offer for Pelham's Oak himself. Now that would be a fine thing, wouldn't it? Keep it in the family?'

'Are you serious?' Sophie paused to get her breath.

'Why not? He is half Woodville. If I had a family I would think of it myself, but I haven't.' He paused and solemnly shook his head. 'But it's no place for a bachelor now, is it, Mrs Woodville? No place at all.'

When Sophie got back from her trip to the stone-mason's yard, she was in a state of such high excitement that it alarmed her.

Unused to trips away from Wenham, taking lunch at an inn with a man she hardly knew, she put it down to her little adventure. But as she skipped up the stairs to her room and took off her hat and coat, she was humming a tune under her breath.

'You seem very happy today, ma'am,' her maid observed as she took the discarded coat and hung it carefully on a hanger.

'Why not, Ivy?' Sophie gazed out of the window to see if she could see the back of Bart Sadler's coach, but it was obscured by a drizzling rain which had started on their way home.

'Certainly 't'in't the weather, mum,' Ivy said morosely. 'Also, all the staff have been put on notice.'

'Notice?'

'Apparently Sir Guy is to sell the house.'

'Has he found a buyer?'

'Oh, so you *knew*, madam?' Ivy's voice was reproachful.

'I have heard talk, Ivy. It has been going on for months.' Sophie was now aware that her spurious happiness had completely evaporated. 'But I didn't think anything was decided.'

'What will you do, ma'am?'

'I don't know, and that's the truth.' Sophie abruptly sat down. 'I may go back to the little cottage if it is still free, or I may seek another missionary society and try and persuade them to let me go overseas now that my children are nearly of school age and can be sent away – though I am doubtful about Charlie, and may be allowed to take him with me.'

'Oh, Mrs Woodville, I am *so* sorry.' Impressionable Ivy's eyes filled with tears. ''Tis terrible, ma'am. Woodvilles have been here for hundreds of years.'

'Never mind, Ivy,' Sophie said with forced cheerfulness. 'I have heard a rumour that it is possible someone connected with the Woodville family may buy it. There, what do you think of that? And if he does, he may well provide a home for us all.'

Sophie thought that when the sun came out, the world suddenly seemed a better place. It was awful to be so physically affected by the weather. Compared to her gloom a few days previously, when she had learned that Guy really planned to sell the house, today, as she trotted along the road that lay between Pelham's Oak and Wenham in her little pony and cart, she felt completely different. For half the way it was possible to keep the great house in view. One passed it on a circular bend, and it slowly revealed itself – from the great stone portico to the oak that, tilting a little more each year like the Leaning Tower of Pisa, lay on the lawn to the east. How beautiful the ancestral Woodville home looked now in the summer sunshine, its windows twinkling like so many diamonds, the tall trees throwing their shadows on the white Chilmark stone of the walls.

And for how much longer would she call it home? But even that didn't seem to matter today, and she kept her head and her spirits high as she crossed the bridge and, halfway up the street, turned into the drive of Riversmead. Jo Yewell immediately came out to take her horse.

'Not at work today, Jo?' she asked, alighting from the trap.

'I finished with the butcher, Mrs Woodville,' Jo said, taking the reins.

'Oh, really? Didn't you like it?'

'I liked it well enough, but Mr Yetman has plans for me, Mrs Woodville. Now that Father is getting on, he said that he'd like me to take his place.'

At that moment Sarah-Jane emerged from the house with her youngest child, Felicity, hanging on to her hand. She wore an apron and her hands were white, as though she had been baking in the kitchen. She greeted Sophie with obvious affection, and Sophie returned her kiss and then embraced Felicity.

'You've come to see Laurence?' Sarah-Jane asked. 'He said something about the window.'

'That's what he told me in his note. I think your brother is organising something. It's very good of him.'

'I told you he was good,' Sarah-Jane said. 'He seems distressed that after all these years there is no memorial to George.'

'He took me round his yard,' Sophie knew she was anxious to discuss Sarah-Jane's brother. 'I understand what you meant about your family's feeling towards him. He is kind, but detached. And he does make me a little nervous.'

'I think he likes you.' Sarah-Jane led her into the house.

'Oh?' Sophie flushed with pleasure. 'Why is it he's never married?'

'He said he never found the right person.' Sarah-Jane stopped abruptly and, her face suddenly serious, looked at Sophie. 'Take care, Sophie, that he doesn't hurt you. He can be quite . . . cruel to ladies.'

'Oh dear!' Sophie laughed nervously. 'Like that, is he? I can assure you, Sarah-Jane, I am not in the least interested in your brother. He is certainly not my type and I don't think I am his. For one thing, he isn't a Christian.' And suddenly she remembered her own confession to him and regretted it. How foolishly one could talk at times.

'He said you were thinking still of trying to return to the missions.'

'It's what I really want to do.' Sophie removed her hat and gloves and sat down. 'I feel it must be now or never.'

'And the children?'

'Deborah, at least, will stay here at boarding-school. I shall also try and find a place for Ruth. I'm hoping that you will be very kind and keep an eye on them.'

'Of course we will.' Sarah-Jane scooped Felicity into her arms. '*And* in the holidays they will come and stay with us; but Sophie . . .' She paused awkwardly.

'Yes?'

'Is it wise . . . after what happened to George? Is it *wise* or *kind* to run the risk of leaving the children, perhaps for ever?'

'There is no risk to me,' Sophie said confidently. 'I shall not go into the interior, I assure you, but shall remain at base, teaching the natives as I did before. If I take my quinine tablets regularly I need never have malaria.'

'Did George not take his regularly?'

'George didn't have malaria. He had some kind of fever he had caught in the jungle. It did not seem to me like malaria at all, but jungle fever.' Sophie paused and then gave a deep sigh. 'I feel that I can only be true to the memory of George if I return to the missions.'

'Well, if it is what you must do, you must do it.' Sarah-Jane was a practical, sensible woman and Sophie was grateful for her support and understanding. 'You can rely on us . . .'

With Felicity in her arms Sarah-Jane went to the window and called out, 'Laurence. Sophie is here.' And there was an answering call back.

'He's doing something to one of the stables,' she said. 'He can't sit still. Always buzzing around, full of ideas.'

A few minutes later Laurence entered the room, wiping his hands on a cloth.

'Sophie, it is very good to see you,' he said, kissing her cheek. 'We don't see enough of you.'

'And will see even less.' Sarah-Jane leaned forward as Felicity struggled to free herself, to get into the arms of her father. 'Sophie wants to return to New Guinea.'

Laurence looked puzzled. 'But I thought they had turned you down?'

'That was with the children. Now they are a little older I thought I could send them to boarding-school. I'm not sure about Ruth. She may be too young. Also, you see . . . there's the question of Pelham's Oak. With Sir Guy gone . . .'

'Quite.' Laurence nodded his head and frowned.

'There's a rumour *you* might buy it.'

'Nothing's settled.' Laurence looked embarrassed. 'It's really Mother who is so keen on it. I'm not keen at all. I love this house. I was born here. Mother was born at Pelham's Oak.'

'Then why does *she* not buy it with Julius?'

'That is exactly what I say,' Sarah-Jane nodded vigorously. 'I am perfectly happy here in the house where Laurence was born.'

'The only thing is, it *is* a little small for us.'

Laurence looked pained. 'I am always enlarging and adding, until in the end the buildings will reach down to the river. But there's also the question of affording it.'

'I hope I'm not speaking out of turn . . .' Sophie looked from one to the other '. . . but Bart Sadler was telling me about a contract . . .'

'Oh, of course, you've been talking to him! Yes, he has introduced me to a client who may prove to be one of the biggest I have ever had. He wants to build a big factory near Dorchester, and then another and another. I shall have to take on more men.'

'*And* a big house? I don't think it's wise.'

Sarah-Jane shook her head. 'I don't think we should be pressured by Eliza or anyone.'

'Nothing is settled.' Laurence kissed his daughter's hand.

'Everyone keeps on saying that,' Sophie said fretfully. 'I wish something were settled and then I would know where I was.'

'You need have nothing to fear, Sophie,' Laurence said at once. 'If we ever contemplate buying Pelham's Oak there will be plenty of room for you. Frankly, however, it would not be wise to bank on us. I don't want to expand my business *and* move at the same time. It is *most* unlikely . . .'

'It's kind of you to be so frank. I shouldn't rely on you at all; but all the uncertainty – which has dragged on for nearly six months now – has increased my restlessness. I think I shall definitely try and return to New Guinea. I like to be useful and I was glad to look after my father-in-law, but if he goes as planned to live in Baden-Baden he will have no need of me. Besides, I don't intend for one minute to settle in a German spa!'

Laurence seemed anxious to change the subject. 'Now, I know you're here to talk about the window. Bart discussed it with us the other night and we think the best thing is to open a subscription. The family will, of course, contribute, and then all George's friends, some from school and some from Cambridge, will be sure to want to. Hubert Turner has already offered a hundred pounds.'

'Oh, how generous!' Sophie felt even more embarrassed. 'Everyone is being *so* kind. You know,' she said, suddenly looking around, 'if I do go, I shall miss you all. I was beginning to feel settled again in Wenham.'

Sophie stayed for tea with the Yetmans and the children. She enjoyed their company; relaxed and at ease in their obviously happy family life, she was reminded of the days when she and George and the children shared such contentment. It was hard to be thrown on one's own. She also had now to break the news to her own children about their possible fate, a task she dreaded.

She left the house at about five and, on an impulse, continued her journey into the town. There was just time to make one last visit. She stopped her pony and trap outside Hubert's house and, tying the reins to the garden fence, opened the gate and walked up the path. The door opened before she reached it and Hubert stood there with a welcoming smile, as if he'd been waiting for her.

'Sophie, how very good to see you! What a lovely surprise. I happened to glance out of the window and saw you. Have you come to see your parents?'

'I've come to see *you*,' she said, taking his extended hand. 'I have just heard about your extraordinarily generous gesture. I can't *thank* you enough.'

'Gesture?' Hubert ushered her into the sitting-room, fussing about to make sure she was comfortably seated. 'What gesture?'

'That there is to be a subscription to the memorial window for George, and you are the first to have subscribed. One hundred pounds! It is *most* generous of you, Hubert.'

After she was seated, Hubert clasped his hands behind his back and stood in front of the fireplace where, as it was summer, there was a bowl of flowers in a large urn instead of a fire.

'You know, my dear Sophie, that I was prepared to pay for the window *entirely*.'

'Yes, I know.' Nervously, Sophie studied her hands. 'But there were conditions, were there not, Hubert?'

'No. I wanted to marry you then, and I still do, but it was not a condition, Sophie.' As she was about to speak he held up his hand and, hastening across the room, sat down next to her. 'I want to marry you, as much now as I ever did. I have waited a long time and have respected your reticence. I realised that at first there was the memory of George, and then you wanted, quite rightly, to look after your father-in-law after the death of his wife.' Hubert joined his hands together as if he were in prayer. 'How I admired you for that. How my love and admiration for you increased.' He lowered his gaze, and his eyes, full of love, fastened on her. Here was a woman who could have had all the comforts he could offer, and yet sacrificed herself for others. 'I realise Sir Guy is not easy, and your position has been a difficult one. But now, my dear, the time has come to think of yourself. Pelham's Oak *is* to be sold and Sir Guy is off to live in Germany. Once more you will find yourself cast penniless on a hostile world.' Suddenly he reached out and seized her hand. 'Dearest Sophie, believe me when I say that the passage of time has only increased my ardour. Now I feel I may speak again and ask you to be my wife. Dare I hope that you will say yes?'

Sophie was conscious of Hubert's hand in hers, and her lack of response. She had a mental image of the strong, confident hand of Bart Sadler as he reached out to help her over the stones in the mason's yard. How reassuring his presence had been! She knew, now, that he liked her, and she knew that she more than liked him. She had lied to the Yetmans. Yet it was, she thought, a very little white lie to pretend she was not interested in a person whose own intentions were obscure. It was a way that any woman would take to protect herself. But she knew, oh how she knew, that she had thought of very little else since that day; his face, his presence, his voice and above all his personality obsessed her. Could it possibly be . . . was it love?

And Hubert was so good. Goodness shone out of him, whereas with Bart one wasn't sure. She imagined that what she admired in Bart was not his goodness, but something else. She had been married, and she knew quite well what that something was. Bart was a strong man in the way that neither George nor Hubert were strong. She knew that she felt the heavy pull of carnal desire and wondered if it was evil in the sight of God.

If only poor Hubert Turner had known the thoughts – base ones, too – churning over in her mind, what would he have thought? It was really quite comical to be thinking of one man while being proposed to by another.

And how *good* Hubert was. How nice it would have been to have loved him. Everyone would have approved; but she was too honest. As it was, she suspected that no one really approved of Bart, which made her sensual feeling for him more bold, more dangerous.

She composed her features as best she could and gazed solemnly at her father's curate, gently releasing her hand.

'You do me a great honour, dear Hubert. I am deeply sorry to have to refuse you yet again, but you know I have a strong desire to return to the missions. The sale of Pelham's Oak has unsettled and decided me. It is a call from God and I feel I cannot reject it.'

'But you can't go.' The expression on his face was agonised. 'You *know* you can't go. You were turned down.'

'I was turned down with *children*,' she said gently. 'But that was a while ago. The children are older, I am stronger. I have written to another society and I hope that, if I can offer myself as a single woman, they will accept me . . .'

'But the children?' Hubert sounded desolate.

'The children will be in good hands. They will be sent to boarding-school, and in the holidays the Yetmans have very kindly consented to look after them. I believe I shall have leave every two or three years. Dearest Hubert,' she reached out to press his hand, 'it is a call to which I feel I must respond.'

Hubert bent over her hand and for a moment she thought he would kiss it. She suddenly felt wretched and guilty. She was lying. If God called, and if Bart called . . . She wondered to which one she would respond.

She felt like a woman cast suddenly into sin, resorting to lies and wracked by feelings of desire and lust . . . but not, alas, for the good, kind man, the representative of Christ on earth, who held her hand.

Dear Mrs Woodville,

I am very sorry to tell you that, with reference to your recent application, the board decided, most regretfully, not to call you for interview.

This decision was taken on the most practical and compassionate of grounds, having in mind the age of your children and their need of a mother. Despite the deposition of Mr and Mrs Laurence Yetman that they would be prepared to act as guardians in your absence, to give them a home during holidays and see to their well-being, we do not feel we are justified in taking on the responsibility for the possibility that, as a result of our decision, your children might one day be left orphaned.

Believe me, dear Mrs Woodville, we think that God is asking a greater sacrifice of you than serving Him in the mission field, and we send you our blessing.

Yours devotedly in Christ,
Tristram R. Painter (Rev.)

Sophie let the letter flutter to her lap and sat for some minutes gazing out of the window. It was no less than she had expected.

But also, as the days since her application passed, she had begun increasingly to think that rejection was what she really wanted; and yet how would God reject her plea and leave her open to an occasion of sin?

For the thoughts she entertained were sinful and, maybe, that was why he had rejected her.

She had fallen, indeed, from grace, and in His wrath God had taken her faith from her.

Sophie picked up the letter again, read it through slowly and then, crossing the floor of her room, hurried down the grand staircase to where she knew Guy would have removed to his seat near the fire which was kept going winter and summer.

There Guy would sit for hours, gazing unseeingly at the embers. She knew that on his mind was the thought of leaving his home, and this dread, this fear, seemed to have brought him to the brink of senility. Perhaps after all he might not be fit to travel abroad and, housed in some kind of special dwelling, would need a nurse and companion?

She shuddered at the thought that the duty might be hers.

Sure enough, he was just where she had expected. Only this time he was sitting upright, reading the morning paper; a pile of letters, mostly bills, lay unopened in a heap by his side.

'Good morning, my dear,' he said as Sophie entered the room, her own letter in her hand. 'Did you sleep well?'

'Yes thank you, Father.' She drew up a chair by his side and, reaching out, he took her hand.

'How lucky you are, my dear, how fortunate to have the gift of sleep. It eludes me these days, with all the worry. The trustees are adamant I should accept the offer of this upstart, Mr Lightfoot, because my own nephew will not make up his mind.'

Mr Lightfoot. The apparently flippant name always had a deadening effect when uttered at Pelham's Oak.

Negotiations had been edging forward for Laurence to indicate an interest in the purchase of the estate, and thus keep it in the family, when this hitherto unknown would-be purchaser had appeared. Mr Hector Lightfoot had lately returned from the West Indies, where he had made a fortune in sugar and tobacco. He wished to buy a large estate in the West Country, with the object of flaunting his newly acquired wealth. Or, at least, that was what Guy unkindly supposed.

'Of course I need not sign with Lightfoot,' Guy said stubbornly. 'It is my house. I can refuse. Only he offers cash.'

'But would it be *wise* to wait, Father? Laurence has still not signed his contract to build the factory. That may have something to do with it.'

'Of course he will sign it. Even then he cannot approach the figure offered by Mr Lightfoot.'

'And Eliza can do nothing with her husband?' Sophie enquired.

'Eliza is beginning to discover that the man she married is a mean-minded Scrooge – which I, of course, knew all along.'

'Oh, surely not.'

'A hard-headed man of business and nothing more. I worked for him, don't forget.'

He looked menacingly at Sophie when there was a knock on the door and Arthur put his head round.

'Come in, come in, Arthur.' Guy beckoned to him amiably.

Arthur entered the room and, with a conspiratorial air, closed the door carefully behind him.

'What is it, man, for goodness' sake?' Guy asked irritably. 'You act like a cat-burglar.'

Arthur crossed the room, bowed to Sophie, and then approaching very close, said to Guy:

'Miss Fairchild is in the hall, sir.'

'Miss who?' Guy frowned.

'Fairchild,' Sophie said. 'Connie's guardian.'

'Oh, Miss *Fairchild*.' Guy's face cleared. 'What on *earth* does that dear lady want?'

'She appears rather agitated, Sir Guy. Maybe it is because she has called on you unexpectedly and is afraid you might be annoyed.'

'Miss Fairchild has called on me unexpectedly?' Guy appeared more bewildered than ever. 'Go and see what she wants, Sophie. Doubtless collecting for some good cause or other. Tell her I am engaged and give her a shilling. No, better, sixpence seeing we are so hard up.' He began to feel in his pocket as Arthur cleared his throat.

'Miss Fairchild said explicitly, Sir Guy, that she wished to talk to you on a matter of some importance.'

'Just arriving like this? Who does she think we are?'

'Father,' Sophie put a hand on his arm, 'perhaps you should see her. After all, she is a person of some consequence in the town. It must be something very important for her to come like this.'

'She said she wouldn't detain you more than a few moments, sir.'

'Oh very well,' Guy sighed, 'show her in. But say I am extremely busy . . .'

Sophie rose as Arthur left the room. 'I had better leave you alone with Miss Fairchild, Father . . .'

'Nonsense, you stay here and see what she has to say. And then make sure she goes.'

'Oh, Miss Fairchild.' He rose to his feet as she was shown into the room by Arthur, and ambled across the room all affability, hands outstretched. 'How nice to see you. How good of you to call.'

'Oh, Sir Guy,' Miss Fairchild nervously clutched his hand, 'I *do* apologise for this interruption. It is not the way I normally conduct my business, I assure you. But what I have to say is of such a delicate nature that I wished to delay it no longer, especially as I understand something very serious, very important is about to happen.'

'And what is that?' Guy took her arm and led her over to the chair next to him, vacated by Sophie who stood smiling at her.

'Good morning, Miss Fairchild. I was just about to go and leave you with Sir Guy.'

'Oh no, *do* stay.' Miss Fairchild appeared more agitated and flustered than ever. She was not at all her usual self. 'I am sure you might be able to help, Sophie. To give us your good advice.'

'Advice?' Sophie found it difficult to hide her own bewilderment. 'Are you in trouble, Miss Fairchild?'

'In trouble?' Miss Fairchild clutched at a navy-blue straw bag she had on her lap as if she needed it for support. '*I* am in no trouble, Sophie, I assure you.' She turned to Guy, who was looking at her with some bewilderment. 'I felt *you* were the one in trouble, Sir Guy.'

'Oh indeed, I *am* in trouble.' Guy flapped a hand in her direction. 'But I don't think you can help me, Miss Fairchild, alas.'

Miss Fairchild put a finger to the livid scar, where as a child she had had an operation for a hare-lip, and rubbed it thoughtfully. Sophie wondered if it still pained her, or maybe she did it unconsciously.

'I think I *may* be in a position to help you.' Her voice now had a tremor in it. 'This is why I am here. I am, however, at a loss how to begin. It is a matter of some delicacy.'

'Well, do say what you have to say, Miss Fairchild.' Guy looked at Sophie for support.

'Begin at the beginning,' Sophie said encouragingly. 'Come right out with whatever it is.'

'It is this.' Miss Fairchild's courage returned and her voice assumed its customary timbre. 'Together, Constance and I are worth well over a million pounds.'

'A million *pounds*,' gasped Guy.

'Yes. I say so with some pride, as my parents' origins were very humble. They were storekeepers, and worked hard all their lives. When they died they left me a considerable sum of money for those days, and the freeholds of two properties: the shop in Wenham High Street and the house where I live. I invested most of the money and it produced a tidy income, but recently some shares my parents purchased many, many years ago increased in value ten-fold. They were for a South African gold mine long thought to contain no gold. However, recently the precious metal was found, *and* in abundance.'

'That *is* splendid news, Miss Fairchild, and believe me, I am very glad for you. But if by coming here so kindly your purpose is to offer me a loan,' Guy gestured helplessly in the air, 'I am afraid I am *quite* unable to accept it. I could never pay you back, my dear lady. I am utterly broke and have to sell my house.'

'I know that, Sir Guy. I am not here to offer you a *loan*.' Miss Fairchild's voice grew more and more excited. She moved to the edge of her seat and clutched her bag so hard that her knuckles turned white. 'I know you have to sell this beautiful mansion, this home of the Woodvilles, to a parvenu, a common creature utterly unworthy of such a prize.'

'Utterly,' Guy agreed, surprised that she knew so much.

'Therefore,' Miss Fairchild began to gabble, 'I am here to offer the hand of my ward, Constance, in marriage to Carson. In that way I believe you will be able to keep this house. And I hope you will consider dearest Constance not unworthy of the honour of one day being its chatelaine.'

There followed a silence as Sophie and Guy tried to digest the implications of what she had said.

'I believe the two young people *are* fond of each other.' Miss Fairchild felt her uncertainty returning as the minutes passed and nothing but a stunned reaction seemed to be forthcoming. 'Otherwise I would not have suggested it. I am not trying to *buy* love and position for my ward. But on the occasions when I have seen them together they seemed, if not enamoured, certainly fond.' Miss Fairchild sat back, visibly relaxed, sure of her ground and her moral position.

Finally Sir Guy made an attempt to pull himself together.

'I didn't even know that Carson and Constance were well acquainted.'

'Oh dear me, yes.' Miss Fairchild glanced at Sophie, perhaps hoping for her support. 'Much better acquainted that you suppose. Carson has occasionally had tea with us. He once was *very* kind and went to all the trouble of fetching an umbrella for Connie, who was sheltering in the church from the rain, and escorting her home. At the wedding of Roger and Emma Martyn he went out of his way to be kind, even asking her to dance and escorting us to our cab. I can assure you I have seen glances pass between the young people, whose meaning it would not be difficult to guess. Otherwise I would, naturally, never have made this suggestion.'

'Glances?' Guy looked at Sophie who, however, kept her eyes firmly on the ground.

'Have you put this to Constance, Miss Fairchild?' Sophie finally found her voice. 'After all, she too must be consulted.'

'Not yet. Were it to be a flat "no" I would not wish to crush her feelings, for I know her to be extremely fond of Carson. But I will be frank with you, Sir Guy. I am seventy-seven years of age, and though in good health and, thank God, strong in mind and body, I don't know how long that happy state will continue. My dear parents were hale and hearty, and then they went very suddenly. It would give me the greatest happiness to know that, were I to go, the person I love most in the world would be in the safe and tender hands of a husband who also loved her and is, I believe, worthy of her. You see,' she looked dispassionately from one to the other, 'were I not to suggest it, it might never occur to either of them, or if it did, it might be much too late to save this beautiful house.'

'Save the *house*?' Guy stammered, as if the penny had only just begun to drop.

'Save the house,' Miss Fairchild nodded. 'Because, of course, to Constance's own not inconsiderable fortune would be added mine, to be entirely at the disposal of her *and* her husband.'

15

Carson lay gazing at the face of the sleeping woman and wondered if he were in love again. There had been Nelly, and Elizabeth – though that had been quickly nipped in the bud – and one or two others since; but Prudence, he thought, was different. Prudence had taken Elizabeth's place at the Sadlers' farm and had lost no time in letting him know she favoured him.

She was a striking brunette with a creamy skin, and he fancied her mightily. Suddenly she opened her eyes and gazed into his.

'What you looking at, Carson?'

'You,' he said.

An amorous look came into her eyes and he put his hand inside her thighs and kissed her lingeringly on the mouth. Then he jumped out of bed and drew on his shirt which lay, along with Prudence's clothes, on the floor.

'If Mrs Sadler finds me here I'll get the sack, and so will you.'

'Why should she find you here?' Prudence asked petulantly. She was a lascivious girl and his caress had given her ideas.

'Because it is time we both got back to work.' Impulsively, he bent over her and put his arm round her. 'You know that we have to sell where I live?'

'So'm you said.'

'I may buy a little farm of my own. I shall have some money then. Or I may farm one on my uncle's estate. At any rate, I may want to settle down.'

'You proposin'?' Her eyes widened hopefully.

'Not yet.' He patted her face and straightened up. 'Just putting it in your mind. I may not have any money, but one day I'll be a baronet and you would be called "lady". Lady Woodville. What do you think about that?'

'*Lady Woodville!*' Prudence gasped and then started to laugh raucously. 'Just *wait* until I tell my pa.'

'Well, don't tell him yet,' Carson said anxiously. 'I don't want him after me with a gun.'

Carson rode home in good humour. He would wait, of course, until the house was sold and all the formalities were completed, his father settled in Baden-Baden or wherever he was going. Then he could do what he liked. With no Pelham's Oak to consider, there would be no problems about having a milkmaid as the chatelaine, no fuss from the family. There would still be the baronetcy, but the home of the Woodvilles would be gone.

Carson had never had the affection for his family home that his father had. In many ways it had been an embarrassment. He might have been born a gentleman, but he had never felt like one. He enjoyed the company of working men, and the beds of working women. He thought of himself, really, as an unpretentious man. Many people said he was like his Uncle Ryder whom he could scarcely remember.

He spurred his horse across the fields, clearing hedges and jumping ditches until at last he came to the house and, vaulting over the final fence, cantered up to the stable.

He was in a good humour, replete and hungry. He had made love and done a good day's sheep-dipping. This was what his life as a farmer with a smallholding of his own would be like, and a buxom woman like Prudence to keep him warm in bed, to provide him with healthy children who would have none of the airs and graces that his family had had in the past. His father and elder brother had been educated at university, but he hadn't, and if he had his way, nor would his sons. They would be honest, unpretentious working men; and the girls would be simple and straightforward like their mother.

Reaching the stable, Carson flung the reins to the stable lad and clapped him on the shoulder.

'What then, Andy.'

'What then, Carson,' Andy said, as always treating the son of the master of the house as a familiar. They went drinking together, and in past days had even shared women. But Andy was engaged to be married and soon, Carson thought, he would be too.

His thoughts turned to Prudence. Whether it was love or not, he wasn't sure. He hadn't known her long enough; but once the home was broken up he knew it would seem strange, and he would feel like putting down new roots.

It would be a good time to make a fresh start, and he was pretty sure that basic, solid, down-to-earth but beautiful Prudence was the one for him. Carson went in by the back door, through the kitchen where cook was preparing the evening meal.

'So here I am again, cook,' he said, plonking a kiss on her rosy cheek.

'Now then, Master Carson!' She was of the old school, and disapproved of his freedom with the lower orders of his father's house. 'Your father has asked for a special dinner this evening.'

'Oh?' Carson's eyes widened.

'Roast beef and salmon-trout, champagne . . .'

'What's the occasion?'

Cook shrugged. 'Maybe he's feeling in a happier frame of mind now the worry about the house has been taken from his shoulders.'

'Oh?' Carson took a small roast potato from the pan and popped it into his mouth. 'Has something happened?'

'I believe it might have done, sir.' Cook finished basting the beef before putting it back in the oven. She hoped Carson had burnt his mouth, but he wouldn't let on if he had. 'But I don't know what. Whatever it is, I believe it's good, and means we shall all stay on at Pelham's Oak.'

'Well, in that case I'd better find out.'

But when Carson got upstairs there was no one about. No sign of his father, nor of Sophie.

Asking Arthur, who was hovering in the hall, where they were, he was told they were changing for dinner and the same was expected of him.

'Changing for dinner!' Carson groaned with dismay. 'I can't remember *when* we last changed for dinner.'

'I have put out your dress-suit, sir,' Arthur said loftily. 'I gave it a good brushing and airing. I also ironed your dress-shirt.'

'Well, well, something good must have happened.' Carson began to run upstairs, then he paused. 'Have you any idea what it is, Arthur?'

'I believe all will be revealed in time,' Arthur replied and, turning his back on Carson, made for the green baize door off the hall.

Carson continued up the stairs, this time more slowly. If his father were staying on at Pelham's Oak he was certainly pleased for him; but he had no intention of allowing it to spoil his plans.

When Carson, having shaved and changed into evening-dress, reached the drawing-room, his father and Sophie were already there, talking to an additional guest.

'Aunt Eliza.' Carson greeted her with pleasure and went up to kiss her. 'No one told me you were coming.'

'It was to be a special surprise,' she said, giving him a decidedly knowing look.

'Is *that* the special surprise? Is that why we're all dressing up?' He looked from one to the other as Arthur handed him a glass of sherry.

'Dry as usual, Mr Carson?'

'Thank you, Arthur.'

Carson lifted the glass and looked round.

'Well, here's to you all, *and* the surprise.' He drank from the glass and then scratched his head. 'I'm at a loss to know . . . but I understand the house has been saved.'

'How do you know?' Guy appeared not only irritated but also nervous. He looked ill at ease in his dinner-jacket, rather as Carson himself felt.

'Cook made a remark to that effect as I passed through the kitchen on my way to the house. Do *tell*, Father.'

'All will be revealed,' Guy said mysteriously, 'in due course. It is a complex matter. *Very* complex.'

A few minutes later Arthur announced dinner, and they went into the grand dining-room which was only used for special occasions.

The table, set for four, was covered with a cloth of Brussels lace that had been part of Margaret's dowry, as had the solid silver cutlery, the cut glass winking in the lights of the candles glowing from an ornate candelabra in the centre of the table.

It was a very large table for four people. Guy sat at one end, Sophie at the other, Eliza and Carson faced each other across the centre.

'I can't remember eating here for years,' Carson said, smiling at his aunt. 'I am all agog to know what the news is and why it is so mysterious. Can it be that *you* are the new purchaser of the family home, Aunt Eliza? Don't tell me that mean old Uncle Julius has been prevailed upon to open the money-bags?'

Eliza averted her eyes and Carson thought that, yet again, he had gone too far and offended her. He was about to apologise when Arthur entered to direct the proceedings.

There were no footmen left at Pelham's Oak. The staff had been reduced to Arthur, cook, a couple of maids, a groom and two gardeners. But, with great pomp, Arthur supervised the maids as they served first the soup, which was followed by fish and then the roast sirloin which Carson had seen cook preparing. With this Arthur poured a fine burgundy which he had decanted some hours before.

'One of the last *great* bottles in Sir Guy's cellars,' he murmured with a scarcely audible sigh.

'All that will change,' Guy said with satisfaction. 'We shall stock up the cellar again with the finest vintages. Now, would you leave us alone, Arthur?'

'Certainly, Sir Guy.' Arthur's eyes roamed over the table to make sure that everything was correct and then, bowing deeply, he withdrew.

'Now, Father.' Carson leaned over the table, projecting his

voice so that his father at the other end could hear. 'What have you to tell us?'

'I have to tell you that we have a chance to save Pelham's Oak.' Guy's voice was solemn, almost sepulchral. 'We have the chance to remain in it as we are, in the comfort and style which we were used to in the days of your dear mother. How heartbroken she would be to see us reduced to this state of near poverty. I can hardly ever remember so few servants, even when Father was alive and, God knows, we were hard up enough then.'

'So what has happened to change this sad state of affairs?' Carson put a piece of succulent beef into his mouth, his eyes on his father.

Guy hesitated and looked at Eliza, who seemed equally uncomfortable and eyed Sophie – who was assiduously applying herself to the food. Carson now felt he knew what was happening: Uncle Julius was the new purchaser of Pelham's Oak, and he and his father did not get on. No wonder there was tension.

'Well, we have had a proposal,' Guy said at last.

'Proposal?' Carson looked up. 'What kind of proposal? Why *are* you being so mysterious, Father?'

'Because the proposal, as a matter of fact, concerns you,' Eliza said, coming at last to her brother's rescue.

'It's a proposal of marriage,' Guy went on, almost stumbling over his words. 'With it goes a considerable sum of money.'

'And who is the fortunate lady?' Carson's tone was acid.

'Connie Yetman.'

'Who?'

'You heard, Carson.'

'I think my ears are deceiving me.'

'No, they are not.' Once more Eliza entered the fray on the side of her brother.

'Someone expects *me* to marry Connie Yetman!' Carson cried, his face scarlet with rage. 'That frumpish old maid? Can someone please tell me why?'

'Because she is *very* wealthy.' Eliza sensed that Guy was

unable to proceed. 'Quite how wealthy we did not know until Miss Fairchild came to see your father . . .'

'Miss *Fairchild* is behind all this?' Carson spluttered. 'Poor Connie, doubtless the sacrificial lamb, probably knows nothing about it. Well, thank heaven for that. She will reject me.'

'We have reason to think she will not.' Guy's courage, aided by Eliza, seemed to be returning. 'It appears she is very fond of you, and Miss Fairchild is of the opinion that you are fond of her. She was at pains to emphasise it was not solely a commercial proposition.'

'But she realised it might not *quite* be love,' Eliza said delicately. 'So . . .' She paused.

'Miss Fairchild is a millionairess.' Guy took over from his sister. 'Connie is wealthy too, and she is Miss Fairchild's sole heir. Miss Fairchild is seventy-seven,' he explained as an afterthought.

'How despicable. How simply disgusting.' Carson put down his knife and fork with a bang and drained the wine in his glass. 'And you, Aunt Eliza, and *you*, Sophie,' he looked at each in turn, 'to be a party to this . . . this . . .'

'Miss Fairchild thought you were so fond of Connie because you have been very kind to her.' Sophie spoke at last.

'Of course I'm *kind* to her, as one is kind to children and dumb animals. Connie is not a woman, she is a girl. How can *I* be expected to marry someone who is an object of pity? No, no, no, a thousand times *no*.' Carson banged the table and stood up. 'I'm revolted and disgusted.'

'Please.' Guy flapped his hand towards his son. 'Sit down, Carson, and let us discuss this rationally.'

'There is nothing to discuss. Absolutely nothing.'

Guy's voice changed into a whine. 'Not to *save* Pelham's Oak for yourself, your children?'

'No, I don't want the house. It means nothing to me . . .'

'How can you say it means nothing to you?' Guy spluttered. 'It has been in our family for three centuries.'

'It meant a lot to George,' Sophie said. '*And* to your mother.'

'I'm amazed at *you*, Sophie; that you, a deeply religious

woman, should connive at selling a man and a woman. Did not Christ drive people out of the temple for attitudes like this?'

'Please.' Sophie looked distinctly uneasy. 'It is not as you think, Carson. Well, not quite. I *do* see your father's point of view, and we all feel . . . We know Constance is a very amiable person. She is talented and clever; married to the right man, she might blossom.'

'I am *not* the right man,' Carson thundered. 'What about the weedy Mr Turner?'

'He is *not* weedy,' Sophie said indignantly. 'In fact, the very reverse.'

'I'm sorry if I offended you, Sophie,' Carson's voice was heavy with sarcasm. 'Maybe you had your eyes on him yourself?'

'There is no need to be rude and hurtful, Carson,' Sophie replied quietly. 'In fact Mr Turner *has* offered for me, and I have declined, twice.'

'Oh really?'

'Yes, really.'

'Then you would not sell yourself? Because, God knows, you need money.'

'Certainly not.'

'Then why should I? Can you tell me that?'

'More is at stake.' Sophie's voice was faltering. 'This is a great house, a great institution; but I am sure that your father would not wish you to marry *anyone* you felt was loathsome.'

'I don't find her loathsome. I just don't want to marry her.'

'Then you disappoint me, Carson,' Guy said reproachfully.

'And you disappoint *me*, Father,' Carson roared, pushing back his chair and jumping up again. 'I know you married for money. I know very well you did. You married for money and then you treated my mother in a disgusting way, and you want *me* to do the same. No one in his senses would be faithful to poor Connie. But I like her too much to hurt her that way. I respect her. And I won't do it. I say shame on you, Father, shame on the three of you.'

Carson pushed back his chair even further so that it toppled onto the floor and then, flinging his napkin on the table, he rushed out of the room, slamming the door violently after him.

For a few moments there was complete silence round the table, then Guy spoke in a voice that trembled.

'What a disgraceful exhibition.'

'It was the way we did it,' Eliza was also shaken. 'We were wrong. The whole approach was wrong. You should have talked to him yourself, Guy, intimately, without all this,' She gestured round the table. 'We were cowards.'

'I thought he would be pleased,' Guy replied defensively. 'He told me he wanted to settle. Far better, then, to settle in his own home; but the way he spoke to me was unforgivable.'

'Guy,' Eliza said softly, 'it *is* common knowledge that, although you may have loved her very much by the time she died, you married Margaret for her money. Everyone knows that, including Carson. He sees that he is repeating your life and he doesn't want to.'

'At least he knows Connie. I had never even met Margaret when I agreed to marry her.'

'I didn't know you could be so cynical,' Sophie murmured.

'It was not cynicism but practicality,' Guy snapped back. 'And family honour. Don't forget that. Very important to an Englishman.'

'Well, what will we do now?' Guy went on. 'I have mishandled the whole affair.'

'Perhaps I can do something?' Sophie drew back her chair and rose from the table. 'Carson and I have been good friends. I will go to him and have a little talk. Unless you prefer to, Eliza?'

'No, you certainly are the one to do it,' Eliza said. 'He thinks I am much too much in league with Guy.'

Sophie found Carson in the drawing-room, his hand on the whisky decanter. Like father, like son, she thought. The Woodvilles when in trouble always seemed to reach for the decanter. Not George, though; George would have prayed. What a singular Woodville dearest George had been.

Carson glared at her and, pouring a stiff measure of whisky into his glass, put it to his lips and drained it. He then began to refill the glass, behaving as though Sophie were not there.

'It won't help, you know, Carson,' she said. 'Drink never solved anything.'

'Spare me your sermons, Sophie,' Carson replied rudely. However, he did not refill his glass but put the top on the decanter instead. Instantly Sophie felt rewarded.

She liked Carson, but she was also a little afraid of him. He was a violent man, and he reminded her a little of Bart Sadler. Maybe that was why she liked them both – because she was, in some way she couldn't fathom, attracted to violence.

'I apologise,' Carson turned abruptly to her. 'That was rude.'

'I understand your feelings.' Sophie indicated a chair and they sat opposite each other. 'Believe me, I do.'

'But you side with Father. As for Aunt Eliza, I thought she was one of my best friends.'

'She is, and so am I, and so is your father. I don't think any of us thought you would be so offended, although, with hindsight, maybe your father should have talked to you privately and alone, not in front of two women.'

'I might have killed him if he had. It was the length of the table between us that saved him.'

'But is it *really* so bad, Carson? In days not so long ago parents played a great part in arranging marriages for their children. If there's affection and respect . . .' She leaned her elbow on the arm of her chair and gazed earnestly at him. 'Do you not have the slightest shred of affection for Connie? I don't think any of us would have entertained the idea if we thought you disliked her so much.'

'I don't dislike her so much,' Carson said. 'I simply don't want to marry her.'

'Maybe love would come?' Sophie suggested. 'They say sometimes it does.'

'I know. Father married my mother to save the house, and he thinks I should do the same.'

'It shows,' she said, in an attempt at cheerfulness, 'that marriages not always based on love can be nonetheless successful for that. We genuinely thought there was a degree of affection on your part for Constance.'

'If there had been, I would have said so, and I didn't even

know she had money. A million pounds.' Carson took a deep breath. 'It's a fortune.'

'At least,' Sophie murmured.

'At *least*?'

'A million is the minimum. Miss Fairchild had shares in South African gold-mines which, once worthless, have greatly appreciated. They are still rising. Is it such a sacrifice, Carson? Think of what it would mean to your father.'

'And you,' he said, reverting to his rough manner. 'It's very nice for you here, isn't it, with maids and things that you never had before?'

'I did have them before,' Sophie coloured violently. 'I have always had maids and I lived in a big house, the rectory, which has fourteen bedrooms. In New Guinea we had plenty of native servants. Such things mean nothing to me, Carson. As I told you, I had the chance to marry Mr Turner, who is well known to be of independent means. He is no humble, impoverished clergyman. My vocation was to serve God in the missionary field. After God, my real love was your brother George, who gave up everything to serve Him. I am completely uninterested in worldly things. You must believe that . . .'

'Then why do you think I should marry a woman I don't love, just to keep this house?'

'Because if you don't, the whole estate will be broken up. Your children and your children's children will have nothing to inherit. Have you thought of that?'

'I have, and I don't care.'

'Really?' She looked at him closely. 'You surprise me. You, who so loved your mother.'

'What has my mother to do with it?' he asked roughly.

'She felt passionately about Pelham's Oak. She did so much to it.'

'She wasn't very nice to you.'

'That's not the point. She was a mother,' Sophie corrected him, 'to her adored eldest son. She felt I took him away and was responsible for his death. I was not; I have prayed about it and forgiven her.'

'I can't understand you, really I can't.'

'It is God,' Sophie said. 'He really does govern our lives. He shows us the way. Maybe if you had a little more humility He would show the way to *you* too, Carson.'

'Humility?' Carson looked bewildered.

'Yes, humility,' Sophie said firmly. 'You are too proud and too selfish. Your father and mother tolerated so much from you because they loved you. You were a bad son and you know it, because you frequently show repentance.

'You blamed yourself for your mother's early death, and now that you have one chance to make up for all the harm you did to your family in the past, you refuse. As well as your father you would make a rather lonely girl very happy. I think Constance *is* very fond of you. And she brings out the best in you. Sometimes I think you are a tormented young man, yet when I have seen you together with her, you do look at her with an expression I seldom see on your face.'

'Pity,' Carson suggested.

'No, it is tenderness, friendship. Connie seems to bring out your best side. She has a childlike air, but she is a woman, the same age as you. Might it not be very nice to have someone as devoted as she is by your side, loving and supporting you for the rest of your life?'

Carson put his head in his hands and, like that, as though he were in a deep state of meditation, she left him.

Carson stood at the back of the church, just inside the door listening to the pure sounds of the organ as they filtered high up into the rafters. His mind went back to a similar occasion some months before when, sheltering from the rain, he did the same thing and, taking pity on the person playing the organ, he had run through the storm to fetch her umbrella and escort her home. He wished now that it had never happened.

Through mischance, through pity, he was being driven to a much more hazardous exercise on behalf of the same person.

Just then the organ stopped, yet its notes still seemed to linger with a singular sweetness in the air. It was true, she did play beautifully. She had a gift which, undoubtedly, Sophie would have said, came from God. At that moment, completely unselfconscious and unaware of his presence, Connie stepped from the sanctuary, her sheet music as usual under her arm, and began to walk down the aisle. He banished from his mind the reflection that one day she would take the same walk on his arm, and stepped forward.

'Why, Carson!' Connie exclaimed, but this time – perhaps more accustomed to his presence – she didn't blush. 'Have you been visiting your family's vault again?'

Carson shook his head as together they walked out into the warm summer sunshine.

As he stood at the door, his imagination returned to haunt him, as if he could see the cheering crowds press forward to welcome him and the future Lady Woodville. He shuddered, and as he turned to Connie she saw the expression on his face, and hers changed to one of concern.

'Are you not well, Carson?'

'I think I have a chill coming,' he lied. 'May I see you home, Connie?'

'Of course.' She nodded her head with pleasure and didn't flinch as he took her arm and escorted her down the path to the church gate.

'I don't *think* you should take my arm,' she whispered conspiratorially, brushing his hand away. 'The rector might see or, worse, Mrs Lamb.'

'Oh!' Carson smiled and looked up at the windows of the rectory. 'Does he spend his time with his nose pressed to the windowpanes to see who goes in and out of church?'

'You never know,' she said. 'If he doesn't, maybe his wife does. Since his gout got so bad he is confined most of the time indoors. They say Mr Turner has a chance of being appointed to the living in his place.'

'Oh really?' Carson removed his hand, which had been supporting her elbow. 'And do you like Mr Turner?'

'Very much.' Connie sounded enthusiastic.

'Oh, as much as that?' He gazed at her with pretended concern.

'No, not as much as *that*! Anyway, he has eyes only for

another, even suppose I liked him in *that* way, which I don't.'
Now, at last, she blushed.

'Mrs Woodville?' Carson stopped and, picking a blade of
grass, stuck it in his mouth.

'Oh! You know?'

'I heard only recently he had proposed to her twice, but each
time she turned him down.'

'*Indeed!*' Connie – not inured to parish gossip – appeared very
interested in this information and carefully studied her feet.

'Do you mind?' Carson looked carefully at her face. If she
was in love with Mr Turner, maybe there was hope that she
would refuse him.

'Mind? *I* don't mind at all. You greatly misunderstand,
Carson, if you think I care particularly for Mr Turner just
because he is the curate and I play the church organ. I
don't.'

'Could you . . .' Carson stopped by the gate and rested his
arm on it. Bracing himself, he took a deep breath. 'Could you
care for *me*, Connie?'

Connie's face now went the colour of a beetroot and she
dropped her music with a thud on the ground.

'Carson,' she faltered, 'I *do* care for you, but . . .'

'Not in *that* way?' he asked, ever hopeful. He had never
considered there was a real chance she might refuse him.

'Oh Carson, what is it you're saying?'

'Look, Connie.' He took her arm firmly again and propelled
her away from the gate, and the possibly prying eyes of the
Lambs, into the shadow of the chestnut tree. 'I'm asking you
to marry me.' He began to stammer. 'I don't know if you ever
considered . . . that I *am* very fond of you, Connie. I think
we suit.'

'Oh Carson!' The colour now drained rapidly from her face
and she slumped against the tree. 'Oh I *cannot* believe it.'

'But why not?' She was indeed an appealing little thing, not
a woman, a child. Gazing at him in that startled, selfconscious
way, she looked about sixteen. She had a skinny body with
no bosom, and he couldn't help a fleeting, invidious comparison with the voluptuous breasts of Prudence. Prudence, who

16

Emma ran up the steps, followed by the chauffeur staggering beneath the weight of an armful of parcels. She had shopped in Knightsbridge, Kensington, Regent Street and Bond Street. She was greeted at the door by Johnson the butler, who opened his eyes wide when he saw the chauffeur staggering up the steps.

'You have been *busy*, madam,' Johnson observed politely. And this, he thought, when she had not long returned from the extended honeymoon trip with boxes full of presents for the family.

No doubt about it, Emma was a spendthrift. She loved to shop. From her earliest years she had been indulged by her parents, and everything she wanted, she had. Marriage to a wealthy man like Roger Martyn had been a prerequisite for a girl with Emma's extravagant tastes.

'Is Mr Martyn in, Johnson?' she enquired.

'He is in the drawing-room, madam, with . . .' Johnson replied with a supercilious lift of the eyebrows '. . . an animal, madam.'

'An animal?' Emma cried. 'What sort of animal?'

'I'm afraid it's a cat, madam.' Johnson looked rueful.

'A cat! That's it!' Emma rapidly crossed the hall and threw open the door of the drawing-room. Roger sat by the open French window, his back to her.

'Roger!' Emma called sharply, running across the room and standing in front of him, staring at Coral curled up peacefully on his knee. 'I can't have that *thing* here.'

'What thing?' Roger, imperturbable, looked up at her, his hand resting on Coral's back.

'*That!*' she pointed.

'That is my cat, Coral,' Roger said coldly, 'and you knew very well that I was going to give her a home when we returned from honeymoon. I made that quite plain.'

'I never take you seriously,' Emma said crossly, unbuttoning the jacket of her two-piece.

'You must always take me seriously, my dear,' Roger said gravely. 'I never say anything I don't mean.'

'Really?' Emma gave him a look and, removing her hat, tossed it on the sofa. 'You surprise me.'

Roger began to stroke Coral, who stretched her paws luxuriously, digging her claws more firmly into his lap.

'Don't talk in riddles, Emma, and please don't let's quarrel so soon after our honeymoon. I would hate the servants to think . . .' He paused, as if uncertain what to say.

'Think? Think what?' Emma thrust her chin in the air.

'Think . . . that all was not well,' he concluded.

'Let them think what they like,' she said petulantly, flinging herself into a chair. 'But get rid of that cat.'

Roger, carefully holding Coral so as to disturb her as little as possible, stood up and gently placed her again on the chair where he had been sitting. Then he put his hands in his pockets and turned with a deceptive air of nonchalance to face his wife.

'Don't you talk to *me* like that,' he said. 'This is my house, and my cat, and if you don't like them you can leave.'

'How dare you talk to *me* like that,' she hissed, rising from her chair. 'And how dare you say it is "your" house. It was bought for *us*.'

'Nevertheless, it is in my name.'

'A mere formality,' she stormed.

'No, no, no formality,' Roger said coldly. 'My uncle is a man of business, also a student of human nature. He knew exactly what he was doing when he put the house in my name.'

'I understood the house was a wedding-present for *us*,' Emma insisted, 'and anyway, we are to share it, and I refuse to share it with *that*!' She pointed a quivering finger at Coral again. 'I can't stand cats.' She agitatedly began to stroke her arms. 'I have a thing about them.'

'I'm very sorry, Emma,' Roger pitched his tone more sympathetically, 'but you didn't make your distaste clear, otherwise I should have told you about my own strong feelings in the matter. Coral has been a companion and friend to me since I was twelve. She is now a very old cat and, as Lally lives constantly in the country, there is no one in Montagu Square to take the interest in her she expects.'

'Let Lally have her in the country.'

'Lally accepts, and has done for some time, that Coral belongs to me. We have a bond, a deep tie of affection. I would not give up my cat for anything . . . or anyone.'

Emma adopted a petulant whining tone. 'I think you love the cat more than me, Roger.'

'It's a different kind of love,' Roger said tactfully.

'But it is true, isn't it?'

'It's not true.'

'Then why are you so cold to me and so warm to the cat?'

With a sigh, Roger sat on the arm of the chair so as not to disturb Coral.

'Emma, you are behaving like a child. If all has not gone well with our marriage, you must give it time.'

'How much time?' she hissed again. 'How much time before I know I am loved, wanted like a woman? How much time does one have to wait for *that*, Roger?'

Roger crossed his arms and with a look of disdain on his face, gazed at her.

'I said if you were not happy you could go.'

'Go? Are you serious? Go back to my father and mother?'

'If you wish.'

'Tell them our marriage is a failure; our honeymoon was a disaster?'

'You can tell them what you like, Emma. But you can't blackmail me.' He rose and, striding to the door, paused. 'But if you do leave, you will never be welcome back, and in the eyes of society, which you seem to care so much about, it is *you* who will appear the fool, not I. So think about it, Emma, before you do, or say, anything you may later regret.'

*

The site was just north of Dorchester in the Piddle Valley, and at the moment was a field put to pasture, with a stream and woodland at one boundary, and some old farm buildings in a state of dereliction at the other. From where they stood they could see the spire of All Saints church in the High Street of the town immortalised by the celebrated novelist Thomas Hardy.

Richard Wainwright, known as Dick, was a northerner; a bluff man from the Yorkshire Dales who invented a novel and economic threshing-machine after watching the old-fashioned implement at work on his father's farm in Wharfedale. He had gone on to invent a number of other farm gadgets and implements, so that by his present age of fifty he had become a millionaire. Some said he was one several times over.

Dick Wainwright had met Bart Sadler when he was looking for property in the West Country. He had first of all thought of building a dwelling for himself and his family in keeping with his wealth and prestige, and Bart, a fixer and dabbler as well as a stone-mason, had introduced him to his brother-in-law Laurence, who was looking for the chance to expand.

However, Wainwright wanted to build a factory to make his inventions and, as it happened, Bart Sadler had just the place – a field he had bought speculatively several years before which, since it had once contained farm dwellings, could be built on without tiresome bureaucratic wrangling.

The sale for the construction of a factory had been completed, architectural plans had been drawn up, and now, with Wainwright and Laurence Yetman, Bart was pacing the site, discussing the timetable for the erection of the factory.

Laurence had already spent weeks costing the project with the help of the architect and his surveyor. Now he stood with the plans in his hand, an arm stretched before him.

'You see, we can build without destroying the coppice. The whole thing will be curtained from the road by trees.

'Capital,' Mr Wainwright said, 'we don't want to upset the locals.'

'You won't upset them because you'll be providing them with work.' Bart sucked on a large cigar in his mouth. 'I don't think there'll be many complaints.'

'And when can all this be achieved, Laurence?' Wainwright looked eagerly at him.

'I would say in eighteen months' time, provided we can start straightaway.'

'Start as soon as you like.' Wainwright thrust a massive hand into Laurence's. 'That can't be soon enough for me.'

Laurence and Bart parted from Wainwright after lunch at the King's Arms and then set off in Bart's pony and trap for the drive to Wenham, the two men discussing the details of the business on the way.

Laurence, well satisfied with the day, began to hum while Bart, the reins in his hand, chewed on the butt of his cigar.

'I think I might buy a motor-car,' Laurence said after a while. 'We'll soon be left behind.'

'I think horseflesh is more reliable.' Bart gently touched his pony's back with his whip.

'You surprise me. A man like you.'

'How do you mean, "a man like me"?' Bart looked questioningly at his companion.

'A go-ahead fellow, ambitious to be wealthy.'

'Oh, I'm not all that ambitious.' Bart flicked the whip again.

'I bet you've got quite a bit on the side already?' Laurence continued his gaze, but Bart kept his eyes on the road.

'You could say I have a pound or two on one side, but I am by no means wealthy. Anyway, looks as if with Wainwright you'll be able to afford your car, a big one, any time you like.'

Laurence put his hands behind his head and leaned back. 'Wainwright seems a reasonable sort of fellow.'

'Seems so.'

'What do you mean, "seems so"?' Laurence again glanced sideways at Bart.

'Yes, he seems a good sort of fellow. I don't 'zactly know him very well.'

'You don't – 'zactly know him very well?' Laurence looked perplexed. 'But you introduced us, Bart.'

'It still doesn't mean I know him very well. He's a business acquaintance of Prosper Martyn.'

'Then his banking references will be good.'

Bart turned his level, rather disturbing gaze on Laurence for a moment or two. 'Why should they not be?'

'Well, a lot of money is involved.'

'He will pay in stages.'

'Of course; that's the normal procedure.'

Bart was to go on to Sadlers' Farm to visit his relations, but they halted at Laurence's gate.

'Why not come in and have a bite with us? We can iron out the details of the business.'

'If you're worried, if you're not happy,' Bart said in a firm, decisive tone, 'you don't need to go on.'

'But I'm too involved to back out! I don't *want* to back out. But maybe in my enthusiasm I've rushed ahead. Anyway, come in and at least say "hello" to Sarah-Jane. Besides, I think there is someone else at our house who you might like to see.'

'Oh? And who might that be?'

'You'll see.' Laurence's face broke into a smile.

'In that case, how can I refuse?'

It was still daylight, and there were two women sitting on a bench outside the house while the Yetman children capered on the lawn in front of them.

They were deep in conversation, but as the pony and cart rattled up the drive they both looked round, and as the trap stopped and the two men alighted, Sarah-Jane jumped up and ran towards Laurence, who greeted her with a hearty kiss on the lips.

'Did all go well?' she asked.

'I think so,' Laurence replied. 'Didn't it, Bart?'

'I think so.' Bart, sounding non-committal, kissed his sister and then waved his hand at Sophie Woodville, who sat watching the scene, her arm resting casually on the back of the bench.

She had an odd expression in her eyes, the twist of her body seemed provocative, and Bart found his interest in her increasing by leaps and bounds as he returned her quizzical gaze.

'Hello!' she called, waving back.

'So *this* is the surprise?' Bart murmured to Laurence as he left his side and strolled over to Sophie. 'Hello, Mrs Woodville. How nice to see you.'

'Nice to see you, Mr Sadler.' Her tone was aloof rather than warm. He thought she was a cold woman in whom an inner fire burned, like a volcano topped with snow and ice. She challenged him, and the friction between them intrigued, nay excited him.

'Isn't it time you two used Christian names?' Sarah-Jane asked as she joined them. 'Sophie, Bart.'

They exchanged distant smiles which seemed to acknowledge the fact that, in reality, they knew each other quite well.

'So you're in this venture too, are you?' Sophie moved along the bench so that Bart could sit next to her.

'Venture? What venture?'

'To build a huge factory.'

'Oh, I'm not in the plan, I merely introduced the builder to the buyer.'

'I *beg* your pardon?' Laurence, who had been greeted with rapture by his children, had Martha's hand in his. He couldn't help overhearing the conversation. '*I* thought we were going to be partners?'

'Oh, did you?' Bart, looking surprised, turned round to face him. 'What gave you that idea?'

'That's what I mean by discussing details. I simply assumed that you were in with me.'

'You shouldn't make assumptions,' Bart chuckled, and put a match to a fresh cigar.

'Seriously.' Laurence told Martha to run and play, and gently pushed her off. Then he walked over to Bart and Sophie. 'Could we talk about this in private, Bart?'

'By all means.' Bart rose, and with a smile to Sophie murmured: 'Shan't be long.'

'Dinner will be ready quite soon.' Sarah-Jane, sensing trouble, looked anxiously at Laurence. 'You're staying to dinner, aren't you, Bart?'

'If I may.' Bart put his arm around Laurence's shoulder as they walked towards the house. 'We shall sort this out in a few minutes.'

Laurence had a workroom at the top of the house. It was cluttered with plans and drawings and no one was allowed there, not even a maid to clean it. A long, low table stood in front of the window, and he now threw down on it copies of the plans he had taken with him to Dorchester. Then he slumped in an easy-chair, inviting Bart to sit opposite him. But Bart seemed to prefer to stand, his back to the window, resting his weight on the sill.

'Now, what is troubling you?' Bart said.

'I think there's a misunderstanding,' Laurence began.

'I never said I'd be a partner,' Bart butted in.

'I assumed you would want to share the profit . . . and the risk.'

'Risk?' Bart looked startled. 'Look, there *is* no risk. Wainwright is a millionaire. Check with your relations.'

'Oh, I shall do that all right. But still, your reluctance to come in makes me uncomfortable about the whole thing.'

'I can't think why.' Bart used his cigar like a baby's dummy, swivelling it from one side of his mouth to the other.

'Well, it's good to have a partner.'

'But you have one. Wainwright. Frankly, I think too many cooks spoil the broth.'

'But it's a *very* big undertaking for me, unsupported . . .'

'Now that Pelham's Oak is not to be sold, and there's no pressure on you to buy it, I should have thought you were quite comfortably off. Remember, although you run the risk – and, frankly, I don't think there is much of a risk – you get all the profits.'

'I'm not a risk-taker.' Laurence shook his head.

'Then you shouldn't be in business. All builders take risks. Sure you can do it, Laurence! You've got cold feet, man.'

'I've never done anything so big. I'll have to have bank support. I don't like doing it on my own.'

'Well.' Bart put his hands in his pockets, his expression slightly contemptuous. 'As you say, you're already involved. Frankly, I haven't got the money to spare, even if I wanted to. I never keep loose change. I'm sorry you misunderstood.'

'Then why did you bring Wainwright and me together?'

'Because you're my brother-in-law. Wainwright and I were talking stone for the house he thought of building. Then he decided to buy.' Bart extended a hand in Laurence's direction. 'The rest you know.'

'I always thought it was a partnership.'

Emphatically Bart shook his head. 'That's not my line of business. I leave that sort of thing to the experts. But if you ask me, if you back out, apart from being thought a fool, you'll regret it all your life. You're on the way to being a very wealthy man.'

Dinner was rather a subdued affair. There was obvious tension between the two men and it was left to the women to make small talk.

In desperation to get the conversation going, Sophie talked about her life as a missionary. She mentioned George's name frequently, yet she could not help noticing Bart's interest in her.

'I think you told me you hoped to go back?' Bart said when she appeared to have finished, and, sadly, she nodded her head.

'But I am not allowed to.'

'And why not?'

'They will not have me with children, and they will not have me without them. I am barred from the field until they are grown up, after which I feel I may be too old.'

'But may you not just go, if that's what you wish to do?'

'I'm afraid not. You have to be sent by a church society, and to go alone would be out of the question. Besides, it is very costly.'

Dinner finished soon after that, because Sophie wished to go back to Pelham's Oak before dark. Laurence was putting on his coat to take her home when Bart stopped him.

'Do let me escort Mrs Woodville home. It is on my way. That is, if she doesn't mind a pony and trap and the company of a strange man?'

'Of course I don't mind.' Sophie gave a gracious smile. 'And, really, you're not strange. You're *almost* a friend.'

There seemed an irony in the way she said it. At the door Bart held out his hand to Laurence.

'It was a good day, Laurence. No hard feelings, then?'

'Of course not.' Laurence smiled good-humouredly. 'As you said, a misunderstanding. But I dare say I will check with the Heering bank, just to be sure . . .'

'Oh yes, do that.' Bart shrugged into his coat. 'I'm sure you'll find everything is in order. Wainwright strikes me as straight.'

He looked out towards the pony and trap being held by the groom.

'It is still light and a fine evening. Will you be warm enough, Mrs Woodville?'

'Oh, I should think so.' She took her shawl from Sarah-Jane and kissed her cheek. 'Thank you for a lovely day.'

'I enjoyed it,' Sarah-Jane said. 'And next time, be sure to bring the children.'

'I would have brought them today, but their grandfather loves to have them without me. He spoils them. I'm rather strict,' she added with a sideways glance at Bart.

But he was clambering into his seat while Laurence helped her up beside him; and Bart then drove off, raising his whip in farewell.

Laurence watched them until they were by the bridge and out of sight. Then, his wife following, he went inside, putting out the lights methodically, one by one.

Laurence Yetman was the least complex of the three children of Eliza and Ryder Yetman. On him, as the eldest, had fallen the mantle of responsibility when his father unexpectedly died. He had wanted to leave school and work in order to support his mother, who had found that her husband's death meant that she had fallen on lean times. Within a year or two of Ryder's death the family cupboard was bare.

Eliza had taken many years to decide to marry Julius Heering. She was a proud woman who had not wished to be thought of as a fortune-hunter. As proud as his mother, and as independent, Laurence would never have asked a penny from his stepfather, who would probably not have given it to him anyway. It took the family some time to realise how close Julius was with his money.

But up to now there had been no need to borrow. Laurence, with his father's foreman, Perce Adams, had built up a successful business. But building was a risky, speculative trade, and cash flow was always a problem. Building materials had to be bought and paid for long before the first revenues came in. It was this that had made him concerned about what he considered to be the reneging of his brother-in-law.

As he turned off the last of the lights, he and Sarah-Jane popped their heads into the children's bedrooms to be sure they were asleep. As they reached the privacy of their room, Sarah-Jane put an arm round his shoulder and shut the door.

'You're out of sorts tonight, dear,' she said, resting her head briefly against his shoulder. 'It's something between you and Bart, isn't it?'

Laurence gently disengaged himself from her and, going over to the bed, sat down and began taking off his shoes.

'You could say that.' He carefully removed his left shoe and sat with it in his hand, looking at her.

'Is it about the Dorchester plot and Mr Wainwright?'

'Yes, it is; but I'd rather not involve you in it, if you don't mind, my dear. This is between men.'

Sarah-Jane swiftly crossed the room and stood in front of him.

'Oh no it's not, Laurence Yetman. It is also between husband and wife. What worries you worries me. You know that.'

'I know that, dearest.' He put his shoe on the floor and reached for her hand. 'But why should I trouble you with my business worries; especially as Bart is your brother?'

'It makes no difference,' she said, sitting next to him. 'I am your wife. That is the closest union, the closest bond imaginable, is it not?'

'Yes it is,' he said, his eyes filling with love as he gently kissed her cheek.

'Then tell me what it is.'

'This is a very big project.' Laurence carefully removed his right shoe. 'I am unsupported if Wainwright doesn't pay.'

'But he will pay?' Her eyes anxiously searched his.

'There is no reason to doubt it; but I imagined Bart and I would be in this as equal partners. But he said that was never his intention. I don't know whether to believe him or not, and that's the truth.'

Sarah-Jane, head in her hands, stared for some seconds at the floor. Then she raised her head and her eyes were troubled.

'Bart is my brother. I know he can be difficult, but I don't think he is dishonest. There must be a misunderstanding between you.'

'I'm quite sure he isn't dishonest.' Laurence's brows knitted together in bewilderment. 'As you say, it *may* be a misunderstanding.'

'But usually Bart is so clear.'

'The problem is that up to now I have built houses, halls, a school, but never a factory the size Mr Wainwright has in mind. It will be a huge building, of complex construction because of the heavy machinery Mr Wainwright will be using and also making. I have never undertaken anything so big and, frankly, it is a little beyond my capacity; but, of course, I don't want to turn it down. Mr Wainwright intends to build more factories in the West Country and I want to be in on it. If I succeed in this one, I may well be asked to do the others. So you see, Sarah-Jane,' he turned to her and put a hand on her cheek, 'it is a very worthwhile and important venture which I understood I was to share jointly with Bart, who introduced me to Wainwright.'

'But what makes you think Bart would take the risk? He is a loner and always has been.'

'I thought he would because there are handsome profits to be made. He tells me now he is only interested in supplying the stone, and that has always been the case.'

'I see.' Sarah-Jane's expression was grave. 'It is complicated. Will you go ahead without him?'

'I shall really want to go ahead without him, but I shall have to borrow heavily. Up to now I have never needed to. We always paid our way. It is against my instincts.'

'But all business people borrow,' Sarah-Jane said encouragingly. 'That is what banks are for.'

'Yes, but I am not one of them. I don't trust them.'

'Not trust the banks?' Sarah-Jane looked shocked.

'Well, let's say I would rather not be in their hands.'

'But Laurence.' She nuzzled her face close to his and ran her hand up and down his back. 'Surely the Heerings . . .'

'I would never approach them,' Laurence said vehemently. 'I would never go near my stepfather for help in a matter like this. I would not want to, and I am sure my mother would not want me to. I would not give him the satisfaction of turning me down. Look at the way he behaved over Pelham's Oak. He wouldn't lift a finger for Uncle Guy.'

'That was a different matter. That was buying something he didn't want, or helping out a man he didn't believe deserved it.'

'But still my mother was shocked by his attitude,' Laurence said gravely. 'As far as Julius is concerned, the scales are falling rapidly from her eyes.'

'You will have to go to the bank.' Sarah-Jane yawned, got off the bed and began to get undressed.

'Which bank?'

'Our bank. The bank in Wenham.'

'And have them all know my affairs? No thank you.'

'Laurence, be reasonable.' Sarah-Jane sat on the bed and began to remove her stockings. 'We are local people, known and, I think, highly respected. Mr Becket is fairly new, and doubtless anxious to please, to make an impression. He wants to establish himself as part of the town. I am sure he will be delighted to lend you money to finance the project. It will be a chance for him too. So why don't you go and ask him?'

Laurence sat beside her and took her in his arms.

'Let's put business out of our minds for the moment,' he said, 'and think of something else.'

After they left the house, Sophie and Bart Sadler drove for some moments in silence. It was just light enough to see the way ahead, but in any case Sophie felt very comfortable and secure sitting next to the driver. She felt happy; a quiet exhilaration possessed her, and she had not felt like this since she had known that George loved her. But Bart seemed unmoved. He sat with the reins in his hands, his hat pulled down well over his forehead, and a scowl on his face.

'So you don't mind coming alone with a man?' he said suddenly, as if to tease her.

'Of course I don't,' Sophie replied spiritedly. 'Why should I?'

'Some people would mind.'

'Maybe a young girl, and in that case it would not be wise. But I am a married woman, a widow. Why, I daresay I'm even older than you are. There is no harm in that, is there? Surely no one would talk.'

'You never know with folk,' Bart muttered. 'Specially hereabouts. I'm thirty-five.'

'And I'm thirty-six.'

'Are you now?' He didn't look at her, but went on gazing steadily in front of him. 'A good-looking woman, so you are, Sophie Woodville. Pleasing to the eye.'

'Thank you,' she said, grateful for the cover of twilight because she imagined a blush was stealing up her face.

'Your husband George now, was he a good-looking man?'

'Oh, I thought so,' she replied. 'Yes he was; but –' she wanted him to be quite clear about this ' – he was also a *godly* one. He was a saint, a martyr.'

'I see.' Bart appeared to ruminate on this for a moment or two, and then he said:

'I appreciate your words of religion, Mrs Woodville, but your God hasn't been very kind to you lately, has he?'

'I don't know what you mean.'

'I mean,' Bart said slowly, 'it seems to me He left you destitute, without a home. I hear you're to be made homeless again. Now He's not looking after you. Is He?'

'Well,' she paused, 'it's not quite decided.'

'But you wouldn't want to stay on with the newly-weds, would you?' Bart glanced quickly at her and quickly glanced away again.

'I don't think so,' she replied cautiously. 'I don't *think* it would be very wise. The late Lady Woodville never hit it off with her mother-in-law. Not that I am in a similar relationship to Connie, but I'm sure she will want to establish her own rules . . .'

'Huh!' Bart laughed out loud, and his tone was not kindly.

'Why do you laugh?' Sophie gave him a reproving look.

'I can't see that young woman establishing anything. Now that *is* a misalliance if ever there was one – that's if you're asking me.'

'I am certainly not asking you.' Sophie's tone was cold. 'And I don't think it's an idea you should put about. As far as I am concerned, having observed them together, I feel they are two young people *who* are indeed very fond of each other. I'm sure Connie would make an excellent Lady Woodville when the time came. Of course we must all hope that will not be for many years.'

'I hear Sir Guy drinks,' Bart said, 'and is not a well man. If you ask me, Carson will inherit the title sooner than he thinks.'

'You *do* seem full of a lot of misinformation, Mr Sadler.' Sophie's observation was caustic. 'I think Sir Guy has many years' life left in him yet. And to be well looked after by his son and daughter-in-law will be an excellent arrangement. I shall not be needed.'

'"Arrangement". That's the word. That's 'zactly what it is. An arrangement.' Bart suddenly stopped his horse in a wide bend in the road so that if there were any traffic following them, it could pass. As it was nearly nightfall this seemed unlikely, and the reins remained loosely held in his hands while the horse began to munch the leaves of an overhanging tree.

'I hear there is a lot of money involved,' he said darkly, as if he were discussing a crime.

'I never thought of *you* as a gossip, or likely to listen to it,' Sophie said derisively, but even in the dusk she saw his eyes flash and moved nervously along the bench away from him. He placed an arm loosely round her waist to restrain her.

'Sophie.'

'Yes, Mr Sadler?'

'I think you're trembling.'

'I am not. It is merely getting a little cold.' She pulled her shawl more closely around her shoulders. 'Do please drive on.'

'I can't drive on and say what I want to say,' he murmured huskily. 'But I can tell you, you won't come to any harm with me.'

'I should think not.' She raised her chin in the air and gazed boldly and defiantly at him.

'I want to tell you that I *do* like you, Sophie. I want you to know that.'

'Oh . . .' She did not know how to proceed.

'I like you very much. Do you like me?'

'I do, a little,' she ventured, and Bart flung back his head and laughed heartily.

'Only a little? Those are *not* the signals I feel I have been getting from you.'

'I've given you no signals.' She pursed her mouth prudishly.

'Oh yes you have, maybe without realising it. Men and women send signals to each other when they're interested, just as the animals do. Surely you must have been aware of that, even with the saintly George?'

'I don't like the way you refer to my late husband,' she replied stiffly.

'But you said he was a saint. You told me that yourself only a few minutes ago. I don't connect saints with fleshly matters.'

She was silent. His hand tightened round her waist. She felt the pricking of desire that she thought only engaged or married people felt, or should feel, when they were close to each other. She wanted him to take her and hold her; to lie down with her and love her, and almost immediately she felt sickened and ashamed of her thoughts and tried to banish them with a quick mental prayer.

'Oh Lord, take these evil thoughts and temptations away from me and leave my heart pure for thee.'

But the prayer remained unanswered. She felt his breath

against her cheek, his mouth on her mouth, and she surrendered herself to blind, overwhelming passion of a previously unknown intensity, even when she was married.

When eventually he released her, it was quite dark. He placed his hand on her bosom but she brushed it angrily away.

'We can't stop *here*,' he protested.

'We can,' she managed to reply, shaken by the rapid pounding of her heart. 'Please, Bart.' The pleading look she gave him was anguished. 'Please drive on.'

'But nothing is decided.' He reluctantly released her and, moving away, took up the reins.

'How do you mean, nothing is decided?' Her voice shook, so complete was her feeling of disorientation.

'Well.' He flicked the reins and the sleepy horse trotted slowly out on to the road. 'I would like your permission to court you, Sophie.' Slowly he turned his face round to gaze solemnly at her. 'With a view eventually to making you my wife.'

Gerald Becket had worked his way doggedly up the bank's hierarchy from being a junior messenger-boy at the age of sixteen. He was thus very proud of his position as manager even of a branch as small as Wenham, where, besides himself, there was one cashier.

But Mr Becket was not yet forty and he was intensely ambitious, firstly for a bigger branch, then, maybe, an administrative position with head office. After that, who knew? It was not beyond the bounds of speculation that he might end up on the board.

The Two Counties Bank of Dorset and Somerset – to give it its full title – was a private bank which had been started in the middle of the nineteenth century when Great Britain stood on the crest of a wave of optimism and prosperity. Queen Victoria was securely on the throne – unlike some Continental monarchs whose bases were often precarious. The government and the opposition had much in common, so that when one succeeded another in power, nothing much changed. They were all gentlemen. Disraeli, Gladstone: who could tell the difference except the dear Queen, who loved one as much as she hated the other?

To some extent this euphoria, despite one or two hiccups, had continued during the reign of good old Teddy. But the death of that jolly monarch had really seemed to mark the end of an age. There were rumblings abroad; anxiety was in the air. The working-classes in England were beginning to chaff against restraint, and in London the suffragettes carried unrest into the streets.

But Dorset, sleepy for centuries, scarcely seemed to have woken up. The poor continued poor and the rich were very rich. The country folk were stalwart, conservative, and upholders of the status quo.

Gerald Becket fitted in well with this philosophy and the rural environment. He was a Wiltshire man, who had married the comely daughter of the landlady whose lodgings he occupied in Dorchester where he was training.

They had been married after a courtship of several years, when Mr Becket was twenty-five and had been made head cashier. He had also saved prudently, with a fervour that was akin to meanness. He was a careful, cautious man, as became an official of the bank. Even his wife was thrifty. She had trained as a seamstress, and was able to mend his clothes, make his shirts and, eventually, all the clothes for the three children with whom in time they were blessed.

Mr Becket's appearance was an uninspiring one, except to the eye touched by love; or to his employers, who discerned in his very lack of looks or personality those qualities which were deemed important in a custodian of the fortunes of the bank.

He was of medium height, with a lean, cautious-looking face, a narrow, parsimonious mouth that would give nothing away, and small pig-like eyes that would guard closely the bank's secrets.

His thinning hair was obvious testimony to his lack of vanity, and his dress was sombre and restrained, though not restrained enough to make people lose confidence. Nothing about Mr Becket was flamboyant, colourful or extravagant.

He was the perfect bureaucrat, created, it might have seemed, in his mother's womb. He had made his way to the top not only by the correctness of his presentation, but by using the right amount of fawning and cajolery to impress his superiors.

Naturally, because marital harmony was seen as an asset, Mr Becket was a devoted family man, a church-goer, and quickly became a supporter of several local causes: treasurer of this society and that. In short, a pillar of the community where he had now been for about three years, having bought the house which had once belonged to Miss Bishop, the village schoolmistress, now dead.

Mr Becket was standing at the counter counting a sheaf of notes when Laurence Yetman entered the bank one morning not long after his conversation with his wife.

'Good morning, Mr Yetman,' Mr Becket cried genially, and leaned across the counter to shake his hand. 'Not often we have the pleasure of seeing you personally in here.'

'Well, there is a purpose for my visit today.' Laurence decided to come to the point at once. 'I wonder if I could have a word in private with you, Mr Becket?'

'Most certainly.' Mr Becket opened the gate in the counter and beckoned Laurence through. Then he turned to his assistant and said: 'Nigel, will you take over, and if anyone asks, say I am engaged.'

'Yes, Mr Becket,' Nigel said with the deference due to his superior.

Laurence followed Mr Becket into a tiny room behind the bank, whose single window, high up in the wall, was protected by iron bars. In the corner was a large safe, beside which there was a desk and two hard chairs. It was not the sort of place, Laurence thought, sitting down, where one would be inclined to linger: state your business and be gone, it seemed to say.

'Now,' Mr Becket sat down at his desk and clasped his hands together, 'to what do I owe the pleasure of this visit?'

'I am here to see you,' Laurence leaned back with the ease of a man come to bestow a favour, 'on a matter of business.'

'Just let me see.' Mr Becket got up and went to a drawer

from which he produced a thin folder. This he took back to his desk and, on resuming his seat, opened it.

'Your account is naturally in good standing, Mr Yetman. How are we able to assist you?'

'I am about to embark on one of the most ambitious and important projects in my life,' Laurence said. 'It could well make me a fortune.'

'That *is* excellent news.' Mr Becket rubbed his hands as though anticipating a share in that good fortune – for his bank, of course. 'Please tell me about it.'

Laurence then went on to explain about Mr Wainwright, the factory, the development near Dorchester, and the prospect of more. As he continued, Mr Becket's face grew thoughtful.

'I see,' he said when Laurence had finished. 'It is a very big project indeed.'

'So I shall need a bank facility,' Laurence concluded, 'or I shall have to take my business to some other bank.'

'Oh, there is no need for that.' Mr Becket was at pains to reassure his client. 'I am sure that this branch of the Two Counties Bank would be delighted to accommodate you.' He reached for a piece of paper and, his pencil poised over it, gazed at Laurence. 'Let me see, what facility would you be requiring?'

'About ten thousand pounds. Maybe fifteen.'

Mr Becket appeared unperturbed and scribbled a note on his piece of paper. 'As much as that?'

'Maybe twenty,' Laurence said aggressively.

'Well!' It was a large sum for such a small branch to deal with, and Mr Becket could be seen to be under some stress.

'I shall have to refer this to head office, Mr Yetman. However, I am sure that I can say there should be *no* difficulty for a person of your standing and consequence in this community.'

'Thank you.' Laurence was about to get up. 'When will I know for sure?'

'Oh, in a day or two. Tell me, Mr Yetman, I suppose you have no doubt as to the credit-worthiness of your client?'

'None at all,' Laurence replied robustly. 'He is a millionaire who has had dealings with the Martyn-Heering Bank.'

'Ah, the family business.' Mr Becket's ambitious eyes brightened. 'Tell me, did you never think of approaching *them* for such a large facility?'

'I never deal with the family bank,' Laurence replied abruptly. 'It would involve my mother and I have my pride. However, I am sure I could provide a reference as to Mr Wainwright's credit-worthiness.'

'That would be useful.' Mr Becket, growing in confidence by the minute in his ability to handle business of such magnitude, doodled on his blotter. 'And it would strengthen your case, certainly with my superiors, if you could put up your own private account, and your house, as further security. Then I think,' he finished with a charmless smile, 'there will be no problem at all.'

'My house?' Laurence looked startled.

'It is owned by you outright, is it not, Mr Yetman? There is no mortgage on it?'

'No, it is mine outright. The deeds were a wedding-present.'

'Why, that's excellent. If you have every confidence in your client, and with this extra security we have every confidence in *you*, it should produce a very happy partnership. Don't you think, Mr Yetman? And then, once the job is finished and you have made what you expect to be a very nice profit, you will doubtless use this to finance further projects, and then we can relinquish the deeds of your house.'

PART THREE

The Power of Money

17

The carriage drew up at the door of the Crown Hotel and the head porter hurried out to open the door. Having been warned in advance of the importance of the visitor, he was followed by an assistant porter and a boy. For a moment they all stood gazing up at the window of the carriage which had brought the distinguished visitor from Blandford Station, while she remained for a moment looking down at them.

She was not young but neither was she old. At one time she might even have been a beauty. But it was difficult to tell because her face was partly obscured by her hat. It was, however, possible to see her eyes, which were undeniably compelling. As the door was opened and the steps put down, and she began to alight, one thing was certain: the visitor was a very fine lady, a woman of consequence. There was no doubt about that at all.

She wore a hobble-skirt dress with a matching coat, and a large picture hat which turned up at the back, with a long ostrich feather sweeping over the brim. She held on to it tightly with her gloved hand as though she were frightened it might fall off.

It was difficult to tell how old the lady was exactly; maybe forty, maybe fifty – not more. Her face had a few lines, but her complexion was clear, and her eyes, dark blue flecked with grey, were surmounted by a pair of pencil-thin, imperiously arched eyebrows. She smiled graciously, even regally, around her and, as the manager came to the door, extended a hand over which he bowed low. 'Welcome to the Crown Hotel, Mrs Gregg. I trust you had a good journey?'

'Passable,' Mrs Gregg murmured in an accent which was hard

to place. 'Passable. The English trains are so *dirty* compared to those in America.'

The manager looked crestfallen, as though it was his personal responsibility.

'I hope we shall make up for the discomforts of your journey from Southampton, Mrs Gregg. Your suite is prepared and your personal maid is waiting for you.'

'Good.' Mrs Gregg again smiled graciously, beginning to remove her gloves as they entered the lobby of the hotel. 'Please have tea sent up to my room immediately.'

'*Immediately*, Mrs Gregg.' The manager snapped his fingers at the underlings and began barking orders.

'Mrs Gregg's luggage up to her room . . . A tray of tea for Mrs Gregg with hot buttered toast. She is tired after her journey.'

Mrs Gregg swept up the stairs to the first floor, preceded by the manager who, on the way, had collected the housekeeper who brought up the rear. He swung open the door of the suite he had reserved for the visitor, and had filled with fresh flowers. He then stood aside and bowed.

'I hope this pleases you, Mrs Gregg. We are only a small market town and this is the best we have to offer.'

Mrs Gregg looked critically round, a frown on her face. The manager winced. The housekeeper, clutching her bunch of keys, hovered nervously.

'There are some very fine hotels in Bournemouth, Mrs Gregg,' he ventured.

'This hotel will suit perfectly well, for the time being. I am in Blandford for a particular purpose.' Mrs Gregg, still frowning, turned on him. 'You could call it business.'

'Ah you *have* been here before, madam?'

'Many years ago,' Mrs Gregg said, as the housekeeper ushered in a girl dressed in the uniform of a maid.

'This is your personal maid, Elizabeth, Mrs Gregg,' the housekeeper said. 'She is to look after you exclusively, and will help you in any way she can.'

Mrs Gregg scarcely glanced at the girl.

'I wish to rest now,' she said to the manager. 'I have had a very tiring journey all the way from Florida. I will have dinner in my room at eight.'

'Yes, Mrs Gregg.'

'You may send up the menu now.'

Mrs Gregg was obviously keen on her food, although her figure, slightly plump and voluptuous, was well-corseted.

'Very well, Mrs Gregg.'

'And you, girl, run my bath.' Mrs Gregg appeared to notice for the first time the young woman who stood gawping at her from the far side of the room.

'Yes, 'm.' The girl bobbed, and rushed into the bathroom to do the bidding of this mysterious and awe-inspiring stranger.

She stood over the bath as the hot steam rose and brushed her hair back from her face.

Elizabeth Yewell had never acted exclusively as a lady's maid at the hotel, and she didn't know quite what was expected of her. The housekeeper, Mrs Buttle, had run through a few formalities with her: how to fold, iron and care for clothes; how to dress a lady's hair and prepare her toilet; but, mainly, how to keep out of the way, and be seen only when needed.

Elizabeth had been working at the Crown for some six months in various capacities, though not at the bar. Her parents had refused to allow her to work in the bar, so she spent a lot of time in the kitchen, in the laundry and in the linen-room which, in many ways, she liked best. She slept with the other staff in the attic under the rafters, sharing her room with two maids who did most of the rough housework.

The life of a busy hotel appealed to Elizabeth. She liked being far enough away from Wenham, but not too far. She enjoyed hotel life better than life on a farm; though what she would really have preferred was a life of ease, such as Mrs Gregg seemed accustomed to.

Elizabeth glanced through the bathroom door and saw Mrs Gregg carefully remove her large hat, then her coat, before glancing at herself critically in the mirror. Clearly she liked what she saw, hair which might or might not have been natural, rather elaborately coiffured with a fringe of little curls. Her features were strong, and she had a full bust. She was about five foot five inches tall and carried herself with authority; a woman, clearly, whom it would be unwise to anger.

But Elizabeth would take good care not to do that and, perhaps, she thought to herself idly, she might well find a permanent position with Mrs Gregg, or someone like her, and travel the world; but that would mean leaving Frank. It would be difficult to explain to Frank that she would like to see the world before settling down. Frank would most certainly not understand.

Elizabeth bore some resentment towards her parents for removing her so abruptly from Sadlers' Farm and forbidding her to see Carson Woodville. There had been nothing except flirtation between them.

She was a servant-girl, this action seemed to suggest, not good enough for him. But she soon forgot him – she was like that – and Frank Sprogett, a brewer's drayman, was just as strong as Carson and even better-looking. Anyway, to have become involved with a Woodville would have been too complicated and, essentially, Elizabeth was a simple girl who sought only simple happiness from life.

'Girl!' came the shrill tones from the next room.

'Yes, 'm?' Elizabeth broke her reverie and scuttled through the door of the bathroom into the bedroom.

'Help me undress.'

'Yes, 'm.'

Mrs Gregg turned, and Elizabeth began to unfasten the silk buttons of her dress right down to her waist. She unhooked the whalebone brassière and tugged at the laces of the formidable corset. When this was loose, Elizabeth was instructed to fetch her gown and, in the privacy of this all-enveloping garment, Mrs Gregg completed the removal of her corset and flung it on the bed. Then with the relieved sigh of one who has unburdened herself of a horrible constriction, she went and sat on the stool in front of the dressing-table mirror and began to unfasten her earrings.

Elizabeth gazed at her with fascination until she realised that Mrs Gregg was looking at her.

'Have you done this sort of work before, girl?'

'No, 'm,' Elizabeth murmured.

'I thought not. I suppose a town like Blandford doesn't have much call for ladies' maids. Where are you from, girl?'

'Wenham, 'm.'

'Wenham?' Mrs Gregg paused, and seemed about to go on when there was a knock on the door. Elizabeth went to it, half-opened it, and brought in a tray on which was Mrs Gregg's tea.

'Thank heaven for that.' Mrs Gregg stretched herself out on the bed and lit a cigarette. 'I'm absolutely *parched*.'

Elizabeth carefully poured milk and tea into a cup and, taking it over to the bedside, gingerly placed it beside Mrs Gregg.

'Will that be all, 'm?'

'Will it be all?' Mrs Gregg looked at her sharply. 'I should think it would not be all. While I'm in the bath you may unpack my things, and while I'm having dinner you can press them. I've come a very long way, you know . . . What's your name, girl?'

'Elizabeth, 'm.'

'I've come from America, from a city called New Orleans. Do you know how far away that is, Elizabeth?'

Mrs Gregg put her hand over her eyes as if she was uninterested in the reply. She was clearly very tired. Elizabeth gazed with some fascination at the cigarette; she had never seen a woman smoke before.

'Four thousand miles. It's a long way.'

'That *is* a long way, madam.' Elizabeth, who had never been further than Bournemouth, was impressed. 'Did you know this part of the country before, ma'am?'

'I did,' Mrs Gregg said firmly, but she seemed disinclined to say more. Somehow she was not the sort of person of whom one dared ask questions; one only answered them.

Mrs Gregg was, indeed, an exacting mistress. She kept Elizabeth constantly at her beck and call until after her dinner when, wishing to go early to bed, she dismissed her.

On the whole Elizabeth felt pleased with her day, and that she had acquitted herself well. She rushed up to her room where one of her room-mates was already slumbering and, tearing off her uniform apron, flung a coat over her shoulders and tumbled down the back staircase to the yard. There were one or two horses tethered, awaiting their owners, but otherwise it was deserted and, opening the back gate, she crept along the hedge that bordered the field by the river. It was a bitterly cold night and she shivered.

Suddenly an arm shot out and grabbed her by the waist; she gave a little shriek but otherwise did not resist.

'Frank!' she gasped, 'you startled me.' But Frank silenced her with kisses and for several seconds they clung together, forgetful of the cold.

Frank Sprogett then leaned her against the wall and covered her body with his while she pulled her coat around both their shoulders. It was the only way they could meet without being seen.

'Wher've ye bin?' he enquired, looking anxiously at her. 'I was worried.'

'This Mrs Gregg arrived late this afternoon.'

'What's she like?'

'You can tell she'm a lady,' Elizabeth said thoughtfully, 'and yet there is something about her.'

'How do you mean?' Frank, using their close proximity, tried to insert his hand under her dress, but she didn't allow that sort of thing yet, and she smacked it sharply so that, shamefacedly, he withdrew it.

'Not *quite* a lady; it's hard to say why. Lady Woodville and Mrs Heering – now they are ladies, or rather, Lady Woodville was when she was alive. I can tell a lady when I see one, and Mrs Gregg . . .' Elizabeth screwed up her nose '. . . Mrs Gregg is not refined enough to be a lady. If anyone was to ask *me*, I'd say she was in some kind of business.'

'What do you mean?'

'Someone who works, has a shop maybe, like Miss Fairchild used to have in Wenham. Miss Fairchild became very wealthy.' Elizabeth's eyes widened dramatically. '*Very* wealthy. No one had any idea she had so much money and, if you ask me, I think Mrs Gregg is like that. Maybe she had a shop and she's sold it, and so she's got all this money; or she had gold shares, like Miss Fairchild . . .'

'Well . . .' Frank, not unusually for him, was at a loss for words.

'Don't say I said, though,' Elizabeth warned him anxiously. 'I may be quite wrong. I'd hate to lose my job.'

'I wouldn't say a word,' Frank assured her virtuously. 'When can we name the day, pet?'

'Oh *Frank* . . .' Elizabeth nestled her head against his shoulder. 'We can't get wed until you've got some more money. You've said it yourself.'

Frank sighed and pressed his body up against his beloved's again, and they both stood there, anticipating yet not daring to perform the act of being two in one flesh.

Frank worked for the brewery up the road. He drove the horse that pulled the dray, and he had first noticed Elizabeth in the yard of the Crown one bright day a few months before.

Elizabeth, though liking the work, found her days, but particularly her nights, at the Crown extremely dull. At weekends Ted came to fetch her and take her back to Wenham, and on Sunday nights he drove her back to Blandford again.

Elizabeth loved her parents but she resented the tight hold they kept on her. After all, she was nearly twenty-two, and many of the women of her age she knew were married and mothers of children.

But in Frank Sprogett she thought at last she had found someone of whom her parents – when they were eventually told – would approve. He was a year older than she was, a native of the town and a man of the working classes. He had good prospects at the brewery, and his intentions towards her were serious. He treated her with respect and, although he tried his chances, he knew he would get nowhere until a gold band was firmly around Elizabeth's finger.

'Best be getting back,' she said to Frank, giving a huge yawn. 'Besides, I'm frozen stiff. Mrs Gregg'll keep me hopping about all tomorrow, that's for sure.'

'What's she doing here?' Frank asked idly, not really interested.

'She's visiting. I wonder if maybe she knew the Portmans, or important people like that.'

'How long's she staying?'

'Indefinite, she says.' Elizabeth paused. 'She's brought so much luggage that if you'm ask me she'm in no hurry to go back. Now *Frank*,' she said as he refused to let her go, but he hugged her tighter.

'Come on,' he wheedled, 'give us one last kiss.'

Mrs Gregg had dined that night in her room: English roast beef washed down by half a bottle of wine. There had been one or two whiskies beforehand and there would be one or two after. She was a woman used to hard drink, and she liked it. But she was seldom drunk. It had been necessary all her life to have her wits about her.

She dressed for dinner, even though it was in her room, and afterwards she dismissed the little maid Elizabeth and got into her nightgown and lay on the bed, smoking.

After a while she got up and poured herself another generous measure of whisky. Then she drew back the bedclothes and lay there for some time, smoking and thinking.

Wenham.

So the little creature came from Wenham? So did she, Agnes Gregg.

Agnes was her real name, but Gregg was assumed. There had never been a Mr Gregg; but it suited Agnes Yetman, returning to the place of her birth, to let people think that there had; to give the appearance of being a wealthy widow who had been a long time away from her native land.

The town on the banks of the River Wen was a place she had never forgotten during all the years of her wandering, in the Middle and Far East and, finally, in the United States.

Wenham; she had frequently thought about it, particularly in moments of stress when times had not been so good. It had seemed like a haven of rest, of peace and security; and perhaps, in the harsh circumstances of her life, she endowed it with a mystique it had never really had. It was only in recent years that times had been good, that they had improved sufficiently for her to have made enough money to be able to go home again; home, after more than twenty years, to Wenham.

But what would Wenham say about her? Would it remember her and the events that had made her desert the town of her birth so many years before?

That was what she did not, as yet, know.

Miss Fairchild, normally a person so well in control of herself, appeared extraordinarily nervous. Already, when Carson entered the room, her colour was high, her hands and fingers fluttered about, never still.

Carson had escorted Connie to her organ practice in the church and, at Miss Fairchild's invitation, had come to tea alone in order, she had suggested, that they could get to know each other better.

Miss Fairchild's grey hair, rather sparse now, was carefully arranged over her head in tight grey curls, so as to disguise the thin patches where her skull showed through. Yet her eyes were as clear and as shrewd as when she had cut the cloth for the customers in the back room of her parents' haberdashery shop; and her chin was firm – though the surrounding skin was wrinkled into tiny folds, clear evidence of her age.

She wore a rather pretty grey chiffon tea-gown that reached her ankles. Miss Fairchild had seldom in her life bought a dress, but had them made by her dressmaker. Never profligate, she had kept yards of material from the bales in her shop, when she had finally sold it, as a provision against hard times. Fortunately those times had never occurred, and apparently, now, never would. How little idea she had had, in those far-off days, that she would ever be in a position to save the mighty Woodvilles from the ignominy of having to sell their ancient and noble family home!

Carson, who had on his best suit for the occasion, and had taken care to give himself a close shave – something he seldom did – stood awkwardly, aware of Miss Fairchild's nervousness as she fussed unduly over the tea-table, giving a rapid set of instructions one after the other to the bewildered maid, then confusing her even further by contradicting them. Finally, she invited him to sit down.

'Thank you, Miss Fairchild,' Carson said. This was the first time he and Miss Fairchild had been alone since the engagement was announced. Hitherto there had always been an over-excited Connie hovering, listening, anxious that she should not be discussed behind her back.

'Milk and sugar, Carson?' Miss Fairchild enquired as a formality; but, of course, she should know. They had had tea together at least a half-dozen times in their curious acquaintanceship, but today she had forgotten.

'Both, please, Miss Fairchild.'

She passed him his teacup and the bowl of sugar, and he saw that her thin, veined hand shook.

'Thank you, Miss Fairchild,' he said, taking two large spoonfuls. She then passed him the plate of thinly cut cucumber sandwiches; he took two, and then sat gazing at her.

'Well?' he said at last.

'Well,' Miss Fairchild replied with her nervous, twittery smile, 'this is the first time we have been alone together since you and Connie were engaged, Carson.'

'Yes, it is.'

She leaned forward confidentially. 'I wanted to tell you alone how happy I am that you two dear people are to form a marriage alliance.' She had thought carefully about how to put it, as 'falling in love' was a term that seemed so inexact.

Carson nervously ran his finger round his collar, too ill at ease to reply.

Miss Fairchild realised that she didn't feel like eating and, leaving her sandwiches untouched, she took a sip of tea. Then, taking care her cup didn't wobble, she carefully placed it on the table beside her.

'You know, of course, Carson,' she ventured after a while, 'that I am settling a great deal of money on dearest Connie on her marriage.' Miss Fairchild choked on the word 'marriage', as though it were one she had never dared hope to hear uttered in connection with her beloved ward. 'In addition to which,' she continued, since Carson still couldn't find his tongue, 'she has a great deal of money of her own.'

'I am aware of that.' Carson hung his head. He was not at all proud of himself, even though he had been used in the interests of the family. 'Not,' he added as an afterthought, 'that it is all that important a factor in my desire to marry Connie.'

Miss Fairchild ignored this sentiment, knowing it to be quite untrue.

'Carson!' Suddenly she threw pretence aside and leaned towards him. 'She must never *know* . . . You know what I mean. She must never *know* that I approached Sir Guy. You *do* know what I am trying to say, don't you, Carson?'

She took up her teacup again and her hand shook more violently than ever, spilling some of the tea into the saucer.

'I do know what you mean,' he said, still avoiding her eyes. It was one of the most painful occasions he could remember, and he wished he had declined the invitation.

'Nevertheless,' Miss Fairchild continued, 'I hope you care a little for Connie. I hope you will do what you can to make her happy. She is devoted to you, Carson, and I happen to love her very much. For so many years she has been my life, and all I want is her happiness, now and when I am gone.'

'I care a great deal about Connie.' Carson was aware of a constriction in his throat. 'I really like her.'

'Oh, you do?' Miss Fairchild prayerfully clasped her hands together. 'I was sure you must. I was convinced that her feeling for you could only be reciprocated. She is a dear girl. She is unique.'

'I will do everything in my power to make her happy,' Carson said solemnly. Then he heard the front door open, and someone came flying along the corridor, bursting into the room where they were sitting.

'Oh, I'm sorry.' Connie seemed dismayed to see them. 'Did I interrupt anything?'

Miss Fairchild, perfectly composed and equal to the occasion, patted the place beside her, gazing reassuringly into Connie's anxious face. 'We were talking about when the banns should be called, matters like that. There are all sorts of things to consider when you are about to be a married woman. There is the date, for instance. That is very important.'

She put an arm around Connie as if to protect her from the

harsh facts of life, even though, sooner or later, she must know them.

'Did we not think May a good month, Carson? If so, the banns had better be called now.'

'May?' Carson gulped. 'Is it not a little soon?'

'For what?'

'To arrange everything.'

'Not soon enough to arrange *everything*.' There was a peculiar emphasis in Miss Fairchild's voice, which Carson took to refer to the financial arrangements between her and his father. Creditors were beginning to press on the master of Pelham's Oak, who kept on fending them off with promises.

'Quite. May it is. Is that all right, Connie?'

'May.' Connie seemed afraid of the proximity too. 'There is so much to be done, Aunt. How can I ever get everything done by May?'

'Such as what, my dear?' Her aunt's tone was mild, assured. 'I, who have so little to do, will see to everything for you. Never fear that.'

'And the music for the wedding . . .'

'Well, you certainly won't be playing *that*.' Carson was eager to break the ice.

'Oh no, of course I won't.' Connie smiled too, and the love in her eyes showing plainly, continued, 'I can't really believe I shall be the next mistress of Pelham's Oak.'

'And there is a lot for you to look at there.' Carson stood up abruptly. 'My father asked me to invite you and Miss Fairchild to lunch. Should we say next Wednesday?'

'That seems *most* suitable,' Connie replied, aware of her dignity as a soon-to-be-married woman. 'Is that all right for you, Aunt?'

'Wednesday is most suitable,' Miss Fairchild replied, rising to her feet. 'Won't it be exciting?'

Then, Miss Fairchild's arm still tightly round Connie's waist, they escorted Carson to the door, where he stood for a moment before turning abruptly and walking briskly along the garden path.

His horse was tethered to the fence outside, and he unfastened the reins with a preoccupied expression on his face. He then swung himself onto his horse and, without looking at the house again, cantered down the street. Connie remained looking after him, her hand half-raised in farewell. But when he didn't respond she lowered it, crestfallen, to her side.

Miss Fairchild tried to draw her back into the house, her arm still round her waist, but Connie remained stubbornly where she was.

'Come in, dear,' Miss Fairchild urged, releasing her grip. 'It's a touch draughty with that door open.'

Reluctantly Connie turned, shut the door and followed her guardian along the passage.

'You didn't finish your tea, Connie,' Miss Fairchild admonished, glancing at her cup. 'I expect you were too excited. Would you like me to have some more freshly made?'

'No thanks, Aunt.' Connie slumped into the chair and gazed morosely at the pot.

'Connie, what *is* it, dearest?' Miss Fairchild enquired uneasily, pouring herself a cup, though she knew that by now it would be cold.

'He didn't look back to wave.'

'Oh my dear, don't be *silly*! That's of no importance.'

'He looked as though he'd completely forgotten me as soon as his back was turned.'

'My dear.' Miss Fairchild perched on the arm of her chair and began to stroke the hair back from her forehead. 'He has so many things on his mind, a young man on the verge of matrimony. It's a big step.'

'It's a big step for me too, Aunt.' She looked up with eyes that were full of doubt and pain. 'It is a *very* big step for me.'

'I know, dearest, I know.' The movement of Miss Fairchild's hand became rather more agitated, as if expressive of her own inner turbulence. 'But, for a man introducing a new woman to his home, it is a *very* big step. Carson may well be rather reluctant to give up the carefree ways of a bachelor . . .'

'Then why is he doing it?' Connie's tone betrayed her bewilderment.

'Well, my dear, because he loves you . . . of course.'

'Do you really think he loves me, Aunt?' Connie's voice was flat, her expression as she looked at her guardian searching.

'Oh, I'm *sure* of it,' Miss Fairchild said with emphasis.

'Did he tell you?'

'Not in so many words, but I wouldn't expect him to.'

'But he didn't tell me either, and I would have expected that. He has never told me he loves me.'

'But, my dear, he is shy. Men *are* shy creatures. They may not appear to be, but they are. Of course Carson loves you. Why else would he marry you?'

'Why else indeed?' Connie said, but from her expression it looked as though she were asking a question to which she did not know the answer.

'My little chick . . .' Miss Fairchild squatted with difficulty by her side '. . . don't be unhappy when such a glorious event is about to befall you. Why, you should be ecstatic! You are about to be the mistress of Pelham's Oak, Lady Woodville . . . Who would ever have imagined that? Little Connie Yetman.'

'The shy spinster with glasses who blushes at the drop of a hat,' Connie said bitterly. 'Who, indeed, would have imagined it – particularly when Carson Woodville is so handsome and so much sought-after.'

Miss Fairchild rose to her feet as if in despair and, turning to Connie, tapped her gently on the wrists.

'Enough of this, my girl! You are being morbid, and also very silly. Carson is devoted to you. He told me.'

'"Devotion" and "love" are not the same thing.'

'They *are*, Connie, they are. People have different ways of showing their emotions. Now don't you be getting silly thoughts about your marriage, or I shall be very cross with you. In fact, the sooner the banns are read the better.' She looked at the clock on the wall, and the notion of the passage of time seemed to confirm her resolution. 'I shall go and see the rector this very moment and discuss it with him.'

Mrs Lamb went once a week to Blandford to do her shopping in the market. The shops in Blandford had a better variety than those in Wenham, and the market was also larger.

Mrs Lamb was in her middle seventies, and although a brisk and active woman, and in much better shape mentally and physically than her husband, she was beginning to feel her age. Sometimes Sophie accompanied her and sometimes she went alone. She enjoyed the company of her daughter because they met so seldom. Their relationship, strained since Sophie's return to England, had grown worse because the Lambs had become jealous of her attachment to Guy, and the fact that their own grandchildren seldom visited them.

On this day, however, Sophie had called for her mother in Sir Guy's coach, and the rector's wife was ready and waiting as it drove up to the door.

'Won't you come in and have a word with your father?' Mrs Lamb gestured indoors. But Sophie, who had not got out of the coach, replied:

'I have to get back, Mother. We have an important luncheon tomorrow and I have much to do. Tell Father I'll pop in and say "hello" when we come back. I'll have time for a quick cup of tea.'

'Oh, very well, dear.' Mrs Lamb, who already had on her coat and hat, turned to the servant who stood by the door.

'Tell the rector Mrs Woodville will be back for tea. And make sure he has that cold pork for lunch.'

'Yes 'm.' The maid bobbed, and ran off to give the message to her master before she forgot it. Mrs Lamb herself closed the door behind her and walked to the coach, which stood right outside the door.

She was helped up the steps by the coachman, who then folded the steps, put them inside the carriage and firmly closed the door. He got into the driving-seat and took up the reins of the two bays, who knew practically every inch of the way between Wenham, Pelham's Oak and Blandford.

'Whoa there!' the coachman cried, flicking his whip lightly across their backs while he turned in the square outside the church, then trotted off down the main street towards the bridge.

Mrs Lamb found her daughter preoccupied as she studied a long list of purchases and errands in her hand.

'Who is coming to luncheon tomorrow, Sophie? May one ask?'

'You may certainly ask, Mother. Connie and Mrs Fairchild.' Sophie busily ticked one of the items with her pencil.

'I wouldn't have thought *that* was so important. I should consider someone like the mayor, or the chairman of the parish council, more important.' She sounded disappointed.

'Connie and Miss Fairchild are *very* important,' Sophie corrected her mother. 'Connie is going to marry Carson and this is her first official visit to the house since they became engaged.'

'I can't imagine that funny, spinsterish little girl as mistress of that huge house.' Mrs Lamb shook her head. 'I can't understand it at all.'

'Mother, don't call her a "funny little girl".' Sophie sounded irritated. 'She is a woman of twenty-four years of age. She is a very special person.' She looked sideways at her mother. 'I thought you always liked Connie Yetman?'

'Oh, I *do* like her,' Mrs Lamb protested, 'I like her *very* much; but as the wife of Carson Woodville . . .' She shook her head. 'It beggars the imagination; unless, as some people are saying, there is an ulterior motive,' she suggested darkly.

'And what can you mean by that?' Sophie still sounded cross.

'Money. Money is a singularly potent factor, is it not?'

'Mother, I do think that is unworthy of you.'

'I am human, and I am not a fool,' Mrs Lamb continued. 'A few weeks ago Pelham's Oak was for sale. Everyone knew that. Now Carson is to marry someone he hardly knows, who happens to be the plainest girl in town, but wealthy and with prospects of more wealth; and the house is no longer for sale.'

'That's a cruel insinuation, Mother.'

'Nevertheless, it *is* true.' The rector's wife was quite firm about this. 'Good and sweet Connie is, a wonderful musician, but plain. You cannot deny it, Sophie. The last woman in the world for a man of Carson's reputation.'

'Maybe Carson sees a beauty in her that you don't appreciate,' Sophie observed tactfully as the coach drew towards the town.

'You must know the reason if anyone does.' Mrs Lamb looked at her suggestively. 'If anyone knows what goes on at Pelham's Oak, you must. Wasn't it sudden? Wasn't it unexpected? And now there is this terrible rush to call the banns. Miss Fairchild came running round to see your father last week at five in the afternoon!'

'What's wrong with five in the afternoon?'

'Nothing is wrong with the time. It's the state she was in. I don't suppose there's any chance the marriage act has been anticipated?'

'That is a most disgraceful suggestion!'

'It's usually the reason for such haste. But in this case I favour money over fornication. "Oh, rector, they must be called quickly," she insisted. "There is *no* time to lose . . ." I never *heard* such a carry-on. Perhaps it was because she was afraid Carson would change his mind.'

'I don't think there's any chance of that. Carson and Connie are quite devoted to each other. Now, Mother,' Sophie briskly patted her mother's arm, 'forget about all this gossip and ill-informed speculation. Concentrate on your shopping list, otherwise you'll forget something and then you'll blame me.'

'Besides,' her mother went on grumbling, taking no notice of Sophie, 'what is to become of *you*? Have you thought of that?'

'I have been told I am welcome to stay in the house. Sir Guy was at pains to assure me on that point.'

'And what will Connie have to say about that? She, after all, is to be the new mistress.'

'We shall see, Mother.' Sophie looked skittishly at her mother. 'After all, I may not want to stay for very long myself. I too may have other plans.'

'Plans? What plans are you talking about?' Mrs Lamb turned on her sharply.

'You never know whether *I* may be thinking of marrying again.' Then, with a mischievous smile, Sophie opened the door as the carriage arrived in the market-place, and quickly jumped out.

Blandford on market-day was a bustling place. The people

came in from all the villages around to buy and to sell, to beg and to barter. There was a steady procession of carts, carriages and horses through the main street, accompanied by a general cacophony of abuse, exhortation and encouragement, the cries of children and the barking of dogs.

Agnes Gregg had been woken at dawn by the noise and had sent for her maid to find out what was happening. Market-day, Elizabeth, bleary-eyed, explained. Of course, how it brought back memories. Nostalgic memories.

Agnes had had her morning tea early and then dressed and breakfasted in the dining-room where, as usual, she didn't talk to anyone other than those who served her. But she was always an object of considerable interest wherever she went.

At The Crown she was already regarded as a woman of some mystery, and it was a reputation she enjoyed cultivating. The fewer people who knew her business, to her mind, the better. But market-day. Oh, *that* was the day she used to drive into the town on various errands, sometimes with her mother, sometimes with her sister-in-law Eliza, sometimes alone. There was the hilarious occasion when she had been propositioned by Herbert Lock. How she'd teased him! How angry he had been. But oh, there were far, far bigger fish to fry now.

Agnes had already, in the days she'd been in Blandford, walked the streets – pausing outside the offices of Yetman Bros Ltd in Salisbury Street, which she thought continued to look prosperous even though her brother Ryder was long dead. She guessed his son, Laurence, ran it now.

On this morning Agnes left the hotel early and went to the market, pausing at the stalls to examine the glass and the *objets d'art*, for she was an ardent collector of bric à brac.

She felt an unusual sense of excitement, as though there was something in the wind, something untoward and interesting about to happen. She wore the fashionable outfit she had worn the day she arrived, and it drew a number of glances from jealous females and one or two catcalls from lewd men which she ignored. Leaning on her parasol, she realised she felt completely at home as she stopped before one stall and then another, inspecting the wares.

She saw the carriage in the market-place stop and the doors at each side open as the two women emerged. One she didn't recognise, but the other . . .

She tried to move out of sight, but there was no refuge except the gutter. The elder woman, who was handed down by the coachman, stopped for a moment or two to give instructions, and then turned in the direction of the market and found herself looking straight into the eyes of Agnes Yetman.

For a moment it seemed as though she was about to pass on. But Mrs Lamb and Agnes Yetman had been well acquainted, even friends – that was, until Agnes mysteriously disappeared, never to be heard of or seen again until this moment: the object of much rumour and speculation.

Mrs Lamb gazed at Agnes as though searching the deep recesses of her memory. Agnes, having recognised her immediately, returned her gaze, but with a mocking smile, as though wondering if the rector's wife would penetrate her mask perfected over so many years.

Sophie, after also instructing the coachman, came and stood behind her mother, and she appeared also to join in the guessing-game, even though she had been a girl of fifteen when Agnes vanished.

'Agnes!' Mrs Lamb said suddenly. 'Agnes *Yetman*. I do believe it *is* Agnes Yetman.'

'Mrs Lamb!' Agnes put out a strong, confident hand. 'And don't tell me behind you we have little Sophie?'

'Little' Sophie, vaguely amused by the adjective, also extended her hand.

'I didn't think you'd recognise me, Miss Yetman . . . Is it still Miss Yetman?' she ventured, glancing at the gloved hand.

'No, it is not,' Agnes said, the tone of her voice faintly American. 'Mrs Gregg. Mrs Wendell Gregg.'

'Mrs Gregg.' Mrs Lamb clasped her hand affectionately. 'Well, Agnes, you look a very fine lady indeed. One who has made her mark in the world. I would certainly not have recognised you except, perhaps, for your eyes. They give you away. But no one told us you were home.'

'No one knows,' Agnes said conspiratorially. 'I have not

331

been back to Wenham, but wished to spend a few quiet days in Blandford familiarising myself with the scene of a county I had almost forgotten.'

'I can tell by your accent you've lived abroad,' Sophie said.

'I made America my home and have lived there nearly twenty years . . .'

'Your family will be thrilled to see you again.'

'Will they?' Agnes sounded sceptical. 'I understand my father and my brother Ryder are now dead. That his widow, Eliza, is married to a very wealthy man. No one told me these things or, as far as I know, tried to find me. For twenty years I have been cut off. Naturally, I feel hurt.'

'Maybe you cut yourself off?' Mrs Lamb suggested. 'Personally, I should love to have heard from you.'

To this Agnes made no reply, the difference between her former life and that of the virtuous wife of the rector seemed so marked.

'And why return now?' Sophie asked.

'Because there is business to be done,' Agnes said. 'Unfinished business, you might say. I also understand that Sir Guy is now a widower?'

'Yes, indeed,' Mrs Lamb sighed sadly. 'Lady Woodville passed away eighteen months ago.'

'Do give him my condolences.' Agnes extended a hand first to the mother and then the daughter. 'And be *sure* to let him know that you saw me.'

She then inclined her head in the manner of one about to pass on, but Mrs Lamb impulsively put a hand on her arm.

'Agnes, do get in touch with us. We are still at the rectory and my husband will be overjoyed to see you. I assure you, everyone would – your sister-in-law, your brothers in Bournemouth. All the people of the parish would welcome you back. And Sophie – ' she turned to her daughter ' – married Sir Guy's son, George. Alas, she is now a widow . . .'

'So sorry,' Agnes murmured.

'It happened years ago,' Sophie said with a rush. 'We have two children and live at the Oak.'

'How very interesting.' Agnes looked speculatively at her.

'Remember to give Sir Guy my *warmest* regards. Now don't forget, Sophie.'

'Oh, certainly I shall,' Sophie assured her. 'I am sure he will be delighted to hear of your return.'

Sophie and her mother talked of nothing else on the way back but the person they had seen and, above all, why she should be there in such mysterious circumstances, and so unforthcoming and mysterious herself.

'Why did she go away, Mama?' Sophie asked, her eyes gazing appreciatively out of the window at the beauty of the passing scene.

'I never knew the truth,' Mrs Lamb replied. 'Certainly your father and I were never told it. But there were rumours . . .'

'What sort of rumours?' Sophie looked curiously at her mother.

'Rumours . . . You know what rumours are; and one should be wary of listening to, never mind believing, parish gossip. Agnes was a discontented girl, dissatisfied with her lot, jealous of Eliza and Ryder. She went to work for Lord and Lady Mount as a governess and stayed there, apparently happy enough, for several years. Then she left without a word of farewell.'

There was an inquisitive light in her mother's eyes.

'You can't wonder the gossips started. But my dear . . .' she placed a hand on Sophie's arm '. . . at the moment I am more interested in a remark *you* made just before we bumped into Agnes. You said that you might be thinking of marrying again. Can it be true?'

'Oh, I wasn't really serious, Mother.' Sophie, wishing she had never made such a flippant remark, gazed at the floor of the swaying carriage. 'There may be someone. I can't be sure.'

'Oh Sophie.' Mrs Lamb's clasp tightened. 'I do hope you are serious. There is nothing in the world that would give your father and me more pleasure, I assure you. We feel we have grown away from you in your sadness, that we have not been of sufficient real help to you. We so long for you to be happy again.' She put her head on one side and gazed speculatively at her daughter. 'Dare one *hope* that it is dear

Hubert Turner? He is *so* devoted to you, and we to him. You have so much in common. Besides, Hubert may well be your father's successor.'

'Is it decided?' Sophie looked surprised. 'Has he been offered the living?'

'When your father hands in his resignation the post becomes open, and is given at the discretion of Sir Guy and the bishop. But we so *hope* that with our influence Hubert might be appointed to take the place of your father.

'There *are* difficulties, because he is still a curate, but they may be overcome. Oh my dear, how much joy there would be in our hearts if our daughter were to be the wife of the next rector of Wenham, as you assuredly would have been had poor dear George been alive.'

18

Guy Woodville, with an air of scarcely suppressed excitement, walked into the lounge of The Crown in Blandford and, taking a seat, stretched out his long legs encased in the trousers of his best suit, and spats. It was mid-morning, and he had announced his intention of visiting Agnes by telephone the day before. She would not speak to him directly, but the hall porter as intermediary had confirmed that Mrs Gregg would receive him the following day at precisely eleven.

Guy was even a few minutes ahead of time.

Agnes. How his mind flew back to those days more than twenty years before. After a three-year affair she had been spirited away to a secret place to have her baby, the fruit of her shame.

It had been several years after Agnes's disappearance that Guy had realised that Elizabeth, adopted daughter of Ted and Beth Yewell, was their child. He had known about Agnes's pregnancy but he had thought the child had been adopted, like his son by Lally.

Guy had been irresponsible, as a husband, a lover and a father; yet in his way he had cared too much, and grieved for the consequences of his behaviour. In his middle-age this had turned him to religion, and love for his lawful wife.

But God was a vengeful God, and had punished him by depriving him of the two children he loved best: dearest Emily and George.

No use dwelling on the past. Guy had produced a handkerchief for the anticipated tears and then thought better of it and replaced his handkerchief in his pocket. It would never do for

335

Agnes to see him weeping, or with so much as a trace of tears on his face.

He had loved Lally and, in the end, he had loved Margaret. There had been other women too, but there had never been anyone like Agnes.

The door opened and he rose quickly to his feet. But it was the hall porter again.

'Mrs Gregg will be down in a few minutes, Sir Guy.'

'That's perfectly all right, my good fellow.' Guy felt a little deflated, though he didn't quite know what he'd say to her when she appeared. He felt as nervous as a kitten.

Twenty years. More. It was a long time. Then he had been thirty-six and in good condition. Now he was nearly fifty-six and the condition was not so good. A long time. A long, long time.

The big clock on the wall ticked and the minutes seemed to pass slowly – very slowly in Guy's opinion. He had spent a lot of time on his toilet, his selection of clothes, aided by Sophie; what suit to wear, what shirt, which tie. But Sophie was not in the know about his illicit relationship with Agnes, so she couldn't possibly be expected to understand why he was so excited, hopping first on one foot then the other, like a schoolboy.

He rose from his chair and began slowly to walk round the room, to ease the tension he felt at the prospect of seeing Agnes again. Why had she come to Blandford, of all places? Mrs Gregg. Where was Mr Gregg? Who above all *was* Mr Gregg? *What* was Mr Gregg? Agnes had appeared to Sophie and her mother to be a woman of some consequence, maybe of wealth. Yet her father had left her nothing when he died. Agnes had disappeared, and John Yetman's whole estate had gone to her half-sister Connie.

Guy began impatiently to examine the prints on the wall and was halfway through when he heard the door slowly open. His heart did a somersault, but when he turned to face the door he saw the hall porter again.

'Mrs Gregg sends her apologies, sir.' The minion bowed, but he had a smirk on his face. 'She hopes to be with you very soon.'

'Thank you,' Guy said, pointedly looking at his watch. 'It is twenty minutes since I arrived.'

'Mrs Gregg has been *very* busy on the telephone, sir. To London,' he added, as though few things could be more important than telephonic contact with the capital.

Guy completed his tour of inspection of the prints and then sat down again. Ten more minutes passed, slowly. Agnes was paying him back. Maybe this was the beginning of a slow retribution for the way he had left her with child all those years ago. Was he, after all, wise to have come? His boyish enthusiasm began to ebb. There would be more to their meeting than mere waiting. He began to be sure of that.

Finally, after the passage of another half-hour, Guy was about to return to the hall with a message that he was going when the door opened again and a handsome woman he didn't recognise stepped in. His disappointment and chagrin returned.

The stranger wore a simple beige two-piece suit, the hem down to her ankles, and high-heeled shoes. Her belt was slightly below her waist and there was a large jewel at the neck of the white blouse she wore under her suit. Her shoes were dark brown and so was her hat, from which two large ostrich feathers, dyed beige, projected at an angle. A fox-fur was slung over one arm as though she had been, or was about to go, walking, and she carried a large dark-brown leather handbag.

Guy bowed slightly, murmured a polite 'good morning' and continued on his way to the door, past the woman who had stopped and, with an expression of tolerant amusement on her face, was staring at him.

Guy had just reached the door when a voice behind him called out:

'Guy!'

He turned and looked more carefully at the stranger. Could it be? But no. There was no resemblance between this elegant but amply-proportioned matron and the slight, initially shy young woman he had once introduced to the arts of love.

'Guy,' the stranger said in a rather deep, melodious voice, 'it is I, Agnes.' Suddenly she threw the fox-fur onto the leather-covered sofa and went towards him with a mysterious, slightly teasing smile on her face.

'I don't believe it is Agnes.' Yet Guy clasped her hand between his, almost mesmerised by her stateliness, the flinty quality in her eyes and the subtlety of her smile.

'Twenty years *is* a long time,' he muttered suddenly, letting go her hand and sitting down. Taking out a handkerchief, he began to mop his brow. 'I didn't know you, Agnes. You must forgive me. I am altogether *bouleversé*.'

She sat with equal care on the edge of the sofa next to him, gently placing a gloved hand on his.

'I didn't mean to give you such a shock. Are you quite well, Guy?'

She saw, indeed, somewhat to her dismay, that he was not the man he had been; that handsome, even elegant figure from her past. He was the man she had dreamed all her life of marrying, even when she was a girl and there was no possibility, no hope at all. When he was married to another she had continued to dream.

The Woodvilles, even with no money, were so much grander than the Yetmans who had plenty. But what was money made through trade compared to centuries of tradition and breeding? So the noble family of Pelham's Oak had dominated her entire life and, in the interval since she had left, she had never forgotten them or her ambition: one day to be Lady Woodville, wife of a baronet.

Guy sat patting his forehead, almost breathless with emotion. 'Oh yes, I am quite well,' he said at last. 'As well as can be expected. Margaret left me, you know . . .' He sighed deeply. 'Died of a disorder of the blood. I relied on her a great deal, more than I knew.' He shook his head. 'I am, sadly, not the man I used to be.' He sighed again. 'Emily was taken from us. Then George. I often wondered if God was punishing me. I reformed, Agnes. I came close to God. Oh dear.' Guy violently blew his nose as the tears, long held back, trickled resolutely down his cheek. 'What a *fool* I am making of myself . . .'

'You mustn't say that,' Agnes said in that gentle, melodious yet almost motherly tone. 'We are *very* old friends; much time has passed. I want you to feel free to talk to me just as you wish, to say whatever you like. After all, dear Guy, what are old friends for?'

Feverishly Guy clasped her hands. 'Oh Agnes, you are so good. I know you understand. I can't tell you how much I wanted to see you when Sophie told me you were here. I was beside myself with eagerness to renew our friendship. I have been very . . . lonely, Agnes.'

'Poor Guy!' Agnes gazed thoughtfully at him as he sat dejectedly staring at the ground. 'I can see you are lonely, and neglected . . .'

'And sad, Agnes.' Soulfully he raised his eyes to meet hers.

'And sad,' she echoed. 'With only Carson, Sophie and her children for company.'

'No one *really* to love . . . and no money. The fates have turned against me, dearest Agnes. I was to lose my house; but Carson has found an heiress to marry, so once again we are to be saved, as my dear Margaret saved us all those years ago.'

'History repeating itself,' Agnes murmured.

'Indeed . . . And the heiress is your half-sister, little Connie.'

'Constance to marry *Carson*?' Agnes looked astounded. That was one piece of information that had escaped her.

'She was made Miss Fairchild's ward. She is worth a million pounds! Imagine that.'

'And *she* is to live at Pelham's Oak. Dear, dear.' Agnes did not sound at all pleased at this news.

'About our baby, Agnes . . .' Guy began, but her attitude suddenly changed and he felt her figure, partly encased in whalebone, stiffen beside him.

'Guy, I must make one thing clear. I *never* want that matter referred to, ever, do you understand?'

'But Agnes . . .'

'Never, ever . . . If we are to be friends, and I hope we are, that must be quite clear. The chapter is closed. It is in my past and I want no reference to it.'

'Very well, Agnes.' Guy bowed his head. 'It shall be as you

wish.' He gave her hand a compulsive squeeze. 'How long are you going to stay here for, my dear?'

'As long as it suits me,' she replied, still rather horrified at the news about Connie. 'I may move from this place; but for the time it suits me. I may even consider purchasing property in Dorset; but I haven't decided. I, too, am newly widowed, Guy.'

'Oh my dear, I'm so sorry.'

'Yes.' She gave a realistic sniff and applied her handkerchief to the tip of her nose. 'As you know, it leaves one feeling so sad, so bereft. One longs for roots, which is why I came home – though not knowing how I would be received, having neglected my family for so long.'

'You will *always* be welcome with me, Agnes.'

'Thank you, my dear.' She gave him a melting glance. 'Happily, my late husband, Wendell, was a railroad millionaire and left me well provided for. Sadly, we had no children, but in my old age I shall have sufficient means to live most comfortably.'

'Oh Agnes!' Guy fervently pressed her hand to his lips. 'How good it is to see you again. I believe God has meant us to be together.'

'I'm sure of it, dear Guy.' Agnes, who had never entered a church since she left Wenham, uttered a pious sigh. 'I am sure that it was meant by One on high.' And then she bent her face towards him and allowed him to kiss her cheek.

Guy lost little time in spreading the news about Agnes. From that moment he was a changed man. He became obsessed with the idea of seeing her, and arrived at The Crown almost daily at about eleven in the morning to take her out to lunch. There were occasions when she went up to London for a day or two, and he fretted until she returned, always meeting her at the station.

It was soon quite obvious to Sophie that her father-in-law was deeply in love.

It was now only a few weeks before the marriage of Carson and Connie, and there was a good deal of excitement in the town. Connie had been several times to Bournemouth, and once as far as London to choose a trousseau. Her wedding-dress was being made from silk woven in Siam, a gift from Lally and Prosper Martyn. The banns had been called three times, Connie and Carson sitting side by side in the church, selfconsciously listening to their names being called, the whispers of the congregation. How awkwardly they walked from the church, in dread of the gazes of the curious. Indeed, they were a curious couple themselves; shy, secretive and oddly insecure.

They had had a solemn talk with the rector on the singular grace conferred by the state of matrimony, their responsibilities and duties in the matter of bringing up children, as well as towards each other. Each had listened gravely, as if they were embarking on an onerous task rather than an adventure of the heart and spirit.

The reception was to be at Pelham's Oak, and already the invitations had been sent out to the lucky ones – half the people of the parish, and many others:

Miss Victoria Fairchild requests the pleasure of the company of

on the occasion of the solemnisation of the
marriage between her beloved ward
Constance Euphemia Yetman and
Matthew Julius Carson Woodville
on May 15 1912 at St Mark's Church Wenham at 11.15 a.m.
and afterwards at Pelham's Oak.
RSVP.

The cards were beautifully embossed and, as a sign of the importance of the occasion, Miss Fairchild had addressed every envelope by hand. In fact she felt that she had never known such happiness as she had in those weeks preparing for the nuptials of her beloved companion. Nor, she felt, had she ever seen Connie so pretty.

Away from Carson, Connie was joyful; but when the pair were together she seemed subdued. Miss Fairchild felt that Connie was still overawed by her future husband, but that once they were married tenderness and love would replace her understandable anxiety, even fear.

As Connie could not play the music at her own wedding, she coached Jasper Pringle, the organist of a nearby church, in the task, and she spent her days running happily backwards and forwards; rehearsing, planning, and trying on the beautiful clothes her aunt was buying her. Yes, Connie had every reason to be happy.

'Beautiful,' Aunt Vicky sighed as the wedding-dress itself was pinned to Connie and, slowly, she revolved around the room. The dressmaker, her mouth full of pins, knelt on the floor critically regarding the creation she herself had designed from the wedding-dress of one of the royal princesses.

Connie certainly looked nice in it; a little drab, but still a bride. Well, who had ever seen a bride who wasn't beautiful? It was unthinkable, even with Connie. Her veil would disguise her timidity, and her long train, carried by six bridesmaids and two pages – the little Woodvilles and Yetmans among them – would enhance her confidence.

The beautiful folds of the Siamese silk cascaded to the ground; the plain, almost virginal bodice ended in a high, stiff collar from which tiny pearl buttons ran down to the waist. The long sleeves were tapered, the shoulders slightly puffed so that it added much-needed fullness to Connie's figure. Indeed, nothing of the dressmaker's art was spared to try and make a swan-princess out of an ugly duckling.

The veil, which would be surmounted by a diamond tiara worn at her wedding by every Lady Woodville, or future Lady Woodville, for over a century, had a twelve-foot train which would be carried by her small attendants. There would be no senior bridesmaid. The best man was to be Laurence Yetman, and Sarah-Jane was to keep a motherly eye on all the proceedings while, of course, Miss Fairchild would not be far in the background.

'Perfect!' Miss Fairchild's admiration was unstinting as Connie carefully revolved yet again after the hem had been slightly altered. 'Now you must get out of it very carefully, Constance dear . . .'

'And I should like her to try on the dress for the dinner-party next week,' the dressmaker muttered, mouth still full of pins. 'I understand that is to be a very special occasion.'

'It is given by Sir Guy especially for the bridal pair, to introduce Connie formally to what will soon be her home and, I expect, to show her how she should behave once she is chatelaine of that great mansion.'

It was obvious from the levity of Miss Fairchild's tone that this was said with tongue in cheek, but the idea seemed to offend Connie, who burst out:

'I know *quite* well how to behave, thank you, Aunt, and I know what to do. I am *not* a child, as I have to keep on reminding you. Besides, Sophie is to continue living there and, in effect, she runs Pelham's Oak.'

'Oh dear!' Miss Fairchild joined her hands together and emitted a profound sigh.

'Oh dear what, Aunt?' Connie rather roughly eased herself out of the dress which was still full of pins and tacks – to the horror of her dressmaker, who gently urged caution.

'I wonder if it *is* a good idea that Sophie should continue to live there,' Miss Fairchild ended in another prolonged sigh.

'But it's her home.'

'Well, it is at the moment, I suppose.' Miss Fairchild looked very worried indeed. 'But how long is she to go on living there? And *is* it a good thing that she should? What do you think, Mrs Pond? Is it a good thing or not?'

'I'm sure *I* don't know.' Mrs Pond didn't want the responsibility of voicing an opinion on such a delicate matter. 'There are good things and bad, I suppose, as there is in everything. It's certainly not for *me* to say.'

Needless to say, Mrs Pond, as a good citizen of Wenham, a member of the Ladies' Guild and a regular church attender, knew everything there was to know that went on in the town; but if she had opinions about the place of Sophie Woodville at Pelham's Oak, she certainly would not voice them to the woman who would supplant her.

'My feeling is,' Miss Fairchild said with the utmost delicacy, 'that at the back of Sophie Woodville's mind there must always be the idea that being mistress of Pelham's Oak is her rightful place. Had George lived she would have been Lady Woodville.

As it is,' she smiled with quiet pride at her ward, '*that* will now be the position of my dearest Constance.'

Connie made no reply as Mrs Pond gently slipped over her head the dress to be worn at the dinner. This was made of satin and had the fashionable underskirt and tunic, and – for Connie – rather a daring plunge at the back; though it was chaste enough in the front.

'Beautiful!' Miss Fairchild was in ecstasies once again, though Connie was looking critically at herself in the mirror.

'Isn't it a little old for me?' she said, still staring at herself.

'Old?' Mrs Pond looked surprised. 'I wouldn't have *said* so, Connie.' But a doubt now placed in her mind, she turned to the older woman. 'Would *you* say so, Miss Fairchild?'

Miss Fairchild, in fact, also had her doubts about the dress. 'I'm not *sure*,' she opined. 'I like the pattern well enough. But the colour worries me, especially on Connie.'

The dress was pink, the colour of a certain kind of petunia. Bright pink; and indeed, on Connie's skeletal form, and in conjunction with the pallor of her face, the effect was slightly startling. It was a beautiful colour in itself, but somehow looked altogether different when draped on a small, slender person such as Connie.

'It's certainly bold,' Mrs Pond said briskly, beginning to gather together her bits and pieces, her scissors, tape-measure and precious box of pins. 'But I like it. After all, Connie is soon to be a married woman. She is no longer a girl.' Mrs Pond stood up and looked critically at Connie. 'And *that* is how married women dress, in fine, bold colours, Connie, and you had better accustom yourself to the fact.'

'I'll wear it just this once,' Connie said sulkily as Mrs Pond helped to ease her head out of it, 'and then I'll see.'

Mrs Pond said no more, but carefully folded the dresses into a large box and her bits and pieces into a copious bag. Promising that everything would be ready by the day, especially the big day, the wedding, she was seen by Miss Fairchild and Connie to the door. They then turned slowly back and walked along the corridor to the sitting-room, where the maid, Nancy, had just put out the tea-things. It was a cold afternoon, with overcast skies, and smoke from the fire rose briskly up the chimney.

'Oh dear, I do hope you soon settle at Pelham's Oak.' Miss Fairchild reached emotionally for Connie's hand. 'I shouldn't say it, but I *shall* miss you.'

'And I'll miss you, Aunt Vicky.' Connie knelt on the floor, resting her head against her aunt's knee, as she often did when they sat by the fire together. 'More than you know.'

'But you have no regrets, child?' Miss Fairchild looked alarmed. 'Carson is the best of men . . .'

'I *am* very, very frightened, Aunt Vicky.' Connie hugged her knees and started to shiver. 'I won't hide it from you. I feel I am not ready for marriage; but I *do* love Carson, however he feels about me. More importantly . . .' she gazed up at her aunt with eyes that seemed suddenly wise '. . . it is the thing I must do. I don't want to be . . .' She stopped and bit her lip as Miss Fairchild leaned forward and began stroking her head:

'A spinster all your life? Is that what you were going to say, dearest?'

Connie avoided a straight answer. 'I love you and admire you so; but you have been lonely, Aunt Vicky. If you hadn't had me you would have been lonelier still.'

'Never lonely with you, my precious darling.' Miss Fairchild had a catch in her voice as she put her arm tenderly round Connie's shoulders. 'Never for a single moment lonely with you. You have been the light, the joy of my life. But it *is* right for you, Connie, more than anybody. It is a wonderful, wonderful opportunity. To be Lady Woodville, mistress of Pelham's Oak! How proud your dear father and mother would have been. How I wish *they* could be there on that happy day . . .'

'But does Carson care for me at all?' Connie went on, almost as though to herself. 'It is a very formal relationship, Aunt. Sometimes I don't know how he feels, honestly I don't.'

'What do you mean, dearest?' Again Miss Fairchild looked alarmed.

'It is not at all as though we were going to be married. He is so very . . . detached with me.'

'My dear, he is behaving as gentlemen should behave. Doubtless he is nervous too, and hesitates to show emotion. I quite approve of that. And Connie . . . dearest . . .' Miss Fairchild shifted a little uneasily '. . . talking about matters of intimacy, are you aware . . . do you know . . .?' She put a hand nervously to her head. 'I have never been married, so I cannot tell you. But, what happens between a man and a woman . . . well, do you know, my dear Connie? With the utmost delicacy, that is what I am trying to discover.'

'Oh, dearest Aunt.' Connie seized her hand, feeling as embarrassed as she was. 'Do not distress yourself about *that*.'

'I thought perhaps Sophie, as a married woman . . .' Miss Fairchild seemed to be searching for words with which to express herself.

'Oh, I could never ask Sophie!' Connie seemed indignant at the idea. 'Besides, it's not necessary. Other people have found out after they were married, haven't they, Aunt?'

'I suppose so.' Miss Fairchild looked doubtful. 'But most girls have a mother; you do not.'

And for a long while neither spoke, as though remembering with grief, affection and regret the woman who, in giving birth to Connie, gave her life as well: Euphemia Yetman, formerly spinster of the parish, and happily married for but a single year.

Guy stood impatiently in the hall while Agnes remained in the empty drawing-room with the estate agent who had shown them round the house. It seemed to him an interminable length of time and made him decidedly nervous. He only hoped she didn't *commit* herself to anything; but if he knew the new Agnes she would proceed with caution. Every house they saw she discussed with him: its size, suitability, location. Guy remained unenthusiastic because each house seemed further away from Wenham, further and more remote. This one was on the eastern side of Salisbury, towards London, and although it was a beautiful house in a park landscaped by no less a person than Capability Brown, it was ridiculous to think of a woman like Agnes living here all alone by herself, staff or no staff.

When at last she appeared, Guy gave a sigh of relief and put on his hat. They went down the stairs of the imposing porch from which in the distance could be seen the spire of Salisbury Cathedral.

'Beautiful, isn't it?' the agent enthused, extending a hand in a wide, sweeping gesture.

'Enchanting,' Guy said perfunctorily, not really taking the trouble to look.

'Out of this world.' Agnes was the most positive. 'Furthermore, they say the army is encamped not so very far away.'

'Oh, the army will not disturb you, madam,' the agent hastened to reassure her.

'I shall not be disturbed,' Agnes replied sweetly. 'I mean, one meets the nicest sort of person in the army. I believe I may have an introduction, through mutual friends, to the commander-in-chief.'

They stood now on the gravel of the drive where Agnes's hired Hispano-Suiza, complete with chauffeur, stood awaiting them. She had been most assiduous in recent days in her search for property, relentlessly dragging Guy with her hither and yon, inspecting notices and orders to view, visiting agents, consulting solicitors. It had become a fixation with her, to find a suitable home; and each one she saw was bigger, finer, better than the one before.

Agnes now paused by the car and looked towards the house, a gracious Palladian mansion that had come on the market through the death of the last surviving member of a family of prosperous Wiltshire merchants.

'It needs a lot doing to it,' she said sharply, biting her lip. 'That might lower the asking price. In places the stone is very much corroded by the weather.'

'It would cost a fortune to repair,' Guy said. 'It stands too high up. Besides, it is too far. Much, much too far.'

'Too far?' Agnes looked enquiringly at him.

'Too far?' the agent echoed, not understanding.

'Too far from *Wenham*,' Guy explained emphatically and, as the chauffeur opened the door of the limousine, he stepped inside and invitingly patted the seat beside him. 'Agnes, come. It will soon be dark.'

The agent had arrived in a pony and cart which, upon seeing the imposing limousine, he had hastily left round the corner near the old stables. Even then Mrs Gregg and her escort were so involved in each other and the house that they didn't seem to notice they might be leaving him high and dry, five miles from Salisbury. Maybe they thought that, as he had made his own way there, he could make his own way back. However, they made no offer of a lift. The rich were rather thoughtless, he told himself, watching the car as it disappeared down the drive, conscious at the same time that, for reasons he could only guess at, a sale of the property would not be made this time.

The car bowled in stately fashion down the drive, which was of immense length. It seemed to go on forever, until it came to the huge wrought-iron gates which were held open by a lodge-keeper, respectfully touching his forelock in time-honoured fashion at a gracious nod from Agnes.

'I liked it very much,' she enthused, pulling on her gloves, a far-away look in her eyes. 'The nicest by far we've seen. Don't you think so, Guy?'

'Beautiful for a large family,' Guy said drily, '*dozens* of servants and the like. For a woman on her own, ridiculous. As for what you said about the army, I didn't think that in very good taste.'

'Really, Guy!' Agnes gave him a bewitching smile. 'I do think you're jealous. To be perfectly honest, I do have an introduction to the major-general . . .'

'Agnes!' Guy clamped his hand firmly over hers. Then turning his face towards her, he gazed for a long time into her eyes. 'This is ridiculous, Agnes. This must stop.'

'I don't understand you, dear,' she said, trying to remove her hand from beneath his.

'Agnes, I have a very large house and, even with other people in it – my son, his future wife, or wife as she will be then, my daughter-in-law and grandchildren – there is still room to accommodate a beautiful and most desirable woman I happen to love very much.'

'What are you suggesting, Guy?' Agnes pretended surprise, yet her eyes glinted with amorous intrigue.

'I am suggesting, Agnes Gregg . . .' Guy glanced at the chauffeur in the front but decided to ignore him. 'No, I am asking you to make me the happiest man alive; to complete something that was begun many years ago but never finished.' He seized her hands and, after kissing them feverishly, held them to his heart. 'Oh dearest Agnes, I am asking you to be my wife.'

Much later, after they had been into Salisbury to look at rings, and had dined at a hotel on the way; and after Guy had kissed her goodnight at the door of her suite at The Crown, promising to be there at first light in the morning, Agnes stood in her room in front of her mirror and gazed at herself.

What she saw did not displease her. She saw a fine-looking woman of some fifty-one summers, with blonde hair carefully waved and a fringe in front. Its colour owed a little to artistry, which was why she made her occasional visits to London; visits which poor Guy was meant to misinterpret. What woman would wish to admit to dyeing her hair? She saw also the lustrous, vampish eyes which had gained her so many admirers, the complexion which, though a little withered, some people still thought flawless. She saw a firm bust, a thickened waist and rather ample hips, the result of years of good living. But then there were her legs, long, firm, shapely, though seldom seen now beneath her ankle-length dresses. In many ways these had been her fortune, and for a good many years, more than she could count, they had been much admired by the multitude of gentlemen who had paid for her favours.

There never had been a Mr Wendell Gregg, railroad millionaire, although there was a faked wedding-certificate to suggest there had. There had never been millions left to her from the railroad, but she had acquired real estate in New Orleans, and had run an extremely profitable business as the owner of first one brothel, then two, then three.

When she had read in the London papers of the death of Lady

Woodville, she had realised that the fulfilment of her lifetime's ambition was near at hand.

She had sold her brothels, she had sold her real estate, her investments in stocks, bonds and shares. She did not have millions, or anything like it, but she had enough to pretend, to give the impression of someone who could afford the trappings of great wealth.

She had come back to Dorset to claim that title for which she had waited all her life, and which many years ago Guy had told her she should have. He had promised then to divorce his wife, but of course his promise was meaningless. He had left her with a child, without a future or a penny to her name.

That night, Agnes Yetman went to bed a very happy woman, dreaming of that goal, once so far distant, which she could now at last see:

A baronet for a husband, and a house set on a hill: Pelham's Oak.

Revenge; oh, revenge would be very sweet indeed.

19

Carson's horse, Prince, drank thirstily from the stream, and watching him, the reins held loosely in his hands, Carson wished he too was a dumb, unthinking animal provided with fresh hay, a warm stall, a groom who watched over him and an owner who loved him. Carson put his hand out and ran it along Prince's sleek neck. Prince's grandmother had been Lady, the horse that had belonged to his Aunt Eliza when she was a girl, and Prince had the same loving, affectionate and faithful nature. Carson, his aunt and his cousin Dora had always shared a love of horses, which made a strong bond between the three of them.

From where he sat he could see Pelham's Oak, surrounded by scaffolding, the decorators busy running up and down their ladders applying fresh coats of paint; the stone-masons working on repairs to the walls. As it had been done over in time for his father's wedding, again to a wealthy heiress, so it was being done over in time for his. It only ever seemed to be thoroughly refurbished when the baronet, or his heir, married money.

Carson sighed and, as Prince raised his head, giving a snort of satisfaction, he gently dug his heels into his flanks and guided him slowly across the fields, past the cottage from which Ryder and Eliza had eloped, past the home farm to the house.

Would that there was some woman he loved so much that he had eloped with her, as Aunt Eliza had eloped with Ryder Yetman in those far-off days before he was born. Every time he thought of marriage to Connie his heart seemed to freeze over like a glacier, and he knew that, intelligent girl that she was, Connie knew this. He was not a diplomat, he was not good at pretence. He showed his feelings too clearly, and Connie knew he didn't love her – rather as his mother must have known, all those years before, that his father hadn't loved her.

History was repeating itself, Carson thought, as Prince effortlessly climbed the last half-mile to the house.

He passed the farmer from the home farm who was clipping his hedge, and stopped to talk to him. Edwin Crook's family had farmed the home farm since the beginning of the previous century, and one of Margaret's first acts when she became Lady Woodville had been to save the family from eviction, since when the Crooks had been grateful and loyal tenants of the Woodvilles.

'Afternoon, Master Carson,' Edwin Crook said, touching his forehead.

'Afternoon, Edwin,' Carson replied. 'I see you've got some fine new heifers in the lower field.'

'Bent on improvin' my stock, zur.' Edwin gestured towards the big house. 'Seems a lot going on at the Oak.'

'Yes.' Carson glanced once more at the workmen scurrying around the scaffolding like busy ants.

'You must be getting very excited 'bout your weddin', zur,' Edwin grinned toothily.

'I am,' Carson affirmed.

'Well, if your bride is anything like your mother you will be a fortunate man, and we shall all be well off. Your mother was a lovely woman and we miss her, zur.'

'I'm sure you will like my bride very much,' Carson said. 'She will be a worthy successor to my mother.'

'I already know Miss Yetman, zur. I sings in the church choir. She has a great gift for music, a beautiful voice.'

'She has indeed,' Carson said wearily. How many times did people appear to be trying to console him for her lack of looks by pointing out her great gift for music.

Of what use was music in the marriage-bed?

'We hope all your family will be there on the day, Edwin.' Carson took up the reins again.

'Oh, we will, zur. And oi'll be singing my 'art out in the choir. We's practising already.'

'That's great news.' Carson raised his whip in a salute and turned swiftly away, watched by a rather puzzled farmer who stood staring after him, scratching his head.

Everyone thought that Connie Yetman was a very odd choice for the heir to Pelham's Oak, known for his liking for pretty girls.

There were some who unkindly said it was on account of her money.

When Carson had stabled his horse, rubbed him down himself and given him his oats, he made his way slowly towards the house, where even now he was conscious of the pre-wedding bustle. Lights were going up in the trees in the grounds, and the location for the marquee for the common people, the estate workers, had already been marked out.

Inside, servants were hurrying about in preparation for the dinner his father was giving for Connie, and about which, for some reason, he appeared inordinately excited. Indeed, for days, weeks even, his father had been a different man from the melancholy creature Carson had known since his mother had died; a man irritable and querulous, driven to drink by debts and his fears for the future. At least now that burden had been taken from his mind, and for this alone Carson, who had sorely tried his parents during his youth, felt he had made compensation. The effect on his father had indeed been remarkable.

Arthur came ambling towards Carson as he entered the house.

'Your father was anxious about you, Mr Carson.'

'Anxious, why?' Carson looked on the hallstand to see if there were any letters or messages for him.

'It's a most important occasion. He thought you might have forgotten, sir.'

'Forgotten the formal party to introduce my future wife? Unlikely!' Carson said with a mirthless laugh and, at that moment, the door of the small parlour opened and Guy emerged, raising his hands with pleasure when he saw his son.

'Carson. I thought . . .'

'Father, I wouldn't forget a night like this.' He looked at his watch. 'There is plenty of time to change before dinner. Besides, everyone knows everyone. Why are you so excited? Why is everyone dashing about as though there was a fire?'

'Ah, but I have a special surprise.' Guy gleefully rubbed his hands together. 'A very special one.'

'And what is that, Father, may one ask?' Carson's voice was distinctly bored.

'It wouldn't be a surprise if I told you now, would it?' Guy gave a schoolboyish giggle and disappeared back into the parlour, shutting the door behind him.

Carson looked at Arthur, who also had raised eyebrows.

'Have you any idea what is the nature of the surprise, Arthur?'

'No, sir.' The butler shook his head. 'But an extra place has been laid for dinner for an unexpected guest. We were given our instructions at the last minute.'

'Well, that can't be very exciting,' Carson replied, and went up the stairs to his room.

When Carson, who had been reluctantly shrugged into white tie and tails at the last moment by the footman sent to fetch him, reached the drawing-room, it seemed already bursting with people. He spotted his Aunt Eliza and Uncle Julius; his cousins Dora, Laurence and Sarah-Jane; Sarah-Jane's brother Bart, Sophie, Connie, of course, and Miss Fairchild – all of whom were grouped around a rather plump but striking woman in a very beautiful evening-gown whom he had never seen before.

He stood on the threshold for a moment, and when he saw Connie gazing wistfully at him he wished so much that he could retreat, go back to his room, throw himself on the bed and go to sleep, forget the whole thing.

However, by now everyone was aware of his presence, and Guy, coming over to him, murmured:

'Last but not least, Carson, as usual.' He then took him by the arm and drew him towards the crowd.

'I am *very* sorry, Father.' Carson bowed nervously to the assembled crowd, but his eyes were held by the strange woman, who also seemed interested in him. She was not tall, but she had presence. She held herself well and added inches by rather high heels. Her hair was piled high on her head in the Edwardian style favoured by women of a certain age. She had a fringe, and loose ringlets clustered to one side of her face behind her ear; her full-skirted gown with its deep neckline was of sapphire-blue, and a necklace of diamonds sparkled at her throat. The mounds of her beautiful breasts were daringly visible. Carson swallowed uncomfortably.

'Well, Carson,' the stranger said after their mutual inspection was over. 'I can see you don't remember me.'

'I . . . er.' Carson searched deeply in the recesses of his memory.

'This is your Aunt Agnes.' Guy seemed bursting with pride. 'Formerly Agnes Yetman, now *Mrs* Wendell Gregg, fresh from the United States of America.'

Agnes extended her hand in a friendly greeting. 'I am your aunt by marriage, as the sister of Ryder Yetman. I was only teasing. You were scarcely three when I left home.' She then enfolded him in an embrace, and he was conscious of an over-powering, almost cloying sweetness. Scent and femininity – something he couldn't quite place. He wanted to rest his head on that comfortable bosom, to encircle that broad waist with his arms. Painfully, instead, he broke away, murmuring: 'How do you do, Aunt Agnes?' And then the spell was broken and everyone started talking at once.

'*And* engaged to be married –' Agnes gave him a roguish look ' – to my little half-sister Connie, of all people!' Agnes reached for Connie's reluctant hand and drew her towards her. 'What a very fortunate young lady you are, Connie dear, to find such a handsome husband.'

'Yes, Agnes,' Connie mumbled, staring at her shoes. She wore the pink satin that Mrs Pond had created especially for this occasion and, as she had known she would, felt horrible in it. It was too old for her; it had too many pleats and flounces; it was a dress for a dowager, and yet the colour was too young. It made her look scraggy, virtually bosomless, and when she saw the well-upholstered breasts, the frank sensuality of her half-sister, and Carson's reaction to her, she had felt she could scream. There were more than twenty-five years between Agnes and herself, yet she felt small, mean, and totally wretched.

Agnes turned deliberately to talk to Julius Heering, Guy fluttering about by her side, clearly delighted at her presence. And, indeed, Agnes did seem quite at home in a house she had seldom visited, and moved at ease from Julius to Sophie, from Laurence to Bart Sadler, to whom she talked for some time. Her poise was assured, elegant, as she stood with a glass of champagne in her hand. She was, she seemed to proclaim, a woman of the world, widely travelled and light-years away from that Agnes Yetman, a spinster of over thirty, who had vanished with an air of mystery about her many, many years before.

'Do *you* remember Agnes?' Carson at last asked Connie as they stood apparently dumbstruck by the apparition.

Connie shook her head. 'Not at all.'

'Why did she go away?'

Miss Fairchild, hovering anxiously behind the betrothed pair like the good fairy at a christening, intervened in a low voice, eager to display her superior knowledge.

'She was a very restless young woman,' she said in a hoarse whisper, 'never satisfied. Agnes always thought herself a cut above everyone else. However, she has done well to go to America and marry a millionaire.'

'Indeed?' Carson looked impressed. 'And where is he?'

'Dead.'

'Ah!' Now he understood. 'Then she has inherited all his money?'

'I suppose so.' Miss Fairchild grew thoughtful.

Dora Yetman, technically Connie's great-niece, though she was older than her by some years, now joined them. Ryder and Eliza's only daughter was a tall girl with strong features, copper-coloured hair and an extrovert personality. She wore for the evening's occasion a long green dress which was not particularly stylish since, like her mother, Dora was much more interested in horses and country pursuits than fashion. Yet her dress became her, it suited her colouring, and Carson idly wondered why his cousin had remained unmarried and even, it seemed, unattached. Her name, as far as he knew, had never been linked to that of a man.

Dora gave the engaged couple a friendly smile, being on good but not intimate terms with both. 'I must say, Uncle Guy seems very taken by Aunt Agnes. He seems to have acquired a new lease of life.'

'I daresay she'll be going back to America,' Miss Fairchild said sharply. 'From what little she told me, it would appear she has business interests there.'

At that moment Arthur, moving in a stately manner like a drum-major, caused everyone to stop talking and made a formal announcement that dinner was served. Forming themselves into pairs, led by Guy and Agnes, the company solemnly processed to reassemble in the dining-room.

Nothing had been spared to impress Agnes with the splendour of the occasion. Guy sat at one end of the long table and Sophie at the other. On Guy's right sat Agnes, and on Sophie's right, placed there intentionally, was Bart who was now considered by those in the know to be walking out with Sophie. His calls to the house were frequent and he behaved punctiliously; taking her for drives, naturally with her children, or calling for tea, naturally with them too. Consequently they were seldom alone, an anomalous state of affairs which Sophie found depressing. She felt she didn't know exactly where she stood with him; whether his intentions were honourable or his mention of marriage sincere.

Yet he attracted her and, slowly, she had found herself unbending with him, and she increasingly thought of him, if not as a prospective husband – he was so reticent on the subject – as a friend. So, as he unfolded his napkin and leaned in a confiding manner towards her, she bent an ear, a smile on her face, as if to a familiar.

'A very wealthy lady, I understand,' he said *sotto voce*.

'So she says.' Sophie's expression was sceptical.

'What do you mean "so she says"?' Bart murmured.

'Well, it's very mysterious, isn't it, for her to come back unannounced, to stay at the Crown in Blandford, not to contact

357

any of her relations at all – after all, she is Wenham-born – and then she is seen merely by chance by my mother and me one day in Blandford.'

'I don't think you should take it so amiss.' Bart still kept his voice low. 'Having left so long ago, she naturally wishes to have time to find her feet. Sophie, when are you coming with me to see the stone?' He lowered his voice even more, and there was a degree of urgency in it. The sudden change of topic surprised her.

'Is it ready?'

'You know it's ready. It's ready to be engraved. All I wait for now is your approval.'

'I have been so preoccupied, so busy,' she replied with evident unease. 'The wedding is almost upon us.'

'Poor little thing,' Bart crooned maliciously, 'a fine bride she'll make.'

'She *will* make a fine bride,' Sophie hissed back. 'Don't be unkind.

'You can hardly say Carson is in love with her. I never saw a bridegroom look so awkward in my life. Half scared to death, if you ask me.'

'Carson has been a bachelor too long.' Sophie looked at her neighbour meaningfully. 'He is probably nervous at such a big step. A big step for any man . . . or woman,' she added. 'Besides, he's slow to show his feelings.'

'That's not what I hear. He has shattered a good many hearts in the district. Prudence Dimmock, who works for my brother, has had her heart broken by him. Says he promised marriage, and has threatened to throw herself into the river.'

'Then it is high time he settled down,' Sophie said reprovingly. 'Besides, Bartholomew Sadler, despite your protests you gossip too much and, if you ask me, pay too much attention to it.'

Sophie's schoolmistressy attitude amused and disarmed Bart. Unlike any woman he had ever fancied, she intrigued him. Getting her into his bed would indeed be a conquest, and one worth waiting for. He pretended to be chastened by her reprimand and applied himself to what was on his plate.

Eliza, on the other side of Carson, was watching Agnes carefully but surreptitiously. Agnes, she knew, blamed her for what had happened to her; her exile in Weymouth, her treatment as a pariah by her family. It was not true, but Eliza could understand the reason for her coolness as they had greeted each other. On the other hand, Agnes's appearance startled her. She doubted that she would have recognised her had she met her on the streets of Blandford. She had always had character, but now she was a personality; distinct, mature, formidable. On Eliza's other side her son Laurence also seemed riveted by the appearance of his father's sister he could scarcely remember; the enigmatic Aunt Agnes, who had left Wenham in the 1880s to be seen and heard of no more.

'Why did Aunt Agnes go to America, Mother?' Laurence asked conversationally.

'She was always ambitious,' Eliza replied. 'Wenham bored her and I think the New World appealed to her.'

'And she was never heard of again?'

'She never kept in touch. We never knew where she went. She left some years before Ryder and her father died. Agnes was always dissatisfied. Always yearning for the moon.'

'Well,' he said with a meaningful nod towards Guy, 'she seems very satisfied now.'

Perhaps, of all people in the room, Eliza was the only one who knew exactly why. She had known of the affair between them. She had arranged for Agnes to be removed to where she had her baby. She knew why – and she observed it with some alarm – her brother Guy was simpering over Agnes, completely excluding from his attentions the bride-to-be, who sat shyly next to him, her importance eclipsed by the vivacity, the grace, the *savoir-faire* of the woman on his other side.

Connie picked at her food; next to her, Carson also lacked appetite both for food and conversation. Miss Fairchild opposite was alarmed by the silence, the lack of rapport, compared to which Guy's absorption with Agnes was irritating. He and Agnes chatted away, openly flirted with each other as though no one else was present. Miss Fairchild simmered. She was also regretfully of the opinion that Connie's dress did not, after all, suit. The colour was wrong, the style ageing. It had also been a mistake to apply the curling tongs so vigorously to her hair, which frizzed up above her face like that of some native from the South Seas. And if only Carson would *smile* . . .

Oh, how apprehensive she was that something would go wrong. How she longed for the day of the wedding, and to know that her little chick was, at last, safely married.

Next to Miss Fairchild was Julius, a man of few words, who also seemed unnaturally preoccupied. Miss Fairchild found she had little to say to him, but on her other side was Laurence and, leaning past her with a polite smile – she took no notice, her eyes on the pair opposite – Julius said:

'How is your project coming along?'

'Which project?' Laurence asked over Miss Fairchild's head. 'We have several.'

'The one in Dorchester.'

'It's coming along very well.' However, an anxious expression flitted over Laurence's face. 'But we don't see too much of your friend Mr Wainwright.'

'He's not my friend,' Julius expostulated indignantly. 'I have never even met the man to my knowledge.'

'But your bank provided us with references.'

'Oh, did it?' Julius's lofty tone implied that he was way above this sort of thing. 'Then he must be all right; but please don't refer to him as "my" friend.'

'I don't know why you're so anxious to disown him.' Laurence sounded annoyed with his stepfather. 'He is already behind with his payment and the situation is a little worrying.'

'Don't worry.' Sarah-Jane, overhearing the conversation, leaned over to her husband. 'I tell you, everything will be well. Bart vouched for him. He knows him very well.'

Whereupon Bart, hearing his name, looked up.

'You vouched for Mr Wainwright, didn't you, Bart?' his sister said.

'Vouched?' Bart looked perplexed. 'I never "vouched". I merely introduced him to Laurence.'

'Everyone seems anxious to distance themselves from my client,' Laurence said angrily, 'and leave me in the lurch.'

'Dearest, I have told you all will be well.' Sarah-Jane frowned at him. 'Let us apply our minds to thinking positively. Nothing was ever gained by worry.'

Laurence, however, did not appear reassured, but the subject was abandoned by general consent and he lapsed into silence.

The Woodvilles made no such claims to the production of fine food as the Martyns (who were out of the country), and the fare served at the dinner was simple: poached Scotch salmon, roast sirloin of beef, and treacle tart. Arthur had managed to find a few good bottles of claret from the diminished stocks in the cellar and, despite Laurence's gloom and Miss Fairchild's apprehension, the meal turned into a jolly one, with frequent bursts of laughter, especially from the doting Guy and the fascinating Mrs Gregg.

After the sweet and before the cheese was served, Guy suddenly stood up and, sharply tapping a spoon against his glass, called for silence. Agnes sat serene and composed beside him, slowly surveying the table, and then her gaze rested calmly on Guy as he began to speak.

'This dinner is an occasion for a double celebration,' he said, glancing first at Carson and Connie and then at Agnes. 'It is to welcome Constance, who has consented to marry my son and given us all great joy. How pleased we are to welcome Constance, who is related to my sister by marriage, into the bosom of the Woodville family, and also her dear guardian, Victoria Fairchild, who has devoted her life to her ward.'

Miss Fairchild visibly flushed and her hand plucked at her napkin, while Connie's eyes remained fixed on her lap. Carson could sense that she was shaking, and his hand stole under the table to clasp hers. She caught it and hung on to it, and he could feel the sticky sweat in her palm.

'Let us drink, therefore, to Constance and Carson.' Guy raised his glass high above his head. 'Let us drink to their happiness.'

Everyone stood, glasses raised in the direction of the shy pair:

'Constance and Carson, Constance and Carson.'

Then, the toast over, they resumed their seats and a buzz of

361

conversation recommenced. But Guy had not finished. Once again he tapped his glass and, even louder, cleared his throat importantly:

'I have yet another announcement to make, so please bear with me. Whereas Carson's engagement gives me great joy, what I am about to say only enhances it.' He stopped and, face flushed with the intensity of his emotion, turned to Agnes and reached for her hand. 'I am overjoyed to tell you that Agnes Gregg, whom I have known for many years and who is now a widow, has consented to make a lonely man a very, very happy one, and to become my wife and, thus, the new Lady Woodville.'

It was hard to tell, in the confusion that followed, who was pleased and who was displeased by the announcement. Clearly, everyone was astounded. Agnes had only been in the country a few months, and yet long enough to capture the vulnerable heart of Sir Guy. In the general hubbub Eliza was the first to recover, to rise from her seat and embrace Agnes, and then everyone fell over themselves to be the next. Only Connie and Miss Fairchild seemed reluctant to leave their seats. To Carson the news also appeared to be a bombshell.

Guy had, by this time, ordered the champagne which had been kept in readiness, and there were more toasts to the happy couples, who were invited to stand next to one another: Connie shy and withdrawn, Agnes confident and radiant, clasping her hand.

Finally, pleading a headache, Connie was the first to leave, accompanied by Miss Fairchild. By now a certain degree of intoxication was evident and no one noticed them creep out except Carson, who saw them to the door.

'A most exciting evening,' Miss Fairchild said insincerely.

'Very exciting,' Carson agreed woodenly.

'And you had no idea about this extraordinary event, Carson?'

'None at all. I didn't even know Aunt Agnes was back. Sophie told me a moment ago that Father has been seeing her secretly, almost every day.'

'It's clear he is very much in love,' Miss Fairchild said jealously. 'Have you considered how this will affect you and Constance, Carson?'

'How can it affect us?' Carson stumbled over the words. 'I hadn't thought of it.'

'Do you suppose Agnes, the new Lady Woodville, will tolerate a younger competitor in the same house?'

'I don't see why not. It is a very large house.'

'But has she been consulted?'

'I must suppose she has, because my father is very keen for Connie and me to marry. Agnes is also Connie's half-sister.'

'That seems to me to be not such a good idea.' Miss Fairchild, clearly put out, looked thoughtful. 'Maybe a house on your own would be the solution.' She brightened perceptibly. 'For the early years of your marriage it would be more suitable to be on your own.' She glanced down at Connie who, having hardly said a word all evening, was staring rather helplessly at Carson, remembering how comforting his hand had felt in hers, grateful to him for his kindness.

'Come along, Constance,' Miss Fairchild said briskly, 'I thought you had a headache.'

'I have, Aunt. Good night, Carson.'

'Good night, my dear,' he said gingerly, putting his lips to her forehead so that they scarcely touched. 'I hope your headache will soon get better.'

He went down the steps and saw them into their carriage, and then he remained in the drive, watching them; watching and waving. But no handkerchief fluttered back.

Then, rather than join the revelry that now continued in the drawing-room, he went upstairs and, his mind a torment of confused thoughts and emotions, lay fully clothed on his bed until the small hours of the morning, taking not one wink of sleep.

Bartholomew Sadler stretched full length on the floor, pretending to be dead. Deborah made a pretence of trying to revive him, while Ruth and Sophie laughed helplessly beside them.

Oh, the rough-and-tumble of children's games! It was such fun, and Bart was so good with them. Better than George, to be truthful. But then the children had been so young, besides which, George had been a serious man. Bart had lots of nieces and nephews and there was clearly a side of him that enjoyed fun.

The Woodville children looked forward to his visits, and Sophie had grown a little dependent on them. That day he had arrived unexpectedly as she sat in the schoolroom where she still taught the children from ten to twelve in the morning and two to four in the afternoon. It was an arrangement that, up to now, up until the bombshell of a few nights before, had worked perfectly.

But now that Agnes was soon to be Lady Woodville, what would happen to them?

That's enough, I think,' Sophie said quietly, sitting up. 'And we'll call a halt to lessons for today, children. Tidy up your books and go and get ready for lunch. Playing with Uncle Bart was a special treat.'

'Yes, Mama,' they chorused obediently.

Bart, still sitting cross-legged on the floor, watched them as they ran out. Then he began to straighten his clothes and ran his hands through his hair.

'Well, that was fun!' he said, standing up and looking round for his hat. 'What do you say to the idea that we go and look at the stone, Sophie? I want to start the inscription and it's a fine day for a drive.' He gestured towards the window, where outside the sky was azure-blue with hardly a trace of cloud.

'Oh yes!' Sophie clapped her hands together. 'I have the inscription written out. And may we take the children, Bart? I will let them off afternoon school and perhaps we can stop and explore the hedgerows for a nature lesson.'

Bart grimaced, his head on one side.

'I *hoped* to have you to myself, Sophie. We are so seldom alone together. Besides, we might stop somewhere for a bite to eat, and it would be late getting back. What do you think? Shall we have some time to ourselves?'

'Oh, all right,' she said, but she felt a little guilty that she was so easy to persuade, knowing how much the children would enjoy an outing with the two of them.

She ran upstairs to get her hat and to tell the children that they would remain at home for the afternoon as she had an errand to do on account of Papa. She set them their tasks of reading and drawing, and gave the nursemaid, who could scarcely read a word herself, instructions as to exactly what to do.

She stood in front of her mirror, adjusting her hat, tucking wisps of hair beneath it, thinking she could see odd streaks of grey. Well, she was thirty-seven . . . and so, nearly, was Bart.

Every time she saw him she felt an excitement sweep through her that lasted until he'd gone. She felt it again now; but more strongly. Every glance, every inflection of his voice was precious to her. And she knew that at last, after years of loyalty to the memory of George, her singular devotion was slipping away and being replaced by another.

She felt guilty and a little sad, and she drew from her bedside drawer a piece of paper on which were the words, much altered and crossed out, of the inscription she had composed to her husband's memory.

But, that done, swiftly her mind flew to Bart again. She thought that, except for his taciturnity, a slight unpredictability, everything about Bartholomew Sadler was perfect. He was no courtier, he was a blunt man who spoke his mind, and she knew, or guessed, that some people didn't like him. But to her he was always charming, considerate, gentle; never making demands of the kind she did not yet feel herself ready for.

Since he had made his announcement that he wished to walk out with her, she had taken it as a form of proposal, yet he had never again mentioned marriage, so nor had she. It didn't do to force a man. She knew enough about life for that. George Woodville, so many years before, had been gently led, rather than pushed, along the path she wished him to follow. Bart's habit was to visit her, frequently staying to take tea and to play with the children; and then, after a leisurely walk round the gardens alone with her, he would take his leave. People now were beginning to invite them out together; they were starting to be seen and thought of as a couple, and this pleased her. The fact that he'd been invited to the dinner-party the other night and placed beside her, was at her instigation, but no one seemed to think it unusual. And, like a couple, they had witnessed the extraordinary events of the evening and shared its dramas.

Securing her hat, she cast a glance over the rest of her trim outfit and then ran down the stairs – to find Bart standing, legs astride, hat between his hands, in the hall, gazing at the oil painting that hung there of Sir Matthew Woodville, Guy's father. Bart was stroking his cheek and his eyes were thoughtful. As Sophie came down the stairs, he turned, and when she went up to him he put an arm lightly round her waist in greeting, and smiled down at her.

It was then that she felt passion, a desire to kiss and be kissed, a stirring in her body for so many years dormant. Bart stared into her eyes for a long time as though he could read her thoughts, sense her feelings. And indeed, he did have a curious quality, almost second-sight, that was disturbing. Disturbing, frightening; but it was very exciting too.

'Shall we go?' he said.

'Ready,' she replied, and she took his arm as they walked down the steps to his pony and gig, waiting in the drive. The pony's reins were in the hands of the groom.

'Has Sir Guy gone out?' Sophie enquired as she mounted the gig. 'I tried to find him to tell him I was going on an errand, and couldn't.'

'He went out very early, ma'am,' the groom replied. 'He took his motor-car and didn't say when he'd be back.'

Since the advent of Agnes, Guy had also acquired a car and chauffeur. Apparently his fiancée didn't like riding about in carriages which, in America, were fast becoming curiosities, such was the speed of change.

Bart made sure Sophie was comfortable, had a rug around her waist; and then, with a light flick of his whip on the pony's back, they set off at a brisk pace down the drive.

Just to be alone with him without talking was enough. She felt their closeness, the harmony between them that would make their union even more natural. Rude and abandoned visions, dreams, long repressed, came tumbling into her mind, and she felt shocked by them. As though, again, he could see these disturbing images, and was encouraged by them, Bart put his arm round her waist – only more tightly this time – and said:

'I think we suit, don't we, Sophie?'

She nodded, her heart, her mind, too full to speak.

'What will happen to you now, with two new women moving into the house?'

'I have not been asked to leave,' she replied, 'but it is true, my future is insecure, though I think Sir Guy would like me to stay on, at least to see the two ladies settled. I must say, it is rather droll, don't you think, Bart, to have two sisters moving in as brides when there is over twenty years between them?'

'Oh, very droll,' Bart replied rather woodenly.

'Sir Guy would also like to have his grandchildren near him,' Sophie prattled on, 'so maybe I shall have some security after all.'

'Which is what you want,' he said.

'Everyone wants security, especially a widow with two young children.'

'I'm amazed that George left you nothing.'

'He had nothing to leave,' she said with surprise. 'Had his mother died before him, doubtless a sum of money would have been settled on George, but even then it would only have been a few hundred pounds and some trinkets, which was all she left Carson.' She sighed deeply. 'You see she never imagined, in her wildest dreams, that the Martyns and Heerings would claw back everything she had. She would turn in her grave if she knew.'

'What they did was very base, but that's businessmen for you. They have no souls.'

'I believe it has caused a rift between Julius and Eliza. Did you notice the other evening how cold they were to each other?'

'I wasn't looking at them, but at you,' Bart replied then, with a chuckle, 'and the lovers. I was looking at how cheerful Sir Guy was and how cheerless his son. The one anticipates marriage with relish, the other does not. But then, for the old man all his troubles are over. Both he and his son are to marry heiresses. What a turn-round from a short while ago when the house was on the market. A curious situation, Sophie, you must agree.'

'Very curious,' she replied. 'But my father-in-law is a man seriously in love, and Agnes is certainly not after him for his money.'

'But his title, I expect.' Bart kept his eyes on the road ahead.

'Do you think so?' Sophie looked at him sharply. 'Oh, I don't at all.'

'Then you are naive, my dear. Agnes Yetman was always ambitious, known as a little gold-digger, so my mother tells me. She didn't find anyone in the town good enough for her. She turned her nose up at everyone who fell for her. She always had that superior air, those fancy manners. But it wasn't money she was after, my mother says, for John Yetman had plenty. What she coveted was a title, position, to be someone of consequence in society. All this was denied her because of the humble origins of her family, of which she was ashamed.'

'But the family were people of consequence in Wenham.'

'Only in the first generation. They had started as estate workers at Pelham's Oak, and only gradually began to make their way up in the world.'

Sophie remained silent, lost in thought. It was true that she scarcely remembered Agnes Yetman, who had left the district when she herself was a girl. But her mother had confirmed what Bart had just told her. Agnes had been known as restless, dissatisfied; she had first worked as a governess, her education convincing her that she was too good for the local farmers and tradesmen who might otherwise have asked for her hand.

Well, what did these things matter now? If she made Guy happy in his final years, that was the important thing.

She realised after a while that the countryside through which they were passing was unfamiliar. They had been so busy talking, and she so preoccupied with her thoughts, that she hadn't been looking where they were going.

But when she realised that they were parallel to Bulbarrow

Hill, twisting and turning up country lanes, past Woolland, Ibberton and Belchalwell, she called out to Bart:

'Where are we going? This isn't the way.'

'We're going to see the stone, like I told you.' He looked at her with a reassuring smile.

'But this isn't the Dorchester road.'

'The stone has been moved, my dear; it's been honed and polished and is now in the garden of my house, where I can better attend to the carving of the inscription undisturbed.'

'Oh.'

'I hope you don't mind that, Sophie?'

'I don't mind at all,' she said, but she experienced, nevertheless, a twinge of unease, a quickening of the heart, a supposition – but only a supposition – as to why he had not wanted her to bring the children. She sighed, and squared her shoulders. Well, she was a mature woman, a widow, and did she not know how to take care of herself?

Finally Bart turned the gig into the yard of what looked like a farmhouse. It was quite a sizeable building, with the outbuildings of the farm. It was practically right underneath Bulbarrow, and from its sloping grounds could be seen breathtaking views of the Dorset plain as far as Somerset.

'You've never been to my home, have you, Sophie?'

'No,' she said, staring straight in front of her.

'It doesn't bother you at all, does it?' He smiled at her quizzically. 'Nothing will happen that you don't want to happen. You know that, Sophie. But I thought 'twas time you saw where I lived. I bet you wus curious.'

Sophie didn't reply but jumped from the gig into the yard; a few hens peered at her curiously before proceeding with their endless forage for food, apparently unperturbed.

'It *is* a nice place,' she said, looking up at the house covered with climbing roses and clematis not yet in bud.

'I'm glad you like it.'

'Now, where's the stone?' she asked briskly and, without another word, Bart led the way round the side of the house to one of the outbuildings, which he appeared to have turned into a workshop. There were several large lumps of stone in various shapes, sizes and degrees of finish; but there was one piece of brown-veined Purbeck marble which stood out. It tapered to the top from the base like an obelisk, and had been honed and polished until it shone.

Sophie took out a handkerchief and blew her nose loudly.

'It is very beautiful,' she murmured, taking a crumpled piece of paper from her pocket and handing it to Bart.

Solemnly he read out:

Sacred to the memory of
George Pelham Woodville
1881–1907
whose body is buried in
Gumbago, New Guinea, but whose
spirit rests forever in his
County of Dorset.
And to those who were martyred
with him, in particular his
beloved servant Kirikeu.
All rest in the bosom of God.

'Those are beautiful words too,' he said softly. 'I like the reference to the servant. Very noble.'

'It was George's wish.' She blew her nose again and he put an arm round her shoulders.

'You have the permission of the rector to place it in the churchyard?'

Sophie nodded. Seeing the stone, George's memorial, had affected her.

'And Sir Guy?'

'Sir Guy doesn't know it's ready, but when it is he will agree. Besides, he has his mind on other things at the moment.'

'Oh yes. Love.' Bart started to laugh and then, seeing Sophie's disapproving gaze, corrected himself.

'I'm sorry, my dear, I didn't wish to be offensive.'

'It's not that you're offensive,' Sophie assured him, 'it is simply that at a moment as solemn as this I don't think one should be light-hearted.'

'Of course not.'

'I meant that Sir Guy's marriage, and Carson's, naturally, preoccupied him; but he has never been enthusiastic about a memorial, otherwise we should have had one long ago. It is almost as though . . .' she paused and then rushed on '. . . he does not wish to be reminded of George.'

'Or the circumstances in which George died.' Bart watched Sophie as she slowly circled the monument, running her hand along the shiny surface of the plinth.

'It is so beautiful,' she murmured again. 'Thank you, Bart.'

She turned towards the door and went into the yard, where she stood looking at the gig, and the pony which had its nose in a bag of oats, as if she were uncertain what to do.

'Will you come in and have a bite to eat? I suggested it, you remember.'

'I didn't think you were referring to your home.'

'Sophie.' He stood before her and looked squarely into her eyes. 'You're not by any chance afraid of me, are you? You told me the first night I drove you home that you were not at all afeared to be alone with a man. I admired that spirit of independence.'

'That was different,' she said, feeling strangely unsure of herself. 'Here, with George's stone . . . it is as if his presence were here too. I feel irreverent . . . to think other things.'

'But my dear, he wouldn't expect you to be a widow all your life, would he? What, is it over four years since you were widowed? And a desperate time you've had of it, too, going from pillar to post, rejected first by this person then that, without money. What sort of future do you really imagine you have now? If I know the reputation of Agnes Yetman, she will have you out of the house in no time, no time at all.'

'But Sir Guy would never . . .'

'Sir Guy will do what she tells him. He is besotted. If ever I saw a woman having dominion over a man, that woman is Agnes Yetman, or Gregg as we must call her now.'

Casually Bart put his arm around her waist and drew her towards the house. The door led directly into a large living-room and kitchen, which had a tiled floor scattered with rugs.

It was a functional, bachelor-style room, sorely in need of a woman's touch. There was a large sofa, some comfortable chairs, and a table in the middle which was already laid with a cloth and knives and forks.

'It seems I was expected,' Sophie said with a trace of amusement, feeling more relaxed as she entered the house.

'I have only very simple fare, some home-killed and home-cured ham, some pickles, cheese and bread. Oh!' He went into a larder off the kitchen and after a few minutes returned with a jug. 'Some ale. Good Dorset ale, straight from the barrel. Will you have a glass, Sophie?'

'I'll try a little,' she said cautiously. 'Just a taste. You know I'm not a drinker.'

'But it's not against your religion, is it?'

'Oh no,' she said quickly. 'Drinking too much *is* against our religion, but certainly not a glass from time to time. However, I do regard drink as a demon and incline to teetotalism. Just half, please, Bart,' she said anxiously as she watched him pouring. He then passed her the half-full glass and, filling his to the brim, put it to his lips.

'Cheers,' he said.

'Your health,' she replied primly.

It was a pleasant enough room, even though the main windows looked directly out on to the side of Bulbarrow and not the glorious view in front. Farmhouses were functional buildings constructed to protect humans and animals from the wind, rather than for the advantage of the view.

Bart produced a side of ham which he sliced with professional skill, and the pickles in a large glass jar. The bread he appeared to have bought in Wenham because it was freshly baked and tasted delicious. For a while they ate in silence. Bart finished his glass of beer, rather too quickly in Sophie's opinion, and fetched another.

'The cheese is made from the cows on my brother's farm,' he said proudly, pushing it towards her. 'You know I have two brothers who farm?'

'Of course I know. Carson worked there for a time. Did farming never appeal to you, Bart?'

'Not as a living,' he replied, leaning back and lighting a cigarette after finishing his cheese. 'I was going into the building business when I was a boy, and was first apprenticed to a builder. Then I became interested in stone, especially the qualities of the marble from our own Isle of Purbeck, which is sent all over the world. At one time they used to haul the stone down from the cliffs and send it by sea to various parts of the country. Now it mainly goes by rail.'

'I would have thought, in a way . . .' Sophie didn't quite know how to proceed and played with a spare knife, her eyes on the white tablecloth '. . . I would have thought you were a more ambitious man.'

'Ambitious?' He seemed surprised. 'How do you mean?'

'Maybe like Laurence, with a big firm . . .'

'Oh, too many risks in that,' Bart replied. 'I don't like having too many workers, big overheads. My small stone-mason's yard is enough for me, and the two men I can lay off if times are bad. And I tell you, I suspect I make more money than Laurence does.'

'Oh! How?' She looked surprised. 'He employs about fifty men.'

'And I employ none.' Bart stood up and leaned against the high slate mantelshelf. 'Only casual labour. Every penny I make, I keep. You see, you don't have to have a large organisation, offices here and offices there, to run a business. I make a bit of money out of my yard, but it's largely by buying cheap and selling at a profit, or making introductions, like Wainwright. I introduced him to Laurence. He paid me for it.'

'Really?' Sophie felt a sense of shock. 'But why should he do that? Surely there are plenty of builders . . .'

'Oh yes, but Wainwright is a speculator. You see, he doesn't really have the resources behind him he says he has, so he needs people who will give him credit and not ask too many questions . . .'

'Oh, but that is awful!' Sophie started to protest. 'Poor Laurence is already alarmed.'

'It's not awful at all.' Bart's brow clouded. 'My recommendation is good enough for both of them without going to any middle-men. There is no need for Laurence to be alarmed. You should see the size of Wainwright's house. You'll see, they'll *both* make a handsome profit, and I haven't done so badly either. But I have taken no risk; Laurence has, so he will get more . . . and deserve it, too.'

'Are you sure?' Sophie still looked doubtful. 'I thought Laurence looked unhappy at the dinner the other night, when both you and Julius Heering were anxious to distance yourself from Wainwright.'

'I made no attempt to distance myself. I said I hardly knew Wainwright, which is true. But his plans seemed good enough to me. He started to talk to me about the manufacture of agricultural machines. He had vision, his eyes on far horizons. I thought Laurence would be prepared to take a risk.'

'But Laurence didn't think there was a risk. He asked Prosper Martyn and Julius Heering.'

'Oh no.' Bart shook his head very firmly. 'I don't think he asked them. I don't really think he asked their bank, either, for a proper reference, though I s'pose he should have done. But you see, my dear, if you don't take no risks, you don't get no reward.'

He threw his cigarette in the empty grate and, going over to her chair, stood behind her and put his arms around her neck, his face pressed close up to hers, his hands making towards her breasts.

'Now, me dear,' he murmured caressingly, 'what say *we* take a risk?'

'A risk?' She tried to turn, but he held her fast.

'You know what risk I mean.' His breath was hot on the side of her face. 'The risk of love. Come, Sophie Woodville, you're no maiden, no virgin. Didn't you ever feel those womanly yearnings in recent times?' He thrust his hand inside the front of her dress. 'Don't you burn inside for a man? Isn't it a long, long time – too long, my dear, since you last had one? 'Sides, you know you like me, Sophie.'

'I do like you.' She tried to prise his fingers away from her breasts, but maybe she was too half-hearted because she didn't succeed.

'Well then? What's stopping you?' He gripped a nipple and rubbed it until it was hard like his finger, calloused and roughened by his trade.

'But I could never . . . Not until we were married.'

'My dear, if we wait that long the fires I feel burning inside you might go out altogether. Don't dampen the flames.' He rubbed her nipple even harder and she could feel the sensation of opening and closing just on the inside of her thighs. 'Besides,' he whispered, close to her ear, 'after being so good all these years, so Christian, would it not be *exciting*, just for once in a while, to do something the world – but not I, mind – might consider wicked?'

20

Carson found it very difficult to get so much as a sight of, never mind an interview with, his father in the days following the announcement of his wedding. Guy was off at first light and returned either in the small hours or, sometimes, it had to be confessed, not at all.

Carson had eventually to write him a note to ask for a meeting, and now at last he stood in his father's study, waiting for him to make his appearance after breakfast, which he always took in his room.

Having shaved carefully and dressed in a suit, Carson wished to present a good appearance to his father. He had rehearsed to himself over and over again what he was going to say; but even so he felt nervous and unsure of himself when his father entered the room, a smile of greeting on his face.

'My dear boy,' he said, coming up to him and clasping his arm. 'Isn't it terrible that a son should have to write and ask his father for an interview? Dear, dear, I feel ashamed.' He then released Carson and went and sat on the sofa, patting it so that Carson should sit beside him. 'But you know, times are not what they were. My dearest Agnes has transformed my life.'

'I can see that, Father,' Carson observed drily, but taking care not to sound too cynical.

'She is such a darling,' Guy went on, heedless of Carson, 'such a gadabout and spendthrift. I can't keep up with her. She is going to do up this entire house inside – which, of course, makes fewer demands on Miss Fairchild, who is already paying for the outside, so we can leave that to her. The inside Agnes will take care of.'

Guy rubbed his hands together as though he had achieved something singular, as perhaps he had, in getting two women to pay for the refurbishment of his home.

Carson had not joined his father on the sofa and stood, instead, with his back to the fireplace in which a fire had been lit, for it was a cold spring day.

'I think you should have told me first, Father.'

'Told you what, Carson?' Guy looked puzzled.

'That you were to marry. It was a great shock . . .'

'It was a shock to me too, my darling boy,' Guy chuckled happily. 'A very pleasant shock, though. I only knew myself a few days before. Dearest Agnes begged me not to announce it until we could tell everyone together. She wished, for some reason, that it should be kept secret, bless her heart. Shyness, I expect,' he concluded, with the expression of a man clearly besotted by love.

'Shyness is hardly the word *I* would use about Agnes, Father. I never saw a woman quite so bold.'

'Carson, please do not speak in that flippant manner about my intended.' Guy's tone was suddenly severe. 'I cannot allow it.'

'But Father, she is not shy. It is the last thing she is. She is a woman of the world, anyone can see that . . .'

'Is it *possible* that you do not like my darling Agnes?' Guy asked suspiciously. 'Or that you are even a little jealous, maybe? To me she is the most beautiful, the most divine woman in the world.'

'I can see you are in love, Father; but to me she appears in the guise not of a woman in love, but a schemer.'

'A schemer! For what?' Guy wrathfully drew his brows together again. 'How dare you suggest she is a *schemer*! *I* haven't a penny. I have confessed this to her and told her the extent of my misfortune. Do you call her generous response to me *scheming*? I have nothing and she has everything, and is prepared to place it all at my, at our, disposal.'

'Are you sure she has the money?' Carson put his hands in his pockets and stared hard at his father.

'Of course I am sure she has the money!' Guy said coldly.

'She lives in some style and has been looking at enormous country mansions to purchase. Her late husband left her his *entire* fortune! But please do not assume that I am marrying Agnes solely for her money. Our relationship goes back many years. Once upon a time . . .' his voice broke slightly with emotion '. . . I loved Agnes.'

'Ah!' Carson said with a note of triumph. 'Now we know that she was one of your women.'

'Don't you dare use that phrase,' Guy snapped. ' "One of my women" indeed. I was in love with Agnes, and she with me . . .'

'While you were married to Mother, I suppose,' Carson sneered.

'Carson, I shall discontinue this conversation if you insist on proceeding in that tone,' his father said. 'I have no need to listen to a young puppy like you.'

'As you wish, Father.' Carson bowed his head to hide his smile.

'And don't you *ever* speak disrespectfully of her again, or you and I will cease to communicate.'

'I merely thought she might be after your title, Father.' Carson assumed a tone of humility. 'My concern was solely for you. Many women pretend to have money to gain some advantage – or so they say. But if you think not . . . If you're happy . . .'

'After my *title*?' Guy thundered. 'What rubbish! You think a little thing like that matters to someone as divine as Agnes? I'll have you know, my dear boy, I had to get down on my knees and *beg* her to marry me. I had to *plead* with her. Even then she wasn't sure, the sweet, bewitching, beguiling darling.' Guy joined his hands together in a paroxysm of emotion which only left Carson feeling renewed disgust at his father's capacity for self-deception.

'Well, if you're happy, Father,' he said, finally sitting by him, 'then I am happy. It also makes what I have to say to you easier.'

'Good, good.' Guy, never a man to bear a grudge, put a hand over Carson's. 'I want you to be happy here, my dear boy, with your little bride. Agnes and I were only talking about it the other day. You shall have your own suite of rooms. We, both being older people who have been married before, would not wish to interfere with young lives.'

There was a pause during which Carson appeared lost in thought.

'Do you like that idea?' His father looked at him anxiously. 'There is no need to make up your mind until you have discussed it with Connie. You may prefer to live in a house on the estate for the first few years. The Richmonds in Lostock Manor Farm are very old. Perhaps I could persuade them to leave for somewhere smaller, a cottage nearby. The house is in good repair, not too large, the animals long dispersed. Is it the fear that there may be some antipathy between Connie and Agnes that worries you?'

Carson ignored his question and asked instead:

'When will you be married, Father?'

'As soon as we can, but certainly after you. We have no wish to steal your thunder. We may well slip away and tie the knot somewhere else. My darling is extremely fond of London and she wishes the London house to be reopened, to have new furnishings and wallpaper.' Guy rubbed his hands together again, like a miser savouring a fortune. 'Oh, I assure you, Carson, we shall have two very fine houses that will recall the Woodville family at its peak.'

'Father,' Carson said in a tense tone of voice, 'now that you are to be married to a woman who you admit has vast wealth, there is no need for me to marry Connie.'

'I beg your pardon?' Guy looked so shocked that Carson had to repeat his statement.

'You now have the money you need to keep Pelham's Oak – if you are sure Agnes has the money, and is not just pretending to be rich to ensnare you . . .'

'Carson, I have warned you!' Guy roared, struggling to his feet. 'I have *forbidden* you to say anything detrimental about my darling. Think what you like, but never, never put it into words, least of all to me. I am quite sure that Agnes has sufficient funds. You should just observe the style in which she lives. Her jewellery alone is worth a small fortune.'

'Then I am happy for you, Father. Truly happy, and I apologise. I withdraw unreservedly my insinuation.' Carson stood up and gazed gravely into his father's eyes. 'But I personally am not happy. The thought of marriage to Connie distresses me beyond words. I shall not be a good husband. I do not love or desire her at all. I shall make her unhappy as you made Mother unhappy.'

'Oh dear.' Guy gnawed thoughtfully at his lip. 'That is very unsettling news. Miss Fairchild has already put considerable funds into the repair of the fabric and the redecoration of the outside of the house.'

'Then they will have to be returned to her, since Agnes has the means.'

'But would not Connie be very upset?'

'I don't know.' Carson, hands in his pockets, strolled to the window, where he stood brooding for a second or two before returning to face Guy. 'I think she does love me sincerely, poor little creature; but someone as intelligent as she is must realise I don't return her love. I don't pretend to. I feel as indifferent to Connie as I did the day you asked me to marry her. I agreed for you, for the family; but now that the future of the house is secured I feel I am released from my obligation.'

'Oh dear, the poor child . . . And what will Miss Fairchild say? She had set her heart on it. This is a complication I hadn't expected. The banns have been called, the trousseau, I understand, is ready; all the preparations are in hand. It will cause a great deal of bother.'

'Father,' Carson said patiently, 'all these things can be undone. A bad marriage can be undone eventually, but it is not easy. I would rather not marry Connie in the first place than do so with the intention of one day divorcing her. That would be wrong.'

'Very wrong,' Guy murmured. Then he reached impulsively for Carson's hand. 'Oh, my poor boy, what an agony of decision for you. Would that you could be as happy, as in love, as contented as my darling Agnes and I. Well.' He let go Carson's hand and sank back, his face thoughtful. 'Do it gently, my dear boy, do it as kindly as you can; but do it soon, before more preparations are made. I'm sure the poor girl will be most dreadfully upset; besides which, I do not wish to jeopardise my own marriage by putting Agnes to vast expense in the repayment of funds before we are even wed.'

The thought of what he had to tell Connie haunted Carson, made him deeply unhappy, and yet he knew he had to do it. He had been wrong to agree to marry her for mercenary reasons, and now he deserved his punishment of endless shame and remorse.

As his father said, he must act quickly, the wedding had but three weeks to go. He toyed with the idea of seeing Miss Fairchild, but he thought that was the coward's way out. He was also more frightened of her reaction than he was of Connie's.

The day following his talk with his father, Carson mounted his horse and rode as slowly as he could across the fields, lingering through the coppices and past the hedgerows, loitering by the stream for his horse to drink; but, delay as he might, he finally and inevitably arrived in Wenham and slowly climbed the hill to the church in the hope that he might catch Connie at her practice, where the influence of music might find her in a mellow mood.

When he got to the church, however, he heard to his chagrin the sound of the choir lustily singing. There was no one about and, dismounting, he took his horse round the side of the church and tethered him to a tree. Then he stood with the horse and himself concealed behind the tree, waiting. The choir was practising and, perhaps, Connie was with them.

Then something about the singing jolted him: they were rehearsing for his wedding! 'My heart is igniting' – glad, joyful hymns, sung with hearts full of hope, pealed forth from the church. Carson felt he could not go through with his task. He would simply disappear. He prepared to mount his horse. He would send a letter, have it delivered by hand and, coward that he was, leave Wenham for a few weeks, or even months. Maybe in that time his father would have the chance to comfort Connie, pacify Miss Fairchild and arrange his own marriage to Agnes. Eventually, in the course of time, everything would be forgotten . . . Forgotten by the town, perhaps, but never forgotten by Connie . . .

The singing came to a glorious climax, and was followed by a silence in which he could hear the choirmaster addressing the choir, but not what he said. Then suddenly the west doors of the church burst open and the members of the choir tumbled out, men and women, chattering and laughing, their whole beings the embodiment of happiness and satisfaction in the anticipation of the exciting event that was to come.

The very joy on their faces sickened him. No one looked behind, and Carson remained where he was, intent on not being seen. There had been no sign of Connie. The chance now was that she would be up at the house with Miss Fairchild, busy with her preparations.

He was about to untie the reins of his horse when the sound of organ music stole upon his ears. But, unlike the music that had preceded it, it was a melancholy sound, almost a dirge; and as he listened it soared and seemed to engulf him, making his eyes unexpectedly fill with tears.

He went round to the door of the church and entered, and the beautiful music continued to crescendo. Carson sank help-lessly onto a pew, then onto his knees, and remained lis-tening.

'Oh God,' he prayed fervently, 'I wish I could love Connie. As I can't, dear Lord, please find her someone else soon.' Then, partly satisfied by this simple prayer, he sat back on the pew and gazed round the church, imagining how it would have been on his wedding-day: the white blossoms, the golden copes of the clergy, the virginal purity of the bride. It was an image that horrified him.

He closed his eyes and the music stopped. Then he heard the sound that he dreaded; footsteps on the floor of the sanc-tuary, taking the two steps down and walking slowly along the aisle.

He opened his eyes and saw that Connie, with an expression of delight on her face, had quickened her steps and was coming towards him. He stood up and moved along the pew, putting out his arm in greeting.

'Carson!' Connie cried, clasping his hand. 'What a lovely surprise to see you! Did you come to listen to the music for the wedding rehearsal? If so, you just missed it.'

Carson said nothing but, continuing to gaze at her, her hand still in his, drew her down beside him on the pew.

'You look worried, Carson,' she said, her smile fading. 'Are you not well? Is something troubling you?'

'Something *is* troubling me, Connie,' he nodded. 'It troubles me very much and I don't know how to say it.'

Connie's features now assumed a look of horror, as though she had seen a ghost.

'Is it that you don't love me?' she whispered at last. 'If it is that, I know; I have always known. But I love you *so* much, Carson, that I hope in time you will come to love me. I have enough love for two of us.'

'Oh Connie, stop, please.' Carson grasped her hand so hard that he crushed her fingers and, to her amazement, tears began to trickle down his cheeks. 'Connie, I love you too; but not in the way you want . . .'

'But in time, Carson . . .' Her voice petered out as he shook his head, avoiding her eyes.

'You are the nicest, best person in the world; but I cannot marry you, Connie. I have wrestled with myself and I cannot do it, however much I want to . . .'

'But why *now* . . .' Suddenly her voice was close to tears.

'Before it was too late,' he said. 'I didn't think it fair to engage you in a loveless marriage.'

'What will people say?' Her voice trembled. 'What will Aunt Vicky say?'

'They will all blame *me*, Connie. They will blame me and they will be right. No blame *at all* attaches itself to you. They will say I am a heartless cad, and I am.'

'It was the dress,' she said, her eyes staring in front of her.

'The dress?' Carson reached for a handkerchief to dry his eyes, and gazed curiously at her. 'What dress?'

'The pink satin I wore at the dinner-party last week. I knew it was all wrong, but Aunt Vicky insisted it suited me. It was too old-looking, and the colour was awful. I knew I shouldn't have worn it, but I said "just once". I felt a frump, and Agnes looked so beautiful, even though she's a bit fat. Sophie and Eliza were so elegant, Dora looked charming. *I* was the ugliest person present.'

'Connie, my dear.' Tentatively Carson put his arm round her back. 'It had nothing to do with the dress. To tell you the truth, I hardly noticed what you were wearing. I had my doubts about the wisdom of our marrying long before this, but lacked the courage to say anything.'

'Then why,' she said, turning to him, her eyes narrowing, 'why did you ever ask me to marry you?'

'Because I do love you,' he stuttered. 'I did it on an impulse. I love you very much. But like a sister, Connie. I can't see myself as a husband, I'm sorry. Frankly, I can't see myself getting married to anyone, and now that father is to marry Agnes, I shall be free.'

'Free?' she cried shrilly. 'How do you mean, "free"? Free from what?'

'Free of my obligations to my father,' he stammered. 'I felt that I should not leave Father, who does not enjoy the best of health. Now there will be someone to look after him.'

'I suppose *I* was to be the nurse in that case.' Connie suddenly stood up and gazed down at him, her lip curled with indignation. 'You did not need to marry *me* if all you wanted was a nurse for your father.'

He put out his hand and clutched hers, but she broke away and, turning her back on him, ran towards the door, her sheet music, which she had forgotten about, scattering in the aisle in her wake.

Carson had a sudden feeling of nausea, and for a few seconds thought he would be physically sick. He sat with his head in his hands until it passed. He then rose, and slowly walked out of the church, mechanically picking up the fallen pages as he went.

He had never in his life felt so terrible, felt such remorse. He felt so wicked, so unworthy; and yet he was troubled, too, about Connie. And so, despite his justifiable fear of her guardian, leaving his horse where it was, he walked past the church towards Miss Fairchild's house, to make sure Connie was all right.

Miss Fairchild sat in her sitting-room in front of the fire, putting some finishing stitches to a pillowcase she was embroidering for Connie's trousseau. She had bought several sets made of the finest Irish linen from the haberdashers in Wenham, which was still called Samuel Fairchild and Co., even though it had been out of the family for many years. 'Fairchild's' was a name for quality and reliability, and the people who had bought it from Miss Fairchild had never regretted their decision not to rename it. Quality and reliability was the keynote of the business, always had been and always would be. It was also the precept that had governed the life of the present holder of the name.

The freehold of the building containing the shop still belonged to Miss Fairchild. It was part of the endowment that, together with the house, the gold shares and other profitable investments, she would leave to Connie, to make her one of the wealthiest women in Wenham – if not *the* wealthiest. If Victoria Fairchild would not be remembered in the parish by children of her own, her name would surely live as that of the woman who promoted the future Lady Woodville to her place of glory and esteem.

Miss Fairchild was an accomplished needlewoman and had already embroidered two full sets of bed-linen in secret whenever Connie was out, or she could manage some hours alone in her room. These were to number among her wedding-gifts but to be a surprise. There was something about sheets that might alert the sensibilities of a reserved young woman and upset her. It rather upset Miss Fairchild, too, to think of the shock, pain and suffering her darling might endure between those sheets; but such was the lot of woman. Miss Fairchild sighed. Fortunately or unfortunately, as the case might be, it was a fate she had escaped, and in many ways she was grateful for it. One did not miss what one had merely glimpsed but never experienced.

She would love to have gone to the rehearsal for the choir, but there was one more pillowcase to go and time was running out.

For a moment she sat back and removed her glasses, rubbing her eyes. Then, to her horror, she heard the front door burst open, and before she had time to hide her sewing Connie rushed into the sitting-room and flung herself against Miss Fairchild, her thin body shaken by violent sobs.

Not caring whether Connie saw the sheets or not, Miss Fairchild rose up in alarm and, enfolding her ward in her arms, drew her gently to the sofa and sat down beside her.

'Constance, dear, what *is* this? What has happened? Was the choir-practice not to your satisfaction? Did something go wrong?'

'Wrong?' Connie stared at her wildly as though she had suddenly become unbalanced, and Miss Fairchild began to feel frightened. 'Carson no longer wishes to marry me,' Connie continued hysterically. 'He said it was a mistake; but I know better, Aunt.' Angrily Connie tried to brush the tears from her eyes. 'It was that *dress*. That hateful pink satin. It was so unbecoming, so old, but I didn't like to say anything. I wore it despite my better judgment. I didn't wish to hurt you or Mrs Pond. But I could see Carson looking at it, the expression in his eyes. All the women there looked so nice, so suitably dressed, except me. Agnes, who is years older than me, and *fat*, was almost beautiful. Carson must have thought *I* was the ugliest woman . . .'

'My dear, calm yourself,' Miss Fairchild commanded in tones of authority. 'It was not the dress, not at all. You looked very charming in it . . .'

'It was the colour . . .' Connie spat out. '*Pink!* So ugly, so unrefined.'

'No, Connie, it was not the colour.' Miss Fairchild was clearly on the verge of hysteria herself, despite her reputation for good sense and control, as well as for quality and reliability. 'It was *Agnes*. When I realised that she had come into a fortune and Sir

Guy had asked her to marry him, I feared something like this might happen. It has haunted me ever since.'

'A fortune . . . Agnes!' Connie ran her hands across her tear-stained face, making it look ten times worse. 'You don't mean that Carson was marrying me for *money*, Aunt Vicky? Please say you don't mean that!'

'But I was sure he loved you. He was always so sweet with you, and you looked so good together. I . . . Yes, as there was a little money I happened to mention it to Sir Guy.'

'You *mentioned it to Sir Guy*?' Connie shouted, now quite clearly out of control, and in a state which Miss Fairchild, so sure that Connie had self-discipline like herself, could never have imagined. 'You went over and *bargained* with him, didn't you, Aunt?' Connie frantically stabbed the air with her forefinger. 'You went over and offered him money for Carson to marry me. The house was up for sale and suddenly it was withdrawn. I never knew why . . . And as for Carson,' suddenly her voice broke completely, 'how could he pretend? How *could* he?'

'My dear.' Miss Fairchild sought desperately for her reserves of inner strength and, to her relief, found them. 'I only did it for the best, I assure you.'

'You did it for the *best*! You dared to *sell* me in marriage . . . and you expected it to work?'

'Yes.' Miss Fairchild raised her head and met Connie's feverish eyes. 'I did think it would work. It worked with Carson's father very well. He married Margaret Heering for her money, and in the end he loved her and relied on her so much that her death nearly broke his heart.'

'Yet now he is marrying someone else! Someone of whom he is enamoured like an old fool in his dotage.'

'Connie, hush.' Miss Fairchild was not used to such strong sentiments. 'Lady Woodville died nearly two years ago. Sir Guy certainly mourned her. It is a decent passage of time for a man to decide to marry another. So *please* don't lose control of yourself, Constance. Maybe, after all, you are better off. I have heard that Carson is not unlike his father when he was young. Sir Guy certainly had other women. Carson . . .'

'And yet you allowed this barter, this sale, to go ahead,

387

knowing that he would be sure to deceive me?' Connie was almost screaming now at her aunt. 'Knowing what you knew, you did what you did. You've blighted my life, Aunt Vicky. I hope you realise it. I loved Carson so much that I thought I could make him love me. What you've done is to ruin my life and embitter me for ever.' Again she pointed an accusing finger at the ashen-faced woman who sat next to her. 'I don't want to spend *my* life as a spinster like you, to have people pity me and say things behind my back . . .'

'They *say* things?' Miss Fairchild looked startled.

'Yes "things". "Poor old spinster, never had a man, never been kissed . . ." All the money in the world can't make up for *that*, Aunt Vicky,' And, with an exclamation, Connie ran out of the room and along the corridor, and Miss Fairchild could hear the heavy sound of her feet racing two steps at a time up the stairs to her bedroom.

She was so afraid of what Connie might do to herself that, despite her hurt, she followed her. Did people *really* say that about her and her friend, the late Miss Barker, and the many other spinsters, worthy women, in the parish? If so, how unfair. They were all most dignified ladies, who did not feel unfulfilled, and many of them had substantial means. They contributed to the church, to orphans and the poor, and to the welfare of the town. How awful to think that the ungrateful townsfolk might laugh at them behind their backs!

Miss Fairchild came to the end of the corridor and was turning to mount the staircase when, through the frosted glass panes of the front door, she observed a familiar shadow, and flinging it open she saw Carson standing by the gate, a look of shame and humiliation on his face.

Miss Fairchild stood for some seconds at the top of the steps, staring at him, and then she ran down them and along the path until her face was about three inches from his. Her gaze never left him, her mouth contorted with wrath.

'I'm terribly sorry,' he began, 'terribly, terribly sorry. I . . .'

The stinging blow he received on his face was given with the kind of force he hadn't imagined a woman capable of. He reeled backwards and clutched at the garden rail for support.

His hands went protectively, but too late, to his face, and he could feel blood trickling out of his nose.

'And that's what I think of *you*, Mr Woodville,' Miss Fairchild's voice rang with scorn. 'Take care you never darken my door again, and if I ever see you anywhere else in this town, God knows what else I shall do to you.'

She then turned her back on him and marched along the path to the steps, mounting them without hurrying, and then slamming the front door behind her. Carson, his hands still clutching his face, stood looking after her, feeling the most wretched man in the world. He turned away and walked along the street, skirting the town so that he would not be seen, past the church to his waiting horse.

His own life ruined, it seemed that all he could do was to ruin the lives of others: innocent sufferers who certainly did not deserve it. And from that moment he knew that he would feel himself cursed.

Laurence Yetman, had he been asked, would have called himself a contented man. He was ambitious, but not over-ambitious, and with the help and support of his mother he had restarted the family building business after his father's death. And in time, like his father, he became a master-thatcher and a master-builder. Yetman Bros (Estab. 1831, re-estab. 1899) in Salisbury Street in Blandford was a business to be proud of, and in a few years he had made it into a success. But he still needed work; bigger and more profitable projects, which was why the prospect of building a factory for Dick Wainwright had proved almost irresistibly attractive.

But before his business and his desire for success Laurence put the love of his family: his mate Sarah-Jane, the three beautiful children she had borne him, and the happy home she had made for him at Riversmead, where his parents had also known the same sort of contentment. The freehold had been given to him as an outright gift by his mother when she married Julius Heering. As the eldest son, she felt it was his birthright.

Now, it was the beloved house, the thought of how he had set it at risk, that gnawed frequently at his mind as the days went by. The factory continued to grow and men had to be paid, materials bought and paid for, but there was no sizeable sum coming from Mr Wainwright.

Laurence walked round the floor of the factory near Dorchester which was now nearly two storeys high. It was well designed, and hidden from the road so that it didn't become a blot on the landscape. Tall trees grew up in front of it, behind was a tributary of the River Piddle and, beyond that, a coppice.

Laurence stood surveying it with Perce Adams, his foreman, the man who had taught him all he knew, his father's old friend and ally.

'It's coming up beautiful,' Perce said. Then, stroking his jaw, he looked thoughtfully at Laurence. 'Did you get any word from Mr Wainwright yet?'

'No.' Laurence threw him a troubled glance. 'I'm going to see him on my way home. I keep on thinking of my house, which I've put up as security for this loan. If I can't meet my commitments, I could lose it.'

'Oh, you'll not lose your house,' Perce protested in amazement. 'A man like you, a solid citizen born in the parish, and also in line to be mayor one day, I hear tell.'

'Oh, I have this and that to do on the town council,' Laurence said modestly, 'but mayor is a long way off, Perce. I have to have grey hairs for that. Besides, I shall be very glad to see this building up and paid for, after which I shall have *no* more to do with speculative deals. Ever,' he concluded firmly. 'You can rely on that, because this has given me too many sleepless nights.' Then he put a hand on Perce's shoulder.

'I'll be off now, Perce. Once I get that money from Dick Wainwright I'll feel a completely different man.'

The men shook hands, and Laurence walked off the site to where he had left his horse. He had toyed with the idea of buying a motor-car like his wealthier relations; had even got as far as inspecting one but, with the commitments he had, he felt that he should be in a sounder financial position before splashing out on luxuries.

A countryman, he had grown up in the saddle and felt

comfortable in the saddle. Still, a fine car with his wife beside him, his three children in the back, might not come amiss one day as a symbol both of status and prosperity.

Laurence unleashed his horse and waved again to Perce, who was watching him; he circled the building with a feeling of pride, and after exchanging greetings with some of the men who were working on it, he set out on the detour that would take him to Wainwright's house.

This was just north of Dorchester on the Sherborne road, and Laurence found it quite easily after he had been riding for about twenty minutes.

He sat for some time in his saddle, looking at the house where it lay in a gentle fold of the hills. It was a fine, large Georgian mansion, parts of it dating back to Elizabethan times; it was imposing, and on the grand scale, rather like Pelham's Oak. It was ridiculous to imagine that a man who could afford to buy and maintain a house like this would not have the money. The very sight of it seemed such a confirmation of strength and security that he decided not to bother Wainwright, who would doubtless be at his lunch with the young wife he had recently married.

A man of substance and fortune, no doubt about that. Sarah-Jane always said he worried too much.

With a feeling of relief Laurence turned away from the house towards Wenham, following the bridle-paths familiar to him since childhood, through woods and across rich fields, over hills and by the side of streams he loved. This was his land, his county: Dorset.

Laurence arrived home about an hour later in a good frame of mind. He was surprised to see his mother's car at the door, and expected it was something to do with what had happened to Connie Yetman. The town had still not recovered from the abrupt cancellation of her marriage, and the younger Yetmans were naturally upset, although they had never been very close to Connie, who had been coddled and protected by Miss Fairchild since she was a little girl.

Yet everyone was indignant about what had happened to her, and Carson's name was even less respected than before.

Miss Fairchild had immediately taken Connie away on what was supposed to be an extended holiday on the Continent; Eliza, who knew and loved Connie, was very distressed, yet she knew it was quite hopeless to try and talk to Guy, a man in love who was trying to press his fiancée into naming the date for their own marriage.

Laurence dismounted to open the gate. He hoped that nothing else was wrong; but he was in such a mellow frame of mind that he walked his horse up the drive and then stood for a few moments admiring the Heering car and thinking about how it would be when he had one like it.

At that moment he looked up and saw Eliza on the steps, gazing down at him. She had Felicity in her arms and Abel clutching one hand.

'Hello, Mother!' he shouted, raising his hat. 'I was admiring your car.'

Eliza came slowly down the steps.

'So I see,' she said, brushing her son's cheeks with her lips.

'I'm going to have one like it one day. Maybe soon.'

'I do hope so.' There was something in Eliza's tone that made Laurence look sharply at her.

'Is there anything wrong, Mother?' he asked, taking Felicity gently from Eliza's arms and giving her a kiss.

'I don't know exactly if something *is* wrong. I'll wait until you see Sarah-Jane.'

'Is she all right?' Laurence, the worrier, was immediately anxious. 'Nothing has happened to her or children? Where's Martha?' Martha was usually the first at the door to greet her father, and she was missing.

'Everyone is *fine*,' Eliza said reassuringly. 'I shouldn't have mentioned it. There is nothing wrong with any member of your family, but Sarah-Jane has a bit of news that may disturb you, I don't know. I hope not.'

She gave him a reassuring smile but knew it was hopeless as Laurence, his daughter clutched in his arms, ran up the steps and shouted through the house:

'Sarah-Jane! Where are you?'

After a few moments Sarah-Jane came running down the

stairs, some laundry in her arms, and stared at him in surprise.

'What are you shouting for?'

'Just to say I'm home.' He put Felicity tenderly down on the floor and then embraced his wife. The smell of her always kindled desire in him, and he thought longingly of the night, when they would be beside each other. Nine years of marriage had done nothing to diminish his ardour.

'My love,' he murmured in her ear, 'how *lucky* I am to have you. Now Mother worried me a little by saying that you had some disturbing news. What might that be? Let's get it out of the way and then perhaps we can have some tea, because I'm thirsty.'

Sarah-Jane broke away from his embrace and walked along the corridor to the kitchen quarters, first of all throwing the laundry into the laundry-room beside the kitchen.

On the kitchen table a newspaper was spread, and without further explanation Sarah-Jane firmly pointed at a particular item.

'I saw this in today's paper. I don't know if it's significant or not, or even if you knew. I didn't *want* to worry you. Your mother's just like you – always jumping to conclusions.'

Laurence was conscious that Eliza had come into the kitchen and stood in the doorway listening.

'It may mean nothing,' she said, uncomfortably aware of Sarah-Jane's implicit reprimand. Her daughter-in-law was always so calm that sometimes she found it irritating. She never anticipated trouble, never let off steam.

Laurence picked up the paper and read aloud the news item his wife indicated: *Pendleton Hall for sale*. (The headline ran over half a column of news.)

Pendleton Hall, the handsome Georgian mansion near Dorchester that has been the home of Mr Richard Wainwright for the past year and a half, is unexpectedly for sale through Dutton, Brock of Weymouth.

The sale is the more curious because Mr Wainwright

has not only recently married for the second time, but had announced his intention of remaining in the locality and investing heavily in it.

In fact he is in the process of building a factory in the Piddle Valley with Yetman Bros of Blandford, which was to be the first of many enterprises intended to revitalise industry in the West Country.

When our reporter called to interview Mr Wainwright, the house appeared to be deserted. There was no answer after prolonged ringing on the doorbell.

Rumour suggests Mr Wainwright may even have gone abroad.

Laurence read the item through again and then sat down heavily at the table, resting his elbows on it, his head in his hands.

'I knew it,' he said. 'I had a premonition. I should never have trusted him.'

'But just because his house is for sale it doesn't mean he won't pay for the factory.' Eliza tried hard to stifle her own worry and doubts as she sat at the table next to him.

'Then where is he?' Laurence looked up at her.

Eliza shook her head.

'The strange thing is,' Laurence continued, 'I went to see him today, on my way home from inspecting the factory.'

'And . . .?' Sarah-Jane asked.

'I didn't go in. You know you always tell me I worry too much. Everything looked so substantial and so indicative of wealth that I thought it was foolish to doubt he would pay. Reassured, I didn't even pass through the gates and made my way home in a happy frame of mind. To this.' He began to read the newspaper again as if committing it to memory.

'Well, don't let's panic,' Eliza said. 'For heaven's sake, there has to be some simple explanation.'

But for once even Sarah-Jane didn't think so.

21

The cottage had no terror for Carson, no memories to make him superstitious.

'You do know,' Lally said, looking at him closely, 'its history. Don't you, Carson?'

Carson, standing as usual with his hands casually in his pockets, gazed with her at the thatched cottage in the grounds of the estate from which Ryder Yetman had fallen to his death, and nodded.

'No one has *ever* lived there,' Lally went on, 'but if you would like to, you are welcome to stay for as long as you like.'

Carson reached out and put his arm around her.

'You're very good, Aunt Lally.' Affectionately he dropped a kiss on her head. Maybe, Carson thought, he had always loved Aunt Lally because she was so thoughtful, so sincere and so feminine.

'I've always been very fond of you, Carson,' she said. 'A maverick; a bad lad, impetuous, impulsive – as far from your Martyn relations as it is possible to be – and all the better for it, in my opinion.'

'You don't mind that then, Aunt Lally?' Carson gave her a wry smile.

'No, I don't. I like it. I can tell you, Carson, when one lives with a man who never acts on impulse and thinks of nothing but facts and figures, it can be irksome.'

'Does it mean, Aunt Lally,' Carson's grip round her shoulders tightened, 'that you and Uncle Prosper are not getting on?'

'Not as well as we should; not as well as we did,' Lally said, turning away, aware of a lump that had suddenly come into her throat. 'It started with the baby, Alexander. Perhaps it *did* seem absurd to adopt a foundling dumped on our doorstep. But I felt there was a purpose, that I was guided by someone or something beyond my control. I . . .' she turned her lovely, limpid eyes on him '. . . I am not religious, Carson, or not particularly so – of course, I go to church at Christmas and Easter, and some Sundays in between – but I felt very strongly as though there were some power at work persuading me to keep little Alexander. And he has transformed my life, given it such meaning and purpose. However, it caused a rift between me and Prosper, a chasm that has deepened, and he now travels incessantly. You see what I mean by impulse? Prosper would never have done such a thing. Sometimes I wonder if he has a mistress on the Continent; but who am I to complain if he has? Formerly I gave everything to him, now I give it to Alexander.'

'He's a nice little fellow,' Carson said absent-mindedly, his attention focused on the cottage which stood a few hundred yards from the Martyns' house. It had been intended to house the servants, but none of them would live there because they were afraid it might be haunted by Ryder Yetman's ghost.

The cottage was much older than the big house, which had been built by Julius Heering as a place in which to entertain his business friends, to impress them by his obvious wealth, the lavishness of his lifestyle. As it turned out, he never lived there. After Ryder's death he realised that the love he had felt for Eliza for many years had a chance of being realised, and he knew she would never live in a place so near to the scene of her late husband's death.

'Could we see inside, Lally?' Carson said, reaching for her hand. 'I feel quite excited. It would be my first home, and it is very good of you to offer it to me.'

'Poor Carson,' Lally said, taking his hand, 'you've been through a lot. I hope you will be very happy here and find the tranquillity you seek.'

'I would never find tranquillity at Pelham's Oak,' Carson said roughly, 'with my new stepmother, that's certain. She is already storming around the place making changes, and that is before they are married.'

They entered the cottage, which had two sizeable downstairs rooms and three upstairs, intended as bedrooms for the staff. A feature that few Dorset cottages possessed was a bathroom and a lavatory with running water, installed to modernise the cottage at the same time as the main house was being rebuilt.

It was sparsely but adequately furnished, and Carson could scarcely get over his delight.

'It's truly lovely, Aunt Lally,' he said, squeezing her hand again. 'You're sure Uncle Prosper won't mind?'

'He won't mind, why should he?' She looked surprised. 'Besides, he and Roger are soon to travel to the Far East.'

'Roger?' It was Carson's turn to be surprised. 'Without his lovely young wife?'

'Without Emma,' Lally nodded. 'The weather would not suit her. She may come and stay with me for a few days, so you will see her again.'

'You had better not tell Roger that *I* shall be making eyes at his wife,' Carson said impetuously; and then hastily corrected himself. 'Of course, I don't mean that, Aunt Lally. I should never dream . . . I can tell you that, after my experience with Connie, it will be a long time before I am involved with another woman. Mrs Roger Martyn is perfectly safe with me.'

They strolled out of the cottage, and as they crossed the paved yard to the house Lally slipped her arm once again companionably through Carson's.

'You must try and put it all behind you, Carson.'

'It is very difficult, Aunt Lally.'

Once in the house, they went straight to Lally's comfortably furnished private sitting-room, its chairs and sofas covered in brightly coloured chintzes.

Carson sank into one of the chairs and, stretching out his feet, stared at them moodily.

'I am not proud of myself, Aunt Lally, or of the distress I caused to Connie. I should never have allowed myself to be browbeaten by Father into proposing to the poor girl. It was a dreadful thing to do, and we are all to blame: Miss Fairchild, Sophie and Aunt Eliza, as well as Father and me. However . . .' he raised his head and looked at her '. . . I feel better for having undone it; purged, cleansed. I would have been a very unhappy man, and made Connie unhappy too.'

'She was certainly not suitable for you.' Lally, tactile like Carson, leaned over to pat his arm. 'And you did the right thing. One day, hopefully, Mr Right will come along for Connie as, indeed, I am sure the right woman will come along for you.'

At that moment the door was pushed violently open, and Alexander stood there with his embarrassed nursemaid behind him.

'Oh Mrs Martyn, I am so sorry, ma'am,' she cried, hand to mouth, as Alexander with a cry of delight saw Carson and toddled over to him. 'I tried to stop him, but he ran away from me. Here, young man.' Just as Alexander reached Carson, his nursemaid caught him and leaned forward to scoop him up into her arms, but Carson, intrigued by the smile on the toddler's face, leaned over and picked him up, placing him on his knee.

'Now then, young Alexander,' he said with mock severity, 'we can't have you behaving like this.'

For reply, Alexander reached out and grabbed the tip of his nose.

'It's you, sir,' the nursemaid said shyly. 'As soon as he knew you were here he was determined to see you.'

'He is *very* fond of you.' Lally laughed indulgently. 'You must have a way with children, Carson. When he knows that you're living at the cottage he will never leave you alone.'

'Young scamp,' Carson said, looking into the beautiful brown eyes that looked so trustfully up at him.

He took Alexander's hand from his nose and held it tightly in his, and a curious feeling overcame him. He looked searchingly into the child's eyes and imagined for a moment that in them he saw the eyes of Nelly. He realised at that moment what it was about the child that had reminded him of someone else;

someone he'd known, but whose name had eluded him. Now he knew who that someone was.

They cuddled and played for a while, until Alexander began to yawn and the nursemaid prised him away from Carson and took him off for his rest.

'See you later,' Carson said, reluctantly relinquishing his hand.

He gazed after Alexander as his nursemaid carried him out of the room and, after the door had closed behind them, he remained silent.

'Penny for them, Carson?' Lally had been watching him. 'Are you thinking, perhaps, that by abandoning the marriage you have missed children of your own?'

'Not at all, Aunt.' Carson jerked himself back to reality. 'I should not particularly have liked children from Connie, and I do not exclude the fact that I may have them in the future, as I am still a young man. It is simply that baby Alexander reminds me very strongly of someone. *How* do you say you came by him?'

'He was left on our doorstep in London.'

'Good gracious!' Carson exclaimed.

'You must have heard the story, surely.' Lally smiled with amusement. 'Perhaps you have forgotten it.' And she told him about the discovery of Alexander and the note pinned to his robe. 'In fact I still have it,' she said, jumping up and going to her bureau. 'I keep it as a treasured memento.' And, opening a drawer, she produced a box of memorabilia, at the bottom of which lay the crumpled note with its pathetic, almost illiterate, message. 'I thought to myself that one day, when Alexander knows the truth, he will be grateful to his mother – poor woman, whoever she was – who was unable to keep him and hoped that, by leaving him outside a well-to-do household, he would have a better future than she could give him, or he would find in an orphanage.'

Carson held out his hand for the note and, his expression deeply thoughtful, studied it.

' "I know as how you are a good wimmin",' he read, and then looked up at Lally. '*How* did she know?'

'I have no idea.' Lally shrugged her shoulders. 'Prosper thought she could have meant anyone; it was a way of softening the heart. But *I* felt it was directed at me by someone who did know me, or knew about me.'

Once he and Nelly had indeed discussed the goodness of Lally as they lay in bed together in the attic room in Carter Lane, Carson recalled. Nelly had been avid for news of him and his family. He was reluctant to tell her too much about himself, but the romance of the dancer who had married a millionaire had appealed to a girl as deprived as Nelly.

Perhaps that was why she had chosen Lally, simply because she knew she was good, and that her instincts, born of her own humble origins, would tell her to keep the baby and not abandon it.

Carson handed the note back to Lally.

'Keep it,' he said solemnly. 'It is indeed a very precious, almost priceless possession. And I think you are right, Aunt Lally. I too think Alexander was meant for you.'

But he did not add aloud: 'And maybe for me, too.'

'And that can go, and that and that,' Agnes pointed with an imperious finger at various pieces of furniture in the room that displeased her. She had walked for some time round the vast drawing-room filled with antiques which had been purchased in happier and more affluent days by a Woodville ancestor. 'And *that*,' she added, indicating a Louis Quinze bureau which somehow failed to find favour.

Guy had trailed round after her with an ingratiating smile on his face, like a dog who, even though it knows it is to be whipped, somehow contrives cheerfully to wag its tail.

But then, he was a man in love.

Every day Agnes arrived at the house in her chauffeur-driven car and began to give orders. This must be done, and that changed or altered in some way. Now she wanted the furniture removed, and replaced by something more modern.

'Who wants this old rubbish, my dear?' she observed to the man she was shortly to marry.

'It is very old, dearest,' Guy ventured cautiously. 'The eighteenth-century stuff is supposed to be quite valuable.'

'Send it to the auction rooms then,' Agnes commanded, 'and maybe we shall get something for it which will pay for its replacement.' Suddenly she threw up her arms as though she were invoking the help of the gods. 'Whoever let this place get into such a state? It is like a museum. I want freshness and light and modern furniture . . .'

'My dear,' Guy grumbled, 'I'm still endeavouring to find ways to pay off Miss Fairchild for what she spent on the outside of the house, or she says she will take me to court.'

'She would never do such a thing,' Agnes said dismissively.

'I think she would. She is out for revenge for the slight cast on her ward.' Guy looked around with a worried frown. 'There *was* talk of a breach of promise action, but no one wanted the publicity, Connie least of all. But Miss Fairchild wants her money back with interest, or she says she will charge me with fraud and deception . . . Ridiculous, really.' Despite his attempt to look cheerful, he was pale with anxiety. 'It amounts to several thousand pounds,' he added weakly.

'Clever old thing.' There was a note of admiration in Agnes's voice. 'Who would have thought that a warped old spinster like that, with parents who were mere haberdashers, could be so clever with money?'

'I should never have called Miss Fairchild a warped old spinster,' Sophie's voice broke in acidly from behind. 'On the contrary, she has always been clever with money just on account of the fact that she *and* her parents were shopkeepers.'

'No one asked your opinion, Sophie.' Agnes turned sharply to her, eyes glinting. 'In fact, I did not even know you were there. What is it you want, snooping around?'

'I was *not* snooping, Agnes,' Sophie retorted heatedly, 'I was merely passing and overheard your unkind remark.'

'But it still does not make it your business.' Agnes gave a dismissive wave of her hand as though to usher Sophie towards the door, but she stayed her ground while Guy anxiously gnawed at a finger, his eyes darting from one powerful woman in his life to the other.

But he knew who would lose. Agnes had money and Sophie did not. The power of money was ruthlessly discriminatory. In the end, it was all that really counted.

'I'm sure we can come to a compromise,' Guy muttered, 'about the furniture.'

'There will be *no* compromise, Guy,' Agnes said firmly. 'Don't be such a weakling. *I* am to live here, after all . . .'

'Sophie has to live here as well. As George's widow she may well have a claim on some of that furniture.'

'Is that so?' Agnes said in a tone of deep sarcasm. 'How *very* interesting. Then perhaps she might like to take it with her.'

'Take it with her?' Guy blinked. 'I wasn't even aware Sophie was going.'

'My dear Guy,' Agnes began to tap her toes impatiently on the floor. 'You must know, and Sophie must know, that she cannot stay here with a newly married bride and groom. I'm sure she would not want to, she is far too sensitive and sensible a person. Carson had the delicacy to remove himself, and I am certain Sophie feels the same. Don't you, Sophie?'

Sophie's flushed face and the angry light in her eyes told a different story.

'I hadn't thought about it until you mentioned it, Agnes.'

'But I was sure you'd feel *de trop*,' Agnes went on in steely tones. '*I* most certainly would not want to be in that situation, intruding, as it were, upon married bliss.'

'I shall certainly not wish to intrude,' Sophie said. 'Besides, it is a very large house. There is also the question of the children to consider.'

'Of course I shouldn't *throw* you out. Indeed, I don't think I have the power.' Agnes glanced at Guy, who had endeavoured to hide his embarrassment by turning to gaze out of the window. 'I thought, anyway, that you yourself might have plans to remarry?'

'Oh?' Guy looked up with interest. 'Surely not, Sophie? I was sure you would be faithful to the memory of George.'

'Don't be silly, Guy.' Agnes marched over to him and gave his shoulder a playful tap. 'A woman cannot expect to remain single forever. It is nearly five years since your son died. Besides, I believe Sophie has a gentleman caller; someone she is seen with quite regularly. You must be careful of your reputation, Sophie,' she said, addressing her directly. 'You don't want to get talked about, to be the subject of speculation and gossip – you, a *rector's* daughter of all things! Do you now?'

Though she put on a bold front in the presence of Agnes, and had marched from the room following her tasteless remark, Sophie felt far from brave inside. Her heart was full of dread: uncertainty about the future, the welfare of the children now that their hold on Guy's affections had diminished in the presence of a woman who was clearly determined to dominate him much more forcefully than his late wife ever had.

But more than either of these was her disgust with herself, her guilt about the fascination that Bartholomew Sadler exercised over her, every bit as irrational and obsessive as that which Agnes wielded over Guy.

She, Sophie Woodville, whose life had been dominated by her Christian zeal, her love of the Lord, her fervour for the gospel and devotion to good works, was engaged in a carnal relationship with a man whose motives she had come increasingly to suspect.

It was carnal, and it was wrong, but she warmed herself at the flame of love like a frozen soul lost in a snowstorm. She could never have enough of it, even though she knew that instead of gaining Bart's love and respect, she was demeaning herself. She could see it in his eyes, even as she craved him and sought his kisses.

There had been no more talk of marriage.

That night Sophie could not sleep, but tossed restlessly in her bed. Through her mind the events of the day tumbled like the slips of paper in a tombola: her hatred of Agnes, her fear of the future and, above all, Bart. Bart. Bart, who had taken her and loved her ruthlessly, passionately, and had made her feel a woman in a way she had never felt with George.

She realised that, for the first time, she had learned the true nature of passion, and that, as well as good and beautiful, it could be evil.

But apart from her guilt about her undoubted sin, what worried her were the rumours about Bart; rumours, whispers, suggestions that he was not all that he should be; that there were other women dotted conveniently around the country. And now there was the suspicion that he had lured Laurence, his own brother-in-law, into a trap over Mr Wainwright, who had sold up and vanished without trace. Consequently, the threat of bankruptcy loomed over Laurence, but not Bart. Had he not told her that he had made money out of the deal? He had not been an innocent bystander as he pretended.

Her knowledge, her guilt, her passion, made her sometimes feel as though she was stoking the flames of everlasting fire.

Sophie tumbled out of bed and threw herself abjectly on her knees beside it.

'Oh God,' she cried, 'be merciful to me, a sinner. Show me the way, dear Lord, out of my torment . . . and give me the strength to abandon this rapid descent into Hell.'

A place, she knew, from which there was no return.

Laurence felt that Mr Becket had grown at least three inches since he had last seen him. He had had the idea that he was a smallish man; small and mild-looking. But now he appeared much taller than before, even fierce and forbidding, as he stood four-square behind his desk and, without a smile or offering his hand in greeting, invited Laurence to be seated.

Puzzled at this curious change, Laurence sat, and when Becket sat down opposite him he seemed the size he had been before, the same mild-mannered man. But there was still no smile and, in a business-like fashion, Becket undid a bulky file he had on his desk, withdrawing from it a bundle of documents over which he pored for several seconds, as if with the deliberate intention of keeping Laurence waiting.

'Yes, Mr Becket?' Laurence said at last impatiently. 'You wanted to see me? You sent for me on a matter of urgency?'

'Indeed I did, Mr Yetman,' Becket intoned, leaning back

in his high chair in a supercilious manner, his thumbs in the pockets of his waistcoat. 'And I expect you know why.'

Then at last he smiled, but it was a malevolent rather than an unctuous smile, that seemed to indicate a decided change of attitude. The tables had been turned.

'I expect it's to do with the factory,' Laurence said laconically.

'Yes it is.' Mr Becket, relishing his power, peered at the paper before him. '*And* a matter of some thirty thousand pounds outstanding. You are in debt by that amount to the bank.'

'It *is* a large sum of money,' Laurence murmured. 'I hadn't realised it was quite as much.'

'We banks, you know,' Mr Becket said pompously, 'are not philanthropic institutions. We lend money to make money, not to lose it.'

'I can understand that.' Laurence refused to be intimidated. 'But still, you have ample security. I am actively seeking a new buyer for the factory, and it would be foolish to abandon it half-finished.'

'Nevertheless, that is what you must do,' Mr Becket said severely. 'You must abandon it *or* find a buyer very quickly.' He leaned over his desk, staring hard at Laurence. 'Or else you will lose your house, sir, and everything you own.'

'You must give me time,' Laurence said angrily. 'You know Wainwright has decamped.'

'I do know he has decamped. Indeed I do . . . And owing money right, left and centre. Yet he seems to have got off scot-free, but *you* would appear to have lost everything.'

'Not yet,' Laurence said firmly. 'I intend to sue Mr Wainwright.'

'When you can find him.' The manager's tone was sarcastic. 'Do you have any idea where he is?'

'No, I do not.' Laurence was overwhelmed by a feeling of helplessness. Sarah-Jane had told him not to worry, but it seemed she had been too optimistic. 'But the estate agent who is handling the sale of his house must know where he is, and I intend to force that knowledge out of him.'

'How?' Mr Becket briskly tapped his fingers on his desk.

'Through my solicitor.'

'And how long do you think it will take, Mr Yetman?'

'I have no idea. Look, I've had quite enough of this inquisition.' Laurence tried to pick up his hat and prepared to rise, but once more Becket leaned across the desk, and put a hand firmly on the hat to stop Laurence from moving it.

'Don't think of leaving yet, Mr Yetman. We have not concluded our business.'

'I am a private citizen and you've no right to detain me,' Laurence protested. 'I am well known in this town. In five or ten years' time, if all goes well, I shall be mayor.'

' "If all goes well",' Mr Becket mimicked, his eyes again on the bulky file. 'But all is not going well, is it? You are practically bankrupt, sir, and I doubt if the people of this parish will want a bankrupt mayor.'

Laurence reached for his hat, wrenched it from Becket's grasp, and stood up.

'I don't like your tone, Becket. I don't like anything about you. I can't believe you are the same person I saw only a few months ago. Some devil has got into you. You are here to help me and you should be giving me a chance. I intend to raise that money, I can assure you, *and* find a purchaser for the factory.'

'Yes,' Mr Becket's tone was soft, almost appealing, 'but how soon? Because I want the money very soon, or rather, the head office of the Two Counties Bank would like to see it very soon. If they don't, my head might be on the block, and yours certainly will be.' He stood up and put out a hand.

'Good day to you, Mr Yetman. I hope when your account is once more in credit we shall again have the pleasure of doing business with you.'

Eliza stood at the window of the drawing-room, watching the figure of her husband as, hands deep in his pockets, he strolled briskly through the grounds with his dog Snap at his heels.

Snap was well named, and everyone who knew him kept clear of him. He liked nothing better than getting his teeth into a pair of ankles or a trouser-leg, and once or twice Julius had

had to pay financial compensation to an angry and wounded victim of Snap's lawlessness.

It was very odd, Eliza thought, that he hung on to an ill-tempered little mongrel like Snap, because he was costly, and Julius hated parting with his money. Yet the dour, rather solitary Dutchman, head of the great Martyn-Heering combine, and the elderly, choleric little dog, seemed well-suited and happy together. Perhaps, after all, they were rather alike.

Eliza went over to the drawing-room fire and pulled her cardigan round her shoulders. A typical English summer was drawing to a close, with rain driving against the windows and a wind roaring down the chimneys, scattering the flames and causing clouds of smoke. It was a large, difficult house to heat, and yet Julius permitted no heating in the summer months, in the interest of economy. During the winter he went round checking all the fires, putting out unused lights and making sure the central-heating system was turned down to minimum.

Eliza sometimes felt that, had she known what she now knew about Julius, she was sure she wouldn't have married him. She had never really been drawn to him, never fallen in love, and her assessment of his character before their marriage had, sadly, turned out to be correct. He had wooed her for a number of years, and there had been something about his persistence that had charmed and then convinced her. She had never been attracted to him for his money, but for the sense of security that he'd given her, the love he offered her. But in their marriage there had been no passion, little tenderness, just a sense of mutual obligation, tolerance and respect.

The children had also found it awkward to come close to Julius, though both sides seemed to try. He was fondest of Dora, and did his best to treat her as a daughter. Eliza often wondered if his cold detachment was defensive, because he had lost so many children before birth, his wife having finally died in childbirth. As if, haunted by the ghosts of the unborn – and also, perhaps, by guilt; who knew? – he found it difficult to make personal connections.

However, today there was an added reason for her nervousness, her feeling of unnatural chill. Laurence was faced with bankruptcy, and she had determined to try and intervene in order to save him.

Restlessly Eliza got up and crossed the room to look out of the window, but it was now raining hard and Julius and Snap had disappeared. Shortly afterwards she heard his footsteps on the stairs, and went to the door to greet him. Snap was barred from the drawing-room.

'My dear, did you get terribly wet?' she asked with wifely concern.

'I changed my shoes and socks.' Julius looked at his feet with a grimace. 'And Snap is drying out in front of the kitchen fire. This terrible English weather.' He rubbed his hands together, blew into them, and went over to the fire to warm them.

'Julius, I wonder if we could have a few words?' Eliza said hesitantly, resuming her seat on the other side of the fire.

'Of course, my dear. Anything important?' Still with his hands to the fire, Julius turned to her, smiling.

'Very important.'

'Then you have all my attention.' He produced his pipe from his pocket and went over to a box of tobacco which, together with the other paraphernalia of smoking, he kept on a side-table. He then began to fill his pipe in the slow, leisurely way that always rather infuriated Eliza. Indeed, there were a lot of things about her husband that irritated her, and they seemed to get worse the longer they were married. Now he looked at her with an expression of such complete detachment that she wondered how many would-be borrowers or defaulters from his bank had seen that expression with dread.

'It is about Laurence, I suppose?' he said impassively. 'I can tell by the gravity of your expression.'

'It is about Laurence,' she agreed, joining her hands around her knees. 'The Two Counties Bank are going to petition for bankruptcy.'

'Oh dear, I am sorry about that.' Julius finished filling his pipe and then began to light it slowly, taking his time, puffing away.

'I wondered if there was anything we could do, Julius?'

'How do you mean, Eliza?' He blew out his match and looked at her with a mystified air.

'If we could help him financially.'

'How much does he need?' Julius asked in a voice that made Eliza's heart bound with hope.

'Several thousand.'

'*I* understand it is in the region of *thirty to forty* thousand.'

'Oh, you know.' Her voice was flat. 'I should have known you would.'

'I make it my business to know these things, and when my stepson is involved you can imagine I take a keen interest. I took care to inform myself in case you should wish to talk to me.'

'Then . . . can you help?'

'My dear Eliza, what *is* the point of throwing good money after bad? My bank certainly won't touch Laurence's debts and, personally, nor would I care to. There is no knowing when it would stop.'

'Just help in paying off the loan. There is the business. He has a half-finished factory to sell, and he says prospects are good.'

'Well, I don't think they are good,' Julius said sombrely. 'The various branches of our bank in Europe detect stirrings of unrest.'

'What kind of unrest?'

'Political and economic. People who want to undermine society: the Bolsheviks in Russia, the communists and anarchists in Germany. Germany is seething with discontent, and the Kaiser is much hated.'

'But my dear Julius, what has that to do with Laurence?'

'Eliza, *if* there is unrest in Europe, who knows what it will do to business worldwide? There will be a fall in demand. Even we will be less profitable. Trust me, I know what I'm saying.' He sat down and, pipe in hand, smiled at his wife. 'It is far better for events to take their course, for Laurence to be made bankrupt – and then he can start all over again. I may be able to help him in a small way then.'

'I don't think he'd want your help *then*,' Eliza said, rising and returning restlessly to the window, where she looked out at the sodden earth. 'And nor should I.' She turned and gazed at her husband.

'Yetmans have a proud name, Julius. Laurence is proud. The business was started over a hundred years ago by his great-grandfather Thomas. Laurence has worked at it since boyhood. It means an enormous amount to him.'

'Then he should have managed it better,' Julius said drily. 'If he had, he would not have been in this predicament.'

'He was taken in by someone recommended by your bank . . .'

'No, my bank did *not* recommend Wainwright,' Julius said firmly. 'To his enquiry they replied that they knew of him, but had not done business with him. If your son took that as a "recommendation" he was a fool.'

'Bart Sadler introduced him.'

'But put no money in the venture, I understand.' Julius sucked at his pipe. 'He acted as a broker without involvement. Now, he is sensible. He *is* a person I might put some money on.'

'I think you're being perfectly horrible,' Eliza burst out. 'Horrible and mean-spirited.'

Julius's eyes narrowed, but he considered his reply before speaking:

'My dear, I think you're being emotional, and I hope those are words you'll regret. Your concern for your son is admirable. But the Woodvilles are hopeless, you know. They can't handle money. When I married you, you didn't have a penny.'

'I didn't marry you for your money,' Eliza expostulated.

'I'm sure you didn't; but I just meant it as an example. Ryder should have made provision for you and left you better-off.'

'Ryder was not a Woodville,' she said acidly.

'Well,' Julius shrugged, 'he'd married one. *Someone* in the Woodville family is always in debt, begging for help. They're absolutely hopeless.' He raised a hand dismissively. 'I really can't see why I, who have been a careful man all my life and amassed a fortune – ' his voice started to rise with emotion as he spoke ' – why *I*, who never got into debt or owed anyone a penny, should bail out the spendthrift Woodvilles. Not long ago I was asked to consider buying Pelham's Oak. As if we hadn't had enough in the past from that free-spending brother of yours and his mistresses.'

'Mistres*ses*?' Eliza spun round. 'I only *knew* of one: Agnes.'

'The really expensive mistress was Lally.'

'*Lally* was *Guy's* mistress?' Eliza reached for the nearest chair and collapsed into it.

'For several years, when she was a penniless dancer in London. He even bought her a house, which was how Margaret found out about him. Now *she* was a real Heering, astute and careful about money. Margaret wished to keep an eye on her husband. However, it didn't prevent him from having an affair with Agnes; but by that time Margaret had become more tolerant. She knew she had him and he would never leave her.'

'Margaret knew about Agnes too?' Eliza looked incredulous.

'Very little escaped Margaret,' Julius said with a superior smile. 'She also knew about Elizabeth and appreciated your tact. She knew, but he never knew she knew. He was very fortunate to have a wife like my sister. I doubt that Agnes will prove such a pearl.'

'Guy and *Lally*!' Eliza could hardly believe it.

'And they too had a child.' Julius shook his head disapprovingly. 'Disgraceful, really.'

'A child?' What more was there to hear, Eliza wondered?

'A son. She had him adopted, but eventually she took him back.'

'Then that could only be Roger,' Eliza murmured.

'It is Roger, and he has turned out well – for a man, that is, whose father is a Woodville. He is financially very sound. We are extremely pleased with Roger. He has a natural instinct with money and will do well.'

'But why was I never told anything about this?'

'Lally wished it to be kept secret. She was very wise.'

'Does Roger know?'

'He does, now. He made the discovery before his marriage

and it naturally distressed him. He found it hard to forgive his mother, and still does, especially in view of her devotion to this foundling, Alexander — the sort of thing which can only be ascribed to a woman in her dotage. One can't blame Roger for his resentment of her. A few months abroad with Prosper will do him the world of good. Now, my dear,' Julius looked at the clock, 'it will soon be time for lunch. Will you have a sherry?'

'I think I will,' Eliza said in a low, vibrant voice. 'I feel I need it.'

Lunch was eaten in virtual silence, Julius and Eliza sitting as they usually did at opposite ends of the large table, waited on by an extensive staff. Their life in the country was regulated by habit and, after lunch, Julius usually lay down while Eliza took the dogs for a walk.

But today she decided to go into town, and after the meal was finished she went up to her room. Julius accompanied her, and as he was about to proceed to his room just beyond hers, he stopped and put a hand on her arm, a kindly, concerned expression on his face.

'I am so sorry, dear, about Laurence. I want you to know that I wish I *could* do something to help; but I really feel that the law should take its course. It would go against the instincts of a lifetime if I attempted to assist him. I know it would be wrong. If, eventually, he would like to come and talk to me, I should be only too pleased to give what advice I can, to save him from similar errors in the future.'

Eliza didn't reply but turned the handle of her bedroom door and went in, shutting it behind her. Julius stood for a few moments looking at it, and then, with a slight shrug of his shoulders, he went along the corridor to his own suite.

Once inside her bedroom, Eliza hastened over to a cupboard which she always kept locked and, unlocking it, drew a silver jewel-box from its velvet pouch.

It was true that, despite her noble birth, she had never been wealthy, never had money of her own — apart from what she had received from both her husbands; and at one time she and Ryder had known real poverty. But she had been left jewellery by her mother, and been given more by the men in her life, some of it of remarkable quality.

Eliza sat on her bed examining the various pieces, remembering – sometimes with a pang of sorrow, sometimes with joy – the significance of each one. The brooch Ryder gave her when Laurence was born, studded with diamonds and amethysts. The diamond necklace Julius had placed round her neck on their wedding-night, asking her to keep it, and only it, on while he made love to her. Excited and amused, she had concurred; but with hindsight she saw new significance in his curious gesture, in that he had made love not only to her but to his money, and the power it gave him.

She would not part with the brooch that had been bought out of Ryder's first earnings, but she would gladly part with the rich man's necklace – the price of her bondage, it seemed to her now.

She placed the necklace in its box, then tucked the box into her handbag and, throwing on a coat, ran downstairs and asked for the car to be sent round to the front door.

Five minutes later she was walking down the steps and through the door held open by the chauffeur, who shut it smartly and then went to his seat.

'Where to, madam?'

'My son's house, please,' she said and, with a sigh and a sense of deep foreboding in her heart, leaned back against the luxuriously cushioned upholstery.

When Eliza reached Riversmead there was a silence about the house that she thought unusual. Usually there was a gaggle of children on the lawn, mothers playing with them or sitting on benches, and maids ferrying trays with cordial, cakes or cups of tea. But today no one was about, even though it had stopped raining and the sun was out.

As the car came to rest outside the porch, however, Sarah-Jane appeared at the door, and when she saw who it was she ran down the steps to greet her mother-in-law with a smile.

There was a feeling of real affection between the two women.

Sarah-Jane was very like Eliza at her age: practical, warm-hearted, keen on helping in the community, a loving mother and, Eliza guessed, a loving wife. There was a closeness between her son and Sarah-Jane that reminded Eliza of herself and Ryder; and the best things in Ryder – his warmth, his humanity, his love of family – she saw in his son.

'What a lovely surprise, Mother,' Sarah-Jane said as she helped her out of the car. She always referred to Eliza as 'Mother', though her own was still alive.

'Where are the children?' Eliza enquired. 'Everything seems so quiet.'

'They've all gone up to Pelham's Oak.'

'Oh!' Eliza looked surprised.

'You know Sophie is leaving very soon, and today she is giving a children's party.'

'Sophie is leaving?' Eliza looked astounded. This was a day for discovering how excluded she was from other people's counsels.

'Agnes has asked her to go, didn't you know? She's going to live temporarily with her parents. She told me she would like to get out of the district altogether, maybe to find a living-in post as a governess or housekeeper, and send the children to boarding-school. Of course, I would help her but – ' Sarah-Jane gestured helplessly around ' – we ourselves may not be here for very much longer either.'

'I can't believe it.' Eliza, having walked with her daughter-in-law into the house, flopped down into one of the comfortable armchairs. 'I simply refuse to believe it . . .'

'What can't you believe, Mother?' Behind her she heard Laurence's cheerful voice, and she rose swiftly from her chair and threw her arms around his neck.

'Oh, darling. It's good to hear you sounding cheerful.'

'Your mother was saying that she couldn't believe the bank would foreclose and we would lose the house.' Sarah-Jane's own cheerfulness had gone, to be replaced by lines of worry on her face.

'Well, it's happening. The hearing is in a few days' time. It will simply be a winding-up operation. I have no defence.' His own voice was not so cheerful now. 'I can't sell the factory, Mother. It's useless to pretend I can do any more. I can't find a buyer for something that is only half-constructed.'

'No one at all?'

'It is designed for a specific purpose, to manufacture agricultural machinery, and it is only someone with a similar interest who would buy it. It will probably be better to raze it to the ground.'

Eliza withdrew her arms from round Laurence's neck and, with his hand in hers, walked with him over to the sofa where they sat down together.

'Julius thinks the outlook for business on the whole is bad.'

'Oh? Why does he say that?'

'He says there are stirrings on the Continent, unrest in the Balkans . . .'

'Not likely to affect us much.' Laurence sounded sceptical.

'Well, that's what he thinks.'

'He always was a merchant of gloom.' Laurence laughed rather gloomily himself. 'Any news of Dora, Mother?'

'A letter a few days ago.' Dora had gone to stay with relations of Julius's in New York. 'She's having a wonderful time.'

'And Hugh?' Hugh was climbing in the Alps, an activity his mother preferred not to think of.

'Well, I don't hear from him, of course. No news is good news.'

Hugh, who had taken a double first at Oxford, was now a Fellow of All Souls and taught philosophy at the university. The only reckless aspect of an otherwise quiet and studious life was this passion for rock-climbing.

'Laurence,' Eliza clung on to his hand, 'I *have* spoken to Julius about you. I said I would. I don't want you to think I didn't try.'

'And I can see by your face it's not good news,' he said, regarding her gravely.

'It isn't, I'm afraid. He says he doesn't want to throw good money after bad, but is willing to help with advice only, after . . .'

'Much good that is.' Laurence rose and gave Sarah-Jane a

despairing look. 'If he could only lend me the money, I know I will repay it.'

'I know you will too. Like your father, you are a worker; but I'm afraid Julius won't budge. I'm sorry. It is hard, and I am very angry with him; but there are two aspects of Julius that never meet: the personal and the business sides. He is able completely to compartmentalise his life in a way that I, who am totally involved with my family, find hard to understand.'

'Don't forget he's a Heering. They're all like that. Remember how tight even Aunt Margaret was?'

'Julius thinks it's better you should go bankrupt and then start again. He says he would be delighted to give his advice then.' Eliza's tone was openly sarcastic, and Laurence laughed mirthlessly.

'I won't *need* his advice then.'

'I thought you wouldn't.'

'I shall have lost my house, my business . . .' Laurence's face darkened '. . . and that Scrooge of a husband of yours is worth millions; not thousands, but millions.'

'Probably.' Eliza, nodding dispassionately, drew her handbag towards her. 'Darling, I have, as you know, no personal wealth, or it would all be yours, but I have a few pieces of jewellery that I was going to distribute among my children anyway on my death.' She opened the box and displayed the dazzling necklace. 'This was a wedding-gift from Julius. The diamonds were cut in Amsterdam. I've hardly ever worn it. I should have thought it would fetch a few thousand. In all . . .'

'Mother, you angel.' Laurence took the proferred box from her and firmly closed the lid. 'I would not dream of letting you deprive yourself of beautiful pieces, many of them of sentimental value.'

'That, I assure you, is of no sentimental value.'

'Nevertheless, I can't accept it.'

'Laurence, I *insist*.'

'And *I* insist.' He kissed her on the cheek as he gave her back the box. 'Besides, what such sacrifice would realise would be insufficient for my needs. The real villain of the piece, after Wainwright, is Bart Sadler who introduced me to that rogue.

By doing that, in my book he vouched for him. Yet it appears he scarcely knew him.'

Eliza looked anxiously at Sarah-Jane, who nodded her head dejectedly.

'My own brother,' she said, 'behaved despicably; he took no risk. I personally feel that Laurence should go and have it out with him.'

'But what good would that do?'

'It will at least make him feel better.' Sarah-Jane reached for Laurence's hand. 'He might be able to shake some regret from that insensitive man – without using violence, of course – and at least make him sorry for what he's done.'

22

Agnes sat on the stool in front of her dressing-table mirror, gazing at the large cluster of diamonds, rubies and sapphires on her finger; Guy's engagement present. He had presented the ring like a courtier, kneeling albeit a little clumsily on one knee. She had had to put a hand to her face to stop herself giggling; it would never have done for him to see she considered the situation farcical.

In the background Elizabeth moved about, packing her things. For she and Guy were to slip away in a few days' time, and marry in London. They would then journey on the Continent, allowing Sophie time to move out of the house, and return for a family Christmas.

Guy was unhappy in his mind about Sophie; but she had assured him she had no wish to stay. She told her father-in-law she was thinking of moving from the district to find work, and thus pay for her children to go to boarding-school.

He wondered if George would have approved; but what could he do? He wished he could help, but explained that he was really so dependent on Agnes. So in love with her, too.

No one else seemed to matter much any more. And Sophie had long ago decided that he had practically forgotten George. It was twelve years since he had left his home, and almost five since he'd died.

'Will there be anything else, madam?' Elizabeth said from behind, her eyes fixed on the ring; but she had been brought up by Beth Yewell to know her place, and that included keeping one's opinions to oneself.

'How do you like my ring, Elizabeth?' Agnes gave her an unexpected chance to comment.

'Oh madam,' Elizabeth gasped, 'I was admiring it but didn't like to say. It is *very* beautiful, madam.'

'It is an engagement ring, Elizabeth. I am to be married.'

'Oh madam.' Elizabeth joined her hands ecstatically together. 'I am *very* happy for you.'

'I would like to have taken you with me, Elizabeth; but at the moment it's not possible. My husband and I shall be taking a long honeymoon on the Continent.'

Elizabeth shyly hung her head and her face slowly reddened. 'S'matter of fact, madam, I *am* hoping to be married myself.'

'Oh Elizabeth!' Agnes spun round and stared at the blushing girl. 'We have *both* been very secretive, haven't we? I didn't tell you of my plan and you didn't tell me of yours.'

'Nothing is settled yet, ma'am.' Elizabeth looked doubtful. 'He has asked, and I have accepted. But he wants to get a better position, so that we can have a little house before we start a family.'

'What does your husband-to-be do?' Agnes asked with interest.

'He works in a brewery, madam. He is a drayman, but he has a way with all horses. He would like something on a farm, maybe with a tied cottage.'

Agnes put a finger to her chin and looked thoughtfully in the mirror.

'Well, who knows, if that is the case we may be able to offer both you and your husband employment in the future. My husband has a number of farms on his estate, and you could serve me as lady's maid. I am to marry Sir Guy Woodville,' she said, proudly raising her head. 'I am to be the new Lady Woodville, just imagine that!'

'Oh madam,' Elizabeth cried, clasping her hands together again. 'That *is* a coincidence, madam. My father used to work for Sir Guy. He married my mother who was maid to Sir Guy's sister, then Mrs Yetman.'

'Beth and Ted,' Agnes murmured, feeling as shocked as if someone had struck her in the face.

'Do you happen to know my mother and father, madam?'

'I knew of them a long time ago,' Agnes said cautiously, 'a very long time ago. Tell me, have you brothers and sisters?'

'A sister Jenny and a brother Jo, madam. Jenny is older, Jo the little 'un.' She gave a bright, perky smile. 'I'm the one in the middle.'

Slowly Agnes turned again, and stared at herself in the mirror as though she had seen a ghost. But no ghost stood behind her. Only her daughter, Elizabeth, to whom she had given birth in Weymouth twenty-two years before, and then completely abandoned.

A uniformed functionary admitted Agnes to the inner sanctum of the manager of a bank tucked discreetly off Piccadilly. It was not a quoted bank, but a private one which had links with the bank that had handled her business affairs in New Orleans. However, it was a British bank, and subscribed to the code of conduct expected of such institutions, especially in respect of the need for strict security and control over its affairs.

Agnes had met Mr Clarke, the manager, only once, on her arrival in England, when she had gone to open an account and deposit some jewellery and shares as security against her drawings. The manager, dressed in a frock-coat and striped trousers, came to the door and welcomed her warmly, his hand outstretched.

'Mrs Gregg, what a *pleasure*. Do come in. How *nice* to see you again.'

He dismissed the functionary, who shut the door quietly and carefully before conducting Agnes to a seat opposite his desk.

'Please sit down, Mrs Gregg. How was your journey to London?'

'Excellent, thank you, Mr Clarke.' Agnes drew off her long kid gloves and, laying them on her lap, managed to ensure that the brilliant sparkle of her engagement ring would not be missed by the astute man of money.

'Are you in London for long?' He sat down and glanced discreetly at a paper that had been placed in front of him only a few moments before.

'I am just passing through on my way to the Continent.'

Agnes raised her head and looked the manager squarely in the eyes. 'I believe I shall have need of further funds, Mr Clarke, considerably more than I anticipated.'

'Ah!' Mr Clarke gravely stroked his chin. 'I'm glad you brought that matter up, Mrs Gregg, because we *are* a little unhappy about the extent of your borrowings. Don't misunderstand me – ' he bent anxiously over his desk towards her ' – but I believe that the securities we have do not nearly cover the amount you owe. Also . . .' his manner became a little more agitated '. . . there's the matter of eventually bringing your account into credit again. How do you propose to do that?' He glanced once more at the paper before him. 'The shares in Consolidated Rail have sunk *very* low in recent weeks. Are further funds expected from America, Mrs Gregg? Would you be thinking of, how shall I put it, injecting either a sum of money, or securities, to finance your borrowings?'

'Indeed I should,' Agnes said haughtily.

He stared up at her, his pale, myopic eyes alight with hope, his tufted moustache quivering with anticipation.

'I'm delighted to hear that, Mrs Gregg.' The manager dipped his pen into a pot of ink and held it poised over his writing-paper. 'May I know the source?'

'I am to be married again, Mr Clarke, within a few days, here in London.'

'Oh, I'm delighted for you, Mrs Gregg . . .' The manager sat back, ecstatic, his pen still poised in the air.

'To a very wealthy man. You may know of him. Sir Guy Woodville of Pelham's Oak in Dorset.'

'Mmmmm.' Mr Clarke shook his head, tactfully replacing his pen in its stand. 'I don't *think* . . .'

'His mother was a member of the wealthy Martyn family . . . You may well have heard of them.'

'Of the Martyn-Heering Bank?' Mr Clarke was immediately alert.

'Precisely.'

'Well, of course I've heard of *them*.'

Agnes raised her hand to her hat so that he could not miss the sparkle of her sapphire, diamond and ruby cluster. 'My husband-to-be's engagement gift to me . . . a mere part of his mother's treasure-chest of jewels.'

She extended her hand for Mr Clarke to inspect the magnificent ring.

'*Exquisite*, Mrs Gregg. Well . . .' He picked up his pen and drew a line firmly under whatever he had been reading on the page in front of him. 'In view of what you have just told me, I feel there will be no problem, none at all, about our increasing your facility immediately, Mrs Gregg.'

'Good,' Agnes replied in a voice with a ring of steel. 'And let us hope that Sir Guy does not get to hear of this encounter, or he may well advise me to place my account elsewhere, where I shall not be subjected to what I can only call an uncomfortable and inconsiderate scrutiny of my circumstances.'

Agnes rose and began drawing on her gloves as Mr Clarke crept sycophantically around his desk, his face humbled, his shoulders bowed.

'Do forgive me, Mrs Gregg. Please forget that it ever happened. And I should also be most grateful if you would not mention the matter to Sir Guy for fear the Martyn-Heering Bank should get to hear of it.'

'Oh, I forgot to mention,' Agnes said in a flash of inspiration, 'that my fiancé's sister is a Heering, so you see he is doubly related.'

Mr Clarke seemed scarcely able to grasp the extent of such wealthy connections, and almost tripped over his feet in his anxiety to escort a lady of quality, as well as substance, to the door.

Bart Sadler invariably fell asleep after love-making. He turned on his side, emitting loud snores. Sophie, on the contrary, felt very wakeful, delirious at first with the joy and thrill of each experience. But then the sensation wore off, her flesh cooled, the beating of her heart slowed down and, with it, came altogether different and unpleasant sensations: fear, guilt, remorse.

She, Sophie Woodville, pious Christian that she was, was nevertheless a woman living in sin who, if she died, without any doubt would go straight to Hell and remain there forever.

Then the memory of the exultation vanished, and she wished that first time had never happened, or that Bart, who initially seemed to promise so much, had at least wed her before it had.

Bart stirred, his back to her, his head resting on his hand. They were nude in the bed. Once the door was shut she took leave of her senses, allowing him to undress her, to embrace and caress her everywhere, in the most intimate places. She thought that she would never know again anything like the wild abandon that possessed her then. The trouble was that, despite the intensity of the sensation, its sweetness, it was over too soon.

She stretched her toes and then crept out of the bed and started to dress.

It was one thing, Bart seeing her in the nude, stage by stage, before they made love. It seemed quite different afterwards. She never thought it was quite right, or nice. It was certainly nothing that she and George had ever done, and they had had two children. Their love-making had been conducted under the bedclothes, with the lamp or candle out, and she thought that never once had he seen her completely naked, nor would he have wanted or expected to. As for her, her first sight of a completely naked man, other than her infant son, was when she saw Bart. What *would* George have thought? She wondered what on earth he would have thought now.

Bart turned on his back just as she had finished putting her dress over her head, and she quickly drew down the hem as he opened his eyes, rubbed them and then gazed at her.

'Up so soon, Sophie?'

'I must be getting back, dear. I have so much to do in the house.'

'They've gone, then?'

'To be married in London, any day now.' Her voice was apathetic.

'And none of the family to be at the wedding?'

'None. That was the way they both wanted it.'

'I wonder why?' Bart looked speculative. 'You'd think they'd something to hide. Sure she ain't still married?'

'Oh no! It's *nothing* like that.' Sophie began to do up her hair, her pins in her mouth, as she studied herself in the mirror. 'They just preferred it that way. It was arranged when Carson and Connie were to be married, to leave them the limelight. They felt they were older; it was a second marriage for each, and thus more decorous. They are to be married in church, I believe, though.' She turned round and looked at him. 'St George's, Hanover Square.'

'St George's, Hanover Square,' Bart murmured, his hands behind his head. 'Now I've heard of that.'

'Bart.'

'Yes, dear?' He lowered his eyes from the ceiling and looked at her.

'When *are* we to be married, Bart?'

'Oh, it's weddings you have in mind, is it?' he said with a chuckle, and put his arm round her waist as she came to sit on the bed beside him.

'I'm serious, Bart.'

'I can see you are.' He took her hand and brought it to his lips.

'And when is the stone to be finished? Why, you haven't even started engraving it.'

'Oh, it's worrying are we now? Worrying time, is it, Sophie?'

'I have a lot to worry about,' she said, taking her hand away. 'I am to lose my home. I am supposed to be out by the time they come back. I'd hoped that by this time you and I would be wed, Bart, and George's stone, engraved, would be in place in the churchyard. That was the reason you asked me to come here in the first place, to see it. Now I think it was just a ploy.'

'A ploy?' He propped himself up on one arm and she averted her eyes from his nude torso, his excessively hairy chest. In and out of bed were such different things, Sophie thought: chastity and its lack. 'What do you mean by a *ploy*?'

'The day we . . . went to bed together, you brought me over to show me George's stone.'

'So I did.'

'I think it was primarily to seduce me.'

'Sophie!' Bart's tone changed to one of menace and she

felt frightened. 'That is a terrible thing to say. Kindly apologise.'

'I apologise,' she said meekly, 'if it isn't true.'

'It certainly is not true. I had no such intention. I thought you were a virtuous woman. Well, you wasn't. You fell into bed real eagerly with me, Sophie. You talk of the stone, but I think it was just a pretext for *you*. What do you really care about your dead husband if you are so eager to fornicate without being married?'

She felt tears of shame spring to her eyes, but said nothing. He was revealing, at last, his true colours; but he was right.

'Anyway,' he said, lying against the pillows again, 'what are you in such a hurry to get married for?'

' "Hurry" to get married?' Sophie exploded. 'Hurry, do you say? I have been living in this sinful relationship with you for months, and now you accuse me of wilful fornication.'

'But you *like* it, Sophie.' He opened an eye and winked. 'I never knew you were so carnal. I never would have guessed it. The rector's daughter, a missionary. Well, well.'

'Carnal or not – ' she knew her face was scarlet ' – I want now to be a wife. A lawful wife. This relationship makes me uneasy.'

'But why does it make you uneasy, my love? You can't tell me you don't enjoy it.'

'Stop teasing me, Bart. It's wrong,' she said stubbornly. 'I feel unclean. It's against the law of God and, besides, I am afraid of people finding out. You see, I am a hypocrite as well as a wicked fornicator. I am afraid that someone might see me come in here, and see me go out, and they will know what happens.'

'Reckon they already do.'

'Bart!'

He smiled slyly at her, and then his features grew tense as there was a loud knocking on the door.

'Who could it be?' Sophie whispered, ashen-faced.

'Dunno!' Bart remained where he was in the bed. 'Happen they'll go away if we don't move. It will be some man about some job or other.'

Bart snuggled comfortably again into the bedclothes and deliberately shut his eyes.

But then they heard the front door flung open, and steps as someone began to walk about the living-room.

'Bart!' a voice called. 'Are you there, Bart?'

'Hurry up,' Sophie hissed. 'It's *Laurence*. He'll come upstairs looking for you. He must not see me here.'

She felt frozen with fear, yet electrified at the same time. Rapidly she handed Bart his shirt and trousers as he tumbled reluctantly out of bed.

'Quick,' she said, and put her hands over her face as Bart finished dressing and opened the door a crack.

'What do you want, Laurence?' he shouted abruptly.

'I want a word with you.'

'What about?'

'You know what about,' Laurence replied threateningly.

'You've been drinking.'

'I have not been drinking. I don't need beer in my gut to tell you what I think of you, or to make a man of me to administer the hiding you should have had weeks and weeks ago.'

'Don't be so silly. I've done nothing wrong.'

'The Bible says there are sins of omission as well as commission,' Laurence said ominously.

'Oh does it?' Bart turned to Sophie, who was listening horror-struck, and sneered. 'What does it say about forgiveness?'

'An eye for an eye, a tooth for a tooth. I'm coming up to get you, Bart Sadler.'

'Don't be so crazy,' Bart called, but they heard Laurence's feet on the stairs. Sophie looked round, panic-stricken, for a hiding-place. But there was none, and then she found herself staring into Laurence's eyes and saw the expression of incredulity on his face.

'Sophie!' he gasped. 'What are *you* doing here?'

'What do you think she's doing?' Bart said with a louche grin. 'Fornicating, that's what.'

He was unprepared for Laurence's blow to his face, and staggered sideways.

'Oh Laurence, *please*!' Sophie cried.

'You pig,' Laurence snarled, disregarding her, curling his fists and shaking them at Bart, who leaned against the wall, his hands tenderly fingering his lip.

'I think it's bleeding,' he said, taking his hand away to examine it. 'What did you do that for?'

'I did it because I hate you, Bart Sadler. I hate what you did to me, but worse, I hate what you've done to this good woman.'

' "Good woman",' Bart grinned. 'That is a laugh. I'll tell you, Laurence, if I wanted a good tumble in bed, I'd take a missionary's widow any day. She's no "good woman". She's a whore.'

Laurence hit him again with such force that this time Bart fell to his knees.

'Laurence, *please* . . .' Sophie cried once more. 'Please go. I know you're distressed and upset, and so am I; but this brutality doesn't help.'

'Look, man,' Bart muttered through lips that were beginning to swell, 'if this fisticuffs is all about Wainwright rather than Sophie, save your breath. I didn't know he was a bad 'un. Nor do I know where he is. I'm sorry, but I couldn't help it and I can't help you. I did my best. I was taken in too. Sophie is a different matter and none of your business. She's old enough to know what she's doing.'

'Yes, I am, Laurence,' Sophie said, raising her head, 'and to be sorry for it; but you settle your business grievance with Bart – then I think you should go.'

'I should have known when you wouldn't come up with any money something was wrong.' Laurence turned his attention to Bart again. 'And I heard you made a packet out of the commission he gave you for introducing me.'

Bart winced and tenderly touched his face again. 'Not a packet, not a fortune. I stood to make an honest commission when you signed, and again when the factory was completed. Two per cent of the gross. Not a fortune.'

'You recommended him.' Laurence had started to shout again, and Sophie feared more violence. One of them might be killed.

'I thought he was all right.' Bart now seemed scared too.

'He had a large house. He appeared to have money. I thought he was straight . . .'

Laurence leaned down as though to hit him where he lay, but suddenly Bart got to his feet and lunged at him.

Sophie cried out as they fell into each other's arms and, after a brief tussle on the landing, rolled down the stairs to the kitchen where they both lay heaving and panting . . . but at least apparently unharmed and alive. She flew down the stairs and knelt by Laurence's side.

'Laurence, are you all right?'

'He started it.' Bart raised his head and winced again. 'What about me, Sophie? Don't you ask if *I'm* all right?'

'I can see you're all right,' she said contemptuously. 'You were feigning hurt in order to get Laurence to attack you again. Using ploys again, Bart.' She shook her finger at him. 'Little games like you played with me. Never honest, were you? Never capable of honesty to me or Laurence, or anybody, I suppose.'

Groggily, Laurence got to his feet. Blood streamed from a gash on his forehead and Sophie calmly went over to the tap, soaked a cloth in cold water and began to dab at his brow.

'Laurence, this is terrible. It is a terrible thing to happen. The whole thing is awful. But what you think . . . about me, . . . I know it looks bad. It is bad and I am ashamed of it; but we are to be married.'

'Married!' Bart roared. 'We are certainly *not* to be married. Not after this. The way you rushed to defend him, to bathe his head before you even see how I am, or care. Married! I'm not the marrying kind anyway, Sophie. You should have realised that. I've been a bachelor too long.'

'But you *asked* me!' she found herself screaming at him. 'You said you wanted to walk out with me as a preparation to be married.'

'We would never suit, Sophie.' Bart shook his head. 'You're too refined for a stone-mason's wife. You're too much of a prig. I'd always be minding my ps and qs, always be expected to have clean hands at table. Nice you are, but not for me. Sorry you had to find out like this, in this way . . .'

'Come.' Gently Laurence touched her arm. 'I'll take you home. You can't argue with a man without principles or morals. Get your things together, Sophie, and come with me.'

Sophie rode behind Laurence, with her head leaning on his shoulder. She was so tired it was impossible to keep it upright. She thought that, of all the terrible things that had happened to her in her life, this was one of the worst; to be shamed and humiliated in front of an upright young man like Laurence, George's first cousin; a man who had known her all his life as the supposedly virtuous daughter of the Rector of Wenham. Now she really would have to leave the district, because she would never be able to face Laurence or his family again.

They didn't speak, but he kept to the bridle-paths and narrow lanes so that they should avoid meeting anyone. When he got to the drive of Pelham's Oak he reined in his horse and turned round. He looked, she thought, infinitely dejected, and she felt more guilty than ever.

'Are you all right, Sophie?'

'I'm all right,' she said. 'I'm sorry.'

Laurence began gingerly to dismount from his horse, obviously in discomfort, and then he reached up to help her.

'It's better the staff don't see us riding together up the drive,' he said.

'I know.' She dusted herself down as she got to the ground. 'I feel so ashamed, Laurence. So unclean. Don't tell . . .'

'I would never tell a soul. Poor Sophie.' He gently touched her face and her eyes filled with tears. 'We are all of us weak, and we all of us have to answer one day to God, and I can tell you I don't know which is worse: the sin of lust or the sin of despair.'

His words disturbed her, and she was about to ask him what he meant when he kissed her abruptly on the cheek and, rapidly mounting his horse, turned in the direction of the gate and rode away.

She watched him until he was out of sight, but there was no clue to explain his behaviour or what he meant. She imagined, from the way he moved, that he was rather more hurt than he'd let on. Maybe hurt as much mentally as physically.

But she herself felt so totally drained of energy that she could scarcely drag herself up the drive to the house. Then she managed to force herself to stand upright and, with her shoulders back and head erect, walked up to the front door like a woman without a stain on her character or a mark on her soul.

Laurence Yetman woke and lay for some time, as he usually did in the early morning, listening to the sounds of the world outside wakening; conscious of the warm body of his sleeping wife beside him, their children tucked away in dreamland elsewhere in the house,

Usually he would give thanks; but today was different, as all the days had been since the bankruptcy notice was served and he knew that everything he had would be taken away from him; that he and his family would have to seek charity from their relations.

All he felt these mornings was a great void, a blackness, and the fear he felt threatened to overwhelm him until he got out of bed. Would that Mr. Wainwright had never appeared in his life, or that he could turn back the clock and follow a different path!

Except for the death of his father, Laurence had suffered little in his lifetime and was unaccustomed to adversity. He was unused to things going wrong, to unhappiness; and he was a complete stranger to despair.

But for the last few weeks despair had gripped his soul, and although he tried to maintain the appearance of cheerfulness in front of others, especially the children, it got darker and deeper until he could see no way out of it at all.

He felt he had disgraced his family, his great-grandfather who had founded the business with scarcely any capital, his grandfather who had built it up, and above all, his beloved father who had revitalised it. It had been a story of well-being and modest success – until he indulged in a rash speculation without taking a few elementary precautions.

Now all those he loved and who depended on him were to share in his shame. People would pity him, and it was pity he hated. Maybe if he had had more misfortune in life he would have found this easier to bear. As it was, he felt he was being tested, and failing to pass.

He had been born in this house, and he loved it almost as much as he loved his family. Now he was to see it knocked down at auction, the victim of the harsh laws of bankruptcy.

Laurence got stealthily out of bed so as not to disturb Sarah-Jane, tiptoed across the room to his dressing-room and, after sluicing his face and hands, got into a shirt and trousers and went downstairs to make a cup of tea.

It was only six o'clock and no one in the household stirred. The servants still slept in the loft and the outbuildings. Soon they would all be given notice, together with Beth and Ted Yewell, who had served the Yetman family for nearly thirty years. Well, there was no problem there. Eliza would gladly have them again.

Then there were the groom, the two gardeners and the coachman. They would all be found new positions and then, finally, the house and its contents, the offices and the half-finished factory would all come under the hammer.

Laurence lit the fire and made his tea, and then he sat at the table by the window drinking it, trying hard to see some sort of light through the haze that engulfed his mind. He shook his head, aware of a muzzy sensation, as though there were some kind of veil between him and reality. He couldn't seem to see straight. He couldn't see straight at all.

His red setter, Kimber, came up, wagging his tail, and Laurence bent down to pat him. He felt a sudden dizziness as though he was going to faint; and then he wondered if, after all, death wasn't preferable to life, fairer to everyone all round? Tears came into his eyes as he stroked Kimber, and then he got up, put on his jacket, rinsed out the cup and saucer, and got Kimber's lead to take him for a walk.

He hesitated while Kimber, wagging his tail, looked excitedly, trustfully up at him.

'There, good boy,' Laurence said and, once again, his eyes

unexpectedly flooded over. He was in very poor shape. Too emotional; over-charged. He shut the door and Kimber abruptly stopped wagging his tail, disappointed that the promised jaunt seemed to be off.

'I shan't be a minute, boy,' Laurence said, stroking his head, and then he went through the kitchen, along the hall to the parlour where Sarah-Jane did her accounts and interviewed servants, and where outdoor coats and boots and a variety of equipment, for indoors and out, was kept.

In the corner was a cupboard which contained fishing-tackle, rods, lines, reels, a couple of tennis rackets, a football or two, and a gun which had belonged to his father.

He stared at it for a few moments and then gripped it firmly; he opened the breech, inspected it, took several cartridges from a box in a drawer at the base of the cupboard, and popped one in. The others he put in his pocket.

Then, with the gun under his arm, he went through the hall back into the kitchen and, calling Kimber, opened the door into the yard.

'Rabbits,' he said to Kimber, 'rabbits,' and the dog danced about excitedly and raced across the lawn towards the river, where a bridge crossed to Wen Wood, stretching all the way up the hill to the other side.

It was now daylight, and the sun, rising from over the hill, cast its beams on the frosty meadow which sparkled as though it was full of diamonds. A thick layer of leaves littered the grass, and from a few cottages that lay around him smoke had already started to rise. It was going to be a beautiful day.

Laurence stopped and took a great lungful of air as Kimber halted in the middle of the bridge, vapour coming from his mouth, begging his master to follow him. Laurence looked backwards to the house, to the town of Wenham topped by the square tower of St Mark's Church.

He thought he had never seen the town, the countryside around, his house nestling amid the trees, so beautiful – with a mist rising from the river, and the birds wheeling overhead in search of a dwindling supply of food.

His land.

He crossed the bridge and walked steadily up through the woods. The sunlight cast patches of light on the ground and Kimber began snuffling through the undergrowth in search of the smell of the small animals of the wood; but Kimber was old, and they were usually too quick for him. He would plod up the hill, hoping that the rabbits would wait for him. Needless to say, they always got away.

Laurence went further up, and then paused again and looked back once more. He then continued his slow climb because Kimber was well ahead. In front of him Laurence saw that there was a movement in the undergrowth. He halted and saw a mother rabbit who, with two small babies crouching fearfully by her side, had successfully hidden from the dog, but was unaware of the man with the gun just behind her. Her ignorance of his presence seemed pitiful.

Their little nostrils quivering, the rabbits took a few tentative steps forward, perhaps afraid that Kimber would turn back and see them. Laurence quietly put his gun to his shoulder and took careful aim.

He saw the little family group in his sights and his hand gently squeezed the trigger. He was aware that the tears now were pouring down his face and his vision was momentarily obscured.

He lowered the gun, and the mother, still unaware of her peril, signalled her babies; they ran off, disappearing into the woods.

'God give them life,' Laurence murmured.

But what life was left for him? His span was finished, his day was done.

Kimber was far off now and could not see him, and with slow deliberation Laurence turned the barrel of the gun towards himself and peered down it.

And later it was Kimber who came home alone and told them his master was dead.

The day Laurence Yetman was buried there was nearly a riot in Wenham. All the windows of the Two Counties Bank were broken and someone had tried to drive a ram through the door. The police had to be called in the early morning and they roped off the bank, which, together with most of the shops in the town, remained closed all day.

Almost every citizen of Wenham was in the streets, lining the route of the funeral procession, and all those who could crowded into the church.

Mr Turner led the service and preached the sermon. He took as his text not the Bible, but the passing over the waters of Mr Valiant-for-Truth as described in Bunyan's *Pilgrim's Progress*. The congregation was quite electrified by Mr Turner's sermon; few could recall one like it, even when Mr Lamb had been at the height of his powers, inviting doom, destruction and the awful judgment of a vengeful God to visit the peaceful town.

' "Then he passed over, and all the trumpets sounded for him at the other side." '

There was a hush in the church. Mr Turner descended the steps of the pulpit to join the rector, both of them in black copes. The solitary organ played music from Mendelssohn's *Elijah*, and then the bearers advanced as the rector gave the final blessing, to carry the coffin out of the church to the burial ground, where Laurence was laid next to his father, who had also been the victim of a tragic accident.

Because few people who knew Laurence, his happy nature, his outgoing disposition, thought it was anything else – except perhaps those who damaged the Two Counties Bank and guessed the truth.

One mourner missing from the funeral was Mr Becket, who had stolen out of the town under cover of darkness with his wife and children, never to be seen again.

In time the Wenham branch of the Two Counties Bank was closed and was replaced by another bank which, the citizens hoped, would have a more enlightened attitude towards those of its members who were visited by misfortune.

The sad little party assembled at Riversmead after the funeral. Guy and Agnes were still abroad, and so were Roger and

Prosper, as well as Connie and Miss Fairchild. None of them yet knew that Laurence was dead; but the rest of the family gathered to give support to his grieving widow, his heart-broken mother and his children, who were almost too young to understand.

The Sadlers came, but Bart did not. Maybe he thought that the opprobrium in which Mr Wainwright was held would pass to him. Sophie moved around, handing out cakes and tea, her fortitude as a missionary allowing her to give words of comfort that still seemed automatic, almost pedestrian. It was really hard to bring relief to anyone afflicted by such grief.

Julius attended the funeral but not the reception. He went home, saying he felt unwell. He had scarcely seen his wife since the incident, as Eliza spent all her time with Sarah-Jane and the children.

At the end of the day Sophie took all the children off to Pelham's Oak, although she was in the process of moving, and finally widow and mother were left alone.

'He *can't* have known what he was doing,' Sarah-Jane said, as she had said numerous times before. 'He would never have left me and the children . . . Mother? He must have had a brainstorm, a moment of madness, of complete and utter despair.'

And, again, Eliza repeated what she'd said before in an effort to console not only Laurence's widow but herself:

'My dear,' she said, 'you *know* Laurence would never have killed himself. It can only have been an accident. He had too much hope, too much love, too much to give. He would never have let something like this bankruptcy get him down.'

Then suddenly she burst into tears. Sarah-Jane patted her shoulder almost mechanically; then, when Eliza's tears had subsided, she said in a voice that was curiously vibrant, positive and clear:

'But Mother, Laurence would never shoot rabbits. He never shot rabbits or birds, you know he didn't. He loved wildlife too much; he loved everything that moved. He frequently walked through the woods with Kimber, but never with the gun. I can't remember ever seeing that gun out of the cupboard. It belonged to his father and Laurence has not used it, to my knowledge, in all the time we were married.'

Eliza stared long and hard at her and then, reaching for Sarah-Jane's hand, kept it in hers.

'I know,' she said, 'I know. I have always known but, like you, I shall never understand; so I like to believe it *was* an accident, and I always shall. You must too, my dear, because if we think that Laurence deliberately put the gun to his head and blew out his brains, we shall both go mad. And far too many people need and depend on us, now that our darling is dead.'

The following day Sophie and her children moved in temporarily with Sarah-Jane and hers, to help with the running of the household, and Eliza finally went back to her husband.

She sat for a long time in the car in front of the house, expecting that at any moment he would come to the door, because he must have known she'd arrived.

But when the door did eventually open, it was the butler who gravely descended the steps to help her out of the car.

'Will you be requiring the car again today, Mrs Heering?' the chauffeur asked.

'Not today, thanks, Gerard. I don't know about myyy husband..'

'Mr Heering is in his quarters, madam,' the butler said. 'He is not feeling well.'

'Oh? Still?' Eliza looked up at the windows of Julius's bedroom and saw that the curtains were drawn. 'Have you sent for Dr Hardy?'

'No, madam. Mr Heering insisted it wasn't necessary.'

'Very well. I'd better see to him myself.'

Eliza took her time, once she was in the house, because she had been absent for so many days. She went to see cook in the kitchen, who confirmed that Mr Heering was not eating. She went up to her room, changed her clothes and summoned her maid to unpack her case.

Then, and only then, did she go along the corridor and knock at the door of Julius's room. 'Julius, may I come in? It's Eliza.'

There was no reply, and she was about to enter when the door opened and Julius, fully dressed, stood in front of her.

She saw that his curtains had now been drawn back, though his bed was unmade, and suspected he had hastily risen and dressed when he heard her arrive.

'Are you still unwell, Julius?' she asked, entering the rooom. 'Haad you not better see thee dooctor?'

'You know there is no need for a doctor, Eliza,' Julius said in a sepulchral tone of voice. 'You know quite well what is wrong with me.'

'No.' Eliza walked into the room and stood looking round – it had an air of neglect as though no maid had been admitted to clean it for several days. 'What is wrong with you?' she asked at last, turning towards him.

'I can tell by the way you speak that you know what is wrong with me,' Julius said. 'It is guilt about Laurence.' He then flopped into a chair by the fire and put his head in his hands.

'Well,' Eliza said calmly, sitting opposite her husband, her hands in the pockets of her cardigan, 'I can well understand *that*.'

Suddenly he flung both his arms towards her and, like a man making an impassioned plea, burst out:

'But how on earth was *I* to know he would do a thing like that? Of course I would have helped him.'

'Too late now. Besides, it was an accident,' she said in an unemotional voice.

'Do you really believe that?' Julius looked closely at her.

'No.' She folded her hands in her lap. 'He never shot animals. He hated killing; but few outside the family know that. No one else must know. "Accidental death" will be the verdict at the inquest, and in a way that's what it was, and what we wish it to be: an accident that Laurence was in the wrong place at the wrong time when his final despair took hold of him, and no one was there to comfort him.'

'Everyone has withdrawn their money from the Two Counties Bank,' Julius said. 'I hear the manager has left the town. Whatever the verdict, the people know. *They* know why Laurence died.'

'Well . . .' Eliza got up, suddenly chilled, to stand nearer

437

the fire '. . . that is the best way to leave it. Now, Julius, why don't you come downstairs and have some lunch with me?'

'You're very forgiving, Eliza,' he said humbly, reaching for her hand. 'If I had helped Laurence you know he would be alive. It was against my principles but, nevertheless, his death will be on my conscience forever.'

Eliza had never seen her husband like this. He was always so in control, master of everything; seldom showing emotion, seldom revealing his true feelings. Now he had been reduced to a most uncharacteristic state of humility which she found rather pathetic.

'Julius,' she said, turning away from him towards the fire, where she stood for a few moments staring into the flames. Then she looked at him again. 'Julius, as you feel so bad there *is* something you can do.'

'And what is that, my dear?' he asked with a note of hope in his voice.

'Have I any rights as a wife?'

'Of course you have. Why?'

'In the past it did not seem like that. I have been a slave.'

'Not at all.' He crossed and uncrossed his legs. 'What a ridiculous thing to say.'

'You said "we Woodvilles" were impoverished and you despised us for it. It is true that, in this respect at least, we are not a very clever lot; but there is something that I would like to do.'

'And what is that, Eliza?'

'I would like the money as a gift, mine by right, to buy Riversmead from the receivers so that Sarah-Jane and the children can live in their own home for as long as they wish. I would like to give the house to them.'

'It is done,' Julius said with tears in his eyes. 'The money is there whenever you want it.'

'Thank you, Julius.' She remained for a long time looking at him, contempt in her eyes, as the tears began to trickle down his cheeks. 'But I must tell you this, and I shan't say it again. You're a mean-minded man, Julius, who has made money your god in the place of compassion. You could easily have saved my son, and I'm glad to see you cry. However, your tears will never bring him back, and I hope your guilt does remain with you for the rest of your days, and you never allow yourself to forget it.'

23

The Black Bull was a small, dark, seedy-looking public house that nestled under the north side of Blackfriars Bridge just after it had crossed the Thames. It predated the building of the bridge, so that all day long the whole place rattled as the trains passed overhead on their way to Holborn Viaduct Station.

However, few of the customers noticed the noise because it was a rowdy, cheery place and they made their own kind of commotion – soon, inevitably, heightened by a degree of intoxication.

It was here that Carson, who used to have a drink on his way back to Montagu Square from the City, had met Nelly Allen.

He could recall it now, though not the night he'd first seen her. She hadn't been a raving beauty, not the kind that usually attracted him, but her quiet nature, her elfin appeal, had finally captured his attention. She had seemed uninterested in him, which was also a challenge. It became a further challenge to get her into conversation, and another to ask her out. After that, she was hooked; no mere pretence.

However, there was no sign of Nelly now, and Carson sat at the bar over his beer, thinking of those days and the little room in Carter Lane where he had imagined himself in love with her.

She had loved him. Of that there was no doubt. But he was fickle; the feeling had soon passed and, until he stared into the eyes of little Alexander, he had almost forgotten Nelly. Now it was possible to imagine that she had borne him a son.

He wondered now where she was, and if he'd ever find her again.

'Nelly Allen?' The landlord handed Carson his second pint. 'Never heard of her.'

'Two or three years ago,' Carson explained, putting the frothing head to his lips. 'Dark, quiet sort of girl.'

'No.' The landlord shook his head and began wiping the bar with a wet cloth, a cigarette slung from the corner of his mouth. 'Only bin here eighteen months meself.'

'Thought I didn't recognise you,' Carson said. 'Sorry to have troubled you.'

'No trouble,' the landlord replied. 'Wish I could have helped. Important to you, was she?'

'Not really,' Carson said offhandedly and, as the landlord moved away, he swallowed the rest of his beer and prepared to depart. He felt a pang of guilt at dismissing Nelly so trivially, but what was the point when he didn't know himself?

There was a tug at his elbow and he looked down. It was the barmaid, who had moved round to the saloon side of the bar where she was picking up dirty glasses and putting them on a tray.

'I knew Nelly Allen,' she said out of the corner of her mouth.

'Did you?' Carson spun round. 'What happened to her?'

'She left sudden-like,' the barmaid said slyly.

'Do you know why?'

'Well, someone said she was ill. I don't know if you'd call it an illness.' The barmaid gave a suggestive little snigger.

'Why do you say that?' Carson demanded.

'*Some* say . . .' the barmaid came up to him and put her mouth to his ear '. . . that she was in the family way; but people can be unkind, can't they? You don't really know. May have had a growth or sommink.'

Carson seized her arm and said urgently, 'Look, if you ever see her, say you saw Carson – Carson, remember – and she can get in touch with me through the house in Montagu Square.'

'That all?' The girl sounded disappointed.

'That's all.' Carson tucked a pound note into her hand, 'And have a drink on me.'

'Thanks.' The barmaid hurriedly stuffed it down her bosom. 'Can't say I'll ever see her because I don't really know her, do I?'

Carson shrugged and went out into the street, the busy thoroughfare full of London traffic. He walked along the cobbles of Blackfriars Lane, past the Apothecaries' Hall and into narrow Carter Lane, where he stood for a few minutes looking up at the grimy building, thinking of Nelly.

More than ever, he felt that she was the mother of his child.

Carson went straight back to Blandford from London, and arrived at his cottage just as it was getting dark. He didn't know what to do about the mystery of Nelly and, in a way, he would like to have shared his problem with Lally; but he thought it might be too much of a responsibility for her, probably too great a shock for her to bear. Besides, if Alexander proved to be his child he might wish to reclaim him, and what would Lally say to that?

It was amazing to think that for two years she had perhaps been looking after his son, and he felt a wave of gratitude for the woman who had shown the compassion that saved Alexander from an uncertain fate.

He lit the lamps in his cottage, and was about to light the fire when there was a knock at the door.

'Come in,' he called, looking over his shoulder. It was Lally's underfootman, Paul.

'Yes, Paul? What is it?' Carson asked cheerfully, setting a match to the combination of wood-shavings and paper in the grate.

'Mrs Martyn noticed you had arrived home, sir, and wondered if you would like to dine?'

'Tonight?'

'Dinner is in an hour, sir.'

'Well, that's very kind of her.' Carson jumped up. 'It will just give me time to have a bath and change.'

'Mrs Martyn asked me to tell you there was company, sir. Mrs Roger Martyn is staying in the house, and she would be glad if you would wear a black tie.'

'Certainly, Paul. Thank you.'

Carson smiled to himself as the footman closed the door. Lally, the dancer, was a stickler for etiquette.

Carson had not seen Emma Martyn since her wedding eighteen months before. His and Roger's paths never crossed. While he seemed to go from one misfortune to another, Roger continued on an upward path. It was really quite amazing to think that, in addition to all his other good fortune, he was married to this adorable creature as well.

She sat opposite Carson, looking the very picture of loveliness in a cream evening-gown, cut on the cross so that it emphasised the contours of her slender figure. Her striking golden hair was worn softly waved in front and short at the back. Her skin was almost opaque, her blue eyes the colour of cornflowers. A beautiful diamond necklace was round her slender throat, while on her fingers sparkled a selection of exquisite and clearly extremely expensive rings.

'It's odd that you two haven't met since the wedding,' Lally remarked as the servants withdrew during dinner.

'Roger is busy making money,' Carson said with a smile. 'I'm afraid the country is too dull a place for him. You too, probably, Emma.'

'Oh, I adore the country,' Emma assured him. 'I love the town, but at heart I'm a country girl.'

'Really?' Carson seemed surprised. 'You must miss Roger now.' He looked up from the supreme of chicken in a light lobster sauce which Lally's superb chef had conjured up for them this evening.

But Emma made no reply. Instead it was left to Lally.

'They have made us both widows,' she said. 'You would think they would take their wives on such an exciting and important trip. The Far East!' Her eyes sparkled.

'But Aunt, you know you would not have wanted to leave Alexander,' Carson said. 'What would he do without you for six months?'

'He would have been well looked after. However, I would have missed him, it's true. Babies grow so quickly in six months.'

She gave Emma a meaningful look, but her daughter-in-law kept her eyes on her plate. Carson smiled to himself. Lally wanted to be a grandmother.

'Tell me,' Lally said after a pause, 'was your visit to London a success?'

'Not really,' Carson replied.

'What was its purpose, may one ask?'

'I was looking for someone.'

'And did you find him?'

'No. It was a her.'

The two women exchanged glances and then Lally, sensing he would reveal no more on the subject, began to talk of something else.

After dinner Lally said she had letters to write, and excused herself. She suggested that Carson and Emma might like to amuse themselves with the gramophone. Perhaps they might even like to dance.

Carson was pleased at the chance to be alone with Emma, whom he found most entertaining company. They sat on either side of the fire as Paul served coffee and liqueurs.

'And put back the carpet, please, Paul,' Carson said. 'In a few moments Mrs Martyn and I are going to dance to the gramophone.'

'Very good, sir,' Paul said, moving across the room while Emma gazed at him with a question-mark in her eyes.

'You like to dance, don't you?' Carson asked a short while later when, after Paul had rolled back the carpet and left the room, he rose to select a record and put it onto the machine. Then, after winding it up and carefully putting the needle in the groove, he held out his arms.

'Love it,' she said, as she took his hands, keeping a respectable distance between them.

'What would your husband think if he knew we were doing this?'

'He probably wouldn't notice.' Emma held her head back and, eyes still sparkling, smiled.

They felt comfortable in each other's arms and for a few

moments they twirled around in the otherwise empty room to the sound of the music.

They danced until the record stopped, and then Emma went over to change it, looking one by one at the stack of records. Carson refilled their glasses with cognac and, taking hers over to her, perched on the arm of the chair as she examined the records, gazing intently at her.

'Is Roger keen on dancing?'

Emma gave him an exaggerated look and then, crossing to the machine, put her latest choice on the table and enthusiastically began to wind up the gramophone, tapping her toes. She held out her arms and he stood up and guided her on to the floor.

'I said, is Roger . . .?'

'Why should we talk about Roger?'

For a moment she stopped dancing and looked at him, while the music continued in the background. He found it hard to interpret her expression.

'It's all rather strange,' he murmured as they began dancing again.

'Roger is a very strange man,' Emma replied.

'I see.'

Carson thought enough had been said on the subject for the evening, and then he very lightly placed his cheek against hers; and that way, stopping only to change the records, they continued to dance until the small hours of the morning.

Carson slept late into the next day, having gone to bed late; and he had then been unable to sleep because the thought of Emma haunted his mind.

As he'd first touched her, a sensation like an electric shock had flashed through his fingers, and as they danced close together there was an overwhelming urge to take her in his arms, to embrace her. But he resisted, and when, later, he saw her to the foot of the stairs as she went to her room, he didn't attempt to kiss her.

Now it was almost noon and he still lay in bed, arms clasped behind his head.

Women. They were a terrible problem. First one and then

another. Maybe the best thing, the wisest thing, would be for him to go away, far away. Maybe he should reconsider the idea of joining the army as his uncle had suggested, and be sent overseas away from temptation.

Roger's wife. He sat upright with shock at the thought of the scandal such an affair would provoke if Roger got to hear about it, a man jealous and unpredictable in his moods. But it was not an affair yet; nor must it be. He loved Lally, who would also be affected if he seduced her daughter-in-law. He would become a pariah in the district, spurned by everyone, including his family.

Carson got out of bed and sat on the side, hands clasped in front of him. He must go away, right away from the temptation offered by Emma, and only think of returning when she was safely back in London.

He had a bath, shaved and dressed in a shirt, his riding-breeches and a thick sweater. He would go for a long ride, maybe to see Eliza who was always full of good advice. He might invite himself to dinner with his aunt, and thus avoid seeing Emma again. Late in the night, he would return, and first thing the next morning he would pack his bags, leave Lally a note and get the train from Blandford to London. He might even go to France.

Cheered by his resolution, Carson had a sandwich and a glass of beer, put on his riding-boots and walked from the cottage over to the stables to get his horse. He was waylaid by one of the footmen.

'Excuse me, Mr Carson, Mrs Martyn would like to see you in her room, sir.'

'Oh? I was just about to go riding.'

'I think it might be urgent, sir. Mrs Martyn feels unwell and would like to ask a favour of you.'

'Unwell?' Carson said with concern. 'I am sorry about that. I'll go at once.'

He retraced his steps and went into the house by a side-entrance, and then through the hall and up the main staircase, looking for Lally's room. He was not quite sure which one it was until the footman, who had followed him, pointed it out. Carson tapped on the door and was told in a muffled voice to enter, but as soon as he had, Lally cried: 'Don't come any nearer,' and he saw, at the far end of the large room, her diminutive figure in a huge double bed, holding out her hands as though to ward him off.

'Aunt Lally,' he cried, 'whatever is the matter?'

'I have the most terrible cold, Carson. I felt it coming on last night, which was why I left you. I do hope you and Emma don't get it. I must have been breathing germs on you both during the evening. I hope you were not too bored with each other.'

Carson couldn't determine from her expression whether or not she was serious, and he merely smiled and replied:

'No, not at all. Emma loves to dance. It was a good idea of yours.'

'Oh yes, she does,' Lally replied in a thick voice. '*And* poor Roger hates it. I knew she would find you fun, Carson, and I think you like her too, don't you?'

'Very much, Aunt.' He tried to keep his tone impassive.

'Well then, dear, the favour I am going to ask you won't seem such a chore, in that case.' She raised herself against the pillows and gave him her most winsome smile. '*Dearest* Carson, I wonder, in return for the favour I have done you, would *you* look after Emma for me until I'm better? Paul has sent for Dr Hardy.' She put a hand to her flushed cheeks. 'I think I might even have influenza, so I shall keep well out of your way . . .'

'But Aunt . . .'

'Yes, Carson?' she said, but began to sneeze, and did so several times before he could reply. 'Oh dear,' she said, 'oh dear.'

'Do you think it's wise, Aunt?'

'Wise, dear?' She looked at him from behind her handkerchief. 'I don't think I understand you.'

'Well, if Roger . . .'

'My dear, Roger is your cousin, in a manner of speaking, and Emma is his wife. There is absolutely no question of impropriety, is there, Carson? I am only asking you to entertain her for a day or two, until I am well again, otherwise the poor girl will get so bored she will go back to London. Roger wouldn't like that at all, and I am so attached to my daughter-in-law that I too would hate it to happen. I see little enough of her as it is. So, will you do me a *very* big favour and entertain her for me? She loves riding and, as you know, dancing. She said she was a country girl, though I find it hard to believe, she is so fond of life in town. However, she might like to go walking too, and I will ask chef to prepare specially delicious meals for you both, to while away the evening. It's not *too* much to ask, is it, dear, to entertain Emma?'

'No, Aunt.' Carson carefully studied the shining tops of his boots.' 'It will be a pleasure.'

'And on your walks you could perhaps take Alexander . . .'

'*That* will be a pleasure too.'

'You are such a good boy, Carson,' Lally said emotionally. 'Sometimes I think those who speak harshly of you are so unfair, and that no one really understands you but me.'

Between them, Alexander, clearly delighted at being with his hero, kept on running ahead with his little steps, and then running back again. They were all wrapped up against the cold, and had kept to the shelter of the house so that if it started to rain on this cold January day, they could quickly retreat inside again.

Emma, who had also slept late, seemed to be delighted with the suggestion that she and Carson should take Alexander for a walk, and not at all depressed to hear that her mother-in-law was ill – though the doctor had now been, and a bulletin issued that Mrs Martyn did not have influenza, but a heavy cold that should respond to treatment in a day or two.

'What a really charming little child he is,' Emma said, watching Alexander, who clearly enjoyed showing off.

'I think so.'

'You *do* seem extraordinarily attached to him, Carson.'

'I am.' For a moment Carson was almost tempted to tell her about Nelly, a temptation he was happy, later, that he had resisted.

'I suppose you'd like children, Carson, wouldn't you?'

'One day,' he answered casually.

'You seem awfully good with them.'

'And you?' He looked at her.

'Yes, I'd like children one day, naturally; but I'm still very young.'

'Of course you are. I expect you and Roger want to have a good time first.'

'I expect so,' she said. Then: 'Were you very upset about the break-up of your engagement?'

'Yes, I was.' Alexander ran up to him again and, to hide his confusion, Carson lifted him up, raising him above his head while the child kicked and screamed with delight. 'I was very upset because I hurt someone very much. I like Connie, but I didn't love her.' Gently he put Alexander down again, and there was a tragic expression on his face as he looked at Emma.

If only it had been her.

Lally didn't recover from her cold as quickly as expected, and Carson and Emma began to get into a routine which they both enjoyed. Carson realised that, in a remarkably short time, he was becoming dependent on her company for the joy it brought to his day. They did not breakfast together, but met at about eleven. Then they rode, or took Alexander for a walk. They lunched together, then rode or walked again, and once they visited Sarah-Jane and the children.

Each night they dined *à deux*, looking at each other across the candles on the table. And afterwards they danced, linked in each other's arms, until they had played all the records that Lally had. Then they began to play them all over again.

But the bad news, finally, was that Lally was getting better. After four days confined to her room she announced her intention of coming down to tea, and maybe having dinner with them as well.

On the morning of the announcement that Lally was returning to civilisation, they met as usual, Emma already in her riding outfit, as they had agreed the night before. Carson was waiting for her with her horse saddled in the yard; she came out of the side-door, swinging her crop, and hailed him cheerfully.

'Lovely morning,' she said.

'Lovely,' he cried, thinking the loveliest part of it was her. 'But it's cold. Jump up, Emma.'

The groom appeared to help her into the saddle, and then she and Carson rode slowly out of the yard, round the back of the house towards the wooded banks of a small tributary of the River Stour.

'Mother-in-law is much better,' Emma said.

'I know, isn't that good?'

'It's splendid; but . . .' Emma stopped her horse, and Carson rode on for some moments before he realised she was behind him. Then he looked round and cantered back.

'What is it?'

'I shall miss you, Carson. It's only been a few days . . . I think I should go back to London.'

'No!' he said. 'No. I know what you mean, but *I'll* go. I was going to go anyway. Lally wants you to stay on here for company.'

'Then can't we just go on as we were?'

'You know we can't,' he said. 'You know something is happening that is wrong.'

She came up to him, and when her horse was alongside his, she leaned across and touched his knee.

He also leaned towards her, reaching for her hand. Then he kissed her.

It was dark in the room when Carson woke; but that was only because they'd drawn the curtains against the pale wintry sun. He looked at his watch and saw it was about three in the afternoon. They'd missed lunch, but they must not miss tea because Lally would be there and expecting them.

He looked at her back, and ran his hand along it very tenderly, a little fearfully. Then he lay against her, gently encircling her body with his arm so that he could touch her breast. He could feel her chest heaving gently, and realised that she was not only awake but weeping. He took his hand from her breast and touched her face.

'Emma,' he whispered. 'Don't cry.'

He tried to turn her to him, but she refused to move. He got out of bed and, throwing on his dressing-gown, went round to her side and knelt on the floor beside her. He reached out and gently stroked her brow, smoothed her beautiful blonde hair away from her forehead.

'I'm very, very sorry,' he said.

'It's quite all right.' She tried to smile through her tears, and put out a hand to take his.

'I didn't know you were a virgin, Emma. I never dreamt it. You should have told me.'

'It's a very difficult thing t-to t-tell anyone,' she stammered, 'when you've been married nearly two years.'

'And Roger never . . .?'

She shook her head.

'He can't. He wants to, but he can't. It's awful for him as well as for me, and because we can't talk about it, it's made us strangers. But now I'm glad, Carson.' Her smile this time was more successful, her flow of tears ceasing, and she began to stroke his hand, 'I'm really glad. You can't realise the frustration of sleeping with a man who doesn't want you as a woman.'

Carson rose to his feet and, sitting beside her on the bed, cradled her head on his lap. How beautiful she was. He couldn't believe it: her hair, her mouth, her nose, everything was perfect. Her breasts were like soft, ripe fruit.

'I love you, Emma,' he said.

And he knew, without any doubt at all, that this time it was for real.

Sophie walked slowly through the rooms of Pelham's Oak, thinking that maybe she would never see it again. She intended not just to cross the Dorset border, but to go right away, miles and miles; to Scotland, maybe, or some remote part of Wales where she could cover up her past, change her name, and no one would know who she was or where she had come from.

She had spent the last weeks while Agnes and Guy were on their extended honeymoon, supervising the cleaning of the house from top to bottom. All the curtains had been cleaned, the carpets shampooed, the upholstery of the furniture made to look like new. The servants had been kept busy scrubbing, cleaning, washing, polishing.

And now the whole place shone, a welcome-home for the new bride.

Sophie only did it out of a sense of gratitude to her father-in-law, not out of any love for Agnes, the woman who had peremptorily ordered her out of the house. Some people, out of spite, might have left at once, taking their things and leaving it as it was. With no supervision, the servants would have lazed their days away. But Sophie was a perfectionist, and not someone who would ever care to appear to be motivated by revenge.

Sophie looked for the last time at her bedroom, a room in which, on the whole, she had been happy, except for her guilty dreams and fretful nights. Now it was empty, immaculate, ready for the next occupant, whoever that might be.

Before she left she looked out of the window, across the fields to where Wenham stood on the hill surmounted by the square tower of the church. Very soon she would be living in its shadow once again; but not for long. She had a sense of time passing, and she had to move quickly.

She shut the door firmly behind her and walked along to the children's rooms; they had had one each, the first time in their short lives they had had this luxury. Next to them there had been the nanny. There was no nanny now. Those times had gone. She had been dismissed, and had returned to her parents' home somewhere on the coast of Kent.

There had been a rocking-horse and rows of teddies in Deborah's room, blocks, toys and balls upon the floor. Ruth's dainty little room had dolls and pretty bows and feminine things, lots of dresses in the wardrobes, and books everywhere. Ruth, already fond of reading, was a bluestocking in the making.

On the other side had been the schoolroom. It had been painted a pretty primrose colour, with the letters of the alphabet, carefully painted by the children under Sophie's supervision, arranged around the wall. Six letters on three walls, eight on the fourth. Their little desks were still there, the chairs they had sat on, and a larger one for Sophie. But the cupboards were bare of drawing-paper and exercise-books, and the abacus on which she had taught them numbers.

And then the tears came to her eyes and she wept. It had, after all, been a brief stay. At one time she had thought it would be for life. That she would live there at least until Carson succeeded his father. What would he have done with her then, she wondered?

But she would not allow her mind to dwell on the fact that things would have been so different had George survived. One day, on the death of his father, they would have returned from the missions as Sir George and Lady Woodville, and in all probability she would have lived here until she died.

In many ways the Woodvilles had been right. She was to blame for what had happened; but for her, George would never have gone to the missions. She had been the driving force, and had she not pushed him, he would undoubtedly have been alive now.

She paused for a moment and looked out of the window at the sky. Maybe someone up there was paying her back for what she'd done, and her present predicament was the price exacted from her.

But enough. Sophie dried her tears and shut that door behind her, then she continued slowly along the corridor, down the great staircase to the hall where, beside their luggage, Deborah and Ruth sat patiently waiting for her.

Deborah was nine and Ruth was seven. Deborah was to go to boarding-school as soon as a suitable one could be found for her, and Ruth would follow. Sir Guy had now agreed to help with the fees and there was also help from the missionary fund which, from time to time, sent money to Sophie.

The children rose when they saw their mother, their little faces sad. They loved Pelham's Oak, the freedom, its sheer size that had enabled them to run around inside the house, sliding along the corridors, across the vast rooms, in and out. She held out her arms and, with one accord, they ran towards her, and for a moment mother and children, a sad, dispossessed little group, stood hugging one another. Once again the tears were not very far away.

'Come on now,' she said as she unclasped them. 'There's no

time to linger. The coach won't wait for ever.' Kind Hubert Turner had offered to pick them up, but at the last minute he had been unexpectedly called to Salisbury for a diocesan meeting. Instead she had had to call a cab.

It was very unlike the day she had arrived. However, she was always telling the children that it was no use crying over spilt milk, bemoaning and bewailing the past, and as they clung to her she looked around for some help to get the luggage into the cab.

But, unlike the day she had arrived, there was no one to be seen, no eager servants to scurry down the stairs, anxious to do her bidding as the daughter-in-law of the master. They all knew now that she had been told to go; dismissed. Once again she was nobody, nothing, and doubtless they were lurking in the servants' hall, sniggering at her misfortune – because, although she was fair, she had been a hard taskmaster, and had made them work as they had not worked since Lady Woodville died.

'Mama, *must* we go?' Ruth asked petulantly, her finger in her mouth.

'Yes, we must,' she said. 'Grandpapa has a new wife and he wants to be alone with her.'

'She's *horrible*,' Deborah said with a grimace. 'Fancy choosing *her*.'

Sophie looked round anxiously. It would never do for the servants to hear her criticise her step-grandmother.

'Hush, you mustn't say things like that,' Sophie said with a warning finger on her lips. 'She is your new grandmama and you must be very nice to her. Then she will invite you to come here often, and if you say nasty things about her, she won't.'

She went to the green baize door and put her head round it. She could hear voices from the servants' hall, and went along the corridor and down the stairs to the basement. She opened the door of the hall and, suddenly, there was silence, and the dozen pairs of eyes in the room stared sullenly at her.

'Could someone help me with the luggage?' she called. 'And I would like to thank you all for looking after us while we have lived here, for being so kind to the children and to me. And I want to wish you well.'

There were a few mumbles and bowed heads, but no one said

anything, not even Arthur, who she thought might have said a few words. But she had corrected him about his drinking, his stealing of Guy's brandy and cigars while he was away, and she knew that, like the rest of them, he had no real feeling for her. What they were all looking for was a big tip, but she had no money, nothing left to give.

'Could someone help me with the luggage?' she asked again. 'I'd be most grateful.'

'Henry, you go,' Arthur said, nudging one of the sullen footmen.

'Why should *I*?' Henry exclaimed. 'It's my lunch-time. Egbert, *you* go.'

But Egbert had a similar excuse and, finally, Sophie said:

'If it's too much trouble, I'll ask the cab-driver.' And she turned sharply on her heel and went through the door, feeling those tears, never very far away these days, pricking at the back of her eyes again.

She was walking through the hall towards the door, to call the ancient cab-driver to come and help her, when she heard footsteps behind and Henry appeared, looking as though he'd had his ears boxed.

'Oi'll give you a hand,' he muttered.

'Thank you so much, Henry.' Sophie gave him a bright smile and pointed towards the pile of luggage in the centre of the hall. 'If you would begin with the two valises, that would be *most* helpful.'

She then took each of the children firmly by the hand and descended the steps of Pelham's Oak, ancestral home of her dead husband, probably, she thought, for the last time.

As the coach trotted down the drive she turned to look back at the noble pile that had housed three centuries of Woodvilles. It had only survived so long because of money.

She knew from the Bible and countless works of devotion that money didn't bring happiness; but it certainly made life a little more easy to endure.

Miss Fairchild and Connie sat outside a café in the Piazza di San Marco, drinking tea – English tea. There were some other tourists like them doing the same: the British being the British when abroad. Around them the capillaries and arteries of alleyways and streets that formed the thoroughfare of Venice ran in all directions, each leading to a *campo* with a church and houses that were centuries old, or a view of the Grand Canal, or the Rialto Bridge, or the Arsenal.

They had been there three weeks and had left very little of the city unexplored; and while Miss Fairchild rested in the afternoons, Connie would try and find a church where there was music, a choir rehearsing or an organ soloist practising, as she used to do in Wenham. It was then, in the quiet, in the dim recesses of the church or basilica, that she would think of Carson, though she never mentioned his name to Miss Fairchild.

She would think that, maybe, had Agnes not appeared when she did, they would have come to Venice on their honeymoon, wandering through France and Italy first, as she and Miss Fairchild had done. Then, instead of being two spinsters, always given a corner table or served last, she would have been with a handsome man, a nobleman; but most important of all, her husband. People would have noted the glances they gave each other across the table, the secret signs, and perhaps would have guessed that they were newly married.

Connie fantasised a good deal these days about the honeymoon that had never happened. It helped her to bear the pain.

Miss Fairchild was pleased with the effect of the long holiday on the spirits of her beloved ward, though she had little doubt about what was on her mind, because of the way she moved restlessly in her bed at night; and once or twice she'd cried out his name.

Miss Fairchild knew all about frustrated love, the time the wound took to heal. Even though she had only had a kiss from Christopher, one kiss, the memory, the thrill of simply seeing him had lingered for years. Yet for poor Connie it had gone so much further. She had been engaged to be married, the banns had been called, the trousseau made, each item carefully wrapped in tissue and placed in special drawers. And then she had had the humiliation of being jilted, so that all the people of Wenham and its surrounding villages instantly knew all about it.

She put down her cup upon its saucer and looked at Connie, whose eyes were fastened on a flock of greedy pigeons in the centre of the square. They were a comical sight as they first pecked each other out of the way, then made a dash for the scraps that the tourists threw out to them. But Connie didn't appear to find it amusing, just absorbing, as though in some way their plight was symptomatic of her own. In fact she seldom smiled. More than ever, she had grown into a serious, morbidly shy young woman.

Miss Fairchild patted Connie's hand which lay on the table.

'I think when we return we'll go and live somewhere else, dear child, what do you think? Wenham is such a small, constricting place. How about Cheltenham, or Bath, where you would be able to hear lots of good music and doubtless meet more interesting people. What about it, Constance? Eh?'

'Just as you say, Aunt,' Connie answered impassively.

She didn't really care where she lived, although maybe it would be a good thing to get away from Wenham. What she knew without any doubt was that, cushioned by money, she would from now on lead a life of spinsterly rectitude right to the end, untouched by love, desire, or the ecstasy of carnal knowledge: two in one flesh.

A week after Sophie left, Agnes and Guy returned to Pelham's Oak and were met with the usual show of servility by all the staff, who ranged themselves on either side of the drive to greet the new mistress of the house just as, many years before, their predecessors had greeted Guy's first wife.

Agnes wore a blue travelling-coat and a black hat with a large ostrich feather, and she swept past Guy, through the line of servants, acknowledging their homage with a slight incline of her head. Guy was reminded of the scene with dear Margaret when they returned from their honeymoon, and he drew out his handkerchief to wipe away the tears, which even now sprang instantly to his eyes.

But Margaret was dead, gone, and Agnes was present and he was very much in love with her. They had extended the three months to over four, visiting the spas, the grand hotels of Germany, France, Austria and Switzerland.

Guy followed Agnes up the steps and into the house, where Arthur accompanied them into the drawing-room.

'How *nice* everything looks,' Agnes exclaimed. 'You have been doing terribly well, Arthur, in our absence.'

'I really must say it was all due to Mrs Woodville,' Alfred grudgingly admitted. 'She supervised the entire spring-cleaning of the house. I told her it was all to be repainted, but she insisted.'

'Repainted!' Agnes said sharply, looking round. 'Why is it to be *repainted*, Guy?'

'I thought the whole place was to be done up, my dear,' he said, looking at her, while Arthur bowed and withdrew. 'You said . . .'

'Guy,' Agnes sat down and began carefully to remove her hat. 'There is one thing I want you to understand. I have not married you to throw all my money away on this house. It can be touched up here and there, but that's enough.' She finished pulling off her gloves and laid them on her lap. '*I* intend to spend a *lot* of my time in London, Guy. You won't see very much of me at Pelham's Oak. I find it, frankly, stifling here. London!' She raised her head as though she could see the sights and hear the sounds. 'It is a city I love, and I want to go to all the balls, the parties, the opera, the theatre; and *that* is where I will spend my substance. Not here.'

Guy looked dumbfounded.

'At least I have enabled you to keep on this old house,' she said contemptuously. 'For the time being, that is. But for me, you would have sold it. Be thankful for that. But don't think that is the end of the matter. I have not got an ever-open purse, and in a year or two it may be that if you find a buyer who will give a good price, you may well have to dispose of it.'

Guy sat down with a thud and stared in front of him, a tremor running through his body that manifested itself in shaking hands.

'*And* another thing, Guy. While we're speaking frankly,' Agnes went on, 'I have something else on my mind.'

'And what is that, dear?'

'Guy, what of our child?'

'Our child?' Guy blinked several times in rapid succession as though he did not quite understand.

'We had a child, you and I, a daughter.'

Guy hung his head.

'You told me you did not want her mentioned, dearest. You wished me never to refer to her.'

'You're quite right, and for good reason. It was a painful episode I wished completely to forget. But I find circumstances have forced me to confront the matter. I have discovered she is a maid at the Crown Hotel in Blandford. In fact, she waited on me. Her name is Elizabeth.'

'Oh, you *know*.' Guy, appearing overjoyed, clasped his hands together.

'She is very pretty,' Agnes cut in. 'Remarkably so.'

'Like you, my darling,' he said ingratiatingly.

'But I can't understand why she could not have been sent to an orphanage, Guy, or adopted, so that she could have been out of our lives altogether. Why had she to be *here*? I was incensed when I realised who she was.'

'You never *said* anything, Agnes. I could have explained.'

'I imagined you must feel pretty guilty too. I have, however, been thinking about it since, and I want to get the matter cleared up so that there is nothing between us . . . to mar our happiness,' she added.

'Why should Elizabeth mar our happiness? Might she not *add* to it?' Guy crossed the room and, reaching for her hand, took it tenderly between his. 'Oh my darling, I have longed to acknowledge Elizabeth, the fruit of our love, as my daughter, and now that we are married and good fortune has smiled on us *and* Elizabeth, may we not publicly claim her as our own at last?'

'Are you out of your mind, Guy?' Agnes pushed his hand away and rose to her feet. 'I would *never*, ever want anyone to know that a serving-maid is *our* daughter, a girl brought up by servants. Whose idea, incidentally, was that?'

'Eliza's. She was too kind-hearted and refused to send Elizabeth away. I was not even consulted, left in ignorance.

459

Consequently, Elizabeth was for many years treated by Eliza virtually as one of her own children.'

'Well then, she should have adopted her properly. She did her no favours. None at all. Elizabeth, though beautiful and well-mannered, is little more than a peasant, and she is going to marry a peasant. Did you know that?'

'No.' Guy hung his head shamefacedly. 'I know very little about her. I see her from time to time, but she is ignorant of the fact that I am her father.'

'Good.'

'I do a little to support her.'

'That should cease. Her husband-to-be is merely a man who drives a brewer's dray.'

'It must be stopped,' he said angrily.

'Certainly not. They are going to live in Blandford, so that will keep them out of the area. Now, Guy.' She turned and shook her finger at him. 'I want you to put Elizabeth out of your mind entirely. Do you understand?'

'Yes, Agnes.'

'It is to be as though she *never* existed. Is that clear?'

'Perfectly clear, my dear.'

'Good.' Agnes crossed the room to gather up her things. 'Then don't forget it, because I should never forgive *you* if we were acknowledged as Elizabeth's parents, and our sinful past exposed.'

Agnes walked purposefully towards the door and Guy rushed to open it for her. Then he closed it and tottered back into the room, sinking helplessly into his chair again, aware of the sudden swift and irregular beating of his heart, the fleeting pain across his chest.

The honeymoon was over.

Sophie Woodville sat between her parents at the dinner-table, her head bowed, her appetite completely gone. Her mother was in the middle of one of her interminable lectures about Sophie's misdeeds, her bad judgment, lack of foresight and so on and so forth, while her father just sat and nodded his agreement like a mechanical toy.

The lectures usually began at dinner and continued through-out the evening until Sophie, exhausted, retired to bed, pleading a headache or some other form of sickness.

The import of these nightly dissertations was that Sophie was a disappointment to her parents. She had somewhere taken the wrong turning, mainly because she took no notice of her parents' attempts at guidance.

They could have told her, had she asked, that it was a mistake to marry George Woodville. A blind man could have seen that his parents would object. Having committed such a gross error of judgment, to whisk him off tto the missions – about which, incidentally, he was never very keen – had compounded her initial folly. And then she had been careless enough to allow him to die . . . And all this when one thought she had been well brought up, well educated, the apparently docile child of worthy parents.

The latest stupidity, undoubtedly, was her decision to leave Wenham.

There was no need. The rectory was large enough for her and her family, the schools were near, what nonsense to send them to board! What needless extravagance!

Then there was the fact that she had not been firm enough with Sir Guy; she had given in to Agnes when she should have opposed her. She had done this, she had done that; she had not done this, not done that. There was no end to it.

'Mother!' she would eventually cry out, and leave the table – or the drawing-room, or wherever the scene was of the everlasting peroration.

But tonight, feeling decidedly unwell, she let it all flow over her until she heard the words:

'*And* when your father retires we shall *need* you, Sophie. How selfish can you be?'

'Why will you need me?' she asked, jerking her head up.

'Because we are getting old, dear.' Mrs Lamb made an effort to sound reasonable. 'Your father is nearly eighty. He will soon retire.'

'And when is that to be?' Sophie turned lack-lustre eyes to him.

'Perhaps in the next few months,' he said. 'It was agreed at the diocesan meeting last week and, providing Sir Guy agrees . . .' Mr Lamb stopped and rolled his eyes mysteriously.

'Yes?' Sophie tried to sound encouraging though, in reality, she wasn't interested.

'Well . . . *providing* Sir Guy agrees, as the living of Wenham is in his gift, Mr Turner is to be appointed the new rector.'

'Oh, that *is* excellent news,' Sophie said whole-heartedly. 'I am so pleased for him. But I thought it wasn't possible until he had served a full term as priest in charge ? He has only been a curate.'

'That was the reason he went to see the bishop, and could not help to move you the day you left Pelham's Oak. The bishop has agreed that, in the circumstances and in view of Mr Turner's generosity to the church, he will automatically succeed to the rectorship.'

'What "generosity" to the church?' Sophie asked curiously.

'Oh, Mr Turner is very *generous*,' Mrs Lamb said warmly. 'He gives to all kinds of causes connected not only with this parish but the needs of the diocese as a whole. He gives assistance to needy people. He is one of the kindest men I ever knew, because he does it all without ostentation. He has also agreed that, in our retirement, we shall continue to occupy the rectory, as he is quite happy with his own house. He is the best of men.' Mrs Lamb paused and gazed reproachfully at her. 'It is a *pity*, Sophie dear, that you could not have seen that. That you . . .'

'Oh *Mother*!' Sophie said, banging the table and standing up. 'I am heartily sick of this . . .'

And then she swayed, stumbled and sat down heavily in her chair, her face as pale as chalk.

'Sophie!' her father cried anxiously. 'Are you unwell?'

Sophie sat there for few moments until the dizziness passed, wondering how to answer the question. What would her parents say if she told them the truth? The thought even made her smile, and her colour came back as her courage returned. She got up slowly from her chair and pushed it under the table.

'I think it is all the business of the move, Father, and my own impending departure. Also, this unending criticism of my behaviour tires me. I should like to go to my room. Good night.'

'But my dear, there is no *need*,' the rector began but, by that time, Sophie was already halfway to the door and seemed not to hear him.

A school had been found for Charles; Ruth was to come with her. Sophie had found lodgings in Cheltenham and a possible position as a temporary teacher at a local school. It would not be for long, but it would bring in some money. Then, later, she would travel further away.

Her parents had seen that their daughter was adamant, her mind made up, and already she had started her packing. She felt constantly unwell, and out of their sight spent a lot of time resting. She was, in fact, lying on her bed when there was a tap at the door and she heard her maid saying:

'Are you there, Mrs Woodville?'

'Yes, I'm here,' she called out, sitting up and immediately getting off the bed and touching up her hair. 'Come in, Susie.'

Susie came in and, with a little bob, said:

'Mr Turner is in the front parlour, madam. He wondered if he could have a few words with you.'

'Oh!' Sophie was about to refuse, then she changed her mind. It would only be polite to take her farewell of one who had been a good friend. 'Tell him I shan't be a minute.'

'Yes, madam,' Susie said and, with another little bob, went away again.

Sophie ran a comb through her hair, patted her cheeks to give them a little colour, and straightened her dress. Then she went along the rambling corridors of the big house, down the stairs and across the hall to the front parlour. The house seemed to be in complete silence; it was mid-afternoon, and she guessed her parents too were resting. She opened the door, and Hubert sprang up from a chair by the fire and threw aside the copy of the *Church Times* that he had been reading.

'Hubert, how very nice to see you.' Sophie held out her hands as she went towards him. 'I hear I am to congratulate you.'

'Oh . . . yes.' Hubert smiled shyly. 'I expect so.'

'An excellent choice.' Sophie pointed to his chair. 'Do sit down.'

'I am very fortunate to be offered the living.'

'And my parents are very fortunate to have *you*,' she said sitting down too. 'Who else would have let them keep on their house? You are a very kind man, Hubert, and my parents appreciate it. I appreciate it, too.'

'But I have no need of this huge place,' Hubert said in surprise. 'I am a bachelor. What would I do with all the rooms? No, I hope I am quite happy where I am, and glad to be able to help your parents, who have been equally good to me. There is only one thing that upsets me, however,' he murmured, and then paused while Sophie sat waiting expectantly for his explanation.

'Yes?' she asked encouragingly.

'I am very sorry to hear you are going.'

'Yes.'

'And so soon?'

'I'm afraid so.'

'I'm frankly devastated,' Hubert said in a voice vibrant with emotion, and then abruptly standing up, he began agitatedly to pace the room. 'I so hoped that, as you had returned to the rectory and were no longer at the beck and call of Sir Guy, we would be seeing more of each other, Sophie.'

'Unfortunately it is not to be,' she said, and a feeling of sadness welled up in her that, just when she needed her friend, he would not be there.

For Hubert Turner was a good man, someone of whom it was not wrong to use the word 'gentle'. He was a gentleman in every way: humorous, kind, pious and, she was sure, above all compassionate. Of all the people she could think of, he would not be the first to cast a stone.

'I shall miss you, though,' she added impulsively. 'I don't think you realise how much.'

'In that case,' he protested, '*must* you go?'

'I'm afraid I must. I have engaged rooms in Cheltenham and a temporary post at a school.'

'But *why*?' The strength of his emotion surprised her.

'I simply want to go away, Hubert.' She lowered her voice. 'Is that wrong? I don't wish to live with my parents. I don't wish to remain in Wenham. My time here hasn't been altogether happy

464

and I wish to get away, to put certain things behind me, like the death of Laurence. It affected me deeply.'

'It affected us all,' Hubert said sadly, 'because each of us, in his own way, thinks that he could have prevented it.'

'Exactly.'

'Digging up your roots won't make you forget,' he replied.

'No. And I do not even leave a memorial behind to George. In four years I have not achieved that, and *that*, Hubert, is the measure of my failure.'

She cast her eyes to the floor, and when she looked up Hubert was standing in front of her, his cheeks flushed, hands in his pockets. His wise, grave face looked immeasurably sad, and she thought how dear it was to her. How much dearer than another face, and how foolish she had been to be so swayed by passion that she put it before affection and respect. Heavy-hearted, she put out her hand. But Hubert didn't take it. Instead he said:

'Sophie, would you consider staying behind in order to become my wife? I know you don't love me, and I have asked you before. But I have never ceased to love *you*, Sophie . . .' He moved away and began to pace the floor again. 'I have loved you almost since I met you; but I knew you were too good for me.'

'Too good . . .' She wanted to laugh, but he would misinterpret it.

He hurried on: 'You were filled with the spirit of God and wished to return to the missions. Your forbearance and humility were admirable. In you I see the spirit of supreme self-sacrifice . . .'

'Please don't go on, Hubert,' she pleaded. 'If you knew the truth about me you would not say that.'

'What do you mean, Sophie?' He peered closely at her face.

'You would despise me.'

'I despise you? Impossible.'

'I am to have a child, Hubert,' she said, joining her hands together on her lap. 'That is why I am going away. I want you to know the truth because, otherwise, I think I could have been happy with you. I have always liked you, admired you, felt you were a true friend. But I was a very foolish woman. Not wise at all, or kind, or good, or gracious. I loved a "man" – ' she stumbled over the word because she nearly said his name ' – and he did ask me to marry him. I emphasise this not to excuse my sin but because I did expect him to marry me. I thought that soon, in the eyes of God, we would be one. This was the reason I anticipated the marriage act; but it only made him despise me. So you can imagine the sense of shame and disgrace I feel that now I am to bear the child of such a dishonourable man. I suppose I should have expected nothing better of one who would take such advantage of a woman's weakness.'

She paused because she felt too near tears to go on. Then, standing up, she said:

'I would like you to go now, Hubert, and, as you are a priest, regard this secret as you would a confession. I will leave this place and I never wish to return, so that no one will know about the baby I bear, or bring such shame to the knowledge of my parents.'

She turned her back on him and waited, head bowed, for the sound of him leaving the room. But instead she felt his hand on her shoulder, his breath warm on her cheek.

'I should still like the privilege of taking care of you, your children and the child you are carrying, Sophie. Nothing you can say alters my mind, and I recall the words of Our Lord: "Many sins are forgiven her because she has loved much".'

Sophie slowly turned to look at him, and saw such an expression of tenderness on his dear face that her heart performed a somersault. She didn't know whether or not it was her imagination, but beyond him, through the window, she could see that the sky, which had been overcast, appeared to have brightened.

The dark storm-clouds had cleared, the sun had come out and bathed the earth in a very sweet light.

EPILOGUE

The Window

EPILOGUE

Wenham, Dorset, August 1913.

The sun seemed to catch the exact angle of the cross, and thus to magnify it above the kneeling figures who, hands joined, had their eyes raised towards it. Only two of the figures, etched forever and devoutly in glass, were white; the others were black, clad in the minimum garments of savages.

The rays beamed down in benediction on those who had gathered in the shadow of the cross and who, many years before, had died for it.

Sacred to the memory
of
George Pelham Woodville, born 1881,
his faithful servant Kirikeu
and their companions, who gave their
lives for Christ in Papua,
New Guinea, December 1907.

Also
in loving memory of his cousin
Laurence Thomas Yetman, born 1882,
who died November 13 1912,
both late of this parish.

This window is erected to their memory
by their family and the generous
donations of the people of Wenham.

As the organ struck up a solemn march from Handel's *Saul*, the procession that had assembled at the back of the church began walking slowly down the aisle: the outgoing rector, the incoming rector and the Bishop of Salisbury were all resplendent in white and gold copes. Because, despite the sadness of the dedication of the window, it was also an occasion for rejoicing.

Hubert Turner was to be installed as rector of the parish in place of his father-in-law, the Reverend Austin Lamb, who had served it for over forty years. Preceded by an altar-boy carrying the pectoral cross, the members of the procession arrived at the sanctuary and, after bowing to the altar, grouped themselves at the base of the window, whose wondrous colours, its brilliant blues, reds, amethysts, yellows and greens, had only finally been put in place the day before.

In the front row of the congregation Sophie stood beside her mother, her sturdy infant son in her arms. In a weekend of rejoicing, Samuel George Turner was to be baptised by his father, the new rector, the following day. His father in the eyes of the parish, and certainly, Sophie thought – her eyes lingering on him lovingly as he went solemnly and reverently about his duties – in the eyes of God.

Sophie's heart was full of sadness at the memory of George, yet there was an overwhelming sense of joy and tenderness too. She had been restored to God, she had peace in her heart, and for this she had to thank her husband. Was there ever a man like Hubert Turner, she wondered? So selfless that even George, that epitome of goodness, ran him a close second, but second nevertheless. As he raised his hand in blessing towards the window she knew that, but for his generosity, it would not be there, and nor would she and her children – the two eldest grouped on either side of her, the baby in her arms.

She had been very wicked in her life, but she had been blessed too. She had been married to two remarkable men, and maybe her Lord who, after all, forgave the woman taken in adultery, had not abandoned her. She knew that she would never, ever stray from the path of holiness and righteousness again.

The bishop pronounced the consecration of the window and

followed it with a brief, simple, but moving homily extolling the virtues of those honoured:

'"Their names liveth for evermore."'

Their names lived in her heart, certainly, and in the hearts of her family. Behind her stood Sarah-Jane with her children, then Eliza with Hugh, Dora and Julius – who had contributed substantially towards the funds. Of George's father there was no sign. He had been confined to his home since suffering a severe heart-attack shortly after his honeymoon. But the new Lady Woodville was there, resplendent in an *haute-couture* outfit, and so were the Martyns: Prosper, Lally, Roger and his wife Emma.

Miss Fairchild and Connie Yetman had moved to Bath and were not in church. But they had sent a substantial contribution to the window. George and Laurence had been loved by everybody, and would not easily be forgotten.

Carson stood, in place of his father, alone, taciturn, grim-faced. Maybe he thought about his dead brother, whose successor he was, or maybe his mind was on the many burdens he carried: his fierce passion for a woman who was another man's wife, and whose eyes he was now studiously trying to avoid; his quarrels with his detested stepmother Agnes; and the fate of the house should his father die.

It was thus, on a hot sunny day in August, that all the people of the parish gathered together to honour those who were no longer among them, and to celebrate the induction of their new parish priest.

In exactly a year's time the guns of war would again ring out to disturb their tranquil existence but, happily, they did not have the power to see into the future.

But now, for Sophie Turner, the daughter of the rectory, the wheel seemed to have come full circle. Here she was, again an important and respected member of the community, an integral part of the very fabric of the small, closed society into which she had been born and yet which was, in so many ways, a microcosm of the world.

A Selected List of Fiction Available from Mandarin

While every effort is made to keep prices low, it is sometimes necessary to increase prices at short notice. Mandarin Paperbacks reserves the right to show new retail prices on covers which may differ from those previously advertised in the text or elsewhere.

The prices shown below were correct at the time of going to press.

☐	7493 1352 8	**The Queen and I**	Sue Townsend	£4.99
☐	7493 0540 1	**The Liar**	Stephen Fry	£4.99
☐	7493 1132 0	**Arrivals and Departures**	Lesley Thomas	£4.99
☐	7493 0381 6	**Loves and Journeys of Revolving Jones**	Leslie Thomas	£4.99
☐	7493 0942 3	**Silence of the Lambs**	Thomas Harris	£4.99
☐	7493 0946 6	**The Godfather**	Mario Puzo	£4.99
☐	7493 1561 X	**Fear of Flying**	Erica Jong	£4.99
☐	7493 1221 1	**The Power of One**	Bryce Courtney	£4.99
☐	7493 0576 2	**Tandia**	Bryce Courtney	£5.99
☐	7493 0563 0	**Kill the Lights**	Simon Williams	£4.99
☐	7493 1319 6	**Air and Angels**	Susan Hill	£4.99
☐	7493 1477 X	**The Name of the Rose**	Umberto Eco	£4.99
☐	7493 0896 6	**The Stand-in**	Deborah Moggach	£4.99
☐	7493 0581 9	**Daddy's Girls**	Zoe Fairbairns	£4.99

All these books are available at your bookshop or newsagent, or can be ordered direct from the address below. Just tick the titles you want and fill in the form below.

Cash Sales Department, PO Box 5, Rushden, Northants NN10 6YX.
Fax: 0933 410321 : Phone 0933 410511.

Please send cheque, payable to 'Reed Book Services Ltd.', or postal order for purchase price quoted and allow the following for postage and packing:

£1.00 for the first book, 50p for the second; **FREE POSTAGE AND PACKING FOR THREE BOOKS OR MORE PER ORDER.**

NAME (Block letters) ....

ADDRESS...

....

☐ I enclose my remittance for ....

☐ I wish to pay by Access/Visa Card Number ⬚⬚⬚⬚⬚⬚⬚⬚⬚⬚⬚⬚⬚⬚⬚⬚

Expiry Date ⬚⬚⬚⬚

Signature ....

Please quote our reference: MAND